*"IF THE POWER TO SHOCK MAY
BE TAKEN AS A YARDSTICK OF
FICTION, JOHN UPDIKE HAS
WRITTEN ONE OF THE YEAR'S
MOST IMPORTANT NOVELS. . . .
THE SUREST WRITING IN YEARS."*
—*Time Magazine*

RABBIT, RUN is a shocking novel—not only because of its sexual candor, but because it challenges an image of life still cherished in America.

Original, graphic, and merciless, RABBIT, RUN will be admired and hated with equal intensity. That it cannot be ignored or read with indifference is a tribute to the author's insight and great gift as a novelist.

"UPDIKE'S PUNCH IS POWERFUL"
—*Newsweek*

by John Updike

———

THE POORHOUSE FAIR, *a novel*

THE SAME DOOR, *short stories*

RABBIT, RUN, *a novel*

PIGEON FEATHERS *and other stories*

THE CENTAUR, *a novel*

VERSE, *poetry*

ASSORTED PROSE, *a miscellany*

OF THE FARM, *a novel*

THE MUSIC SCHOOL, *short stories*

COUPLES, *a novel*

John Updike

RABBIT, RUN

A FAWCETT CREST BOOK

Fawcett Publications, Inc., Greenwich, Conn.
Member of American Book Publishers Council, Inc.

A Fawcett Crest Book published by arrangement with
Alfred A. Knopf, Inc.

This book was written with the help of a grant generously
given by the John Simon Guggenheim Memorial Foundation.

Sixteenth Fawcett Crest printing, May 1970

Published by Fawcett World Library,
67 West 44th Street, New York, New York 10036
Printed in the United States of America

The motions of Grace, the hardness of the heart;
external circumstances.

—PASCAL, Pensée 507

BOYS are playing basketball around a telephone pole with a backboard bolted to it. Legs, shouts. The scrape and snap of Keds on loose alley pebbles seems to catapult their voices high into the moist March air blue above the wires. Rabbit Angstrom, coming up the alley in a business suit, stops and watches, though he's twenty-six and six three. So tall, he seems an unlikely rabbit, but the breadth of white face, the pallor of his blue irises, and a nervous flutter under his brief nose as he stabs a cigarette into his mouth partially explain the nickname, which was given to him when he too was a boy. He stands there thinking, the kids keep coming, they keep crowding you up.

His standing there makes the real boys feel strange. Eyeballs slide. They're doing this for their own pleasure, not as a demonstration for some adult walking around town in a double-breasted cocoa suit. It seems funny to them, an adult walking up the alley at all. Where's his car? The cigarette makes it more sinister still. Is this one of those going to offer them cigarettes or money to go out in back of the ice plant with him? They've heard of such things but are not too frightened; there are six of them and one of him.

The ball, rocketing off the crotch of the rim, leaps over the heads of the six and lands at the feet of the one. He

7

catches it on the short bounce with a quickness that startles them. As they stare hushed he sights squinting through blue clouds of weed smoke, a suddenly dark silhouette like a smokestack in the afternoon spring sky, setting his feet with care, wiggling the ball with nervousness in front of his chest, one widespread pale hand on top of the ball and the other underneath, jiggling it patiently to get some adjustment in air itself. The moons on his fingernails are big. Then the ball seems to ride up the right lapel of his coat and comes off his shoulder as his knees dip down, and it appears the ball is not going toward the backboard. It was not aimed there. It drops into the circle of the rim, whipping the net with a ladylike whisper. "Hey!" he shouts in pride.

"Luck," one of the kids says.

"Skill," he answers, and asks, "Hey. O.K. if I play?"

There is no response, just puzzled silly looks swapped. Rabbit takes off his coat, folds it nicely, and rests it on a clean ashcan lid. Behind him the dungarees begin to scuffle again. He goes into the scrimmaging thick of them for the ball, flips it from two weak white hands, has it in his own. That old stretched-leather feeling makes his whole body go taut, gives his arms wings. It feels like he's reaching down through years to touch this tautness. His arms lift of their own and the rubber ball floats toward the basket from the top of his head. It feels so right he blinks when the ball drops short, and for a second wonders if it went through the hoop without riffling the net. He asks, "Hey whose side am I on?"

In a wordless shuffle two boys are delegated to be his. They stand the other four. Though from the start Rabbit handicaps himself by staying ten feet out from the basket, it is still unfair. Nobody bothers to keep score. The surly silence bothers him. The kids call monosyllables to each other but to him they don't dare a word. As the game goes on he can feel them at his legs, getting hot and mad, trying to trip him, but their tongues are still held. He doesn't want this respect, he wants to tell them there's nothing to getting old, it takes nothing. In ten minutes another boy goes to the other side, so it's just Rabbit Angstrom and one kid standing five. This boy, still midget but already diffident with a kind of rangy ease, is the best of the six; he wears a knitted cap with a green pompom well down over his ears and level with his eyebrows, giving his head a cretinous look. He's a natural.

The way he moves sideways without taking any steps, gliding on a blessing: you can tell. The way he waits before he moves. With luck he'll become in time a crack athlete in the high school; Rabbit knows the way. You climb up through the little grades and then get to the top and everybody cheers; with the sweat in your eyebrows you can't see very well and the noise swirls around you and lifts you up, and then you're out, not forgotten at first, just out, and it feels good and cool and free. You're out, and sort of melt, and keep lifting, until you become like to these kids just one more piece of the sky of adults that hangs over them in the town, a piece that for some queer reason has clouded and visited them. They've not forgotten him; worse, they never heard of him. Yet in his time Rabbit was famous through the county; in basketball in his junior year he set a B-league scoring record that in his senior year he broke with a record that was not broken until four years later, that is, four years ago.

He sinks shots one-handed, two-handed, underhanded, flatfooted, and out of the pivot, jump, and set. Flat and soft the ball lifts. That his touch still lives in his hands elates him. He feels liberated from long gloom. But his body is weighty and his breath grows short. It annoys him, that he gets winded. When the five kids not on his side begin to groan and act lazy, and a kid he accidentally knocks down gets up with a blurred face and walks away, Rabbit quits readily. "O.K.," he says. "The old man's going."

To the boy on his side, the pompom, he adds, "So long, ace." He feels grateful to the boy, who continued to watch him with disinterested admiration after the others grew sullen, and who cheered him on with exclamations: "God. Great. Gee."

Rabbit picks up his folded coat and carries it in one hand like a letter as he runs. Up the alley. Past the deserted ice plant with its rotting wooden skids on the fallen loading porch. Ashcans, garage doors, fences of chickenwire caging criss-crossing stalks of dead flowers. The month is March. Love makes the air light. Things start anew; Rabbit tastes through sour aftersmoke the fresh chance in the air, plucks the pack of cigarettes from his bobbling shirt pocket, and without breaking stride cans it in somebody's open barrel. His upper lip nibbles back from his teeth in self-pleasure. His big suede shoes skim in thumps above the skittering litter of alley gravel.

Running. At the end of this block of the alley he turns up a street, Wilbur Street in the town of Mt. Judge, suburb of the city of Brewer, fifth largest city in Pennsylvania. Running uphill. Past a block of big homes, fortresses of cement and brick inset with doorways of stained and beveled glass and windows of potted plants, and then halfway up another block, which holds a development built all at once in the Thirties. The frame homes climb the hill like a single staircase. The space of six feet or so that each double house rises above its neighbor contains two wan windows, wide-spaced like the eyes of an animal, and is covered with composition shingling varying in color from bruise to dung. The fronts are clapboards, weathered and white except for those gaps which individual owners have painted green and barn-red and wheat-color. There are a dozen three-story homes, and each has two doors. The seventh door is his. The wood steps up to it are worn; under them there is a cubbyhole of dirt where a lost toy molders. A plastic clown. He's seen it there all winter but he always thought some kid would be coming back for it.

He pauses in the sunless vestibule, panting. Overhead, a daytime bulb burns dustily. Three tin mailboxes hang empty above a brown radiator. His downstairs neighbor's door across the hall is shut like an angry face. There is that smell which is always the same but that he can never identify; sometimes it seems cabbage cooking, sometimes the furnace's rusty breath, sometimes something soft decaying in the walls. He climbs the stairs to his home, the top floor.

The door is locked. In fitting the little key into the lock his hand trembles, pulsing with unusual exertion, and the metal scratches. But when he opens the door he sees his wife sitting in an armchair with an Old-fashioned, watching television turned down low.

"You're *here*," he says. "What's the door locked for?"

She looks to one side of him with vague dark eyes reddened by the friction of watching. "It just locked itself."

"Just locked itself," he repeats, but bends down to kiss her glossy forehead nevertheless. She is a small woman with a tight dark skin, as if something swelling inside is straining against her littleness. Just yesterday, it seems to him, she stopped being pretty. With the tiny addition of two short wrinkles at the corners, her mouth had become greedy; and her hair has thinned, so he keeps thinking of her skull under it. But he keeps hoping that tomorrow she'll be his girl again. "Watcha fraid of? Who do you think's gonna come in that door?"

Expecting no answer, he carefully unfolds his coat and goes to the closet with it and takes out a wire hanger. The closet is in the living-room and the door only opens half-way, since the television set is in front of it. He is careful not to kick the wire, which is plugged into a socket on the side of the door. One time Janice, who is especially clumsy when pregnant or drunk, got the wire wrapped around her foot and nearly pulled the set, a hundred and forty-nine dollars, down *smash* on the floor. Luckily he got to it while it was still rocking in the metal cradle and before Janice began kicking out in one of her panics. What made her get that way? What was she afraid of? With loving deftness, a deftness as complimentary to the articulation of his own body as to the objects he touches, he inserts the corners of the hanger into the armholes of the coat and with his long reach hangs it on the printed pipe with his other clothes. He presses the door shut and it clicks but then swings open again an inch or two. Locked doors. It rankles: his hand trembling in the lock like some old man and her sitting in here listening to the scratching.

He turns and asks her, "If you're home where's the car? It's not out front."

"It's in front of my mother's. You're in my way."

"In front of your mother's? That's terrific. That's just the God-damn place for it."

"What's brought this on?"

"Brought what on?" He moves out of her line of vision and stands to one side.

She is watching a group of children called Mouseketeers perform a musical number in which Darlene is a flower girl in Paris and Cubby is a cop and that smirky squeaky tall kid is a romantic artist. He and Darlene and Cubby and Karen (dressed as an old French lady whom Cubby as a cop helps across the street) dance.

Then the commercial shows the seven segments of a Tootsie Roll coming out of the wrapper and turning into the seven letters of "Tootsie." They, too, sing and dance. Still singing, they climb back into the wrapper. It echoes like an echo chamber. Son of a bitch: cute. He's seen it fifty times and this time it turns his stomach. His heart is still throbbing; his throat feels narrow.

Janice asks, "Harry, do you have a cigarette? I'm out."

"Huh? On the way home I threw my pack into a garbage can. I'm giving it up." He wonders how anybody could think of smoking, with his stomach on edge the way it is.

Janice looks at him at last. "You threw it into a garbage can! Holy Mo. You don't drink, now you don't smoke. What are you doing, becoming a saint?"

"Shh."

The big Mouseketeer has appeared, Jimmy, an older man who wears circular black ears. Rabbit watches him attentively; he respects him. He expects to learn something from him helpful in his own line of work, which is demonstrating a kitchen gadget in several five-and-dime stores around Brewer. He's had the job for four weeks. "Proverbs, proverbs, they're so true," Jimmy sings, strumming his Mouseguitar, "proverbs tell us what to do; proverbs help us all to *bee* —better—Mouse-ke-teers."

Jimmy sets aside his smile and guitar and says straight out through the glass, "Know Thyself, a wise old Greek once said. Know Thyself. Now what does this mean, boys and girls? It means, be what you are. Don't try to be Sally or Johnny or Fred next door; be yourself. God doesn't want a tree to be a waterfall, or a flower to be a stone. God gives to each one of us a special talent." Janice and Rabbit become unnaturally still; both are Christians. God's name makes them feel guilty. "God wants some of us to become scientists, some of us to become artists, some of us to become firemen and doctors and trapeze artists. And He gives to each of us the special talents to become these things, *provided we work to develop them.* We must *work,* boys and girls. So: Know Thyself. Learn to understand your talents, and then work to develop them. That's the way to be happy." He pinches his mouth together and winks.

That was good. Rabbit tries that, pinching the mouth together and then the wink, getting the audience out front with you against some enemy behind, Walt Disney or the MagiPeel Peeler Company, admitting it's all a fraud but, what the hell, making it likable. We're all in it together. Fraud makes the world go round. The base of our economy. Vitaconomy, the modern housewife's password, the one-word expression for economizing vitamins by the MagiPeel Method.

Janice gets up and turns off the set when the six-o'clock news tries to come on. The little star left by the current slowly dies.

Rabbit asks, "Where's the kid?"

"At your mother's."

"At *my* mother's? The car's at your mother's and the kid's at my mother's. Jesus. You're a mess."

She stands up and her pregnancy infuriates him with its look of stubborn lumpiness. She wears one of those maternity skirts with a U cut in the belly. A white crescent of slip shows under the hem of her blouse. "I was tired."

"No wonder," he says. "How many of those have you had?" He gestures at the Old-fashioned glass.

She tries to explain. "I left Nelson at your mother's on my way to my mother's to go into town with her. We went in in her car and walked around looking at the spring clothes in the windows and she bought a nice Liberty scarf at Kroll's at a sale. Purply Paisley." She falters; her little narrow tongue pokes between her parted rows of dim teeth.

He feels frightened. When confused, Janice is a frightening person. Her eyes dwindle in their frowning sockets and her little mouth hangs open in a dumb slot. Since her hair has begun to thin back from her shiny forehead, he keeps getting the feeling of her being brittle, and immovable, of her only going one way, toward deeper wrinkles and skimpier hair. He married relatively late, when he was twenty-four and she was two years out of high school, still scarcely adult, with soft small breasts that when she lay down flattened against her pliant body that was like a soft smooth boy's. Nelson was born seven months after the Episcopal service, in prolonged labor: this pang of memory turns Rabbit's fright to tenderness. "What did you buy?"

"A bathing suit."

"A bathing suit! Chh. In March?"

She closed her eyes for a moment; he can feel the undertow of liquor sweep over her and is disgusted. "It made it seem closer to when I could fit into it."

"What the hell ails you? Other women *like* being pregnant. What's so damn fancy about you? Just tell me. What *is* so frigging fancy?"

She opens her brown eyes and tears fill them and break over the lower lids and drop down her cheeks, pink with injury, while she looks at him and says "You bastard" with drunken care.

Rabbit goes to his wife and, putting his arms around her, has a vivid experience of her, her tear-hot breath, her bloodshot eyes. In an affectionate reflex he dips his knees to bring his loins against hers, but her belly prevents him. He stands to his full height above her and says, "O.K. You bought a bathing suit."

Sheltered by his chest and arms she says with unexpected earnestness, "Don't run from me, Harry. I love you."

"I love *you*. Now come on, you bought a bathing suit."

"Red," she says, rocking sadly against him. But her body when tipsy has a brittleness, an unconnectedness, that feels disagreeable in his arms. "With a strap that ties behind your neck and a pleated skirt you can take off in the water. Then my varicose veins hurt so much Mother and I went into the basement of Kroll's and had chocolate sodas. They've re-done the whole luncheonette section, the counter isn't there any more. But my legs still hurt so Mother brought me home and said you could pick up the car and Nelson."

"Your legs hell, they were probably her legs."

"I thought you'd be home before now. Where were you?"

"Oh, clowning around. I played ball with some kids down the alley." They have parted.

"I tried to take a nap but I couldn't. Mother said I looked tired."

"You're supposed to look tired. You're a housewife."

"And meanwhile you're off playing like a twelve-year-old?"

He is indignant that she didn't see his crack about being a housewife, based on the "image" the MagiPeel people tried to have their salesmen sell to, as ironical and at bottom pitying and fond. There seems no escaping it: she is dumb. He says, "Well what's the difference if you're sitting here watching a program for kids under two?"

"Who was *shushing* a while ago?"

"Ah, Janice." He sighs. "Screw you. Just screw you."

She looks at him clearly a long moment. "I'll get supper," she at last decides.

He is all repentance. "I'll run over and get the car and bring the kid back. The poor kid must think he has no home. What the hell makes your mother think my mother has nothing better to do than take care of other people's kids?" Indignation rises in him again at her missing the point of why he wanted to watch Jimmy, for professional reasons, to earn a living to buy oranges for her to put into her rotten Old-fashioneds.

She moves into the kitchen, angry but not angry enough. She should be really sore, or not sore at all, since all he had said was what he had done a couple hundred times. Maybe a thousand times. Say, on the average once every three days since 1956. What's that? Three hundred. That often? Then why is it always an effort? She used to make it easier before they got married. She could be sudden then. Just a girl. Nerves like new thread. Skin smelled like fresh cotton. Her girl friend at work had an apartment in Brewer they used. Pipe-framed bed, silver medallions in the wallpaper; a view westward of the great blue gas tanks by the edge of the river. After work, working both at Kroll's then, she selling candy and cashews in a white smock with "Jan" stitched on her pocket and he lugging easy chairs and maple end tables around on the floor above, hammering apart packing crates from nine to five, the itch of the packing excelsior getting into his nose and eyes and making them burn. That filthy black crescent of bins behind the elevators, the floor covered with bent nails, his palms black and Chandler the dandy mincing in every hour on the hour telling him to wash his hands so he wouldn't foul the furniture. Lava soap. It's lather was gray. His hands grew yellow calluses from using the crowbar. After 5:30, the dirty day done, they would meet by the doors, chained to keep customers out, a green-glass-paved chamber of silence between the two sets of doors, in the shallow side windows the bodiless mannequin heads in their feathered hats and necklaces of pink pearls eavesdropping on the echoing farewell gossip. Every employee hated Kroll's; yet they left it slow as swimming. Janice and Rabbit would meet in this chamber, with the dim light and green floor like something underwater, and push at the one unchained door, push up into the light, and walk, never admitting they were going there, toward the silver medallions, hand in hand tired walking gently against the current of homegoing traffic, and make love with the late daylight coming level in the window. She was shy about him seeing her. She made him keep his eyes shut. And then with a shiver come as soon as he was in, her inside softly grainy, like a silk slipper. Lying side by side on this other

girl's bed, feeling lost, having done the final thing; the
wall's silver and the fading day's gold.

The kitchen is a narrow room off the living-room, a tight
aisle between machines that were modern five years ago. She
drops something metal, a pan or cup. "Think you can make
it without burning yourself?" he calls in.

"Are you still here?" is the answer.

He goes to the closet and takes out the coat he hung up
so neatly. It seems to him he's the only person around here
who cares about neatness. The clutter behind him in the
room—the Old-fashioned glass with its corrupt dregs, the
choked ashtray balanced on the easy-chair arm, the rumpled rug, the floppy stacks of slippery newspapers, the kid's
toys here and there broken and stuck and jammed, a leg
off a doll and a piece of bent cardboard that went with
some breakfast-box cutout, the rolls of fuzz under the
radiators, the continual crisscrossing mess—clings to his back
like a tightening net. He tries to sort out picking up his
car and then his kid. Or should he pick up the kid first? He
wants more to see the kid. It would be quicker to walk over
to Mrs. Springer's, she lived closer. But suppose she was
watching out the window for him to come so she could pop
out and tell him how tired Janice looked? Who wouldn't be
tired after tramping around trying to buy something with you
you miserable nickel-hugger? You fat hag. You old gypsy. If
he had the kid along this might not happen. Rabbit likes
the idea of walking up from his mother's place with his boy.
Two-and-a-half, Nelson walks like a trooper, with choppy
stubborn steps. They'd walk along in the day's last light
under the trees and then like magic there would be Daddy's car at a curb. But it will take longer this way, what
with his own mother talking slyly and round-about about
how incompetent Janice is. It ruined him when his mother
went on like that; maybe she did it just to kid him, but he
couldn't take her lightly, she was somehow too powerful,
at least with him. He had better go for the car first and
pick the kid up with it. But he doesn't want to do it this
way. He just doesn't. The problem knits in front of him and
he feels sickened by the intricacy.

Janice calls from the kitchen, "And honey pick up a pack
of cigarettes could you?" in a normal voice that says everything is forgiven, everything is the same.

Rabbit freezes, standing looking at his faint yellow shadow

on the white door that leads to the hall, and senses he is in a trap. It seems certain. In disgust he goes out.

Outdoors it is growing dark and cool. The Norwegian maples exhale the smell of their sticky new buds and the broad living-room windows along Wilbur Street show beyond the silver patch of a television set the warm bulbs burning in kitchens, like fires at the backs of caves. He walks downhill. The day is gathering itself in. He now and then touches with his hand the rough bark of a tree or the dry twigs of a hedge, to give himself the small answer of a texture. At the corner, where Wilbur Street meets Potter Avenue, a mailbox stands leaning in twilight on its concrete post. Tall two-petaled street sign, the cleat-gouged trunk of the telephone pole holding its insulators against the sky, fire hydrant like a golden bush: a grove. He used to love to climb the poles. To shinny up from a friend's shoulders until the ladder of spikes came to your hands, to get up to where you could hear the wires sing. Terrifying motionless whisper. It always tempted you to fall, to let the hard spikes in your palms go and feel the space on your back, feel it take your feet and ride up your spine as you fell. He remembers how hot your hands felt at the top, rubbed full of splinters from getting up to where the spikes began. Listening to the wires as if you could hear what people were saying, what all that secret adult world was about. The insulators giant blue eggs in a windy nest.

As he walks along Potter Avenue the wires at their silent height strike into and through the crowns of the breathing maples. At the next corner, where the water from the ice plant used to come down, sob into a drain, and reappear on the other side of the street, Rabbit crosses over and walks beside the gutter where the water used to run, coating the shallow side of its course with ribbons of green slime waving and waiting to slip under your feet and dunk you if you dared walk on them. He can remember falling in but not why he was walking along this slippery edge in the first place. Then he remembers. To impress the girls—Lotty Bingaman, Margaret Schoelkopf, sometimes June Cobb and Mary Hoyer—he walked home from grade school with. Margaret's nose would often start bleeding, for no reason. She had worn high button shoes.

He turns down Kegerise Street, a narrow gravel alley curving past the blank back side of a small box factory where mostly middle-aged women work, the cement-block face of a wholesale beer outlet, and a truly old stone farmhouse, now boarded up, one of the oldest buildings in town, thick crude masonry of Indianskin sandstone. This building, which once commanded half of the acreage the town is now built on, still retains, behind a shattered and vandalized fence, its yard, a junkheap of brown stalks and eroded timber that will in the summer bloom with an unwanted wealth of weeds, waxy green wands and milky pods of silk seeds and airy yellow heads almost liquid with pollen.

So there is some space between the old farmhouse and the Sunshine Athletic Association, a tall thin brick building like a city tenement misplaced in this disordered alley of backsides and leftovers. The entrance is made ominous by a strange sheathing, the size of an outhouse, erected each winter on the stone steps, to protect the bar from the weather. Rabbit has several times entered the club. There was no sunshine in it. The first floor was a bar and the second was full of card tables where the old bucks of the town sat muttering strategically. Alcohol and cards Rabbit both associates with a depressing kind of sin, sin with bad breath, and he was further depressed by the political air of the place. His old basketball coach, Marty Tothero, who before scandal had ousted him from the high school had a certain grip on local affairs, lived in this building supposedly and still, they said, manipulated. Rabbit dislikes manipulation but he had liked Tothero. Next to his mother Tothero had had the most *force*.

The thought of his old coach crouching in there frightens him. He walks on, past a body shop and an unused chicken house. His progress is always down, for the town of Mt. Judge is built on the east side of the mountain Mt. Judge, whose west face overlooks the city of Brewer. Though the town and the city meet along the highway that skirts the mountain on the south on the way to Philadelphia fifty miles away, they will never merge, for between them the mountain lifts a broad green spine, two miles long north to south, assaulted by gravel pits and cemeteries and new developments but above a line preserved, hundreds of acres of forest Mt. Judge boys can never wholly explore. Much of it is penetrated by the sound of cars climbing the scenic drives in second gear. But in long patches of forgotten pine plantation the needle-hushed floor of land glides up and up, on and on, under endless tunnels of dead green and you seem to have passed through silence into something worse. And then, coming upon a patch of sunlight the branches neglect to keep out or upon a softened stone-filled cellar pit dug by some brave and monstrous settler centuries ago, you become vividly frightened, as if this other sign of life will call attention to yourself, and the menace of the trees will become active. Your fear trills like an alarm bell you cannot shut off, the louder the faster you run, hunchbacked, until distinctly, with a gasp of the clutch, a near car shifts gears, and the stumpy white posts of the guard fence dawn behind the pine trunks. Then, safe on the firm blacktop, you decide whether to walk back down home or to hike up to the Pinnacle Hotel for a candy bar and a view of Brewer spread out below like a carpet, a red city, where they paint wood, tin, even red bricks red, an orange rose flowerpot red that is unlike the color of any other city in the world yet to the children of the county is the only color of cities, the color all cities are.

The mountain brings dusk early to the town. Now, just a few minutes after six a day before the vernal equinox, all the houses and gravel-roofed factories and diagonal hillside streets are in the shadow that washes deep into the valley of farmland east of the mountain. Huts on the shadow's shore, twin rows of ranch-houses blare from their picture windows the reflection of the setting sun. One by one, as suddenly as lamps, these windows dim as the sunlight ebbs, drawing across the development and across the tan fenced land waiting for planting and a golf course that at the distance could be a long pasture except for the yellow beans of sand; drawing upward into the opposing hills on whose westward slopes it still burns with afternoon pride. Rabbit pauses at the end of the alley, where he has an open view. He used to caddy over there.

Pricked by an indefinite urgency, he turns away, going left on Jackson Road, where he lived for twenty years. His parents' home is in a two-family brick house on the corner; but it is their neighbors, the Bolgers, who have the corner half, with a narrow side yard Mrs. Angstrom has always envied. The Bolgers' windows getting all that light and here we sit wedged in.

Rabbit stealthily approaches his old home on the grass, hopping the little barberry hedge and the wire meant to keep kids on the pavement. He sneaks down the strip of grass between the two cement walks that go with the two brick walls; he used to live behind the one and the Zims behind the other. All day long Mrs. Zim, who was plain, with big thyroid eyes and bluish, slack skin, screamed at her daughter Carolyn, who was prettier than you'd think a five-year-old girl could be. Mr. Zim was a thick-lipped redhead, and in Carolyn thick and thin, red and blue, health and high-strungness had blended just right; her beauty was not merely precocious but somehow absolutely, apart from age, exotic. Even Harry, six years older, saw this. All day long Mrs. Zim screamed at her and when Mr. Zim came home from work the two of them would shout together for hours. It would begin with Mr. defending the little girl, and then as the neighbors listened old wounds opened like complicated flowers in the night. Sometimes Mom said that Mr. would murder Mrs., sometimes she said that the little girl would murder them both, as they lay asleep. It was true there was something cold-blooded about Carolyn; when she reached school age, she never left the house without a smile on her little heart-face, swinging herself along like she owned the world, though the Angstroms had just heard her mother throw hysterics at her all through breakfast, the kitchen windows not six feet apart. How does that poor man endure? If Carolyn and her mother don't settle their differences they're going to wake up some fair morning without a protector. But Mom was never proved right in any of her predictions. When the Zims left, it was together, Mr. and Mrs. and Carolyn, vanishing in a station wagon while half their furniture still stood on the sidewalk beside the mover's truck. He had a new job in Cleveland, Ohio. Poor souls, they won't be missed. But they were. They had sold their half-house to an old couple, strict Methodists, and the old man refused to cut the strip of grass between his house and the Angstroms'. Mr. Zim, who worked outdoors rain or shine on weekends, as if it's his only pleasure in life and I don't wonder, had always cut it. The old Methodist cut exactly his half, one swath of a lawnmower, and then pushed his lawnmower back inverted on his own walk, when it would have been just as easy to push it back along the other half of the strip and not leave such a ridiculous job. When I hear that old fool's wheels rattle along his walk so self-righteously, my blood pressure goes up so I hear my ears pop. Mother refused to let him or his father mow their half for one whole summer, and the grass grew knee-high in that little sunless space and stalks of like wheat came up and one or two goldenrod until a man from the town came around in August and said they must cut it on account of an ordinance; he was sorry. Harry had gone to the door and was saying, Sure, O.K., when Mother came up behind him saying, What did he mean? That was her flowerbed. She had no intention of letting it be destroyed. As her son, Rabbit felt terribly embarrassed. The man just looked at her and got a little thumbed book out of his hip pocket and showed her the ordinance. She still said it was her flowerbed. The man read to her what the fine was and went off the porch. That Saturday when she was in Brewer shopping, Pop got the sickle out of the garage and chopped all the weeds down and Harry pushed the lawnmower back and forth across the stubble until it looked as trim as the Methodist's half, though browner. He felt guilty doing it, and was frightened of the fight his parents would have when Mother came back. He dreaded their quarrels: when their faces went angry and flat and words flew, it was as if a pane of glass were put in front of him; cutting off air; his strength drained away and he had to go to a far corner of the house. This time there was no fight. His father shocked him by simply lying, and doubled the shock by winking as he did. He told her the Methodist had at last broken down and cut the strip of grass himself. Mother believed it but wasn't pleased; she talked all the rest of the day and off and on all week about suing the old holy-roller. In a way she had come to think it *was* her flowerbed. From cement to cement the strip is not much more than a foot across. Walking along it feels slightly precarious to Harry, like treading the top of a wall.

He walks back as far as the lit kitchen window and steps onto the cement without the sole of his shoe scraping and on tiptoe looks in one bright corner. He sees himself sitting in a high chair, and a quick strange jealousy comes and passes. It is his son. The boy's little neck gleams like one more clean object in the kitchen among the cups and plates and chromium knobs and aluminum cake-making receptacles on shelves scalloped with glossy oilcloth. His mother's glasses glitter as she leans in from her place at the table with a spoon of smoking beans at the end of her fat curved arm. Her face shows none of the worry she must be feeling about why nobody comes for the boy and instead is narrowed, her nose a faceted beak, into one wish: that the boy eat. Her mouth is focused into white crinkles. They smooth in a smile; Nelson's lips, hidden from Rabbit's angle, must have taken the beans. The others around the table express praise, blurred syllables from his father, piercing from his sister, something thin about both voices. Rabbit, with the intervening glass and the rustle of blood in his head, can't hear what they say. His father, fresh from work, is in an ink-smeared blue shirt and, when his face lapses from applauding his grandson, looks old: tired and grizzled. His throat a loose bundle of cords. The new teeth he got a year ago have changed his face, collapsed it a fraction of an inch. Miriam, dolled up in gold and jet for Friday night, picks at her food indifferently and offers a spoonful to the kid; the reach of her slender white braceleted arm across the steaming table rings a barbaric chord into the scene. She makes up too much; at nineteen she would be good enough without green eyelids. Because she has buck teeth she tries not to smile. Nelson's big whorly head dips on its bright neck and his foreshortened hand, dots of pink, dabbles toward the spoon, wants to take it from her. Pop's face lurches into laughter above his plate, and Mim's lips leap in a grin that cracks her cautious wised-up squint and breaks through to the little girl Rabbit used to ride on his handlebars, her streaming hair tickling his eyes as they coasted down the steep Mt. Judge streets. She lets Nelson take her spoon and he drops it. The kid cries "Peel! Peel!": this Rabbit can hear, and understand. It means "spill." Pop and Mim smile and make remarks but Mom, mouth set, comes in neatly with her spoon. Harry's boy is being fed, this home is happier than his, he glides a pace backward over the cement and rewalks the silent strip of grass.

His acts take on decisive haste. In darkness he goes down another block of Jackson. He cuts up Joseph Street, runs a block, strides another, and comes within sight of his car, its grid grinning at him, parked the wrong way on this side of the street. He taps his pocket and fear hits him. He doesn't have the key. Everything depends, the whole pure idea, on which way Janice was sloppy. Either she forgot to give him the key when he went out or she never bothered to take it out of the ignition. He tries to imagine which is more likely and can't. He doesn't know her that well. He never knows what the hell she'll do. She doesn't know herself. Dumb.

The back but not the front of the big Springer house is lit up. He moves cautiously in the sweet-smelling shadows under the trees in case the old lady is waiting inside the darkened living-room to tell him what she thinks. He crosses around in front of the car, the '55 Ford that old man Springer with his little yellow Hitler mustache sold him for an even thousand in 1957 because the scared bastard was ashamed, cars being his business he was ashamed of his daughter marrying some-body who had nothing but a '36 Buick he bought for $125 in the Army in Texas in 1953. Made him cough up a thou-sand he didn't have when the Buick had just had eighty dollars' worth of work. That was the kind of thing. They de-serve everything they get. He opens the car from the passenger side, wincing at the *pung* of the brittle door spring and quickly ducking his head into the car. Thank God. Be-neath the knobs for lights and wipers the octagon of the ignition key tells in silhouette. Bless that dope. Rabbit slithers in, closing the side door until metal touches metal but not slamming it. The front of the stucco Springer house is still unlit. It reminds him for some reason of an abandoned ice-cream stand. He turns the key through On into Start and the motor churns and catches. In his anxiety to be secret he is delicate on the accelerator and the motor, idle for hours in the air of an early spring day, is cold, sticks, and stalls. Rab-bit's heart rises and a taste of straw comes into his throat. But of course what the hell if she *does* come out? The only thing suspicious is that he doesn't have the kid and he can say he's on his way to pick him up. That would have been the logical way to do it anyway. Nevertheless he doesn't want to be put to the inconvenience of lying, however plausi-bly. He pulls the hand choke out a fraction, just enough to pinch his fingertips, and starts the motor again. He pumps once, and glances aside to see the Springers' living-room light flash on, and lets the clutch out, and the Ford bucks away from the curb.

He drives too fast down Joseph Street, and turns left, ig-noring the sign saying STOP. He heads down Jackson to where it runs obliquely into Central, which is also 422 to Philadelphia. STOP. He doesn't want to go to Philadelphia but the road broadens on the edge of town beyond the electric-power station and the only other choice is to go back

through Mt. Judge around the mountain into the thick of
Brewer and the suppertime traffic. He doesn't intend ever to
see Brewer again, that flowerpot city. The highway turns
from three-lane to four-lane and there is no danger of hitting
another car; they all run along together like sticks on a
stream. Rabbit turns on the radio. After a hum a beautiful
Negress sings, "Without a song, the dahay would nehever
end, without a song." Rabbit wishes for a cigarette to go with
the washed feeling inside and remembers he gave up smoking and feels cleaner still. He slumps down and puts one
arm up on the back of the seat and glides down the twilight
pike left-handed. "A field of corn" the Negress's voice bending dark and warm like the inside of a cello "the grasses
grow" the countryside dipping around the road like a continuous dark bird "it makes no mind no how" his scalp
contracts ecstatically "wihithout a." The smell of parched
rubber says the heater has come on and he turns the little
lever to MOD.

"Secret Love," "Autumn Leaves," and something whose
title he missed. Supper music. Music to cook by. His mind
nervously shifts away from the involuntary vision of Janice's
meal sizzling in the pan, chops probably, the grease-tinted
water bubbling disconsolately, the unfrozen peas steaming
away their vitamins. He tries to think of something pleasant.
He imagines himself about to shoot a long one-hander; but
he feels he's on a cliff, there is an abyss he will fall into
when the ball leaves his hands. He tries to repicture his
mother and sister feeding his son, but the boy is crying in
backward vision, his forehead red and his mouth stretched
wide and his helpless breath hot. There must be something:
the water from the ice plant running in the gutter, yellowish,
the way it curled on stones and ran in diagonal wrinkles,
waving the pretty threads of slime attached to its edges.
Suddenly Janice shivers in memory of the other's girl's bed
in declining daylight. He tries to blot out the sensation with
Miriam, Mim on his handlebars, Mim on a sled in dark snowfall being pulled up Jackson Street by him, the little kid
laughing in her hood, himself the big brother, the red lights in
snowfall marking the trestles the town crew have used to
block off the street for sledding, down, down, the runners
whistling on the dark packed slick, Hold me Harry, the
sparks as the runners hit the cinders spread at the bottom
for safety, the scraping stop like the thump of a great heart

in the dark. Once more Harry, then we'll go home, I promise Harry, please, oh I love you, little Mim only seven or so,
in her dark hood, the street waxy with snow still falling.
Poor Janice would probably have the wind up now, on the
phone to her mother or his mother, somebody, wondering
why her supper was getting cold. So dumb. Forgive me.

He accelerates. The growing complexity of lights threatens
him. He is being drawn into Philadelphia. He hates Philadelphia. Dirtiest city in the world they live on poisoned water.
He wants to go south, down, down the map into orange
groves and smoking rivers and barefoot women. It seems
simple enough, drive all night through the dawn through the
morning through the noon park on a beach take off your
shoes and fall asleep by the Gulf of Mexico. Wake up with
the stars above perfectly spaced in perfect health. But he is
going east, the worst direction, into unhealth, soot, and stink,
a smothering hole where you can't move without killing
somebody. Yet the highway sucks him on, and a sign says
POTTSTOWN 2. He almost brakes. But then he thinks.

If he is heading east, south is on his right. And then, as
if the world were just standing around waiting to serve his
thoughts, a broad road to the right is advertised, ROUTE 100
WEST CHESTER WILMINGTON. Route 100 had a fine ultimate
sound. He doesn't want to go to Wilmington but it's the right
direction. He's never been to Wilmington. The Du Ponts
own it. He wonders what it's like to make it to a Du Pont.

He doesn't drive five miles before this road begins to feel
like a part of the same trap. The first road offered him he
turns right on. A keystone marker in the headlights says 23.
A good number. The first varsity game he played in he
made 23 points. A sophomore and a virgin. Trees overshadow
this narrower road.

A barefoot Du Pont. Brown legs probably, bitty birdy
breasts. Beside a swimming pool in France. Something like
money in a naked woman, deep, millions. You think of millions as being white. Sink all the way in softly still lots left.
Rich girls frigid? Nymphomaniacs? Must vary. Just women
after all, descended from some old Indian-cheater luckier
than the rest, inherit the same stuff if they lived in a slum.
Glow all the whiter there, on drab mattresses. That wonderful
softness they have when they want it. Otherwise just fat
weight. That wonderful softness, but they want you up
and hard on their little ledge. The thing is play them until

just a touch. You can tell: their skin under the fur gets all loose like a puppy's neck.

Route 23 works west through little tame country towns, Coventryville, Elverson, Morgantown. Rabbit likes these. Square high farmhouses nuzzle the road. Soft chalk sides. In one town a tavern blazes and he stops at a hardware store opposite with two gasoline pumps outside. He knows from the radio it's about seven-thirty, but the hardware store is still open, shovels and seeders and post-hole diggers and axes, metal painted blue and orange and yellow, in the window, along with some fishing rods and a string of fielder's gloves. A middle-aged man comes out in boots, baggy suntans, and two shirts. "Yes *sir*," he says, coming down on the second word with forced weight, like a lame man stepping.

"Couldya fill it up with regular?"

The man starts to pump it in and Rabbit gets out of the car and goes around to the back and asks. "How far am I from Brewer?"

The farmer looks up with a look of curt distrust from listening to the gas gurgle. He lifts a finger. "Back up and take that road and it's sixteen miles to the bridge."

Sixteen. He had driven forty miles to get sixteen miles away.

But it was far enough, this was another world. It smells differently, smells older, of nooks and pockets in the ground that nobody's stirred yet. "Suppose I go straight?"

"That'll take you to Churchtown."

"What's after Churchtown?"

"New Holland. Lancaster."

"Do you have any maps?"

"Son, where do you want to go?"

"Huh? I don't know exactly."

"Where are you headed?" The man is patient. His face at the same time seems fatherly and crafty and stupid.

For the first time, Harry realizes he is a criminal. He hears the gasoline rise in the neck of the tank and notices with what care the farmer squeezes every drop he can into the tank without letting it slosh over the lip insolently the way a city garageman would. Out here a drop of gas isn't supposed to escape and he's in the middle of it at night. Laws aren't ghosts in this country, they walk around with the smell of earth on them. Senseless fear cakes over Rabbit's body.

"Check the oil?" the man asks in a voice of startling softness after hanging up the hose on the side of the rusty pump, one of the old style, with the painted bubble head.

"No. Wait. Yeah. You better had. Thanks." Simmer down. All he'd done was ask for a map. Damn dirtdigger so stingy, what was suspicious about that? Somebody was always going somewhere. He better get the oil checked because he wasn't going to stop again until he was halfway to Georgia. "Hey, how far is Lancaster south of here?"

"Due south? Don't know. It's about twenty-five miles on the road. Your oil's all right. You think you're going to Lancaster now?"

"Yeah, I might."

"Check your water?"

"No. It's O.K."

"Batteries?"

"They're fine. Let's go."

The man lets the hood slam down and smiles over at Harry. "That's three-ninety on the gas, young fella": the words are pronounced in that same heavy cautious crippled way.

Rabbit puts four ones in his paw. He disappears into the hardware store; maybe he's phoning the state cops. He acts like he knows something, but how could he? Rabbit itches to duck into the car and drive off. To steady himself he counts the money left in his wallet. Seventy-three. Today was payday. Fingering so much lettuce strengthens his nerves. Switching off the lights in the hardware store as he comes, the farmer comes back with the dime and no map. Harry cups his hand for the dime and the man pushes it in with his broad thumb and says, "Looked around inside and the only road map is New York State. You don't want to go that way, do you now?"

"No," Rabbit answers, and walks to his car door. He feels through the hairs on the back of his neck the man following him. He gets into the car and slams the door and the farmer is right there, the meat of his face hung in the open door window. He bends down and nearly sticks his face in. His cracked thin lips with a scar tilting toward his nose move thoughtfully. He's wearing glasses, a scholar. "The only way to get somewhere, you know, is to figure out where you're going before you go there."

Rabbit catches a whiff of whisky. He says in a level way, "I don't think so." The lips and spectacles and black hairs

poking out of the man's tear-shaped nostrils show no surprise. Rabbit pulls out, going straight. Everybody who tells
you how to act has whisky on their breath.

He drives to Lancaster and all the way his good airy feeling
inside is spoiled. That that guy didn't know a thing but was
just half-crocked makes the whole region sinister. Outside of
Churchtown he passes an Amish buggy in the dark and
catches a glimpse of a bearded man and a woman in black
in this horsedrawn shadow glaring like devils. The beard
inside the buggy like hairs in a nostril. He tries to think of
the good life these people lead, of the way they keep clear
of all this phony business, this twentieth-century vitamin
racket, but in his head they stay devils, risking getting killed
trotting along with one dim pink reflector behind, hating
Rabbit and his kind, with their big furry tail lights. Who
they think they were? He can't shake them, mentally. They
never appeared in his rear-view mirror. He passed them and
there was nothing. It was just that one sideways glance; the
woman's face a hatchet of smoke in the square window. Tall
coffin lined with hair clopping along to the tune of a dying
horse. Amish overworked their animals, he knew. Fanatics.
Hump their women standing up, out in the fields, wearing
clothes, just hoist black skirts and there it was, nothing underneath. No underpants. Fanatics. Worship manure.

The rich earth seems to cast its darkness upward into the
air. The farm country is somber at night. He is grateful
when the lights of Lancaster merge with his dim beams. He
stops at a diner whose clock says 8:04. He hadn't intended
to eat until he got out of the state. He takes a map from
the rack by the door and while eating three hamburgers at
the counter studies his position. He is in Lancaster, surrounded
by funny names, Bird in Hand, Paradise, Intercourse, Mt. Airy,
Mascot. They probably didn't seem funny if you lived in
them. Like Mt. Judge; you get used. A town has to be
called something.

Bird in Hand, Paradise: his eyes keep going back to this
dainty lettering on the map. He has an impulse, amid the
oil-filmed shimmer of this synthetic and desultory diner, to
drive there. Little plump women, toy dogs in the street,
candy houses in lemon sunshine.

But no, his goal is the huge white sun of the south. And
from the map he's been traveling more west than south; if
the dirtdigger back there had had a map he could have gone

due south on 10. Now the only thing to do is go into the heart of Lancaster and take 222 out and take it all the way down into Maryland and then catch 1. He remembers reading in the *Saturday Evening Post* how 1 goes from Florida to Maine through the most beautiful scenery in the world. He asks for a glass of milk and to go with it a piece of apple pie; the crust is crisp and bubbled but the filling is watery and lavender in color. He pays by cracking a ten and goes out into the parking lot feeling pleased. The hamburgers had been fatter and warmer than the ones you get in Brewer, and the buns had seemed steamed.

It takes him a half-hour to pick his way through the city. On 222 he drives south through Refton, Hessdale, New Providence, and Quarryville, through Mechanics Grove and Unicorn and then a long stretch so dull and unmarked he doesn't know he's entered Maryland until he hits Oakwood. On the radio he hears "No Other Arms, No Other Lips," "Stagger Lee," a commercial for Rayco Clear Plastic Seat Covers, "If I Didn't Care" by Connie Francis, a commercial for Radio-Controlled Garage Door Operators, "I Ran All the Way Home Just to Say I'm Sorry," "That Old Feeling" by Mel Torme, a commercial for Big Screen Westinghouse TV Set with One-Finger Automatic Tuning, "needle-sharp pictures a nose away from the screen," "The Italian Cowboy Song," "Yep," by Duane Eddy, a commercial for Papermate Pens, "Almost Grown," a commercial for Tame Cream Rinse, "Let's Stroll," news (President Eisenhower and Prime Minister Harold Macmillan began a series of talks in Gettysburg, Tibetans battle Chinese Communists in Lhasa, the whereabouts of the Dalai Lama, spiritual leader of this remote and backward land, are unknown, a $250,000 trust fund has been left to a Park Avenue maid, Spring scheduled to arrive tomorrow), sports news (Yanks over Braves in Miami, somebody tied with somebody in St. Petersburg Open, scores in a local basketball tournament), weather (fair and seasonably warm), "The Happy Organ," "Turn Me Loose," a commercial for Savings Bank Life Insurance, "Rocksville, P-A" (Rabbit loves it), "A Picture No Artist Could Paint," a commercial for New Formula Barbasol Presto-Lather, the daily cleansing action tends to prevent skin blemishes and emulsifies something, "Pink Shoe Laces" by Dody Stevens, a letter about a little boy called Billy Tessman who was hit by a car and would appreciate cards or letters, "Petit Fleur,"

"Fungo" (great), a commercial for Wool-Tex All-Wool Suits, "Fall Out" by Henry Mancini, "Everybody Likes to Cha Cha Cha," a commercial for Lord's Grace Table Napkins and the gorgeous Last Supper Tablecloth, "The Beat of My Heart," a commercial for Speed-Shine Wax and Lanolin Clay, "Venus," and then the same news again. Where is the Dalai Lama?

Shortly after Oakwood he comes to Route 1, which with its hot-dog stands and Calso signs and roadside taverns aping log cabins is unexpectedly discouraging. The further he drives the more he feels some great confused system, Baltimore now instead of Philadelphia, reaching for him. He stops at a gas station for two dollars' worth of regular. What he really wants is another map. He unfolds it standing by a Coke machine and reads it in the light coming through a window stained green by stacked cans of liquid wax.

His problem is to get west and free of Baltimore-Washington, which like a two-headed dog guards the coastal route to the south. He doesn't want to go down along the water anyway; his image is of himself going right down the middle, right into the broad soft belly of the land, surprising the dawn cottonfields with his northern plates.

Now he is somewhere here. Further on, then, a road numbered 23 will go off to his left—no, his right. That goes up and over and back into Pennsylvania but at this place, Shawsville, he can take a little narrow blue road without a number. Then go down a little and over again on 137. There is a ragged curve then that this road makes with 482 and then 31. Rabbit can feel himself swinging up and through that curve into the red line numbered 26 and down that into another numbered 340. Red, too; he is really gliding and suddenly sees where he wants to go. Over on the left three red roads stream parallel northeast to southwest; Rabbit can just feel them sliding down through the valleys of the Appalachians. Get on one of them it would be a chute dumping you into sweet low cottonland in the morning. Yes. Once he gets on that he can shake all thoughts of the mess behind him.

He gives two dollars for gas to the attendant, a young but tall colored boy whose limber lazy body slumping inside his baggy Amoco coveralls Rabbit has a weird impulse to hug. This far south the air already feels warmer. Warmth vibrates in brown and purple arcs between the lights of the service station and the moon. The clock in the window above the green cans of liquid wax says 9:10. The thin red second hand sweeps the numbers calmly and makes Rabbit's way seem smooth. He ducks into the Ford and in that fusty hot interior starts to murmur, "Ev, reebody loves the, cha cha cha." He drives bravely at first. Over blacktop and whitetop, through towns and fields, past false intersections with siren voices, keeping the map on the seat beside him, keeping the numbers straight and resisting the impulse to turn blindly south. Something animal in him knows he is going west.

The land grows wilder. The road evades great lakes and tunnels through pines. In the top of the windshield the telephone wires continually whip the stars. The music on the radio slowly freezes; the rock and roll for kids cools into old standards and show tunes and comforting songs from the Forties. Rabbit pictures married couples driving home to baby-sitters after a meal out and a movie. Then these melodies turn to ice as real night music takes over, pianos and vibes erecting clusters in the high brittle octaves and a clarinet wandering across like a crack on a pond. Saxes doing the same figure 8 over and over again. He drives through Westminster. It takes forever to reach Frederick. He picks up 340 and crosses the Potomac.

Growing sleepy, Rabbit stops before midnight at a roadside café for coffee. Somehow, though he can't put his finger on the difference, he is unlike the other customers. They sense it too, and look at him with hard eyes, eyes like little metal studs pinned into the white faces of young men sitting in zippered jackets in booths three to a girl, the girls with orange hair hanging like seaweed or loosely bound with gold barrettes like pirate treasure. At the counter middle-aged couples in overcoats bunch their faces forward into the straws of gray ice-cream sodas. In the hush his entrance induces, the excessive courtesy the weary woman behind the counter shows him amplifies his strangeness. He orders coffee quietly and studies the rim of the cup to steady the sliding in his stomach. He had thought, he had read, that from shore to shore all America was the same. He wonders, Is it just these people I'm outside, or is it all America?

Outside in the sharp air, he flinches when footsteps pound behind him. But it is just two lovers, holding hands and in a hurry to reach their car, their locked hands a starfish leaping through the dark. Their license plate says West Virginia. All the plates do except his. On the other side of the road the wooded land dips down so he can look over the tops of trees at the side of a mountain like a cutout of stiff paper mounted on a slightly faded blue sheet. He climbs into his Ford distastefully, but its stale air is his only haven.

He drives through a thickening night. The road unravels with infuriating slowness, its black wall wearilessly rising in front of his headlights no matter how they twist. The tar sucks his tires. He realizes that the heat on his cheeks is anger; he has been angry ever since he left that diner full of mermaids. So angry his cheeks feel parched inside his mouth and his nostrils water. He grinds his foot down as if to squash this snake of a road, and nearly loses the car on a curve, as the two right wheels fall captive to the dirt shoulder. He brings them back but keeps the speedometer needle leaning to the right.

He turns off the radio; its music no longer seems a river he is riding down but instead speaks with the voice of the cities and brushes his head with slippery hands. Yet into the silence that results he refuses to let thoughts come. He doesn't want to think, he wants to fall asleep and wake up pillowed by sand. How stupid, how frigging, frigging stupid it was, not to be further than this. At midnight, the night half gone.

The land refuses to change. The more he drives the more the region resembles the country around Mt. Judge. The same scruff on the embankments, the same weathered billboards for the same insane products. At the upper edge of his headlight beams the naked tree-twigs make the same net. Indeed the net seems thicker now.

The animal in him swells its protest that he is going west. His mind stubbornly resists. The only way to get somewhere is to decide where you're going and go. His plan calls for him to bear left 28 miles after Frederick and that 28 miles is used up now and, though his instincts cry out against it, when a broad road leads off to the left, though it's unmarked, he takes it. It is unlikely that the road *would* be marked, from its thickness on the map. But it is a shortcut, he knows. He remembers that when Marty Tothero began to coach him he didn't want to shoot fouls underhand but that it turned out in the end to be the way.

The road is broad and confident for miles, but there is a

sudden patched stretch, and after that it climbs and narrows. Narrows not so much by plan as naturally, the edges crumbling in and the woods on either side crowding down. The road twists more and more wildly in its struggle to gain height and then without warning sheds its skin of asphalt and worms on in dirt. By now Rabbit knows this is not the road but he is afraid to stop the car to turn it around. He has left the last light of a house miles behind. When he strays from straddling the mane of weeds, brambles rake his painted sides. Tree-trunks and low limbs are all his headlights pick up; the scrabbling shadows spider backward through the web of wilderness into a black core where he fears his probe of light will stir some beast or ghost. He supports speed with prayer, praying that the road not stop, remembering how on Mt. Judge even the shaggiest most forgotten logging lane eventually sloped to the valley. His ears itch; his height presses on them.

The prayer's answer is blinding. The trees at a far bend leap like flame and a car comes around and flies at him with its beams tilted high. Rabbit slithers over into the ditch and, faceless as death, the bright car rips by at a speed twice his own. For more than a minute Rabbit drives through this bastard's insulting dust. Yet the good news makes him meek, the news that this road goes two ways. And shortly he seems to be in a park. His lights pick up green little barrels stenciled PLEASE and the trees are thinned on both sides and in among them picnic tables and pavilions and outhouses show their straight edges. The curves of cars show too, and a few are parked close to the road, their passengers down out of sight. So the road of horror is a lovers' lane. In a hundred yards it ends.

It meets at right angles a smooth broad highway overhung by the dark cloud of a mountain ridge. One car zips north. Another zips south. There are no signs. Rabbit puts the shift in neutral and pulls out the emergency brake and turns on the roof light and studies his map. His hands and shins are trembling. His brain flutters with fatigue behind sandy eyelids; the time must be 12:30 or later. The highway in front of him is empty. He has forgotten the numbers of the routes he has taken and the names of the towns he has passed through. He remembers Frederick but can't find it and in time realizes he is searching in a section due west of Washington where he has never been. There are so many red lines and blue lines, long names, little towns, squares and circles and stars. He moves his eyes north but the only line he recognizes is the straight dotted line of the Pennsylvania-Maryland border. The Mason-Dixon Line. The schoolroom in which he learned this recurs to him, the rooted desk rows, the scarred varnish, the milky black of the blackboard, the sweet pieces of ass all up and down the aisles in alphabetical order. His eyes blankly founder. Rabbit hears a clock in his head beat, monstrously slow, the soft ticks as far apart as the sound of waves on the shore he had wanted to reach. He burns his attention through the film fogging his eyes down into the map again. At once "Frederick" pops into sight, but in trying to steady its position he loses it, and fury makes the bridge of his nose ache. The names melt away and he sees the map whole, a net, all those red lines and blue lines and stars, a net he is somewhere caught in. He claws at it and tears it; with a gasp of exasperation he rips away a great triangular piece and tears the large remnant in half and, more calmly, lays these three pieces on top of each other and tears them in half, and then those six pieces and so on until he has a wad he can squeeze in his hand like a ball. He rolls down the window and throws the ball out; it explodes, and the bent scraps like disembodied wings flicker back over the top of the car. He cranks up the window. He blames everything on that farmer with glasses and two shirts. Funny how the man sticks in his throat. He can't think past him, his smugness, his *solidity,* somehow. He stumbled over him back there and is stumbling still, can't get him away from his feet, like shoelaces too long or a stiff stick between his feet; the man mocked, whether out of his mouth or in the paced motions of his hands or through his hairy ears, somewhere out of his body mocked the furtive wordless hopes that at moments made the ground firm for Harry. Decide where you want to go and then go: it missed the whole point and yet there is always the chance that, little as it is, it is everything. At any rate Rabbit feels if he'd trusted to instinct he'd be in South Carolina now. He wishes he had a cigarette, to help him decide what his instinct is. He decides to go to sleep in the car for a few hours.

But a car starts up in the petting grove behind him and the headlights wheel around and press on Rabbit's neck. He stopped his car right in the middle of the road, for a glance at the map. Now he must move. He feels unreasoning fear of being overtaken; the other headlights swell in the rear-view mirror and fill it like a cup. He stamps the clutch, puts the shift in first, and releases the handbrake. Hopping onto the highway, he turns instinctively right, north.

The trip home is easier. Though he has no map and hard-ly any gas, an all-night Mobilgas magically appears near Hagerstown and green signs begin to point to the Pennsylvania Turnpike. The music on the radio is soothing now, lyrical and unadvertised, and, coming first from Harrisburg and then from Philadelphia, makes a beam he infallibly flies in on. He has broken through the barrier of fatigue and come into a calm flat world where nothing matters much. The last quarter of a basketball game used to carry him into this world; you ran not as the crowd thought for the sake of the score but for yourself, in a kind of idleness. There was you and sometimes the ball and then the hole, the high perfect hole with its pretty skirt of net. It was you, just you and that fringed ring, and sometimes it came down right to your lips it seemed and sometimes it stayed away, hard and re-mote and small. It seemed silly for the crowd to applaud or groan over what you had already felt in your fingers or even in your arms as you braced to shoot or for that matter in your eyes: when he was hot he could see the separate threads wound into the strings looping the hoop. Yet at the start of the night when you came out for warm-up and could see all the town clunkers sitting in the back of bleachers elbowing each other and the cheerleaders wisecracking with the racier male teachers, the crowd then seemed right inside you, your liver and lungs and stomach. There was one fat guy used to come who'd get on the floor of Rabbit's stomach and really make it shake. "Hey, Gunner! Hey, Showboat, shoot! Shoot!" Rabbit remembers him fondly now; to that guy he had been a hero of sorts.

Throughout the early morning the music keeps coming and the signs keep pointing. His brain feels like a frail but alert invalid packed inside among a lot of deep pillows with mes-sengers bringing him down long corridors all this music and geographical news. At the same time he feels abnormally senstive on the surface, as if his skin is thinking. The steering wheel is thin as a whip in his hands. As he turns it lightly he can feel the shaft stiffly pivot, and the differential gears part, and the bearings rotate in their sealed tunnels of grease. The phosphorescent winkers at the side of the road beguile him into thinking of young Du Pont women: strings of them winding through huge glassy parties, potentially naked in their sequined sheath gowns.

He wonders why there are so many signs coming back and so few going down. Of course he didn't know what he was going toward going down. He takes the Brewer turnoff off the Pike and the road takes him through the town where he first bought gas. As he takes the road marked BREWER 16 he can see cattycornered across the main street the dirt-digger's pumps and his dark window full of glinting shovels and fishing rods. The window looks pleased. There is just a touch of light in the air. The radio's long floe of music is breaking up in warm-weather reports and farm prices.

He comes into Brewer from the south, seeing it as a gradual multiplication of houses among the trees beside the road and then as a treeless waste of industry, shoe factories and bottling plants and company parking lots and knitting mills converted to electronics parts and elephantine gas tanks lifting above trash-filled swampland yet lower than the blue edge of the mountain from whose crest Brewer was a warm carpet woven around a single shade of brick.

He crossed the Running Horse Bridge and is among streets he knows. He takes Warren Avenue through the south side of town and comes out on 422 near City Park. He drives around the mountain in company with a few hissing trailer trucks. As he turns left from Central into Jackson he nearly sideswipes a milk truck idling yards out from the curb. He continues up Jackson, past his parents' house, and turns into Kegerise Alley, and in the clear dawn light he glides past the old chicken house, past the silent body shop, and parks the car in front of the Sunshine Athletic Association, a few steps from the boxed-in entrance, where anyone coming out would have to notice. Rabbit glances up hopefully at the third-story windows but no light is showing. Tothero, if he is in there, is still asleep.

Rabbit settles himself to sleep. He takes off his suit coat and lays it over his chest like a blanket. But the daylight is growing, and the front seat is far too short, and the steering wheel crowds his shoulders. He doesn't move to the back seat because that would make him vulnerable; he wants to be able to drive away in a second if he must. Further, he doesn't want to sleep so heavily he will miss Tothero when he comes out.

So there he lies, his long legs doubled up and no place really for his feet, gazing up with crusty vision across the steering wheel and through the windshield into the sky's flat fresh blue. Today is Saturday, and the sky has that broad bright blunt Saturday quality Rabbit remembers from boyhood when the sky of a Saturday morning was the blank scoreboard of a long game about to begin.

A car goes by up the alley, and Rabbit closes his eyes, and the darkness vibrates with the incessant automobile noises of the night past. He sees again the woods, the narrow road, the dark grove full of cars each containing a silent coupling. He thinks again of his goal, lying down at dawn in sand by the Gulf of Mexico, and it seems in a way that the gritty seat of his car is that sand, and the rustling of the waking town the rustling of the sea.

He must not miss Tothero. He opens his eyes and tries to rise from his stiff shroud. He wonders if he has missed any time. The sky is the same.

He becomes anxious about the car windows. He hoists his chest up on one elbow and checks them all. The window above his head is open a crack and he cranks it tight and pushes down all the lock buttons. This security relaxes him hopelessly. He turns his face into the crack between seat and back. This twisting pushes his knees into the tense upright cushion, and annoyance that for the moment makes him more wakeful. He wonders where his son slept, what Janice has done, where his parents and her parents hunted. Whether the police know. He feels the faded night he left behind in this place as a net of telephone calls and hasty trips, trails of tears and strings of words, white worried threads shuttled through the night and now faded but still existent, an invisible net overlaying the steep streets and in whose center he lies secure in his locked windowed hutch.

Cotton and gulls in half-light and the way she'd come on the other girl's bed, never as good on their own. But there were good things: Janice so shy about showing her body even in the first weeks of wedding yet one night coming into the bathroom expecting nothing he found the mirror clouded with steam and Janice just out of the shower standing there doped and pleased with a little blue towel lazily and unashamed her bottom bright pink with hot water the way a women was of two halves bending over and turning and laughing at his expression whatever it was and putting

her arms up to kiss him, a blush of steam on her body and
the back of her neck slippery. Rabbit adjusts his position
and returns his mind to its dark socket; the back of her
neck slippery, the pit of her back pliant, both on their
knees together, contortions that never were. His shin knocks
the door handle, the pain becoming oddly mixed with the
knocks of metal on metal down in the body shop. Work
had begun. Eight o'clock? Rabbit writhes and sits up, the
covering coat collapsing to his warm lap, and indeed through
the splotched windshield there *is* Tothero's figure, walking
away down the alley. He is up beyond the very old farmhouse; Rabbit jumps from the car, puts on his coat, and
runs after him. "Mr. Tothero! Hey Mr. Tothero!" His voice
sounds flaked and rusty after hours of disuse.

The man turns, looking more tired than Rabbit had expected. A short man with a big balding head, he had
played when basketball was still a quick man's game. He
seems foreshortened: this big head and a massive checkered
sports coat and then stubby legs in blue trousers that are too
long, so the crease buckles and zigzags above the shoes. As
he brakes his run, and walks the last strides, Rabbit fears
he's made a mistake.

But Tothero says the perfect thing. "Harry," he says,
"the great Harry Angstrom." He puts out his hand for Harry
to seize and with the other squeezes the boy's arm in a clasp
of rigor. It comes back to Rabbit how he always had his
hands on you. Tothero just stands there holding on and looking at him, smiling crookedly, the nose bent, one eye wide
open and the other heavy-lidded. His face has grown more
lopsided with the years. He is not going bald evenly; brushed
strands of gray and pale brown patch his skull.

"I need your advice," Rabbit says, and corrects himself. "What I really need is a place to sleep."

Tothero is silent before replying. His great strength is in
these silences; other men hasten to respond instantly, as if
they were always embarrassed, but Tothero has the disciplinarian's trick of waiting a moment. As if he considers
everything. It gives him great weight. At last he asks,
"What's happened to your home?"

"Well it kind of went."

"How do you mean?"

"It was no good. I've run out. I really have."

Another pause. Rabbit narrows his eyes against the sunlight that rebounds off the asphalt. His left ear aches. His teeth on that side feel as if they might start hurting.

"That doesn't sound like very mature behavior," Tothero states.

"It was a mess as it was."

"What sort of mess?"

"I don't know. My wife's an alcoholic."

"And have you tried to help her?"

"Sure. How?"

"Did you drink with her?"

"No sir, never. I can't stand the stuff, I just don't like the taste." He says this readily, proud to be able to report to his old coach that he has not abused his body.

"Perhaps you should have," Tothero offers after a moment. "Perhaps if you had shared this pleasure with her, she could have controlled it."

Rabbit, dazed by the sun, numb through weariness, can't follow this thought.

"It's Janice Springer, isn't it?" Tothero asks.

"Yeah. God she's dumb. She really is."

"Harry, that's a harsh thing to say. Of any human soul."

Rabbit nods because Tothero himself seems certain of this. He is beginning to feel weak under the weight of the man's pauses. These pauses seem longer than he remembered them, as if Tothero too feels their weight. Fear touches Rabbit again; he suspects his old coach is addled, and begins all over. "I thought maybe I could sleep a couple hours somewhere in the Sunshine. Otherwise I might as well go home. I've had it."

To his relief Tothero becomes all bustling action, taking his elbow, steering him back along the alley, saying, "Yes of course, Harry, you look terrible, Harry. Terrible." His hand holds Rabbit's arm with metallic inflexibility and as he pushes him along Rabbit's bones jolt, pinned at this point. Something frantic in so tight a grip diminishes the comfort of its firmness. Tothero's voice, too, having turned precise, hasty, and gay, cuts into Rabbit's woolly state too sharply. "You asked me for two things," he says. "Two things. A place to sleep, and advice. Now, Harry, I'll give you the place to sleep provided, provided, Harry, that when you wake up the two of us have a serious, a long and serious talk about this crisis in your marriage. I'll tell you this now, it's not so much you I'm worried about, I know you well enough to know you always land on your feet, Harry; it's not so much you as Janice. She doesn't have your co-ordination. Do you promise?"

"Sure. Promise what?"

"Promise, Harry, we'll thrash out a way between us to help her."

"Yeah, but I don't think I can. I mean I'm not that interested in her."

They reach the cement steps and the wood weather-box of the entrance. Tothero opens the door with a key he has. The place is empty, the silent bar shadowy and the small round tables looking rickety and weak without men sitting at them. The electrical advertisements behind the bar are unplugged and dead: dusty tubing and tinsel. Tothero says, in a voice too loud, "I don't believe it. I don't believe that my greatest boy would grow into such a monster."

Monster: the word seems to clatter after them as they climb the stairs to the second floor. Rabbit apologizes: "I'll try to think when I get some sleep."

"Good boy. That's all we want." What does he mean, we? All these tables are empty. Sunlight strikes blond squares into the drawn tan shades above a low radiator dyed black with dust. Men's steps have worn paths in the narrow bare floorboards.

Tothero leads him to a door he has never entered; they go up a steep flight of attic stairs, a kind of nailed-down ladder between whose steps he sees sections of insulated wire and ragged gaps of carpentry. They climb into comparative light. "Here's my mansion," Tothero says, and fidgets with his coat pocket flaps.

The tiny room faces east. A slash in a window shade throws a long knife of sun on a side wall, above an unmade Army cot. The other shade is up. Between the windows stands a bureau cleverly made of six beer cases wired together, three high and two wide. In the six boxes are arranged shirts in their laundry cellophane, folded undershirts and shorts, socks balled in pairs, handkerchiefs, shined shoes, and a leatherbacked brush with a comb stuck in the bristles. From two thick nails some sport coats, jarringly gay in pattern, are hung on hangers. Tothero's housekeeping stops at caring for his clothes. The floor is dotted with rolls of fluff. Newspapers and all kinds of magazines, from the *National Geographic* to teen-age crime confessions and comic books, are stacked around. The space where Tothero lives merges easily with the rest of the attic, which is storage space, containing old pinochle tournament charts and pool tables and some lumber and metal barrels and broken chairs with cane bottoms and a roll of chickenwire and a rack of softball uniforms, hung on a pipe fixed between two slanting beams and blocking out the light from the window at the far end.

"Is there a men's?" Rabbit asks.

"Downstairs, Harry." Tothero's enthusiasm has died; he seems embarrassed. While Rabbit uses the toilet he can hear the old man fussing around upstairs, but when he returns he can see nothing changed. The bed is still unmade.

Tothero waits and Rabbit waits and then realizes Tothero wants to see him undress and undresses, sliding into the rumpled lukewarm bed in his T shirt and Jockey shorts. Though the idea is distasteful, getting into the old man's hollow, the sensations are good, being able to stretch out at last and feeling the solid cool wall close to him and hearing cars moving maybe hunting him far below. He twists his neck to say something to Tothero and is surprised by solitude. The door at the foot of the attic steps has closed and footsteps diminish down one, two flights of stairs, and a key scratches in the outside door and a bird cries by the window and the clangor of the body shop comes up softly. The old man's standing there was disturbing but Rabbit is sure that's not his problem. Tothero's problem he knows is in the other direction, female. Why watch? Suddenly Rabbit knows. It takes Tothero back in time. Because of all the times he had stood in locker rooms watching his boys change clothes. Solving this problem relaxes Rabbit's muscles. He remembers the couple with linked hands running on the parking lot outside the diner in West Virginia and regrets that it hadn't been him about to nail her. Feel her open up in the cavity of the car, her seaweed hair sprawling. Red hair? There? He imagines West Virginia girls as coarse hard-bodied laughers, like the young whores in Texas. Their sugar drawls always seemed to be poking fun but then he was so young. Coming down the street Hanley and Jarzylo and Shamberger the tight khaki making him feel nervous and the plains breaking away on all sides the horizon no higher than his knees it seemed and the houses showing families sitting on sofas inside like chickens at roost facing TV's. Jarzylo a maniac, cackling. Rabbit couldn't believe this house was right. It had flowers in the window, actual living flowers innocent in the window and he was tempted to turn and run. Sure enough the woman who came to the door could have been on television selling cake mix. But she said, "Come on in boys, don't be shaaeh, come on in and heyiv a good taam," said it so motherly, and there they were, not as many as he had pictured, in the parlor on old-fashioned-looking furniture with scrolls and knobs. That they were pretty homely made him less timid, just ordinary factory-looking women, you wouldn't even call them girls, with a glaze on their faces like under fluorescent lights. They pelted the soldiers with remarks like balls of dust and the men sneezed into laughter and huddled together surprised and numb. The one he took, but she took him, came up and touched him, hadn't buttoned her blouse more than one button from the last one and upstairs asked him in her gritty sugar voice if he wanted the light on or off and when out of choked throat he answered "Off" laughed, and then now and then smiled under him, working around to get him right, and even speaking kindly: "You're all right, honey. You're gone along all right." So that when it was over he was hurt to learn, from the creases of completion at the sides of her lips and the hard way she wouldn't keep lying beside him but got up and sat on the edge of the metal-frame bed looking out the dark window at the green night sky, that she hadn't meant her half. Her mute back showing in yellow-white the bar of a swimming-suit bra angered him; he took the ball of her shoulder in his hand and turned her roughly. It was kid stuff; the weighted shadows of her front hung so careless and undefended he looked away. She said down into his ear, "Honey, you didn't pay to be no two-timer." Sweet woman, *she* was money. The clangor of the body shop comes up softly. Its noise comforts him, tells him he is hidden and safe, that while he hides men are busy nailing the world down, and toward the disembodied sounds his heart makes in darkness a motion of love.

His dreams are shallow, furtive things. His legs switch. His lips move a little against the pillow. The skin of his eyelids shudders as his eyeballs turn, surveying the inner wall of vision. Otherwise he is as dead, beyond harm. The slash of sun on the wall above him slowly knifes down, cuts across his chest, becomes a coin on the floor, and vanishes. In shadow he suddenly awakes, his ghostly blue irises searching the unfamiliar planes for the source of men's voices. These voices are downstairs, and a rumble suggests that they are moving the furniture, tramping in circles, hunting him. But a familiar bulbous basso rings out, it is Tothero, and around this firm center the noises downstairs crystallize as the sounds of card-playing, drinking, horse-play, companionship. Rabbit rolls in his hot hollow and turns his face to his cool companion, the wall, and through a red cone of consciousness falls asleep again.

"Harry! Harry!" The voice is plucking at his shoulder, rumpling his hair. He rolls away from the wall, squinting upward into vanished sunshine. Tothero sits in the shadows, a hulk of darkness dense with some anxiousness. His dirty-milk face leans forward, scarred by a lopsided smile. There is a smell of whisky. "Harry, I've got a girl for you!"

"Great. Bring her in."

The old man laughs, uneasily? What does he mean? "You mean Janice?"

"It's after six o'clock. Get up, get up, Harry; you've slept like a beautiful baby. We're going out."

"Why?" Rabbit meant to ask "Where?"

"To eat, Harry, to dine. D-I-N-E. Rise my boy. Aren't you hungry? Hunger. Hunger." He's a madman. He jumps off the bed, pivots a few times on his quick man's little feet, and goes through the motions of bringing things to his mouth. "Oh Harry, you can't understand an old man's hunger, you eat and eat and it's never the right food. You can't understand that." He walks to the window and looks down into the alley, his lumpy profile leaden in the dull light.

Rabbit slides back the covers, angles his naked legs over the edge, and holds himself in a sitting position. The sight of his thighs, parallel, pure, aligns his groggy brain. The hair on his legs, once a thin blond fur, is getting dark and whiskery. The odor of his sleep-soaked body rises to him. "Whatsis girl business?" he asks.

"What is it, yes, what is it?" he asks and utters three obscenities in a stream touching a woman in her three parts, and in the gray light by the window his face falls; he seems amazed to hear himself. Yet he's also watching, as if this was some sort of test. The result determined, he corrects himself, "No. I have an acquaintance, an acquaintance in Brewer, a ladylove perhaps; whom I stand to a meal once in a blue moon. But it's nothing more than that, little more than that. Harry, you're so innocent."

Rabbit begins to be afraid of Tothero, these phrases are so inconsequential, and stands up in his underclothes. "I think I just better run along." The floor-fluff sticks to the soles of his bare feet.

"Oh Harry, Harry," Tothero cries in a rich voice mixed of pain and affection, and comes forward and hugs him with one arm. "You and I are two of a kind." The big lopsided face looks up into his with confidence, but Rabbit sees no resemblance. Yet his memory of the man as his coach still disposes him to listen. "You and I know what the score is, we know—" And right here, arriving at the kernel of his lesson, Tothero is balked, and becomes befuddled. He repeats, "We know," and removes his arm.

Rabbit says, "I thought we were going to talk about Janice when I woke up." He picks up his trousers from the floor and puts them on. Their being rumpled disturbs him; reminds him that he has taken a giant step, and makes nervous wrinkles in his stomach and throat.

"We will, we will," Tothero says, "the moment our social obligations are satisfied." A pause. "Do you want to go back now? You must tell me if you do."

Rabbit remembers the dumb slot of her mouth, the way the closet door bumps against the television set. "No. God."

Tothero is overjoyed; it is happiness making him talk so much. "Well then, well then; get dressed. We can't go to Brewer undressed. Do you need a fresh shirt?"

"Yours wouldn't fit me, would it?"

"No, Harry, no? What's your size?"

"Fifteen three."

"Mine! Mine exactly. You have short arms for your height. Oh, this is wonderful, Harry. I can't tell you how much it means to me that you came to me when you needed help. All those years," he says, taking a shirt from the bureau made of beer cases and stripping off the cellophane, "all those years, all those boys, they pass through your hands, and into the blue. And never come back, Harry; they never come back."

Rabbit is startled to feel and to see in Tothero's mirror

that the shirt fits. Their difference must be all in their legs. With the rattling tongue of a proud mother Tothero watches him dress. His talk makes more sense, now that the embarrassment of explaining what they're going to do is past. "It does my heart good," he says. "Youth before the mirror. How long has it been, Harry, now tell me truly, since you had a good time? A long time?"

"I had a good time last night," Rabbit says. "I drove to West Virginia and back."

"You'll like my lady, I know you will, a city flower," Tothero goes on. "The girl she's bringing I've never met. She says she's fat. All the world looks fat to my lady—how she eats, Harry: the appetite of the young. That's a fascinating knot, you young people have so many tricks I never learned."

"It's just a Windsor." Dressed, Rabbit feels a return of calm. Waking up had in a way returned him to the world he deserted. He had missed Janice's crowding presence, the kid and his shrill needs, his own walls. He had wondered what he was doing. But now these reflexes, shallowly scratched, are spent, and deeper instincts flood forward, telling him he is right. He feels freedom like oxygen everywhere around him; Tothero is an eddy of air, and the building he is in, the streets of the town, are mere stairways and alleyways in space. So perfect, so consistent is the freedom into which the clutter of the world has been vaporized by the simple trigger of his decision, that all ways seem equally good, all movements will put the same caressing pressure on his skin, and not an atom of his happiness would be altered if Tothero told him they were not going to meet two girls but two goats, and they were going not to Brewer but to Tibet. He adjusts his necktie with infinite attention, as if the little lines of this juncture of the Windsor knot, the collar of Tothero's shirt, and the base of his own throat were the arms of a star that will, when he is finished, extend outward to the rim of the universe. *He* is the Dalai Lama. Like a cloud breaking in the corner of his vision Tothero drifts to the window. "Is my car still there?" Rabbit asks.

"Your car is blue. Yes. Put on your shoes."

"I wonder if anybody saw it there. While I was asleep, did you hear anything around town?" For in the vast blank of his freedom Rabbit has remembered a few imperfections, his home, his wife's, their apartment, clots of concern. It seems impossible that the passage of time should have so soon dissolved them, but Tothero's answer implies it.

"No," he says. He adds, "But then of course I didn't go where there would have been talk of you."

It annoys Rabbit that Tothero shows no interest in him except as a partner on a joyride. "I should have gone to work today," he says in a pointed voice, as if blaming the old man.

"What do you do?"

"I demonstrate a kitchen gadget called the MagiPeel Peeler in five-and-dime stores."

"A noble calling," Tothero says, and turns from the window. "Splendid, Harry. You're dressed at last."

"Is there a comb anywhere, Mr. Tothero? I ought to use the can."

Under their feet the men in the Sunshine Athletic Association laugh and catcall at some foolishness. Rabbit pictures passing among them and asks, "Say, should everybody see me?"

Tothero becomes indignant, as he used to now and then at practice, when everybody was just fooling around the basket and not going into the drills. "What are you afraid of, Harry? That poor little Janice Springer? You overestimate people. Nobody cares what you do. Now we'll just go down there and don't be too long in the toilet. And I haven't heard any thanks from you for all I've done for you, and all I *am* doing." He takes the comb stuck in the brush bristles and gives it to Harry.

A dread of marring his freedom blocks the easy gesture of expressing gratitude. Rabbit pronounces "Thanks" thin-lipped.

They go downstairs. Contrary to what Tothero had promised, all of the men—old men, mostly, but not very old, so that their impotence has a nasty vigor—look up with interest at him. Insanely, Tothero introduces him repeatedly: "Fred, this is my finest boy, a wonderful basketball player, Harry Angstrom, you probably remember his name from the papers, he twice set a county record, in 1950 and then he broke it in 1951, a wonderful accomplishment."

"Is that right, Marty?"

"Harry, an honor to meet you."

Their alert colorless eyes, little dark smears like their mouths, feed on the strange sight of him and send acid impressions down to be digested in their disgusting big beer-tough stomachs. Rabbit sees that Tothero is a fool to them, and is ashamed of his friend and of himself. He hides in the lavatory. The paint is worn off the toilet seat and the washbasin is stained by the hot-water faucet's rusty tears; the walls are oily and the towel-rack empty. There is something terrible in the height of the tiny ceiling: a square yard of a dainty metal pattern covered with cobwebs in which a few white husks of insects are suspended. His depression deepens, becomes a kind of paralysis; he walks out and rejoins Tothero limping and stiffly grimacing, and they leave the place in a dream. He feels affronted, vaguely invaded, when Tothero gets into his car. But, just as in a dream he never stops to question, Rabbit slides in behind the wheel and, in the renewed relation of his arms and legs to the switches and pedals, puts on again the mantle of power. His wet-combed hair feels stiff on his head.

He says sharply, "So you think I should've drunk with Janice."

"Do what the heart commands," Tothero says. "The heart is our only guide." He sounds weary and far away.

"Into Brewer?"

There is no answer.

Rabbit drives up the alley, coming to Potter Avenue, where the water from the ice plant used to run down. He goes right, away from Wilbur Street, where his apartment is, and two more turns bring him into Central Street heading around the mountain to Brewer. On the left, land drops away into a chasm floored by the slick still width of the Running Horse River; on the right, gasoline stations glow, twirlers flicker on strings, spotlights protest.

As the town thins, Tothero's tongue loosens. "The ladies we're going to meet, now Harry, I have no conception of what the other one will be like, but I know you'll be a gentleman. And I guarantee you'll like my friend. She is a remarkable girl, Harry, with seven strikes against her from birth, but she's done a remarkable thing."

"What?"

"She's come to grips. Isn't that the whole secret, Harry; to come to grips? It makes me happy, happy and humble, to have, as I do, this very tenuous association with her. Harry?"

"Yeah?"

"Do you realize, Harry, that a young woman has hair on every part of her body?"

"I hadn't thought about it." Distaste, like an involuntary glandular secretion, has stained his throat.

"Do," Tothero says. "Do think about it. They are monkeys, Harry. Women are monkeys."

He says it so solemn, Rabbit has to laugh.

Tothero laughs too, and comes closer on the seat. "Yet we love them, Harry, don't we? Harry, why do we love them? Answer that, and you'll answer the riddle of life." He is squirming around, crossing and uncrossing his legs, leaning over and tapping Rabbit's shoulder and jerking back and glancing out the side window and turning and tapping again. "I am a hideous person, Harry. A person to be abhorred. Harry, let me tell you something." As a coach he was always telling you something. "My wife calls me a person to be abhorred. But do you know when it began? It began with her skin. One day in the spring, in nineteen forty-three or four, it was during the war, without warning it was hideous. It was like the hides of a thousand lizards stitched together. Stitched together *clumsily*. Can you picture that? That sense of it being *in pieces* horrified me, Harry. Are you listening? You're not listening. You're wondering why you came to me."

"What you said about Janice this morning kind of worries me."

"Janice! Let's not talk about little mutts like Janice Springer, Harry boy. This is the night. This is no time for pity. The real women are dropping down out of the trees." With his hands he imitates things falling out of trees. "Plippity, plippity."

Even discounting the man as a maniac, Rabbit becomes expectant. They park the car off Weiser Avenue and meet the girls in front of a Chinese restaurant.

The girls waiting under crimson neon have a floral delicacy; like a touch of wilt the red light rims their fluffy hair. Rabbit's heart thumps ahead of him down the pavement. They all come together and Tothero introduces Margaret, "Margaret Kosko, Harry Angstrom, my finest athlete, it's a pleasure for me to be able to introduce two such wonderful young people to one another." The old man's manner is queerly shy; his voice has a cough waiting in it.

After Tothero's build-up, Rabbit is amazed that Margaret is just another Janice—that same sallow density, that stubborn smallness. Scarcely moving her lips, she says, "This is Ruth

Leonard. Marty Tothero, and you, whatever your name is."
Ruth is fat alongside Margaret, but not *that* fat. Chunky,
more. But tall. She has flat blue eyes in square-cut sockets.
Her upper lip pushes out a little, like with an incipient blis-
ter, and her thighs fill the front of her dress so that even
standing up she has a lap. Her hair, kind of a dirty ginger
color, is bundled in a roll at the back of her head.

"Harry," Rabbit says. "Or Rabbit."

"That's right!" Tothero cries. "The other boys used to call
you Rabbit. I had forgotten." He coughs.

"Well you're a big bunny," Ruth remarks. Beyond her the
parking meters with their red tongues recede along the curb,
and at her feet, pinched in lavender straps, four sidewalk
squares meet in an x.

"Just big outside," he says.

"That's me too," she says.

"God I'm hungry," Rabbit tells them all, just to say something. From somewhere he's got the jitters.

"Hunger, hunger," Tothero says, as if grateful for the
cue. "Where shall my little ones go?"

"Here?" Harry asks. He sees from the way the two girls
look at him that he is expected to take charge. Tothero is
moving back and forth like a crab sideways and bumps into
a middle-aged couple strolling along. His face shows such
surprise at the collision, and he is so elaborately apologetic,
that Ruth laughs; her laugh rings on the street like a handful
of change thrown down. At the sound Rabbit begins to loosen
up; the space between the muscles of his chest feels filled
with warm air. Tothero pushes into the glass door first, Margaret follows, and Ruth takes his arm and says, "I know
you. I went to West Brewer High and got out in fifty-one."

"That's *my* class." Like the touch of her hand on his arm,
her being his age pleases him, as if, even in high schools on
opposite sides of the city, they have learned the same things
and gained the same view of life. The Class of '51 view.

"You beat us," she says.

"You had a lousy team."

"No we didn't. I went with three of the players."

"Three at once?"

"In a way."

"Well. They looked tired."

She laughs again, the coins thrown down, though he feels
ashamed of what he has said, she is so good-natured and

maybe was pretty then. Her complexion isn't good now. But her hair is thick. A young Chinaman in a drab linen coat blocks their way past the glass counter where an American girl in a kimono sits counting threadbare bills. "Please, how many?"

"Four," Rabbit says, when Tothero is silent.

Unexpected, generous gesture, Ruth slips off her short white coat and gives it to Rabbit: soft, bunched cloth. The motion stirs up a smell of perfume on her.

"Four, yes please this way," and the waiter leads them to a red booth. The place has just recently reopened as Chinese; pink paintings of Paris are still on the wall. Ruth staggers a little; Rabbit sees from behind that her heels, yellow with strain, tend to slip sideways in the net of lavender straps that pin her feet to the spikes of her shoes. But under the shiny green stretch of her dress her broad bottom packs the cloth with a certain composure. Her waist tucks in trimly, squarely, like the lines of her face. The cut of the dress bares a big V-shaped piece of her fat fair back. In arriving at the booth, he bumps against her; the top of her head comes to his nose. The prickly smell of her hair stitches the store-bought scent behind her ears. They bump because Tothero is ushering Margaret into her seat so ceremoniously, a gnome at the mouth of his cave. Standing there waiting, Rabbit is elated to think that a stranger passing outside the restaurant window, like himself last night outside that West Virginia diner, would see him with a woman. He seems to be that stranger, staring in, envying himself his body and his woman's body. Ruth bends down and slides over. The skin of her shoulders gleams and then dims in the shadow of the booth. Rabbit sits down too and feels her rustle beside him, settling in, the way women do, fussily, as if making a nest.

He discovers he has held on to her coat. Pale limp pelt, it sleeps in his lap. Without rising he reaches up and hangs it on the coat-pole hook above him.

"Nice to have a long arm," she says, and looks in her purse and takes out a pack of Newports.

"Tothero says I have short arms."

"Where'd you meet that old bum?" This so Tothero can hear if he cares.

"He's not a bum, he's my old coach."

"Want one?" A cigarette.

He wavers. "I've stopped."

"So that old bum was your coach," she sighs. She draws a cigarette from the turquoise pack of Newports and hangs it between her orange lips and frowns at the sulphur tip as she strikes a match, with curious feminine clumsiness, away from her, holding the paper match sideways and thus bending it. It flares on the third scratch.

Margaret says, *"Ruth."*

"Bum?" Tothero says, and his heavy face looks unwell and lopsided in cagey mirth, as if he's started to melt. "I am, I am. A vile old bum fallen among princesses."

Margaret sees nothing against her in this and puts her hand on top of his on the table and in a solemn dead voice insists, "You're nothing like a bum."

"Where is our young Confucian?" Tothero asks and looks around with his free arm uplifted. When the boy comes he asks, "Can we be served alcoholic beverages here?"

"We bring in from next door," the boy says. Funny the way the eyebrows of Chinese people look embedded in the skin instead of sticking out from it. Their faces look washed always.

"Double Scotch whisky," Tothero says. "My dear?"

"Daiquiri," Margaret says; it sounds like a wisecrack.

"Children?"

Rabbit looks at Ruth. Her face is caked with orange dust. Her hair, her hair which seemed at first glance dirty blond or faded brown, is in fact many colors, red and yellow and brown and black, each hair passing in the light through a series of tints, like the hair of a dog. "Hell," she says. "I guess a Daiquiri."

"Three," Rabbit tells the boy, thinking a Daiquiri will be like a limeade.

The waiter recites, "Three Daiquiri, one double whisky Scotch on the rocks," and goes.

Rabbit asks Ruth, "When's your birthday?"

"August. Why?"

"Mine's April," he says. "I win."

"You win." As if she knows how this makes him feel warmer; you can't feel master, quite, of a woman who's older.

"If you recognized me," he asks, "why didn't you recognize Mr. Tothero? He was coach of that team."

"Who looks at coaches? They don't do any good, do they?"

"Don't do any good? A high-school team is all coach; isn't it?"

Tothero answers, "It's all boy, Harry. You can't make gold out of lead. You can't make gold out of lead."

"Sure you can," Rabbit says. "When I came out in my freshman year I didn't know my feet from my, elbow."

"Yes you did, Harry, yes you did. I had nothing to teach you; I just let you run." He keeps looking around. "You were a young deer," he continues, "with big feet."

Ruth asks, "How big?"

Rabbit tells her, "Twelve D. How big are yours?"

"They're tiny," she says. "Teeny weeny little."

"It looked to me like they were falling out of your shoes." He pulls his head back and slumps slightly, to look down past the table edge, into the submarine twilight where her fore-shortened calves hang like tan fish. They dart back under the seat.

"Don't look too hard, you'll fall out of the booth," she says, ruffled, which is good. Women like being mussed. They never say they do, but they do.

The waiter comes with the drinks and begins laying their places with paper placemats and lusterless silver. He does Margaret and is halfway done on Tothero when Tothero takes the whisky glass away from his lips and says in a freshened, tougher voice, "Cutlery? For Oriental dishes? Don't you have chopsticks?"

"Chopsticks, yes."

"Chopsticks all around," Tothero says positively. "When in Rome."

"Don't take mine!" Margaret cries, slapping her hand with a clatter across her spoon and fork when the waiter reaches. "I don't want any sticks."

"Harry and Ruth?" Tothero asks. "Your preference?"

The Daiquiri does have the taste of limeade, riding like oil on the top of a raw transparent taste. "Sticks," Rabbit says in a deep voice, delighted to annoy Margaret. "In Texas we never touched metal to chicken hoo phooey."

"Ruth?" Tothero's facial attitude toward her is timid and forced.

"Oh I guess. If this dope can I can." She grinds out her cigarette and fishes for another.

The waiter goes away like a bridesmaid with his bouquet of unwanted silver. Margaret is alone in her choice, and this preys on her. Rabbit is glad; she is a shadow on his happiness.

"You ate Chinese food in Texas?" Ruth asks.

"All the time. Give me a cigarette."

"You've stopped."

"I've started. Give me a dime."

"A dime! The hell I will."

The needless urgency of her refusal offends him, it sounds as if she wants a profit. Why does she think he'd steal from her? What would he steal? He dips into his coat pocket and comes up with coins and takes a dime and puts it into the little ivory tune-selector that burns mildly on the wall by their table. Leaning over, past her face, he turns the leaves listing titles and finally punches the buttons for "Rocksville, P-A." "Chinese food in Texas is the best Chinese food in the United States except Boston," he says.

"Listen to the big traveler," Ruth says. She gives him a cigarette. He forgives her about the dime.

"So you think," Tothero says steadily, "that coaches don't do anything."

"They're worthless," Ruth says.

"Hey come on," Rabbit says.

The waiter comes back with their chopsticks and two menus. Rabbit is disappointed in the chopsticks; they feel like plastic instead of wood. The cigarette tastes rough, a noseful of straw. He puts it out. Never again.

"We'll each order a dish and then share it," Tothero tells them. "Now who has favorites?"

"Sweet and sour pork," Margaret says. One thing about her, she is very definite.

"Harry?"

"I don't know."

"Where's the big Chinese-food specialist?" Ruth says.

"This is in English. I'm used to ordering from a Chinese menu."

"Come on, come on, tell me what's good."

"Hey cut it out; you're getting me rattled."

"You were never in Texas," she says.

He remembers the house on that strange treeless residential street, the green night growing up from the prairie, the flowers in the window, and says, "Absolutely I was."

"Doing what?"

"Serving Uncle."

"Oh, in the Army; well that doesn't count. Everybody's been to Texas with the Army."

"You order whatever you think is good," Rabbit tells Tothero. He is irritated by all these Army veterans Ruth seems to know, and strains to hear the final bars of the song he spent a dime to play. In this Chinese place he can just make out a hint, coming it seems from the kitchen, of the jangling melody that exhilarated him last night in the car.

Tothero gives the waiter the order and when he goes away tries to give Ruth the word. The old man's thin lips are wet with whisky, and saliva keeps trying to sneak out of the corner of his mouth. "The coach," he says, "the coach is concerned with developing the three tools we are given in life; the head, the body, and the heart."

"And the crotch," Ruth says. Margaret, of all people, laughs. She really gives Rabbit the creeps.

"Young woman, you've challenged me, and I deserve the respect of your attention." He speaks with grave weight.

"Shit," she says softly, and looks down. "Don't sob on *me*." He has hurt her. The wings of her nostrils whiten; her coarse make-up darkens.

"One. The head. Strategy. Most boys come to a basketball coach from alley games and have no conception of the, of the *elegance* of the game played on a court with two baskets. Won't you bear me out, Harry?"

"Yea, sure. Just yesterday—"

"Second—let me finish, Harry, and then you can talk— second, the body. Work the boys into condition. Make their legs hard." He clenches his fist on the slick table. "Hard. Run, run, run. Run every minute their feet are on the floor. You can't run enough. Thirdly"—he puts the index finger and thumb of one hand to the corners of his mouth and flicks away the moisture—"the heart. And here the good coach, which I, young lady, certainly tried to be and some say *was*, has his most solemn opportunity. Give the boys the will to achieve. I've always liked that better than the will to win, for there can be achievement even in defeat. Make them feel the, yes, I think the word is good, the *sacredness* of achievement, in the form of giving our best." He dares a pause now, and wins through it, glancing at each of them in turn to freeze their tongues. "A boy who has had his heart enlarged by an inspiring coach," he concludes, "can never become, in the deepest sense, a failure in the greater game of life." Confident that he has sold them, he draws on his glass, which is mostly ice cubes. As he tilts it up they ride forward and rattle against his lips.

Ruth turns to Rabbit and asks quietly, as if to change the subject, "What do you do?"

He laughs. "Well I'm not sure I do anything any more. I should have gone to work this morning. I uh, it's kind of hard to describe, I demonstrate something called the Magi-Peel Kitchen Peeler."

"And I'm sure he does it well," Tothero says. "I'm sure that when the MagiPeel Corporation board sits down at their annual meeting, and ask themselves 'Now who has done the most to further our cause with the American public?' the name of Harry Rabbit Angstrom leads the list."

"What do you do?" Rabbit asks her in turn.

"Nothing," Ruth answers. "Nothing." And her eyelids make a greasy blue curtain as she sips her Daiquiri. Her chin takes something of the liquid's green light.

The Chinese food arrives. Delicious saliva fills his mouth. He really hasn't had any since Texas. He loves this food that contains no disgusting proofs of slain animals, a bloody slab of cow haunch, a hen's sinewy skeleton; these ghosts have been minced and destroyed and painlessly merged with the shapes of insensate vegetables, plump green bodies that invite his appetite's innocent gusto. Candy. Heaped on a smoking breast of rice. Each is given such a tidy hot breast, and Margaret is in a special hurry to muddle hers with glazed chunks; all eat well. Their faces take color and strength from the oval plates of dark pork, sugar peas, chicken, stiff sweet sauce, shrimp, water chestnuts, who knows what else. Their talk grows hearty.

"He was terrific," Rabbit says of Tothero. "He was the greatest coach in the county. I would've been nothing without him."

"No, Harry, no. You did more for me than I did for you. Girls, the first game he played he scored twenty points."

"Twenty-three," Harry says.

"Twenty-three points! Think of it." The girls eat on. "Remember, Harry, the state tournaments in Harrisburg; Dennistown and their little set-shot artist."

"He was tiny," Harry tells Ruth. "About five two and ugly as a monkey. Really a dirty player too."

"Ah, but he knew his trade," Tothero says, "he knew his trade. He had us, too, until Harry went wild."

"All of a sudden the basket looked big as a well. Everything I threw went in. Then this runt trips me."

"So he did," Tothero says. "I'd forgotten."

"He trips me, and over I go, bonk, against the mat. If the walls hadn't been padded I'da been killed."

"Then what happened, Harry? Did you cream him? I've forgotten this whole incident." Tothero's mouth is full of food and his hunger for revenge is ugly.

"Why, no," Rabbit says slowly. "I never fouled. The ref saw it and it was his fifth foul and he was out. Then we smothered 'em."

Something fades in Tothero's expression; his face goes slack. "That's right, you never fouled. Harry was always the idealist."

Rabbit shrugs. "I didn't have to."

"The other strange thing about Harry," Tothero tells the two women. "He was never hurt."

"No, I once sprained my wrist," Rabbit corrects. "The thing you said that really helped me—"

"What happened next in the tournaments? I'm frightened at how I've forgotten this."

"Next? Pennoak, I think. Nothing happened. They beat us."

"They won? Didn't we beat them?"

"Oh hell no. They were good. They had five good players. What'd we have? Just me, really. We had Harrison, who was O.K., but after that football injury he never had the touch, really."

"*Ronnie* Harrison?" Ruth asks.

Rabbit is startled. "You *know* him?" Harrison had been a notorious bedbug.

"I'm not sure," she says, complacently enough.

"Shortish guy with kinky hair. A little bitty limp."

"No, I don't know," she says. "I don't think so." She is pleasingly dexterous with the chopsticks, and keeps one hand lying palm up on her lap. He loves when she ducks her head, that thick simple neck moving forward making the broad tendons on her shoulder jump up, to get her lips around a piece of something. Pinched with just the right pressure between the sticks; funny how plump women have that delicate touch. Margaret shovels it in with her dull bent silver.

"We didn't win," Tothero repeats, and calls, "Waiter." When the boy comes Tothero asks for another round of the same drinks.

"No, not for me, thanks," Rabbit says. "I'm high enough on this as it is."

"You're just a big clean-living kid, aren't you, you," Margaret says. She doesn't even know his name yet. God, he hates her.

"The thing, I started to say, the thing you said that really helped me," Rabbit says to Tothero, "is that business about almost touching your thumbs on the two-handers. That's the whole secret, really, getting the ball in front of your hands, where you get that nice lifty feeling. Just zwoops off." His hands show how.

"Oh, Harry," Tothero says sadly, "you could shoot when you came to me. All I gave you was the will to win. The will to achievement."

"You know my best night," Rabbit says, "my best night wasn't that forty-pointer that time against Allenville, it was in my junior year, we went down to end of the county real early in the season to play, a funny little hick school, about a hundred in all six grades; what was its name? Bird's Nest? Something like that. You'll remember."

"Bird's Nest," Tothero says. "No."

"It was the only time I think we ever scheduled them. Funny little square gymnasium where the crowd sat up on the stage. Some name that meant something."

"Bird's Nest," Tothero says. He is bothered. He keeps touching his ear.

"Oriole!" Rabbit exclaims, perfect in joy. "Oriole High. This little kind of spread-out town, and it was early in the season, so it was kind of warm still, and going down in the bus you could see the things of corn like wigwams out in the fields. And the school itself kind of smelled of cider; I remember you made some joke about it. You told me to take it easy, we were down there for practice, and we weren't supposed to try, you know, to *smother* 'em."

"Your memory is better than mine," Tothero says. The waiter comes back and Tothero takes his drink right off the tray, before the boy has a chance to give it to him.

"So," Rabbit says. "We go out there and there are these

five farmers clumping up and down, and we get about
fifteen points up right away and I just take it easy. And
there are just a couple dozen people sitting up on the stage
and the game isn't a league game so nothing matters much,
and I get this funny feeling I can do anything, just drifting
around, passing the ball, and all of a sudden I know, you
see, I *know* I can do anything. The second half I take
maybe just ten shots, and every one goes right in, not just
bounces in, but doesn't touch the rim, like I'm dropping stones
down a well. And these farmers running up and down getting
up a sweat, they didn't have more than two substitutes, but
we're not in their league either, so it doesn't matter much to
them, and the one ref just leans over against the edge of the
stage talking to their coach. Oriole High. Yeah, and then
afterwards their coach comes down into the locker room
where both teams are changing and gets a jug of cider out
of a locker and we all passed it around. Don't you remember?" It puzzles him, yet makes him want to laugh, that
he can't make the others feel what was so special. He resumes eating. The others are done and on their second
drinks.

"Yes, sir, Whosie, you're a real sweet kid," Margaret tells
him.

"Pay no attention, Harry," Tothero says, "that's the way
tramps talk."

Margaret hits him: her hand flies up from the table and
across her body into his mouth, flat, but without a slapping
noise.

"Socko," Ruth says. Her voice is indifferent. The whole
thing is so quiet that the Chinaman, clearing their dishes
away, doesn't look up, and seems to hear nothing.

"We're going," Tothero announces, and tries to stand up,
but the edge of the table hits his thighs, and he can stand no
higher than a hunchback. The slap has left a little twist
in his mouth that Rabbit can't bear to look at, it's so ambig-
uous and blurred, such a sickly mixture of bravado and
shame and, worst, pride or less than pride, conceit. This
deathly smirk issues the words, "Are you coming, my dear?"

"Son of a bitch," Margaret says, yet her little hard nut
of a body slides over, and she glances behind her to see if
she is leaving anything, cigarettes or a purse. "Son of a
bitch," she repeats, and there is something pretty in the

level way she says it. Both she and Tothero seem calmer now, determined and kind of rigid.

Rabbit starts to push up from the table, but Tothero sets a rigid urgent hand on his shoulder, the coach's touch, that Rabbit had so often felt on the bench, just before the pat on the bottom that sent him into the game. "No no, Harry. You stay. One apiece. Don't let our vulgarity distract you. I couldn't borrow your car, could I?"

"Huh? How would I get anywhere?"

"Quite right, you're quite right. Forgive my asking."

"No, I mean, you can if you want—" In fact he feels deeply reluctant to part with a car that is only half his.

Tothero sees this. "No no. It was an insane thought. Good night."

"You bloated old bastard," Margaret says to him. He glances toward her, then down fuzzily. She is right, Harry realizes, he is bloated; his face is lopsided like a tired balloon. Yet this balloon peers down at him as if there was some message bulging it, heavy and vague like water.

"Where will you go?" Tothero asks.

"I'll be fine. I have money. I'll get a hotel," Rabbit tells him. He wishes, now that he has refused him a favor, that Tothero would go.

"The door of my mansion is open," Tothero says. "There's the one cot only, but we can make a mattress—"

"No, look," Rabbit says severely. "You've saved my life, but I don't want to saddle you. I'll be fine. I can't thank you enough anyway."

"We'll talk sometime," Tothero promises; his hand twitches, and accidentally taps Margaret's thigh.

"I could kill you," Margaret says at his side, and they go off, looking from the back like father and daughter, past the counter where the waiter whispers with the American girl, and out the glass door, Margaret first. The whole thing seems so *settled:* like little wooden figures going in and out of a barometer.

"God, he's in sad shape."

"Who isn't?" Ruth asks.

"You don't seem to be."

"I eat, is what you mean."

"No, listen, you have some kind of complex about being big. You're not fat. You're right in proportion."

She laughs, catches herself, looks at him, laughs again

and squeezes his arm and says, "Rabbit, you're a Christian gentleman." Her using his own name enters his ears with unsettling warmth.

"What she hit him for?" he asks, giggling in fear that her hands, resting on his forearm, will playfully poke his side. He feels in her grip the tension of this possibility.

"She likes to hit people. She once hit me."

"Yeah, but you probably asked for it."

She replaces her hands on the table. "So did he. He likes being hit."

He asks, "You know him?"

"I've heard her talk about him."

"Well, that's not knowing him. That girl is dumb."

"Isn't she. She's dumber than you can know."

"Look, I know. I'm married to her twin."

"Ohhh. Married."

"Hey, what's this about Ronnie Harrison? Do you know him?"

"What's this about you being married?"

"Well, I was. Still am." He regrets that they have started talking about it. A big bubble, the enormity of it, crowds his heart. It's like when he was a kid and suddenly thought, coming back from somewhere at the end of a Saturday afternoon, that this—these trees, this pavement—was life, the real and only thing.

"Where is she?"

This makes it worse, picturing Janice, where would she go? "Probably with her parents. I just left her last night."

"Oh. Then this is just a holiday. You haven't left her."

"I think I have."

The waiter brings them a plate of sesame cakes. Rabbit takes one tentatively, thinking they will be hard, and is delighted to have it become in his mouth mild elastic jelly, through the shell of bland seeds. The waiter asks, "Gone for good, your friends?"

"It's O.K., I'll pay," Rabbit says.

The Chinaman nods and retreats.

"You're rich?" Ruth asks.

"No, poor."

"Are you really going to a hotel?" They both take several seasame cakes. There are perhaps twenty on the plate.

"I guess I'll tell you about Janice. I never thought of leaving her until the minute I did; all of a sudden it seemed obvious. She's about five-six, sort of dark-complected—"

"I don't want to hear about it." Her voice is positive; her many-colored hair, as she tilts back her head and squints at a ceiling light, settles into one grave shade. The light was more flattering to her hair than it is to her face; on this side of her nose there are some spots in her skin, blemishes that make bumps through her powder.

"You don't," he says. The bubble rolls off his chest. If it doesn't worry anybody else why should it worry him? "O.K. What shall we talk about? What's your weight?"

"One-fifty."

"Ruth, you're tiny. You're just a welterweight. No kidding. Nobody wants you to be all bones. Every pound you have on is priceless."

He's talking just for happiness, but something he says makes her tense up. "You're pretty wise, aren't you?" she asks, tilting her empty glass toward her eyes. The glass is a shallow cup on a short stem, like an ice-cream dish at a fancy birthday party. It sends pale arcs of reflection swimming across her face.

"You don't want to talk about your weight, either. Huh." He pops another sesame cake into his mouth, and waits until the first pang, the first taste of jelly, subsides. "Let's try this. What you need, Mrs. America, is the MagiPeel Kitchen Peeler. Preserve those vitamins. Shave off fatty excess. A simple adjustment of the plastic turn screw, and you can grate carrots and sharpen your husband's pencils. A host of uses."

"Don't. Don't be so funny."

"O.K."

"Let's be nice."

"O.K. You start."

She plops a cake in and looks at him with a funny fullmouth smile, the corners turned down tight, and a frantic look of agreeableness strains her features while she chews. She swallows, her blue eyes widened round, and gives a little gasp before launching into what he thinks will be a remark but turns out to be a laugh, right in his face. "Wait," she begs. "I'm trying." And returns to looking into the shell of her glass, thinking, and the best she can do, after all that, is to say, "Don't live in a hotel."

"I got to. Tell me a good one." He instinctively thinks she

knows about hotels. At the side of her neck where it shades into her shoulder there is a shallow white hollow where his attention curls and rests.

"They're all expensive," she says. "Everything is. Just my little apartment is expensive."

"Where do you have an apartment?"

"Oh a few blocks from here. On Summer Street. It's one flight up, above a doctor."

"It's yours alone?"

"Yeah. My girl friend got married."

"So you're stuck with all the rent and you don't do anything."

"Which means what?"

"Nothing. You just said you did nothing. How expensive is it?"

She looks at him curiously, with that alertness he had noticed right off, out by the parking meters.

"The apartment," he says.

"A hundred-ten a month. Then they make you pay for light and gas."

"And you don't do anything."

She gazes into her glass, making reflected light run around the rim with a rocking motion of her hands.

"Whaddeya thinking?" he asks.

"Just wondering."

"Wondering what?"

"How wise you are."

Right here, without moving his head, he feels the wind blow. So this is the drift; he hadn't been sure. He says, "Well I'll tell ya. Why don't you let me give you something toward your rent?"

"Why should you do that?"

"Big heart," he says. "Ten?"

"I need fifteen."

"For the light and gas. O.K. O.K." He is uncertain what to do now. They sit looking at the empty plate that had held a pyramid of sesame cakes; they have eaten them all. The waiter, when he comes, is surprised to see this; his eyes go from the plate to Rabbit to Ruth, all in a second. The check amounts to $9.60. Rabbit puts a ten and a one on top of it, and besides these bills he puts a ten and a five. He counts what's left in his wallet; three tens and four ones. When he looks up, Ruth's money has vanished from the slick table. He stands up and takes her little soft coat and holds it for her, and like a great green fish, his prize, she heaves across and up out of the booth and coldly lets herself be fitted into it. He calculates, a dime a pound.

And that's not counting the restaurant bill. He takes the bill to the counter and gives the girl a ten. She makes change with a frown; the frightening vacancy of her eyes is methodically ringed with mascara. The purple simplicity of her kimono does not go with her frizzly permed hair and rouged, concave, deprived face. When she puts his coins on the pink cleats of the change pad, he flicks his hand in the air above the silver, adds the dollar to it, and nods at the young Chinese waiter, who is perched attentively beside her. "Thank you very much, sir. Thank you very much," the boy says to him. But his gratitude does not even last until they are out of sight. As they move toward the glass door he turns to the cashier and in a reedy, perfectly inflected voice completes his story: "—and then this other cat says, 'But man, mine was *he*lium!'"

With this Ruth, Rabbit enters the street. On his right, away from the mountain, the heart of the city shines: a shuffle of lights, a neon outline of a boot, of a peanut, of a top hat, of an enormous sunflower erected, the stem of green neon six stories high, along one building to symbolize Sunflower Beer, the yellow center a second moon, the shuffling headlights glowworms in the grass. One block down, a monotone bell tolls hurriedly, and as long as knives the red-tipped railroad-crossing gates descend, slicing through the soft mass of neon, and the traffic slows, halts.

Ruth turns left, toward the shadow of Mt. Judge, and Rabbit follows; they walk uphill on the rasping pavement. The slope of cement is a buried assertion, an unexpected echo, of the land that had been here before the city. For Rabbit the pavement is a shadow of the Daiquiri's luminous transparence; he is gay, and skips once, to get in step with his love. Her eyes are turned up, toward where the Pinnacle Hotel adds its coarse constellation to the stars above Mt. Judge. They walk together in silence while behind them a freight train chuffs and screaks through the crossing.

He recognizes his problem; she dislikes him now, like that

whore in Texas. "Hey," he says. "Have you ever been up to the top there?"

"Sure. In a car."

"When I was a kid," he says, "we used to walk up from the other side. There's a sort of gloomy forest, and I remember once I came across an old house, just a hole in the ground with some stones, where I guess a pioneer had had a farm."

"The only time I ever got up there was in a car with some eager beaver."

"Well, congratulations," he says, annoyed by the self-pity hiding in her toughness.

She bites at being uncovered. "What do you think I care about your pioneer?" she asks.

"I don't know. Why shouldn't you? You're an American."

"How? I could just as easy be a Mexican."

"You never could be, you're not little enough."

"You know, you're a pig really."

"Oh now baby," he says, and puts his arm around the substance of her waist, "I think I'm sort of neat."

"Don't tell me."

She turns left, off Weiser, out of his arm. This street is Summer. Brick rows, not so much run down as well worn. The house numbers are set in fanlights of stained glass above the doors. The apple-and-orange-colored light of a small grocery store shows the silhouettes of some kids hanging around the corner. The supermarkets are driving these little stores out of business, make them stay open all night.

He puts his arm around her and begs, "Come on now, be a pleasant piece." He wants to show her that her talking tough won't keep him off. She wants him to be content with just her heavy body, but he wants whole women, light as feathers. To his surprise her arm mirrors his, comes around his waist. Thus locked, they find it awkward to walk, and part at the traffic light.

"Didn't you kind of like me in the restaurant?" he asks. "The way I tried to make old Tothero feel good? Telling him how great he was?"

"All I heard was you telling how great *you* were."

"I *was* great. It's the fact. I mean, I'm not much good for anything now, but I really was good at that."

"You know what I was good at?"

"What?"

"Cooking."

"That's more than my wife is. Poor kid."

"Remember how in Sunday school they'd tell you everybody God made was good at something? Well, that was my thing, cooking. I thought, Jesus, now I'll really be a great cook."

"Well aren't you?"

"I don't know. All I do is eat out."

"Well, stop it."

"It's in the trade," she says, and this really stops him. He doesn't think of her this bluntly. It frightens him to think of her this way. It makes her seem, in terms of love, so vast.

"Here I am," she says. Her building is brick like all the others on the west side of the street. Across the way a big limestone church hangs like a gray curtain under the streetlamp. They go in, passing beneath stained glass. The vestibule has a row of doorbells under brass mailboxes and a varnished umbrella rack and a rubber mat on the marble floor and two doors, one to the right with frosted glass and another in front of them of wire-reinforced glass through which he sees rubber-treaded stairs. While Ruth fits a key in this door he reads the gold lettering on the other: F. X. PELLIGRINI, M.D. "Old Fox," Ruth says, and leads him up the stairs.

She lives one flight up. Her door is the one at the far end of a linoleum hall, nearest the street. He stands behind her as she scratches her key at the lock. Abruptly, in the cold light of the streetlamp which comes through the four flawed panes of the window by his side, blue panes so thin-seeming the touch of one finger might crack them, he begins to tremble, first his legs, and then the skin of his sides. The key fits and her door opens.

Once inside, as she reaches for the light switch, he knocks her arm down, pulls her around, and kisses her. It's insanity, he wants to crush her, a little gauge inside his ribs doubles and redoubles his need for pressure, just pure pressure, there is no love in it, love that glances and glides along the skin, he is unconscious of their skins, it is her heart he wants to grind into his own, to comfort her completely. By nature in such an embrace she grows rigid. The small moist cushion of slack willingness with which her lips had greeted his dries up and turns hard, and when she can get her head back and her hand free she fits her palm against his jaw and pushes as if she wanted to throw his skull back into the hall. Her fingers curl and a long nail scrapes the tender skin below one eye. He lets her go. The nearly scratched eye squints and a tendon in his neck aches.

"Get out," she says, her chunky mussed face ugly in the light from the hall.

He kicks the door shut with a backwards flip of his leg. "Don't," he says. "I had to hug you." He sees in the dark she is frightened; her big black shape has that pocket in it, that his instinct feels like a tongue probing a pulled tooth. The air tells him he must be motionless; for no reason he wants to laugh. Her fear and his inner knowledge are so incongruous; he knows there is no harm in him.

"Hug," she says. "Kill felt more like it."

"I've been loving you so much all night," he says. "I had to get it out of my system."

"I know all about your systems. One squirt and done."

"It won't be," he promises.

"It better be. I want you out of here."

"No you don't."

"You all think you're such lovers."

"I am," he assures her. "I am a lover." And on a tide of alcohol and stirred semen he steps forward, in a kind of swoon. Though she backs away, it is not so quickly that he cannot feel her socket of fear healing. The room they are in, he sees by streetlight, is small, and two armchairs and a sofa-bed and a table furnish it. She walks into the next room, a little larger, holding a double bed. The shade is half drawn, and low light gives each nubbin of the bedspread a shadow.

"All right," she says. "You can get into that."

"Where are you going?" Her hand is on a doorknob.

"In here."

"You're going to undress in there?"

"Yeah."

"Don't. Let me undress you. Please." In his concern he has come to stand beside her, and touches her arm now.

She moves her arm from under his touch. "You're pretty bossy."

"Please. Please."

Her voice grates with exasperation: "I have to go to the *john.*"

"But come out dressed."

"I have to do something else, too."

"Don't do it. I know what it is. I hate them."

"You don't even feel it."

"But I know it's there. Like a rubber kidney or something."

Ruth laughs. "Well aren't you choice? Do you have the answer then?"

"No. I hate them even worse."

"Look. I don't know what you think your fifteen dollars entitles you to, but I got to protect myself."

"If you're going to put a lot of gadgets in this, give me the fifteen back."

She tries to twist away, but now he holds the arm he touched. She says, "Say do you think we're married or something the way you boss me around?"

The transparent wave moves over him again and he calls to her in a voice that is almost inaudible, "Yes; let's be." So quickly her arms don't move from hanging at her sides, he kneels at her feet and kisses the place on her fingers where a ring would have been. Now that he is down there, he begins to undo the straps of her shoes. "Why do you women wear heels?" he asks, and yanks her one foot up, so she has to grab the hair on his head for support. "Don't they hurt you?" He heaves the shoe, sticky web, through the doorway into the next room, and does the same to the other. Her feet being flat on the floor gives her legs firmness all the way up. He puts his hands around her ankles and pumps them up and down briskly, between the boxy ankle bones and the circular solid fat of her calves. He has a nervous habit of massage.

"Come on," Ruth says, in a voice slightly tense with the fear of falling, his weight pinning her legs. "Get into bed."

He senses the trap. "No," he says, and stands up. "You'll put on a flying saucer."

"No, I won't. Listen, you won't know if I do or don't."

"Sure I will. I'm very sensitive."

"Oh Lord. Well anyway I got to take a leak."

"Go ahead, I don't care," he says, and won't let her close the bathroom door. She sits, like women do, primly. At home he and Janice had been trying to toilet-train Nelson, so leaning there in the doorway he feels a ridiculous paternal impulse to praise her. She is so tidy.

"Good girl," he says when she rises, and leads her into

the bedroom. The edges of the doorway they pass through seem very vivid and sharp. They will always be here. Behind them, the plumbing vibrates and murmurs. She moves with shy stiffness, puzzled by his will. Trembling again, shy himself, he brings her to a stop by the foot of the bed and searches for the catch of her dress. He finds buttons on the back and can't undo them easily; his hands come at them reversed.

"Let me do it."

"Don't be in such a hurry; I'll do it. You're supposed to enjoy this. This is our wedding night."

"Ha ha."

He hates this mocking reflex in her. He turns her roughly, and, in a reflex of his own, falls into a deep wish to give comfort. He touches her caked cheeks; she seems small as he looks down into the frowning planes of her set, shadowed face. He moves his lips into one eye socket, gently, trying to say this night has no urgency in it, trying to listen through his lips to the timid pulse beating in the bulge of her lid. With a careful impartiality he fears she will find comic, he kisses also her other eye; then, excited by the thought of his own tenderness, his urgency spills; his mouth races across her face, nibbling, licking, so that she does laugh, tickled, and pushes away. He locks her against him, crouches, and presses his parted teeth into the fat hot hollow at the side of her throat. Ruth tenses at his threat to bite, and her hands shove at his shoulders, but he clings there, his teeth bared in a silent exclamation, crying out against her smothering throat that it is not her crotch he wants, not the machine; but her, her.

Though there are no words she hears this, and says, "Don't try to prove you're a lover on me. Just come and go."

"You're *so* smart," he says, and starts to hit her, checks his arm, and offers instead, "Hit me. Come on. You want to, don't you? Really pound me."

"My Lord," she says, "this'll take all night." He plucks her limp arm from her side and swings it up toward him, but she manages her hand so that five bent fingers bump against his cheek painlessly. "That's what poor Maggie has to do for your old bastard friend."

He begs, "Don't talk about them."

"Damn men," she continues, "either want to hurt somebody or be hurt."

"I don't, honest. Either one."

"Well then undress me and stop screwing around."

He sighs through his nose. "You have a sweet tongue," he says.

"I'm sorry if I shock you." Yet in her voice is a small metallic withdrawal, as if she really is.

"You don't," he says and, business-like, stoops and takes the hem of her dress in his hands. His eyes are enough accustomed to the dark now to see the cloth as green. He peels it up her body, and she lifts her arms, and her head gets caught for a moment in the neck-hole. She shakes her head crossly, like a dog with a scrap, and the dress comes free, skims off her arms into his hands floppy and faintly warm. He sails it into a chair hulking in a corner. "God," he says, "you're pretty." She is a ghost in her silver slip. Dragging the dress over her head has loosened her hair. Her solemn face tilts as she quickly lifts out the pins. Her hair falls out of heavy loops.

"Yeah," she says. "Pretty plump."

"No," he says, "you are," and in the space of a breath goes to her and picks her up, great glistening sugar in her sifty-grained slip, and carries her to the bed, and lays her on it. "So pretty."

"You lifted me," she says. "That'll put you out of action."

Harsh direct light falls on her face; the creases on her neck show black. He asks, "Shall I pull the shade?"

"Please. It's a dismal view."

He goes to the window and bends to see what she means. There is only the church across the way, gray, somber, confident. Lights behind its rose window are left burning, and this circle of red and purple and gold seems in the city night a hole punched in reality to show the abstract brilliance burning underneath. He feels gratitude to the builders of this ornament, and lowers the shade on it guiltily. He turns quickly, and Ruth's eyes watch him out of shadows that also seem gaps in a surface. The curve of her hip supports a crescent of silver; his sense of her weight seems to make an aroma.

"What's next?" He takes off his coat and throws it; he loves this throwing things, the way the flying cloth puts him in the center of a gathering nakedness. "Stockings?"

"They're tricky," she says. "I don't want a run."

"You do it then." In a sitting position, with the soft-pawed irritable deftness of a cat, she extricates herself from a web of elastic and silk and cotton; he helps clumsily. His uncertain touches gather in his own body, bending him into a forest smelling of spice. He is out of all dimension, and in a dark land, and a tender entire woman seems an inch away around a kind of corner. When he straightens up on his knees, kneeling as he is by the bed, Ruth under his eyes is an incredible continent, the pushed-up slip a north of snow.

"So much," he says.

"Too much."

"No, listen. You're good." He kisses her lips; her lips expect more than they get. Into their wet flower he drops a brief bee's probe. Cupping a hand behind her hot sheltered neck, he pulls her up, and slides her slip over her head. In just the liquid ease it comes off with he feels delight; how clothes just fall from a woman who wants to be stripped. The cool hollow his hand finds in the small of her back mixes in his mind with the shallow shadows of the stretch of skin that slopes from the bones of her shoulders. He kisses this expanse. Where her skin is whiter it is cooler. She shrugs off her bra. He moves away and sits on the corner of the bed and drinks in the pure sight of her. She keeps her arm tight against the one breast and brings up her hand to cover the other; a ring glints. Her modesty praises him; it shows she is feeling. The straight arm props her weight. Light lies along her right side where it can catch her body as it turns in stillness; this pose, embarrassed and graceful, she holds; rigidity is her one defense against his eyes and her figure does come to seem to him inviolable; absolute; her nakedness swings in tides of stone. So that when her voice springs from her form he is amazed to hear a perfect statue, unadorned woman, beauty's home image, speak: "What about you?"

He is still dressed, even to his necktie. While he is draping his trousers over a chair, arranging them to keep the crease, she scurries under the covers. He stands over her in his underclothes and asks, "Now you really don't have anything on?"

"You wouldn't let me."

He remembers the glint. "Give me your ring."

She brings her right hand out from under the covers and he carefully works a thick brass ring, like a class ring, past her bunching knuckle. In letting her hand drop she grazes the distorted front of his Jockey shorts.

He looks down at her, thinking. The covers come up to her throat and the pale arm lying on top of the bedspread has a slight serpent's twist. "There's nothing else?"

"I'm all skin," she says. "Come on. Get in."

"You want me?"

"Don't flatter yourself. I want it over with."

"You have all that crust on your face."

"God, you're insulting!"

"I just love you too much. Where's a washrag?"

"I don't want my God-damned face washed!"

He goes into the bathroom and turns on the light and finds a facecloth and holds it under the hot faucet. He wrings it out and turns off the light. As he comes back across the room Ruth laughs from the bed. He asks, "What's the joke?"

"In those damned underclothes you *do* look kind of like a rabbit. I thought only kids wore those elastic kind of pants."

He looks down at his T-shirt and snug underpants, pleased and further stirred. His name in her mouth feels like a physical touch. She sees him as special. When he puts the rough cloth to her face, it goes tense and writhes with a resistance like Nelson's, and he counters it with a father's practiced method. He sweeps her forehead, pinches her nostrils, abrades her cheeks and, finally, while her whole body is squirming in protest, scrubs her lips, her words shattered and smothered. When at last he lets her hands win, and lifts the washrag, she stares at him, says nothing, and closes her eyes.

Her wet face, relaxed into slabs, is not pretty; the thick lips, torn from most of their paint, are the pale rims of a loose hole. He stands and presses the cloth against his own face, like a man sobbing. He goes to the foot of the bed, throws the rag toward the bathroom, peels out of his underclothes, bobs, and hurries to hide in the bed. The long dark space between the sheets buries him.

He makes love to her as he would to his wife. After their marriage, and her nerves lost that fineness, Janice needed coaxing; he would begin by rubbing her back. Ruth submits warily when he tells her to lie on her stomach. To lend his hands strength he sits up on her buttocks and leans his weight down through stiff arms into his thumbs and palms as they work the broad muscles and insistent bones of the spine's terrain. She sighs and shifts her head on the pillow. "You should be in the Turkish-bath business," she says. He goes for her neck, and advances his fingers around to her throat, where the columns of blood give like reeds, and massages her shoulders with the balls of his thumbs, and his fingertips just find the glazed upper edges of her pillowing breasts. He returns to her back, until his wrists ache, and flops from astride his mermaid truly weary, as if under a sea-spell to sleep. He pulls the covers up over them, to the middle of their faces.

Janice was shy of his eyes so Ruth heats in his darkness. His lids flutter shut though she arches anxiously against him. Her hand seeks him, and angles him earnestly for a touch his sealed lids feel as red. He sees blue when with one deliberate hand she pries open his jaw and bows his head to her burdened chest. Lovely wobbly bubbles, heavy: perfume between. Taste, salt and sour, swirls back with his own saliva. She rolls away, onto her back, the precious red touch breaking, twists. Cool new skin. Rough with herself, she forces the dry other into his face, coated with cool pollen that dissolves. He opens his eyes, seeking her, and sees her face a soft mask gazing downward calmly, caring for him, and closes his eyes on the food of her again; his hand abandoned on the breadth of her body finds at arm's length a split pod, an open fold, shapeless and simple. They enter a lazy space. He wants the time to stretch long, to great length and thinness. As they deepen together he feels impatience that through all their twists they remain separate flesh; he cannot dare enough, now that she is so much his friend in this search; everywhere they meet a wall. The body lacks voice to sing its own song. Impatience tapers; she floats through his blood as under his eyelids a salt smell, damp pressure, the sense of her smallness as her body hurries everywhere to his hands, her breathing, bedsprings' creak, accidental slaps, and the ache at the parched root of his tongue each register their colors.

Nudge enters his softness, "Now?" Her voice croaky. He kneels in a kind of sickness between her spread legs, her body blurred white, distended willingly under him. With her help their blond loins fit. Something sad in the capture. He braces himself on his arms above her, afraid, for it is here he most often failed Janice, by being too quick. Yet, what with the alcohol drifting in his system, or his good fortune stunning him, his love is slow to burst in her warmth. He hides his face beside her throat, in her mint hair. With thin,

thin arms she hugs him and presses him down and rises above him. From her high smooth shoulders down she is one long underbelly erect in light above him; he says in praise softly, "Hey."

She answers, "Hey."

"You're pretty."

"Come on. Work."

Galled, he shoves up through her and in addition sets his hand under her jaw and shoves her face so his fingers slip into her mouth and her slippery throat strains. As if unstrung by this anger, she tumbles and carries him over and he lies on top of her again, the skin of their chests sticking together; her breathing snags. Her thighs throw open wide and clamp his sides and throw open again so wide it frightens him, she wants, impossible, to turn inside out; the muscles and lips and bones of her expanded underside press against him as a new anatomy, of another animal. She feels transparent; he sees her heart. She suspends him, subsides, and in the folds of her withering, his love and pride revive. So she is first, and waits for him while at a trembling extremity of tenderness he traces again and again the arc of her eyebrow with his thumb. His sea of seed buckles, and sobs into a still channel. At each shudder her mouth smiles in his and her legs, locked at his back, bear down.

She asks in time, "O.K.?"

"You're pretty."

Ruth takes her legs from around him and spills him off her body like a pile of sand. He looks in her face and seems to read in its shadows a sad expression of forgiveness, as if she knows that at the moment of release, the root of love, he betrayed her by feeling despair. Nature leads you up like a mother and as soon as she gets her little price leaves you with nothing. The sweat on his skin is cold in the air; he brings the blankets up from her feet.

"You were a beautiful piece," he says from the pillow listlessly, and touches her soft side. Her flesh still soaks in the act; it ebbs slower in her.

"I had forgotten," she says.

"Forgot what?"

"That I could have it too."

"What's it like?"

"Oh. It's like falling through."

"Where do you fall to?"

"Nowhere. I can't talk about it."

He kisses her lips; she's not to blame. She lazily accepts, then in an afterflurry of affection flutters her tongue against his chin.

He loops his arm around her waist and composes himself against her body for sleep.

"Hey. I got to get up."

"Stay."

"I got to go into the bathroom."

"No." He tightens his hold.

"Boy, you better let me up."

He murmurs, "Don't scare me," and snuggles more securely against her side. His thigh slides over hers, weight on warmth. Wonderful, women, from such hungry wombs to such amiable fat; he wants the heat his groin gave given back in gentle ebb. Best bedfriend, done woman. Bit of bowl about their bellies always. Oh, how! when she got up on him like the bell of a big blue lily slipped down on his slow head. He could have hurt her shoving her jaw. He reawakens enough to feel his dry breath drag through sagged lips as she rolls from under his leg and arm. "Hey get me a glass of water," he says suddenly.

She stands by the edge of the bed, baggy in nakedness, and goes off into the bathroom to do her duty. There's that in women repels him; handle themselves like an old envelope. Tubes into tubes, wash away men's dirt, insulting, really. Faucets cry. The more awake he gets the more depressed he is. From deep in the pillow he stares at the horizontal strip of stained-glass church window that shows under the window shade. Its childish brightness seems the one kind of comfort left to him.

Light from behind the closed bathroom door tints the air in the bedroom. The splashing sounds are like the sounds his parents would make when as a child Rabbit would waken to realize they had come upstairs, that the whole house would soon be dark, and the sight of morning would be his next sensation. He is asleep when like a faun in moonlight Ruth, washed, creeps back to his side, holding a glass of water.

During this sleep he has an intense dream. He and his mother and father and some others are sitting around their kitchen table. It's the old kitchen. A girl at the table reaches with a very long arm weighted with a bracelet and turns a handle of the wood icebox and cold air sweeps over Rabbit. She has opened the door of the square cave where the cake of ice sits; and there it is, inches from Harry's eyes, lopsided from melting but still big, holding within its metal-black bulk the white partition that the cakes have when they come bumping down the chute at the ice plant. He leans closer into the cold breath of the ice, a tin-smelling coldness he associates with the metal that makes up the walls of the cave and the ribs of its floor, delicate rhinocerous gray, mottled with the same disease the linoleum has.

Having leaned closer he sees that under the watery skin are hundreds of clear white veins like the capillaries on a leaf, as if ice too were built up of living cells. And further inside, so ghostly it comes to him last, hangs a jagged cloud, the star of an explosion, whose center is uncertain in refraction but whose arms fly from the core of pallor as straight as long eraser-marks diagonally into all planes of the cube. The rusted ribs the cake rests on wobble through to his eyes like the teeth of a grin. Fear probes him; the cold lump is alive.

His mother speaks to him. "Close the door."

"I didn't open it."

"I know."

"She did."

"I know. My good boy wouldn't hurt anyone." The girl at the table fumbles a piece of food and with terrible weight Mother turns and scolds her. The scolding keeps on and on, senselessly, the same thing over and over again, a continuous pumping of words like a deep inner bleeding. It is himself bleeding; his grief for the girl distends his face until it feels like a huge white dish. "Tart can't eat decently as a baby," Mother says.

"Hey, hey, hey," Rabbit cries, and stands up to defend his sister. Mother rears away, scoffing. They are in the narrow place between the two houses; only himself and the girl; it is Janice Springer. He tries to explain about his mother. Janice's head meekly stares at his shoulder; when he puts his arms around her he is conscious of her eyes being bloodshot. Though their faces are not close he feels her breath hot with tears. They are out behind the Mt. Judge Recreation Hall, out in back with the weeds and tramped-down bare ground and embedded broken bottles; through the wall they hear music on loudspeakers. Janice has a pink dance dress on, and is crying. He repeats, numb at heart, about his mother, that she was just getting at *him* but the girl keeps crying, and to his horror her face begins to slide, the skin to slip slowly from the bone, but there is no bone, just more melting stuff underneath; he cups his hands with the idea of catching it and patting it back; as it drips in loops into his palms the air turns white with what is his own scream.

The white is light; the pillow glows against his eyes and sunlight projects the flaws of the window panes onto the drawn shade. This woman is curled up under the blankets between him and the window. Her hair in sunlight sprays red, brown, gold, white, and black across her pillow. Smiling with relief, he gets up on an elbow and kisses her solid slack cheek, admires its tough texture of pores. He sees by faint rose streaks how imperfectly he scrubbed her face in the dark. He returns to the position in which he slept, but he has slept too much in recent hours. As if to seek the entrance to another dream he reaches for her naked body across the little distance and wanders up and down broad slopes, warm like freshly baked cake. Her back is toward him; he caresses her in an idle trance during which, without moving a muscle but those in her unseen eyelids, she awakes. Not until she sighs heavily and stretches and turns toward him does he know she has felt him.

Again, then, they make love, in morning light with cloudy mouths, her tits silky sacs of milk floating shallow on her ridged rib cage. The nipples sunken brown buds. Her bush a froth of tinted metal. It is almost too naked; his climax seems petty in relation to the wealth of brilliant skin, and he wonders if she pretends. She says not; no, it was different but all right. Really all right. In his shame he goes back under the covers while she pads around on bare feet getting dressed. Funny how she puts on her bra before her underpants. Her putting on her underpants makes him conscious of her legs as separate things, thick pink liquid twists diminishing downward into her ankles. Taking pink light from the reflection of each other as she moves. Her accepting his watching her flatters him, shelters him. They have become domestic.

Church bells ring loudly. He moves to her side of the bed to watch the crisply dressed people go into the limestone church across the street, whose lit window had lulled him to sleep. He reaches and pulls up the shade a few feet. The rose window is dark now, and above the church, above Mt. Judge, the sun glares in a façade of blue. It strikes a shadow down from the church steeple, a cool stumpy negative in which a few men with flowers in their lapels stand and gossip while the common sheep of the flock stream in, heads down. The thought of these people having the bold idea of leaving their homes to come here and pray pleases and reassures Rabbit, and moves him to close his own eyes and bow his head with a movement so tiny Ruth won't notice. *Help me, Christ. Forgive me. Take me down the way. Bless Ruth, Janice, Nelson, my mother and father, Mr. and Mrs. Springer, and the unborn baby. Forgive Tothero and all the others. Amen.*

He opens his eyes to the day and says, "That's a pretty big congregation."

"Sunday morning," she says. "I could throw up every Sunday morning."

"Why?"

She just says, "Fuh," as if he knows the answer. After thinking a bit, and seeing him lie there looking out the window seriously, she says, "I once had a guy in here who woke me up at eight o'clock because he had to teach Sunday school at nine-thirty."

"You don't believe anything?"

"No. You mean you do?"

"Well, yeah. I think so." Her rasp, her sureness, makes him wince; he wonders if he's lying. If he is, he is hung in the middle of nowhere, and the thought hollows him, makes his heart tremble. Across the street a few people in their best clothes walk on the pavement past the row of worn brick homes; are they walking on air? Their clothes, they put on their best clothes: he clings to the thought giddily; it seems a visual proof of the unseen world.

"Well, if you do what are you doing here?" she asks.

"Why not? You think you're Satan or somebody?"

This stops her a moment, standing there with her comb, before she laughs. "Well you go right ahead if it makes you happy."

He presses her. "Why don't you believe anything?"

"You're kidding."

"No. Doesn't it ever, at least for a second, seem obvious to you?"

"God, you mean? No. It seems obvious just the other way. All the time."

"Well now if God doesn't exist, why does anything?"

"Why? There's no why to it. Things just are." She stands before the mirror, and her comb pulling back on her hair pulls her puffy upper lip up so her wet teeth show grayly.

"That's not the way I feel about you," he says, "that you just are."

"Hey, why don't you get some clothes on instead of just lying there giving me the Word?"

This, and her turning, hair swirling, to say it, stir him. "Come here," he asks. The idea of making it while the churches are full excites him.

"No," Ruth says. She is really a little sore. His believing in God grates against her.

"You don't like me now?"

"What does it matter to you?"

"You know it does."

"Get out of my bed."

"I guess I owe you fifteen more dollars."

"All you owe me is getting the hell out."

"What! Leave you all alone?" He says this as with comical speed, while she stands there startled rigid, he jumps from bed and gathers up some of his clothes and ducks into the bathroom and closes the door. When he comes out, in underclothes, he says, still clowning, "You don't like me any more," and moves sadly to where his trousers are neatly laid on the chair. While he was out of the room she made the bed.

"I like you enough," she says in a preoccupied voice, tugging the bedspread smooth.

"Enough for what?"

"Enough."

"Why do you like me?"

" 'Cause you're bigger than I am." She moves to the next corner and tugs. "Boy that used to gripe hell out of me, the way these little women everybody thinks are so cute grab all the big men."

"They have something," he tells her. "They seem easier to get to."

She laughs and says, "I guess that's right."

He pulls up his trousers and buckles the belt. "Why else do you like me?"

She looks at him. "Shall I tell you?"

"Tell me."

" 'Cause you haven't given up. 'Cause in your stupid way you're still fighting."

He loves hearing this; pleasure spins along his nerves, making him feel very tall, and he grins. But the American protest of modesty is instinctive with him, and "The will to achievement" glides out of his mouth mockingly.

"That poor old bastard," she says. "He really is a bastard too."

"Hey, I'll tell you what," Rabbit says. "I'll run out and get some stuff at that grocery store you can cook for our lunch."

"Say, you settle right in, don't you?"

"Why? Were you going to meet somebody?"

"No, I don't have anybody."

"Well, then. You said last night you liked to cook."

"I said I used to."

"Well, if you used to you still do. What shall I get?"

"How do you know the store's open?"

"Isn't it? Sure it is. Those little stores make all their money on Sundays, what with the supermarkets." He goes to the window and looks up at the corner. Sure, the door of the place opens and a man comes out with a newspaper.

"Your shirt's filthy," she says behind him.

"I know." He moves away from the windowlight. "It's Tothero's shirt. I got to get some clothes. But let me get food now. What shall I get?"

"What do you like?" she asks.

The thing about her is, she's good-natured. He knew it the second he saw her standing by the parking meters. He could just tell from the soft way her belly looked. With women, you keep bumping against them, because they want different things, they're a different race. Either they give, like a plant, or scrape, like a stone. In all the green world nothing feels as good as a woman's good nature. The pavement kicks under his feet as he runs to the grocery store in his dirty shirt. What do you like? He has her. He knows he has her.

He brings back eight hot dogs in cellophane, a package of frozen lima beans, a package of frozen French fries, a quart of milk, a jar of relish, a loaf of raisin bread, a ball of cheese wrapped in red cellophane, and, on top of the bag, a

Ma Sweitzer's shoo-fly pie. It all costs $2.43. As she brings the things out of the bag in her tiny stained kitchen, Ruth says, "You're kind of a bland eater."

"I wanted lamb chops but he only had hot dogs and salami and hash in cans."

While she cooks he wanders around her living-room and finds a row of pocketbook mysteries on a shelf under a table beside a chair. The guy in the bunk beside his at Fort Hood used to read those all the time. Ruth has opened the windows, and the cool March air is sharpened by this memory of baking Texas. Ruth's curtains of dingy dotted Swiss blow; their gauze skin gently fills and they lean in toward him as he stands paralyzed by a more beautiful memory: his home, when he was a child, the Sunday papers rattling on the floor, stirred by the afternoon draft, and his mother rattling the dishes in the kitchen; when she is done, she will organize them all, Pop and him and baby Miriam, to go for a walk. Because of the baby, they will not go far, just a few blocks maybe to the old gravel quarry, where the ice pond of winter, melted into a lake a few inches deep, doubles the height of the quarry cliff by throwing its rocks upside down into a pit of reflection. But it is only water; they take a few steps further along the edge and from this new angle the pond mirrors the sun, the illusion of inverted cliffs is wiped out, and the water is as solid as ice with light. Rabbit holds little Mim hard by the hand. "Hey," he calls to Ruth. "I got a terrific idea. Let's go for a walk this afternoon."

"Walk! I walk all the time."

"Let's walk up to the top of Mt. Judge from here." He can't remember having ever gone up the mountain from the Brewer side; gusts of anticipation sweep over him, and as he turns, exalted, away from the curtains stiff and leaning with the breeze, huge church bells ring. "Yeah let's," he calls into the kitchen. "Please." Out on the street people leave church carrying wands of green absent-mindedly at their sides.

When Ruth serves lunch he sees she is a better cook than Janice; she has boiled the hot dogs somehow without splitting them. With Janice, they always arrived at the table torn and twisted, cracked from end to end in wide pink mouths that seemed to cry out they'd been tortured. He and Ruth eat at a small porcelain table in the kitchen. As he touches his fork to his plate he remembers the cold feel in his dream of Janice's face dropping into his hands, and the memory spoils his first bite, makes it itself a kind of horror. Nevertheless he says, "Terrific," and gamely goes ahead and eats, and does regain some appetite. Ruth's face across from him takes some of the white crudity of the table-top; the skin of her broad forehead shines and the two blemishes beside her nose are like spots something spilled has left. She seems to sense that she has become unattractive, and eats obsequiously, with quick little self-effacing bites.

"Hey," he says.

"What?"

"You know I still have that car parked over on Cherry Street."

"You're O.K. The meters don't matter on Sunday."

"Yeah, but they will tomorrow."

"Sell it."

"Huh?"

"Sell the car. Get rich quick."

"No, I mean— Oh. You mean for you. Look, I still have thirty dollars, why don't you let me give it to you now?" He reaches toward his hip pocket.

"No, no, I did *not* mean that. I didn't mean anything. It just popped into my fat head." She is embarrassed; her neck goes splotchy and his pity is roused, to think how pretty she appeared last night.

He explains. "You see, my wife's old man is a used-car dealer and when we got married he sold us this car at a pretty big discount. So in a way it's really my wife's car and anyway since she has the kid I think she ought to have it. And then as you say my shirt's dirty and I ought to get my clothes if I can. So what I thought was, after lunch why don't I sneak over to my place and leave the car and pick up my clothes?"

"Suppose she's there?"

"She won't be. She'll be at her mother's."

"I think you'd like it if she was there," Ruth says.

He wonders; imagines opening the door and finding Janice sitting there in the armchair with an empty glass watching television, and feels, like a small collapse within him, like a piece of food stuck in his throat at last going down, his relief at finding her face still firm, still its old dumb obstinate walnut of a face. "No, I wouldn't," he tells Ruth. "I'm scared of her."

"Obviously," Ruth says.

"There's something about her," he insists. "She's a menace."

"This poor wife you left? *You're* the menace, I'd say."

"No."

"Oh that's right. You think you're a rabbit." Her tone in saying this is faintly jeering and irritable, he doesn't know why.

She asks, "What do you think you're going to do with these clothes?" That's it; she feels him moving in.

He admits, "Bring them here."

She takes in the breath but comes out with nothing. "Just for tonight," he pleads. "You're not doing anything are you?"

"Maybe. I don't know. Probably not."

"Well then, great. Hey. I love you."

She rises to clear away the plates and stands there, thumb on china, staring at the center of the white table. She shakes her head heavily and says, "You're bad news."

Across from him her broad pelvis, snug in a nubbly brown skirt, is solid and symmetrical as the base of a powerful column. His heart rises through that strong column and, enraptured to feel his love for her founded anew yet not daring to lift his eyes to the test of her face, he says, "I can't help it. You're such good news."

He eats three pieces of shoo-fly pie and a crumb in the corner of his lips comes off on her sweater when he kisses her breasts good-by in the kitchen. He leaves her with the dishes. His car is waiting for him on Cherry Street in the cool spring noon mysteriously; it is as if a room of a house he owned had been detached and scuttled by this curb and now that the tide of night was out stood up glistening in the sand, slightly tilting but unharmed, ready to sail at the turn of a key. Under his rumpled and dirty clothes his body feels clean, narrow, hollow. The car smells secure: rubber and dust and painted metal hot in the sun. A sheath for the knife of himself. He cuts through the Sunday-stunned town, the soft rows of domestic brick, the banistered porches calm pools of wood. He drives around the great flank of Mt. Judge; its slope by the highway is dusted the yellow-green of new leaves; higher up the evergreens make a black horizon with the sky. The view has changed since the last time he came this way. Yesterday morning the sky was ribbed with thin-stretched dawn clouds, and he was exhausted, heading into the center of the net, where alone there seemed a chance of rest. Now the noon of another day has burned away the clouds, and the sky in the windshield is blank and cold, and he feels nothing ahead of him, Ruth's delicious nothing, the nothing she told him she did. Her eyes were that blue. Unflecked. Your heart lifts forever through that black sky.

His mood of poise crumbles as he descends into the familiar houses of Mt. Judge. He becomes cautious, nervous. He turns up Jackson, up Potter, up Wilbur, and tries to make out from some external sign if there is anyone in his apartment. No telltale light would show; it is the height of day. No car is out front. He circles the block twice, straining his neck to see a face at the window. Purple opaque panes. Ruth was wrong; he doesn't want to see Janice.

The bare possibility makes him so faint that when he gets out of the car the bright sun almost knocks him down. As he climbs the stairs, the steps seem to calibrate, to restrain by notches, a helpless tendency in his fear-puffed body to rise. He raps on the door, braced to run. Nothing answers on the other side. He taps again, listens, and takes the key out of his pocket.

Though the apartment is empty, it is yet so full of Janice he begins to tremble; the sight of that easy chair turned to face the television attacks his knees. Nelson's broken toys on the floor derange his head; all the things inside his skull, the gray matter, the bones of his ears, the apparatus of his eyes, seem clutter clogging the tube of his self; his sinuses choke, with a sneeze or tears, he doesn't know. The living-room has the feel of dust. The shades are still drawn. Janice drew them in the afternoons to keep glare off the television screen. Someone has made gestures of cleaning up; her ashtrays and her empty glass have been taken away. Rabbit puts the door key and the car keys on top of the television case, metal painted brown in imitation of wood grain. As he opens the closet door the knob bumps against the edge of the set. Some of her clothes are gone.

He means to reach for his clothes but instead turns and wanders toward the kitchen, trying to gather up the essence of what he has done. Their bed sags in the filtered sunlight. Never a good bed. Her parents had given it to them. On the bureau sit a few of her bottles and jars and a fingernail scissors and a spool of white thread and a needle and some brass hairpins and a telephone book and a Baby Ben with luminous numbers and a recipe she never used torn from a magazine and a necklace made of wood beads carved in Java he got her for Christmas. Insecurely tilted against the wall is the big oval mirror they took away when her parents had a new bathroom put in; he always meant to attach it to the plaster above her bureau for her but never got around to buying molly bolts. A glass on the windowsill, half full of stale, bubbled water, throws a curved patch of diluted sun onto the bare place where the mirror should have been fixed. Three long nicks, here, scratched in the wall, parallel; what ever made them, when? Beyond the edge of the made bed a white triangle of bathroom floor shows: the time after her shower, her bottom blushing with steam, lifting her arms gladly to kiss him, soaked licks of hair in her armpits. What gladness had seized her, and then him, unasked?

In the kitchen he discovers an odd oversight. The pork chops never taken from the pan, cold as death, riding congealed grease. He dumps them out in the paper bag under the sink and with a spatula scrapes crumbs of the stiff specked fat after them. The bag, stained dark brown at the bottom, smells of something sweetly rotting. He puzzles, the can is downstairs out back, can't take two trips. He decides to forget it. He draws scalding water into the sink and puts the pan in to soak. The breath of steam like a whisper in a tomb frightens him.

In haste he takes clean Jockey pants, T-shirts, and socks from a drawer, three shirts in cellophane and blue cardboard from another, a pair of laundered suntans from a third, draws his two suits and a sports shirt from the closet, and wraps the smaller clothing in the suits to form a bundle he can carry. The job makes him sweat. Clutching his clothes between two arms and a lifted thigh, he surveys the apartment once more, and the furniture, carpeting, wallpaper all seem darkly glazed with the murk filming his own face; the rooms are filled with flavor of an awkward job, and he is glad to get out. The door snaps shut behind him irrevocably. His key is inside.

Toothbrush. Razor. Cuff links. Shoes. At each step down he remembers something he forgot. He hurries, his feet patter. Jumps. His head almost hits the naked bulb burning at the end of a black cord in the vestibule. His name on the mailbox seems to call at him as he sweeps past; its letters of blue ink crowd the air like a cry. He feels ridiculous, ducking into the sunlight like one of those weird thieves you read about in the back pages of newspapers who instead of stealing money and silver carry away a porcelain wash-basin, twenty rolls of wallpaper, or a bundle of old clothes.

"Good afternoon, Mr. Angstrom."

A neighbor is passing, Miss Arndt, in a lavender church hat, carrying a palm frond in clutched hands. "Oh. Hello. How are you?" She lives three houses up; they think she has cancer.

"I am just splendid," she says. "Just splendid." And stands there in sunshine, bewildered by splendor, flatfooted, leaning unconsciously against the slope of the pavement. A green car goes by too slowly. Miss Arndt sticks in his way, ami-ably confused, grateful for something, her simple adherence to the pavement it seems, like a fly who stops walking on the ceiling to marvel at itself.

"How do you like the weather?" he asks.

"I love it, I love it; Palm Sunday is always blue. It makes the sap rise in my legs." She laughs and he follows; she stands rooted to the hot cement between the feathery shade of two maples. She knows nothing, he becomes certain.

"Yes," he says, for her eyes have snagged on his arms. "I seem to be doing spring cleaning." He shrugs the bundle to clarify.

"Good," she says, with a surprising sarcastic snarl. "You young husbands, you certainly take the bit in your teeth." Then she twists, and exclaims, "Why, there's a clergyman in there!"

The green car has come back, even more slowly, down the center of the street. With a dismay that makes the bundle of clothes double its weight in his arms, Rabbit realizes he is pinned. He lurches from the porch and strides past Miss Arndt saying, "I got to run," right on top of her considered remark, "It's not Reverend Kruppenbach."

No, of course not Kruppenbach; Rabbit knows who it is, though he doesn't know his name. Episcopal. The Springers were Episcopalians, more of the old bastard's social climbing, everyone else was Lutheran or Reformed if they were any-thing. He doesn't quite run; the downward pavement jars his heels at every stride, he can't see the cement under the bun-dle he carries. If he can just make the alley. His one hope is the preacher can't be sure it's him. He feels the green car crawling behind him; he thinks of throwing the clothes away and really running. If he could get into the old ice plant. But it's a block away. He feels Ruth, the dishes done, waiting on the other side of the mountain. Blue beyond blue under blue.

As a shark nudges silent creases of water ahead of it the green fender makes ripples of air that break against the back of Rabbit's knees. The faster he walks the harder these ripples break. Behind his ear a childishly twanging voice pipes, "I beg your pardon. Are you Harry Angstrom?"

With a falling sensation of telling a lie Rabbit turns and half-whispers, "Yes."

The fair young man with his throat manacled in white lets his car glide diagonally against the curb, yanks on the hand-brake, and shuts off the motor, thus parking on the wrong side of the street, cockeyed. Funny how ministers ignore small laws. Rabbit remembers how Kruppenbach's son used to tear around town on a motorcycle. It always impressed him. "Well, I'm Jack Eccles," this minister says, and inconsequently laughs a syllable. The white stripe of an unlit cigarette hanging from his lips makes with the echoing collar a comic picture in the car window. He gets out of his car, a '58 olive Buick four-door, and offers his hand. To accept it Rabbit has to put his big ball of clothes down in the strip of grass between the pavement and curb.

Eccles' handshake, eager and practiced and hard, seems to symbolize for him an embrace. For an instant Rabbit fears he will never let go. He feels caught, foresees explanations, embarrassments, prayers, reconciliations rising up like dank walls; his skin prickles in desperation. He feels tenacity in his captor.

The minister is about his age or a little older and a good bit shorter. But not small; a sort of needless muscularity runs under his black coat. He stands edgily, with his chest faintly cupped. He has long reddish eyebrows that push a worried wrinkle around above the bridge of his nose, and a little pale pointed knob of a chin tucked under his mouth. Despite his looking vexed there is something friendly and silly about him.

"Where are you going?" he asks.

"Huh? Nowhere." Rabbit is distracted by the man's suit; it only feigns black. It is really blue, a sober but elegant, lightweight, midnight blue. While his little vest or bib or whatever is black as a stove. The effort of keeping the cigarette between his lips twists Eccles' laugh into a snort. He slaps the breasts of his coat. "Do you have a match by any chance?"

"Gee I'm sorry, no. I quit smoking."

"You're a better man than I am." He pauses and thinks, then looks at Harry with startled, arched eyebrows. The distention makes his gray eyes seem round and as pale as glass. "Can I give you a lift?"

"No. Hell. Don't bother."

"I'd like to talk to you."

"No; you don't really want to, do you?"

"I do, yes. Very much."

"Yeah. O.K." Rabbit picks up his clothes and walks around the front of the Buick and gets in. The interior has that sweet tangy plastic new-car smell; he takes a deep breath of it and cools his fear. "This is about Janice?"

Eccles nods, staring out the rear window as he backs away from the curb. His upper lip overhangs his lower; there are scoops of weary violet below his eyes.

"How is she? What did she do?"

"She seems much saner today. She and her father came to church this morning." They drive down the street. Eccles adds nothing, just gazes through the windshield, blinking. He pokes the lighter in on the dashboard.

"I *thought* she'd be with them," Rabbit says. He is getting slightly annoyed at the way the minister isn't bawling him out or something; he doesn't seem to know his job.

The lighter pops. Eccles puts it to his cigarette, inhales, and seems to come back into focus. "Evidently," he says, "when you didn't come back in half an hour she called your parents and had your father bring your boy over to your apartment. Your father, I gather, was very reassuring and told her you had probably been sidetracked somewhere. She remembered you had been late getting home because of some street game and thought you might have gone back to it. I believe your father even walked around town looking for the game."

"Where was old man Springer?"

"She didn't call them. She didn't call them until two o'clock that morning, when I suppose the poor thing had given up all hope." "Poor thing" is one word on his lips, worn smooth.

Harry asks, "Not until two?" Pity grips him; his hands tighten on the bundle, as if comforting Janice.

"Around then. By then she was in such a state, alcoholic and otherwise, that her mother called me."

"Why you?"

"I don't know. People do." Eccles laughs. "They're supposed to; it's comforting. To me at least. I always thought Mrs. Springer hated me. She hadn't been to church in months." As he turns to face Rabbit, to follow up this joke, a little quizzical pang lifts his eyebrows and forces his broad mouth open.

"This was around two in the morning?"

"Between two and three."

"Gee, I'm sorry. I didn't mean to get you out of bed."

The minister shakes his head irritably. "That's not to be considered."

"Well I feel terrible about this."

"Do you? That's hopeful. Uh, what, exactly, is your plan?"

"I don't really have a plan. I'm sort of playing it by ear."

Eccles' laughter surprises him; it occurs to Rabbit that the minister is a connoisseur of affairs like this, broken homes, fleeing husbands, and that "playing it by ear" has struck a fresh note. He feels flattered; Eccles has this knack.

"Your mother has an interesting viewpoint," Eccles says. "She thinks it's all an illusion your wife and I have, that you've deserted. She says you're much too good a boy to do anything of the sort."

"You've been busy on this, haven't you?"

"This, and a death yesterday."

"Gee, I'm sorry."

They have been driving idly, at low speed, through the familiar streets; once they passed the ice plant, and at another point rounded a corner from which you can see across the valley. "Say, if you really want to give me a lift," Rabbit says, "you could drive over into Brewer."

"You don't want me to take you to your wife?"

"No. Good grief. I mean I don't think it would do any good, do you?"

For a long time it seems that the other man didn't hear him; his tidy, tired profile stares through the windshield as the big car hums forward steadily. Harry has taken the breath to repeat himself when Eccles says, "Not if you don't want good to come of it."

The matter seems ended this simply. They drive down Potter Avenue toward the highway. The sunny streets have just children on them, some of them still in their Sunday-school clothes. Little girls in pink bell dresses that stick straight out from their waists. Their ribbons match their socks.

Eccles asks, "What did she do that made you leave?"

"She asked me to buy her a pack of cigarettes."

Eccles doesn't laugh as he had hoped; he seems to dismiss the remark as impudence, a little over the line. But it was the truth. "It's the truth. It just felt like the whole business was fetching and hauling, all the time trying to hold this mess together she was making all the time. I don't know, it seemed like I was glued in with a lot of busted toys and empty glasses and television going and meals late and no way of getting out. Then all of a sudden it hit me how easy it was to get out, just walk out, and by damn it *was* easy."

"For less than two days, it's been."

"Oh. There's the law I suppose—"

"I wasn't thinking of that so much. Your mother-in-law thought of it immediately, but your wife and Mr. Springer are dead against it. I imagine for different reasons. Your wife seems almost paralyzed; she doesn't want anyone to do anything."

"Poor kid. She's such a mutt."

"Why are you here?"

" 'Cause you caught me."

"I mean why were you in front of your home?"

"I came back to get clean clothes."

"Do clean clothes mean so much to you? Why cling to that decency if trampling on the others is so easy?"

Rabbit feels now the danger of talking; his words are coming back to him, little hooks and snares are being fashioned. "Also I was leaving her the car."

"Why? Don't you need it, to escape?"

"I just thought she should have it. Her father sold it to us cheap. Anyway it didn't do me any good."

"No?" Eccles stubs his cigarette out in the car ashtray and goes to his coat pocket for another. They are rounding the mountain, at the highest stretch of road, where the hill rises too steeply on one side and falls too steeply on the other to give space to a house or gasoline station. The river down below. "Now if *I* were to leave *my* wife," he says, "I'd get into a car and drive a thousand miles." It almost seems like advice, coming calmly from above the white collar.

"That's what I did!" Rabbit cries, delighted by how much they have in common. "I drove as far as West Virginia. Then I thought the hell with it and came back." He must try to stop swearing; he wonders why he's doing it. To keep them apart, maybe; he feels a dangerous tug drawing him toward this man in black.

"Should I ask why?"

"Oh I don't know. A combination of things. It seemed safer to be in a place I know."

"You didn't come back to protect your wife?"

Rabbit is wordless at the idea.

Eccles continues, "You speak of this feeling of muddle. What do you think it's like for other young couples? In what way do you think you're exceptional?"

"You don't think I can tell ya but I will. I once played a game real well. I really did. And after you're first-rate at something, no matter what, it kind of takes the kick out of being second-rate. And that little thing Janice and I had going, boy, it was really second-rate."

The dashboard lighter pops. Eccles uses it and quickly returns his eyes to his driving. They've come down into the outskirts of Brewer. He asks, "Do you believe in God?"

Having rehearsed that this morning, Rabbit answers promptly, "Yes."

Eccles blinks in surprise. The furry lid in his one-eyed profile shutters, but his face does not turn. "Do you think, then, that God wants you to make your wife suffer?"

"Let me ask you. Do you think God wants a waterfall to be a tree?" This question of Jimmy's sounds, Rabbit realizes, ridiculous; he is annoyed that Eccles simply takes it in, with a sad drag of smoke. He realizes that no matter what he says, Eccles will take it in with the same weary smoke; he is a listener by trade. His big fair head seems stuffed with a gray mash of everybody's precious secrets and passionate questions, a mash that nothing, young as he is, can color. For the first time, Rabbit dislikes him.

"No," Eccles says after thought. "But I think He wants a little tree to become a big tree."

"If you're telling me I'm not mature, that's one thing I don't cry over since as far as I can make out it's the same thing as being dead."

"I'm immature myself," Eccles offers.

It's not enough of an offering. Rabbit tells him off. "Well, I'm not going back to that little dope no matter how sorry you feel for her. I don't know what she feels. I never have. All I know is what's inside *me*. That's all I have. Do you know what I was doing to support that bunch? I was demonstrating a penny's worth of tin called a frigging MagiPeeler in five-and-dime stores!"

Eccles looks at him and laughs, his eyebrows all surprise now. "Well that explains your oratorical gifts," he says.

This aristocratic sneer rings true; puts them both in place. Rabbit feels less at sea. "Hey, I wish you'd let me out," he says. They're on Weiser Street, heading toward the great sunflower, dead in day.

"Won't you let me take you where you're staying?"

"I'm not staying anywhere."

"All right." With a trace of boyish bad temper Eccles pulls over and stops in front of a fire hydrant. As he brakes racily, something clatters in the trunk.

"You're coming apart," Rabbit tells him.

"Just my golf clubs."

"You play?"

"Badly. Do you?" He seems animated; the cigarette burns forgotten in his fingers.

"I used to caddy."

"Could I invite you for a game?" Ah. Here's the hook. Rabbit gets out and stands on the curb and sidesteps, clowning in his freedom. "I don't have clubs."

"They're easy to rent. Please. I mean it." Eccles leans far over, to speak through the door. "It's hard for me to find partners. Everybody works except me." He laughs.

Rabbit knows he should run, but the thought of a game, and his idea that it's safest to see the hunter, make resistance.

Eccles presses. "I'm afraid you'll go back to demonstrating peelers if I don't catch you soon. Tuesday? Tuesday at two? Shall I pick you up?"

"No; I'll come to your house."

"Promise?"

"Yeah. But don't trust a promise from me."

"I have to." Eccles names an address in Mt. Judge and they call good-by at the curb. An old cop walks with a wise squint along the pavement beside the shut, stunned Sunday storefronts. To him it must look like a priest parting from the president of his Youth Group. Harry grins at this cop, and walks along the pavement with his stomach singing. Funny, the world just can't touch you.

Ruth lets him in, a pocket mystery in one hand. Her eyes look sleepy from reading. She has changed into another sweater. Her hair seems darker. He dumps the clothes on her bed. "Do you have hangers?"

"Say. You really think you have it made."

"I made you," he says. "I made you and the sun and the stars." Squeezing her in his arms it seems that he did. She is tepid and solid in his embrace, not friendly, not not. The filmy smell of soap lifts into his nostrils while dampness touches his jaw. She has washed her hair. It pulls back from her forehead in darker straighter strands evenly harrowed by the comb. Clean, she is clean; he puts his nose against her skull to drink in the demure sharp scent. He thinks of her naked in the shower, her hair hanging oozy with lather, her neck bowed to the whipping water. "I made you bloom," he says.

"Oh you're a wonder," she answers, and pushes away from his chest. As he hangs up his suits tidily, Ruth asks, "You give your wife the car?"

"There was nobody there. I snuck in and out. I left the key inside."

"And nobody caught you?"

"As a matter of fact somebody did. The Episcopal minister gave me a ride back into Brewer."

"Say; you *are* religious aren't you?"

"*I* didn't ask him."

"What did he say?"

"Nothing much."

"What was he like?"

"Kind of creepy. Giggled a lot."

"Maybe just *you* make him giggle."

"I'm supposed to play golf with him on Tuesday."

"You're kidding."

"No, really. I told him I don't know how."

She laughs, on and on, in that prolonged way women use when they're excited by you and ashamed of it. "Oh, my Rabbit," she exclaims in a fond final breath. "You just wander, don't you?"

"He got hold of *me*," he insists, knowing his attempts to

explain will amuse her, for shapeless reasons. "I didn't do anything."

"You poor soul," she says. "You're just irresistible."

With keen secret relief, he at last takes off his dirty clothes and changes into clean underwear, fresh socks, the sports shirt, and suntans. He has to put his suede shoes back on. He forgot to steal his sneakers. "Let's go for that walk," he announces, dressed.

"I'm reading," she says from a chair. The book is open to near the end. She reads books nicely, without cracking their backs, though they cost only 35¢.

"Come on. Get out in the weather." He goes over and tries to tug the mystery from her hand. The title is *The Deaths at Oxford*. Now what should she care about deaths at Oxford? When she has him here.

"Wait," she pleads, and turns a page, and reads some sentences as the book is pulled slowly up, her eyes shuttling, and then suddenly lets him take it. "God, you're a bully."

He marks her place with a burnt match and looks at her bare feet. "Do you have sneakers or anything?"

"No. Hey I'm sleepy."

"We'll go to bed early."

Her eyeballs turn on him at this, her lips pursed a little. There is this vulgarity in her, that just couldn't let that go by. Ever so faintly unctuous vulgarity.

"Come on," he says. "Put on flat shoes and we'll dry your hair."

"I'll have to wear heels." As she bows her head to pinch them on, the white line of her parting makes him smile, it's so straight. Like a little birthday girl's parting.

They approach the mountain through the city park. The trash baskets and movable metal benches have not been set out yet. On the concrete-and-plank benches fluffy old men sun like greater pigeons, dressed in patches of gray multiple as feathers. The trees in small leaf dust the half-bare ground with shadow. Sticks and strings protect the newly seeded margins of the unraked gravel walks. The breeze, flowing steadily down the slope from the empty bandshell, is cool out of the sun. Pigeons with mechanical heads flee on pink legs from their shoetips and resettle, chuffling, near their heels. A derelict stretches an arm along the back of a bench to dry, and out of a gouged face sneezes petitely, catlike. A few toughs, fourteen or younger, smoke and jab near the locked equipment shed of a play pavilion on whose yellow boards someone has painted with red paint Tex & Josie, Rita & Jay. Where would they get red paint? Threads of green poke up through matted brown. He takes her hand. The ornamental pool in front of the bandshell is drained and scum-stained; they move along a path parallel to the curve of its cold lip, which echoes back the bandshell's silence. A World War II tank, made a monument, points its guns at far-off tennis courts. The nets are not up, the lines unlimed.

Trees darken; pavilions slide downhill. They walk through the upper region of the park, which thugs haunt at night, scattering candy-bar wrappers. The beginning of the steps is almost hidden in an overgrowth of great bushes tinted dull amber with the first buds. Long ago, when hiking was customary entertainment, people built stairs up the Brewer side of the mountain. They are made of six-foot tarred logs with dirt filled in flat behind them. Iron pipes have since been driven, to hold these tough round risers in place, and fine blue gravel scattered over the packed dirt they dam. The footing is difficult for Ruth; Rabbit watches her body struggle to propel her weight on the digging points of her heels. They catch and buckle on an unevenness hidden below the coating of gravel. Her backside lurches, her arms grab out for balance.

He tells her, "Take off your shoes."

"And kill my feet? You're a thoughtful bastard."

"Well then, let's go back down."

"No, no," she says. "We must be halfway."

"We're nowhere near half up. Take off your shoes. These blue stones are stopping; it'll just be mashed-down dirt."

"With chunks of glass in it."

But further on she does take off her shoes. Bare of stockings, her white feet lift lightly under his eyes; the yellow skin of her heels flickers. Thin ankles under the swell of calf. In a gesture of gratitude he takes off his shoes, to share whatever pain there is. The dirt is trod smooth, but embedded pebbles negligible to the eye do stab the skin, with the force of your weight. Also the ground is cold. "Ouch," he says. *"Owitch."*

"Come on, soldier," she says, "be brave."

They learn to walk on the grass at the ends of the logs. Tree branches overhang part of the way, making it an up-ward tunnel. At other spots the air is clear behind them, and they can look over the rooftops of Brewer into the twentieth story of the courthouse, the city's one skyscraper. Concrete eagles stand in relief, wings flared, between its top windows. Two middle-aged couples in plaid scarves, bird-watchers, pass them on the way down; as soon as they have descended out of sight behind the gnarled arm of an oak, Rabbit hops up to Ruth's step and kisses her, hugs her hot bulk, tastes the salt in the sweat on her face, which is un-responsive. She thinks that is a silly time; her one-eyed wom-an's mind is intent on getting up the hill. But the thought of her city girl's paper-pale feet bare on the stones for his sake makes his heart, fevered with exertion, sob, and he clings to her tough body with the weakness of grief. An airplane goes over, rapidly rattling the air.

"My queen," he says, "my good horse."

"Your what?"

"Horse."

Near the top, the mountain rises sheer in a cliff, and here modern men have built concrete stairs with an iron railing that in a Z of three flights reach the macadam parking lot of the Pinnacle Hotel. They put their shoes back on and climb the stairs and watch the city slowly flatten under them.

Rails guard the cliff edge. He grips one white beam, warmed by the sun now sinking steeply away from the zenith, and looks straight down, into the exploding heads of trees. A frightening view, remembered from boyhood, when he used to wonder if you jumped would you die or be cushioned on those green heads as on the clouds of a dream? In the lower part of his vision the stone-walled cliff rises to his feet foreshortened to the narrowness of a knife; in the upper part the hillside slopes down, faint paths revealed and random clearings and the steps they have climbed.

Ruth's gaze, her lids half-closed as if she were reading a book, rests on the city. The hard silhouette of her cheek-bone in the high vigilant air is still. Is she feeling like an Indian? She said she might be Mexican.

O.K. He brought them up here. To see what? The city stretches from dollhouse rows at the base of the park through a broad blurred belly of flowerpot red patched with tar roofs and twinkling cars and ends as a rose tint in the mist that hangs above the distant river. Gas tanks glimmer in this smoke. Suburbs lie like scarves in it. But the city is huge in the middle view, and he opens his lips as if to force the lips of his soul to receive the taste of the truth about it, as if truth were a secret in such low solution that only immensity can give us a sensible taste. Air dries his mouth.

His day has been bothered by God: Ruth mocking, Eccles blinking—why did they teach you such things if no one believed them? It seems plain, standing here, that if there is this floor there is a ceiling, that the true space in which we live is upward space. Someone is dying. In this great stretch of brick someone is dying. The thought comes from nowhere: simple percentages. Someone in some house along these streets, if not this minute then the next, dies; and in that suddenly stone chest the heart of this flat prostrate rose seems to him to be. He moves his eyes to find the spot; perhaps he can see the cancer-blackened soul of an old man mount through the blue like a monkey on a string. He strains his ears to hear the pang of release as this ruddy illusion at his feet gives up this reality. Silence blasts him. Chains of cars creep without noise; a dot comes out of a door. What is he doing here, standing on air? Why isn't he home? He becomes frightened and begs Ruth, "Put your arm around me."

She carelessly obliges, taking a step and swinging her haunch against his. He clasps her tighter and feels better. Brewer at their feet seems to warm in the sloping sunlight; its vast red cloth seems to lift from the valley in which it is sunk concavely, to fill like a breast with a breath, Brewer the mother of a hundred thousand, shelter of love, ingenious and luminous artifact. So it is in an access of security that he asks, voicing like a loved child a teasing doubt, "Were you really a whore?"

To his surprise she turns hard under his arm and twists away and stands beside the railing menacingly. Her eyes narrow; her chin changes shape. In his nervousness he notices three Boy Scouts grinning at them across the asphalt. She asks, "Are you really a rat?"

He feels the need of care in his answer. "In a way."

"All right then."

They take a bus down.

Tuesday afternoon, overcast, he takes a bus to Mt. Judge. Eccles' address is at the north end of town; he rides past his own neighborhood in safety, gets off at Spruce, and walks along singing in a high voice to himself the phrase, "Oh, *I'm* just *wild* about Har-ry"—not the beginning of the song, but the place at the end where the girl, repeating, goes way up on "I'm."

He feels on even keel. For two days he and Ruth have lived on his money and he still has fourteen dollars left. Furthermore he has discovered, poking through her bureau this morning while she was out shopping, that she has an enormous checking account, with over five hundred dollars in it at the end of February. They have gone bowling once and have seen four movies—*Gigi, Bell, Book and Candle, The Inn of the Sixth Happiness,* and *The Shaggy Dog.* He saw so many snippets from *The Shaggy Dog* on the Mickey Mouse Club that he was curious to see the whole thing. It was like looking through a photograph album with about half familiar faces. The scene where the rocket goes through the roof and Fred MacMurray runs out with the coffee pot he knew as well as his own face.

Ruth was funny. Her bowling was awful; she just sort of paddled up to the line and dropped the ball. *Plok.* Every time, in *Gigi,* the stereophonic-sound loudspeaker behind them in the theater would blare out she turned around and said "Shh" as if it were somebody in the theater talking too loud. In *The Inn of the Sixth Happiness,* every time Ingrid Bergman's face appeared on the screen she leaned over to Rabbit and asked him in a whisper, "Is she really a whore?" He was upset by Robert Donat; he looked awful. He knew he was dying. Imagine knowing you're dying and going ahead pretending you're a mandarin. Ruth's comment about *Bell, Book and Candle* last night was, "Why don't you ever see any bongo drums around here?" He vowed secretly to get some. A half-hour ago, waiting for the bus on Weiser Street, he priced a set in the window of the Chords 'n' Records music store. $19.95. All the way out on the bus he beat bongo patterns on his knees.

"For *I'm* just *wild* about Harrr-ree—"

Number 61 is a big brick place with white wood trim, a little porch imitating a Greek temple, and a slate roof that shines under the clouds' sullen luster. Out back a wire fence encloses a yellow swing frame and a sandbox. A puppy yaps in this pen as Harry goes up the walk. The grass wears that intense greasy green that promises rain, the color of grass in color snapshots. The place looks too cheerful to be right; Rabbit thinks of ministers as living in black shingled castles. But a small plate above the fish-shaped door-knocker says in engraved script *The Rectory*. He bangs the fish twice and, after waiting, twice again.

A crisp little number with speckled green eyes opens the door. "What is it?" Her voice as good as says, "How dare you?" As she adjusts her face to his height her eyes enlarge, displaying more of the vividly clear whites to which her moss-colored irises are buttoned.

At once, absurdly, he feels in control of her, feels she likes him. Freckles dot her little bumpy nose, kind of a pinched nose, narrow and pale under the dots of tan. Her skin is fair, and fine-grained as a child's. She is wearing orange shorts. With a pleasantness that amounts to arrogance he says, "Hi."

"Hello."

"Say, is Reverend Eccles in?"

"He's asleep."

"In the middle of the day?"

"He was up much of the night."

"Oh gosh. The poor guy."

"Do you want to come in?"

"Well gee, I don't know. He told me to be here. He really did."

"He might well have. Please come in."

She leads him past a hall and staircase into a cool room with a high ceiling and silver wallpaper, a piano, watercolors of scenery, a lot of sets of books in a recessed bookcase, a fireplace whose mantel supports one of those clocks with a pendulum of four gold balls that are supposed to run practically forever. Photographs in frames all around. Furniture heavy green and red except for a long sofa with a scrolling back and arms whose cushions are cream white. The room smells coldly kept. From far off comes the warmer odor of cake baking. She stops in the center of the rug and says, "Listen."

He stops. The faint bump that he also heard is not repeated. She explains, "I thought that brat was asleep."

"Are you the babysitter?"

"I'm the wife," she says, and sits down in the center of the white sofa, to prove it.

He takes a padded wing chair opposite. The plum fabric feels softly gritty against his naked forearms. He is wearing a checked sports shirt, with the sleeves turned back to his elbows. "Oh, I'm sorry." Of course. Her bare legs, crossed, show the blue dabs of varicose veins. Her face, when she sits, is not as young as at the door. Double chin when she relaxes, head tucked back. Smug little cookie. Firm little knockers. He asks, "How old is your child?"

"Two children. Two girls, one and three."

"I have a boy who's two."

"I'd like a boy," she says. "The girls and I have personality problems; we're too much alike. We know exactly what the other's thinking."

Dislikes her own children! Rabbit is shocked, this from a minister's wife. "Does your husband notice this?"

"Oh, it's wonderful for Jack. He loves to have women fighting over him. It's his little harem. I think a boy would threaten him. Do you feel threatened?"

"Not by the kid, no. He's only two."

"It starts earlier than two, believe me. Sexual antagonism begins practically at birth."

"I hadn't noticed."

"Good for you. I expect you're a primitive father. I think Freud is like God; you make it true."

Rabbit smiles, supposing that Freud has some connection with the silver wallpaper and the watercolor of a palace and a canal above her head. Class. She brings her fingertips to her temples, pushes her head back, shuts her lids, and through plump open lips sighs. He is struck; she seems at this moment a fine-grained Ruth.

Eccles' thin voice, oddly amplified in his home, cries down the stairs. "Lucy! Joyce is getting into bed with me!"

Lucy opens her eyes and says to Rabbit proudly, "See?"

"She says you told her it's all right," the voice whines on, piercing bannisters, walls, and layers of wallpaper.

Mrs. Eccles gets up and goes to the archway. The seat of her orange shorts is wrinkled from sitting; the hitched-up legs expose most of the oval backs of her thighs. Whiter than the sofa; the blush of pink from the pressure of sitting fades from the skin. "I told her no such thing!" she calls upward while one fair hand tugs the shorts down and smooths the cloth around her mussed but smug rump, a pocket stitched with black thread to the right half. "Jack," she goes on, "you have a visitor! A very tall young man who says you invited him!"

At the mention of himself Rabbit has risen and right behind her says, "To play golf."

"To play golf!" she echoes in a yell.

"Oh, dear," the voice upstairs says to itself, then shouts, "Hello, Harry! I'll be right down."

A child up there is crying, "Mommy did too! Mommy did too!"

Rabbit shouts in answer, "Hello!"

Mrs. Eccles turns her head with an inviting twist. "Harry—?"

"Angstrom."

"What do you do, Mr. Angstrom?"

"Well. I'm kind of out of work."

"Angstrom. Of course. Aren't you the one who disappeared? The Springers' son-in-law?"

"Right," he says smartly and, in a mindless follow-through, a kind of flower of co-ordination, she having on the drop of his answer turned with prim dismissal away from him again, slaps! her sassy fanny. Not hard; a cupping hit, rebuke and fond pat both, well-placed on the pocket.

She swiftly wheels, swinging her backside to safety behind her. Her freckles dart sharp as pinpricks from her shock-bleached face. Her leaping blood freezes her skin, and this rigid effect, of superbly severe stone, is so incongruous with the lazy condescending warmth he feels toward her, that he makes a funny face, pushing his upper lip over his lower in a burlesque of penitence.

A chaotic tumble on the stairs shakes the walls. Eccles jolts to a stop in front of them, off-balance, tucking a dirty white shirt into rumpled suntans. His shadowed eyes weep between his furry lids. "I'm sorry," he says. "I hadn't really forgotten."

"It's kind of cloudy anyway," Rabbit says, and smiles involuntarily. Her ass had felt so good, just right, dense yet springy, kind of smacked back. He supposes she'll tell, which will finish him here. Just as well. He doesn't know why he's here anyway.

Maybe she would have told, but her husband starts annoying her immediately. "Oh, I'm sure we can get nine in before it rains," he tells Rabbit.

"Jack, you aren't *really* going to play golf again. You said you had all those calls to make this afternoon."

"I made calls this morning."

"Two. You made two. On Freddy Davis and Mrs. Landis.

The same old safe ones. What about the Ferrys? You've been talking about the Ferrys for six months."

"What's so sacred about the Ferrys? They never do anything for the church. She came on Christmas Sunday and went out by the choir door so she wouldn't have to speak to me."

"Of course they don't do anything for the church and that's why you should call as you know perfectly well. I don't think anything's sacred about the Ferrys except that you've been brooding about her going out the side door and making everybody's life miserable for months. Now if she comes on Easter it'll be the same thing. To tell you my honest opinion you and Mrs. Ferry would hit it off splendidly, you're both equally childish."

"Lucy, just because Mr. Ferry owns a shoe factory doesn't make them more important Christians than somebody who works in a shoe factory."

"Oh Jack, you're too tiresome. You're just afraid of being snubbed and don't quote Scripture to justify yourself. I don't care if the Ferrys come to church or stay away or become Jehovah's Witnesses."

"At least the Jehovah's Witnesses put into practice what they say they believe." When Eccles turns to Harry to guffaw conspiratorially after this dig, bitterness cripples his laugh, turns his lips in tightly, so his small-jawed head shows its teeth like a skull.

"I don't know what that's supposed to mean," Lucy says, "but when you asked me to marry you I told you what I felt and you said all right fine."

"I said as long as your heart remained open for *Grace*." Eccles pours these words on her in a high strained blast that burns his broad forehead, soils it with a blush.

"Mommy I had a *rest*." The little voice, shyly penetrating, ambushes them from above. At the head of the carpeted stairs a small brown girl in underpants hangs in suspense. She seems to Rabbit too dark for her parents, too somber in the shadows, braced on silhouetted stout legs, baby fat knotted on longer stalks. Her hands rub and pluck her naked chest in exasperation. She hears her mother's answer before it comes.

"Joyce. You go right back into your own bed and have a *nap*."

"I can't. There's too many noises."

"We've been screaming right under her head," Eccles tells his wife.

"*You've* been screaming. About Grace."

"I had a scary dream," Joyce says, and clumsily descends two steps.

"You did not. You were never asleep." Mrs. Eccles walks to the foot of the stairs, holding her own throat gently.

"What was the dream about?" Eccles asks his child.

"A lion ate a boy."

"That's not a dream at all," the woman snaps, and turns on her husband: "It's those hateful Belloc poems you insist on reading her."

"She asks for them."

"They're hateful. They give her traumas."

"Joyce and I think they're funny."

"Well, you *both* have perverted senses of humor. Every night she asks me about that damn pony Tom and what does 'die' means?"

"Tell her what it means. If you had Belloc's and my faith in the supernatural these perfectly natural questions wouldn't upset you."

"Don't harp, Jack. You're awful when you harp."

"I'm awful when I take myself seriously, you mean."

"Hey. I smell cake burning," Rabbit says.

She looks at him and recognition frosts her eyes. That there is some kind of cold call in her glance, a faint shout from the midst of her enemies, he feels but ignores, letting his gaze go limp on the top of her head, showing her the sensitive nostrils that sniffed the smoking case. The compact arc of her skull under her short-clipped fluffed hairdo suggests that she's been turned on an exceptionally precise lathe.

"If only you *would* take yourself seriously," she says to Eccles, and on glimpsey bare legs flies down the sullen hall of the rectory.

Eccles calls, "Joyce, go back to your room and put on a shirt and you can come down."

The child instead thumps down three more steps.

"Joyce, did you hear me?"

"You get it, Dayud-dee."

"Why should I get it? Daddy's all the way downstairs."

"I don't know where it is."

"You do too. Right on your bureau."

"I don't know where my bruro is."

"In your room, sweet. Of course you know where it is. You get your shirt and I'll let you downstairs."

But she is already halfway down.

"I'm frightened of the li-un," she sings with a little smile that betrays consciousness of her own impudence. Her voice has a spaced, testing quality; Rabbit heard this note of care in her mother's voice too, when she was teasing the same man, and wonders why Eccles doesn't go for it; drive a wedge in this chink of fear and make discipline. Not that he could do it either.

"There's no lion up there. There's nobody up there but Bonnie sleeping. Bonnie's not afraid."

"Please, Daddy. Please please please please *please*." She has reached the foot of the stairs and seizes and squeezes her father's knees.

Eccles laughs, bracing his unbalanced weight on the child's head, which is rather broad and flat-topped, like his own. "All right," he says. "You wait here and talk to this funny man." And bounds up the stairs with that unexpected athleticism.

Rabbit says, "Joyce, are you a good girl?"

She waggles her stomach and pulls her head into her shoulders. The motion forces a little gutteral noise, "cukk," out of her throat. She shakes her head; he has the impression she is trying to hide behind a screen of dimples. But she says with unexpectedly prim and positive enunciation, "Yes."

"And is your mommy good?"

"Yes."

"What makes her so good?" He hopes Lucy hears this in the kitchen. The hurried oven sounds have stopped.

Joyce looks up at him and like a sheet being rippled fear tugs a corner of the surface of her face. Really tears seem close. She scampers from him down the hall, the way her mother went. Fled from, Rabbit wanders uneasily in the hall, trying to attach his excited heart to the pictures hanging there. Surfaces of foreign capitals, a woman in white beneath a tree whose every leaf is rimmed in gold, a laborious pen rendering, brick by brick, of the St. John's Episcopal Church, dated 1927 and signed large by Mildred L. Kramer, the letters interlocked artistically. Above a small table halfway down the hall hangs a studio photograph of some old rock with white hair above his ears and a clerical collar staring over your shoulder as if square into the heart of Things; stuck into the frame is a yellow photo clipped from a newspaper showing in coarse dots the same old gent gripping a cigar and laughing like a madman with three others in robes. He looks a little like Jack but fatter and stronger. He holds the cigar in a fist. Further on is a colored print of a painted scene in a workshop where the carpenter works in the light given off by his Helper's head: the glass this is protected by gives back to Rabbit the shadow of his own head; this half-mirroring glass rejects his attention, which slips back and forth clinging nowhere. There is a tangy scent in the hallway of, spot cleaner? new varnish? mothballs? old wallpaper? He hovers among these possibilities, "the man who disappeared." "Sexual antagonism begins practically at birth." What a bitch, really. Yet with a nice low flame in her, lighting up her legs. Those bright white legs. She'd have an anxious little edge and want her own. Cookie. A sharp vanilla cookie. In spite of herself he loves her.

There must be a back stairs, because he next hears Eccles' voice in the kitchen, arguing Joyce into her sweater, asking Lucy if the cake was ruined, explaining, not knowing Rabbit's ears were around the corner, "Don't think this is pleasure for me. It's work."

"There's no other way to talk to him?"

"He's frightened."

"Sweetie, everybody's frightened to you."

"But he's even frightened *of* me."

"Well, he came through that door cocky enough."

This was the place for, *And he slapped my sweet ass, that's yours to defend.*

What! Your sweet ass! I'll murder the rogue. I'll call the police.

In reality Lucy's voice stopped at "enough," and Eccles is talking about if so-and-so called, where are those new golf balls?, Joyce you *had* a cookie ten minutes ago, and at last calling, in a voice that has healed too smooth over the scratches of their quarrel, good-by. Rabbit pads up the hall and is leaning on the front radiator when Eccles, looking like a young owl, awkward, cross, pops out of the kitchen.

They go to his car. Under the threat of rain the green skin of the Buick has a tropical waxiness. Eccles lights a cigarette and they go down, across Route 422, into the valley toward the golf course. Eccles says, after getting several deep drags settled in his chest. "So your trouble isn't really lack of religion."

"Huh?"

"I was remembering our other conversation. About the waterfall and the tree."

"Yeah well: I stole that from Mickey Mouse."

Eccles laughs, puzzled; Rabbit notices how his mouth stays open after he laughs, the little inturned rows of teeth waiting a moment while his eyebrows go up and down expectantly. "It stopped me short," he admits, closing this flirtatious cave. "Then you said you know what's inside you. I've been wondering all weekend what that was. Can you tell me?"

Rabbit doesn't want to tell him anything. The more he tells, the more he loses. He's safe inside his own skin, he doesn't want to come out. This guy's whole game is to get him out into the open where he can be manipulated. But the fierce convention of courtesy pries open Rabbit's lips. "Hell, it's nothing much," he says. "It's just that, well, it's all there is. Don't you think?"

Eccles nods and blinks and drives without saying a word. The trap is there waiting; damn him, he's so sure I'll come down the path. "How's Janice now?" Rabbit asks.

Eccles is startled to feel him veer off. "I dropped by Monday morning to tell them you were in the county. Your wife was in the back yard with your boy and what I took to be an old girl friend, a Mrs.—Foster? Fogleman?"

"What did she look like?"

"I don't really know. I was distracted by her sunglasses. They were the mirror kind, with very wide sidepieces."

"Oh Peggy Gring. That moron. She married that hick Morris Fosnacht."

"Fosnacht. That's right. Like the doughnut. I knew there was something very local about the name."

"You'd never heard of Fosnacht Day before you came here?"

"Never. Not in Norwalk."

"The thing I remember about it, when I was, oh I must have been six or seven, because he died in 1940, my grandfather would wait upstairs until I came down so I wouldn't be the Fosnacht. He lived with us then." He hasn't thought or spoken of his grandfather in years, it seems; a mild dry taste comes into his mouth.

"What was the penalty for being a Fosnacht?"

"I forget. It was just something you didn't want to be. Wait. I remember, one year I was the last downstairs and my parents or somebody teased me and I didn't like it and I guess I cried, I don't know. Anyway that's why the old man stayed up."

"He was your father's father?"

"My mother's. He lived with us."

"I remember my father's father," Eccles says. "He used to come to Connecticut and have dreadful arguments with my father. My grandfather was the Bishop of Providence, and had kept his church from going under to the Unitarians by becoming almost Unitarian himself. He used to call himself a Darwinian Deist. My father, in reaction I suppose, became very orthodox; almost Anglo-Catholic. He loved Belloc and Chesterton. In fact he used to read to us those poems you heard my wife objecting to."

"About the lion?"

"Yes. Belloc has this bitter mocking streak my wife can't appreciate. He mocks children, which she can't forgive. It's her psychology. Children are very sacred in psychology. Where was I? Yes; along with his watered-down theology my grandfather had kept in his religious *practice* a certain color and a, a *rigor* that my father had lost. Grandpa felt Daddy was ex*treme*ly remiss in not having a family worship service every night. My father would say he didn't want to bore his children the way he had been bored with God and anyway what was the good of worshipping a jungle god in the living-room? 'You don't think God is in the woods?' my grandfather would say. 'Just behind stained glass?' And so on. My brothers and I used to tremble, because it put Daddy in a terrible depression, ultimately, to argue with him. You know how it is with fathers, you never get rid of the idea that maybe after all they're *right*. A little dried-up old man with a Yankee accent who was really awfully dear. I remember he used to grab us by the knee at mealtimes with this brown bony hand and croak, 'Has he made you believe in Hell?' " Harry laughs; Eccles' imitation is good; being an old man fits him.

"Did he? Do you?"

"Yes, I think so. Hell as Jesus described it. As separation from God."

"Well then we're all more or less in it."

"I don't think so. I don't think so at all. I don't think

even the blackest atheist has an idea of what real separation will be. Outer darkness. What we live in you might call"— he looks at Harry and laughs—"inner darkness."

Eccles' volunteering all this melts Rabbit's caution. He wants to bring something of himself into the space between them. The excitement of friendship, a competitive excitement that makes him lift his hands and jiggle them as if thoughts were basketballs, presses him to say, "Well I don't know all this about theology, but I'll tell you. I *do* feel, I guess, that somewhere behind all this"—he gestures outward at the scenery; they are passing the housing development this side of the golf course, half-wood half brick one-and-a-half-stories in little flat bulldozed yards with tricycles and spindly three-year-old trees, the un-grandest landscape in the world—"there's something that wants me to find it."

Eccles tamps out his cigarette carefully in the tiny cross-notched cup in the car ashtray. "Of course, all vagrants think they're on a quest. At least at first."

Rabbit doesn't see, after trying to *give* the man something, that he deserves this slap. He supposes this is what ministers need, to cut everybody down to the same miserable size. He says, "Well I guess that makes your friend Jesus look pretty foolish."

Mention of the holy name incites pink spots high on Eccles' cheeks. "He *did* say," the minister says, "that saints shouldn't marry."

They turn off the road and go up the winding drive to the clubhouse, a big cinder-block building fronted with a long sign that has CHESTNUT GROVE GOLF COURSE lettered between two Coca-Cola insignia. When Harry caddied here it was just a clapboard shack holding a wood-burning stove and charts of old tournaments and two armchairs and a counter for candy bars and golf balls you fished out of the swamp and that Mrs. Wenrich resold. He supposes Mrs. Wenrich is dead. She was a delicate old rouged widow like a doll with white hair and it always seemed funny to hear talk about greens and turf and tourneys and par come out of her mouth. Eccles parks the Buick on the asphalt lot and says, "Before I forget."

Rabbit's hand is on the door handle. "What?"

"Do you want a job?"

"What kind?"

"A parishioner of mine, a Mrs. Horace Smith, has about

eight acres of garden around her home, toward Appleboro. Her husband was an incredible rhododendron enthusiast. I shouldn't say incredible; he was a terribly dear old man."

"I don't know anything about gardening."

"Nobody does, that's what Mrs. Smith says. There are no gardeners left. For forty dollars a week, I believe her."

"A buck an hour. That's pretty poor."

"It wouldn't be forty hours. Flexible time. That's what you want, isn't it? Flexibility? So you can be free to preach to the multitudes."

Eccles really does have a mean streak. Him and Belloc. Without the collar around his throat, he kind of lets go. Rabbit gets out of the car. Eccles does the same, and his head across the top of the car looks like a head on a platter. The wide mouth moves. "Please consider it."

"I can't. I may not even stay in the county."

"Is the girl going to kick you out?"

"What girl?"

"What is her name? Leonard. Ruth Leonard."

"Well. Aren't you smart?" Who could have told him? Peggy Gring? By way of Tothero? More likely Tothero's girl Whatsername. She looked like Janice. It doesn't matter; the world's such a web anyway, things just trickle through. "I never heard of her," Rabbit says.

The head on the platter grins weirdly in the sunglare off the metal.

They walk side by side to the cement-block clubhouse. On the way Eccles remarks, "It's the strange thing about you mystics, how often your little ecstasies wear a skirt."

"Say. I didn't have to show up today, you know."

"I know. Forgive me. I'm in a very depressed mood."

There's nothing exactly wrong with his saying this, but it rubs Harry's inner hair the wrong way. It kind of clings. It says, "Pity me. Love me." The prickly sensation makes his lips sticky; he is unable to open them to respond. When Eccles pays his way, he can scarcely negotiate thanking him. When they pick out a set of clubs for him to rent, he is so indifferent and silent the freckled kid in charge stares at him as if he's a moron. As he and Eccles walk together toward the first tee he feels partially destroyed, like a good horse yoked to a pulpyhoofed nag. Eccles' presence drags at him so decidedly he has to fight leaning toward that side.

And the ball feels it too, the ball he hits after a little advice from Eccles. It sputters away to one side, crippled by a perverse topspin that makes it fall from flight as dumpily as a blob of clay.

Eccles laughs. "That's the best first drive I ever saw."

"It's not a first drive. I used to hit the ball around when I was a caddy. I should do better than that."

"You expect too much of yourself. Watch me, that'll make you feel better."

Rabbit stands back and is surprised to see Eccles, who has a certain spring in his unconscious movements, swing with a quaint fifty-year-old stiffness. As if he has a pot to keep out of the way. He punches the ball with weak solidity. It goes straight, though high and weak, and he seems delighted with it. He fairly prances into the fairway. Harry trails after him heavily. The soggy turf, raw and wet from recently thawing, sinks beneath his big suede shoes. They're on a seesaw; Eccles goes up, he comes down.

Down in the pagan groves and green alleys of the course Eccles is transformed. Brainless gaiety animates him. He laughs and swings and clucks and calls. Harry stops hating him; he himself is so awful. Ineptitude seems to coat him like a scabrous disease; he is grateful to Eccles for not fleeing from him. Often Eccles, fifty yards further on—he has an excited gleeful habit of running ahead—comes all the way back to find a ball Harry has lost. Somehow Rabbit can't tear his attention from where the ball should have gone, the little ideal napkin of clipped green pinked with a pretty flag. His eyes can't keep with where it did go. "Here it is," Eccles says. "Behind a root. You're having terrible luck."

"This must be a nightmare for you."

"Not at all, not at all. You're extremely promising. You've never played and yet you haven't once missed the ball completely."

This does it; he aims and in the murderous strength of his desire to knock it out in spite of the root he misses the ball completely.

"You only mistake is trying to use your height," Eccles says. "You have a beautiful natural swing." Rabbit whacks again and the ball flops out and wobbles a few yards.

"Bend to the ball," Eccles says. "Imagine you're about to sit down."

"I'm about to lie down," Harry says. He feels sick, giddily sick, sucked deeper into a vortex whose upper rim is marked by the tranquil tips of the leafing trees. He seems to remember having been up there once. He skids into puddles, is swallowed by trees, infallibly sinks into the mangy scruff at the sides of the fairways.

Nightmare is the word. In waking life only animate things slither and jerk for him this way. He's always had a touch with objects. His unreal hacking dazes his brain; half-hypnotized, it plays tricks whose strangeness dawns on him slowly. In his head he talks to the clubs as if they're women. The irons, light and thin yet somehow treacherous in his hands, are Janice. *Come on, you dope, be calm; here we go, easy.* When the slotted club face gouges the dirt behind the ball and the shock jolts up his arms to his shoulders his thought is that Janice has struck him. *Oh, dumb, really dumb. Screw her. Just screw her.* Anger turns his skin rotten, so the outside seeps through; his insides go jagged with the tiny dry forks of bitter scratching brambles, the brittle silver shaft one more stick, where words hang like caterpillar nests that can't be burned away. *She stubs stubs fat she stubs the dirt* torn open in a rough brown mouth *dirt stubs fat:* with the woods the "she" is Ruth. Holding a three wood, absorbed in its heavy reddish head and grass-stained face and white stripe prettily along the edge, he thinks *O.K. if you're so smart* and clenches and swirls. Ahg: when she tumbled so easily, to balk this! The mouth of torn grass and the ball runs, hops and hops, hides in a bush; white tail. And when he walks there, the bush is damn somebody, his mother; he lifts the huffy branches like shirts, in a fury of shame but with care not to break any, and these branches bother his legs while he tries to pour his will down into the hard irreducible pellet that is not really himself yet in a way is; just the way it sits there in the center of everything. As the seven iron chops down *please Janice just once* awkwardness spiders at his elbows and the ball as he stares with bitten elbows hooks with dismal slowness into more sad scruff further on, the khaki color of Texas. *Oh you moron go home.* Home is the hole, and above, in the scheme of the unhappy vision that frets his conscious attention with an almost optical overlay of presences, the mild gray rain sky is his grandfather waiting upstairs so that Harry will not be a Fosnacht.

And, now at the corners, now at the center of this striving dream, Eccles flits in his grubby shirt like a white flag of forgiveness, crying encouragement, fluttering from the green to guide him home.

The greens, still dead from the winter, are salted with a dry dirt; fertilizer? The ball slips along making bits of grit jump. "Don't stab your putts," Eccles says. "A little easy swing, arms stiff. Distance is more important than aim on the first putt. Try again." He kicks the ball back. It took Harry about twelve to get up here on the fourth green, but this smug assumption that his strokes are past counting irritates him. *Come on, sweet,* he pleads with his wife, *there's the hole, big as a bucket. Everything is all right.*

But no, she has to stab in a panicked way; what was she afraid of? Too much, the ball goes maybe five feet past. Walking toward Eccles, he says, "You never did tell me how Janice is."

"Janice?" Eccles with an effort drags his attention up from the game. He is absolutely in love with winning; *he is eating me up,* Harry thinks. "She seemed in good spirits on Monday. She was out in the back yard with this other woman, and they were both giggling when I came. You must realize that for a little while, now that she's adjusted somewhat, she'll probably enjoy being back with her parents. It's her own version of your irresponsibility."

"Actually," Harry says gratingly, squatting to line up the putt, the way they do it on television, "she can't stand her parents any more than I can. She probably wouldn't've married me if she hadn't been in such a hurry to get away from um." His putt slides past on the down side and goes two or three fucking feet too far. Four feet.

Eccles sinks his. The ball wobbles up and with a glottal rattle bobbles in. The minister looks up with the light of triumph in his eyes. "Harry," he asks, sweetly yet boldly, "why have you left her? You're obviously deeply involved with her."

"I *told* ja. There was this thing that wasn't there."

"What thing? Have you ever seen it? Are you sure it exists?"

Harry's two-foot putt dribbles short and he picks up the ball with trembling fingers. "Well if you're not sure it exists don't ask me. It's right up your alley. If you don't know nobody does."

"No," Eccles cries in the same strained voice in which he told his wife to keep her heart open for Grace. "Christianity isn't looking for a rainbow. If it were what you think it is we'd pass out opium at services. We're trying to *serve* God, not *be* God."

They pick up their bags and walk the way a wooden arrow tells them.

Eccles goes on, explanatorily, "This was all settled centuries ago, in the heresies of the early Church."

"I tell you, I know what it is."

"What is it? What *is* it? Is it hard or soft? Harry. Is it blue? Is it red? Does it have polka dots?"

It hits Rabbit depressingly that he really wants to be told. Underneath all this I-know-more-about-it-than-you-heresies-of-the-early-Church business he really wants to be told about it, wants to be told that it is there, that he's not lying to all those people every Sunday. As if it's not enough to be trying to get some sense out of this frigging game, you have to carry around this madman trying to swallow your soul. The hot strap of the bag gnaws at his shoulder.

"The truth is," Eccles tells him with womanish excitement, in a voice agonized by embarrassment, "you're monstrously selfish. You're a coward. You don't care about right or wrong; you worship nothing except your own worst instincts."

They reach the tee, a platform of turf beside a hunchbacked fruit tree offering fists of taut pale buds. "I better go first," Rabbit says. "Till you calm down." His heart is hushed, held in mid-beat, by anger. He doesn't care about anything except getting out of this mess. He wishes it would rain. In avoiding looking at Eccles he looks at the ball, which sits high on the tee and already seems free of the ground. Very simply he brings the clubhead around his shoulder into it. The sound has a hollowness, a singleness he hasn't heard before. His arms force his head up and his ball is hung way out, lunarly pale against the beautiful black blue of storm clouds, his grandfather's color stretched dense across the east. It recedes along a line straight as a ruler-edge. Stricken; sphere, star, speck. It hesitates, and Rabbit thinks it will die, but he's fooled, for the ball makes this hesitation the ground of a final leap: with a kind of visible sob takes a last bite of space before vanishing in falling. "That's *it!*" he cries and, turning to Eccles with a smile of aggrandizement, repeats, "That's it."

SUN and moon, sun and moon, time goes. In Mrs. Smith's acres, crocuses break the crust. Daffodils and narcissi unpack their trumpets. The reviving grass harbors violets, and the lawn is suddenly coarse with dandelions and broad-leaved weeds. Invisible rivulets running brokenly make the low land of the estate sing. The flowerbeds, bordered with bricks buried diagonally, are pierced by dull red spikes that will be peonies, and the earth itself, scumbled, stone-flecked, horny, raggedly patched with damp and dry, looks like the oldest and smells like the newest thing under Heaven. The shaggy golden suds of blooming forsythia glow through the smoke that fogs the garden while Rabbit burns rakings of crumpled stalks, perished grass, oak leaves shed in the dark privacy of winter, and rosebud prunings that cling together in infuriating ankle-clawing clumps. These brush piles, ignited soon after he arrives, crusty-eyed and tasting coffee, in the midst of the webs of dew, are still damply smoldering when he leaves, making ghosts in the night behind him as his footsteps crunch on the spalls of the Smith driveway. All the way back to Brewer in the bus he smells the warm ashes.

Funny, for these two months he never has to cut his fingernails. He lops, lifts, digs. He plants annuals, packets the old lady gives him—nasturtiums, poppies, sweet peas, petunias.

He loves folding the hoed ridge of crumbs of soil over the seeds. Sealed, they cease to be his. The simplicity. Getting rid of something by giving it. God Himself folded into the tiny adamant structure. Self-destined to a succession of explosions, the great slow gathering out of water and air and silicon: felt without words in the turn of the round hoe-handle in his palms.

Now, after the magnolias have lost their grip but before any but the leaves of the maple have the breadth to cast deep shade, the cherry trees and crabapples and, in a remote corner of the grounds, a solitary plum tree ball with bloom, a whiteness the black limbs seem to gather from the blowing clouds and after a moment hurl away, so the reviving grass is bleached by an astonishing storm of confetti. Fragrant of gasoline, the power mower chews the petals; the lawn digests them. The lilac bushes bloom by the fallen tennis-court fences. Birds come to the birdbath. Busy one morning with a crescent-shape edger, Harry is caught in a tide of perfume, for behind him the breeze has turned and washes down through a thick sloping bank of acrid lily-of-the-valley leaves in which on that warm night a thousand bells have ripened, the high ones on the stem still the bitter sherbet green of cantaloupe rind. Apple trees and pear trees. Tulips. Those ugly purple tatters the iris. And at last, prefaced by azaleas, the rhododendrons themselves, with a profusion increasing through the last week of May. Rabbit had waited all spring for this crowning. The bushes had puzzled him, they were so big, almost trees, some twice his height, and there seemed so many. They were planted all along the edges of the towering droop-limbed spruces that sheltered the place, and in the acres sheltered there were dozens of great rectangular clumps like loaves of porous green bread. The bushes were evergreen. With their zigzag branches and long leaves fingering in every direction they seemed to belong to a different climate, to a different land, whose gravity pulled softer than this one. When the first blooms came they were like the single big flower Oriental prostitutes wear on the sides of their heads, on the covers of the paperback spy stories Ruth reads. But when the hemispheres of blossom appear in crowds they remind him of nothing so much as the hats worn by cheap girls to church on Easter. Harry has often wanted and never had a girl like that, a little Catholic from a shabby house, dressed in flashy bargain clothes; in the swarthy leaves under the pert soft cap of five-petaled flowers he can imagine her face, with its plucked eyebrows, its little black nostrils round as buttons, its eyes made surly by nuns. He can almost smell her perfume as she passes him on the concrete cathedral steps, head bowed, her mincing legs tucked into her tailored suit. Intent on prayer, she has a dumb girl's sweet piercing way of putting her whole body into one thing at a time. Close, he can go so close to the petals. Each flower wears on the roof of its mouth two fans of freckles where the anthers tap. He *can* smell her.

At this climax of her late husband's garden, Mrs. Smith comes out of the house and on Rabbit's arm walks deep into the rhododendron plantation. A woman once of some height, she is bent small, and the lingering strands of black look dirty in her white hair. She carries a cane, but in forgetfulness, perhaps, hangs it over her forearm and totters along with it dangling loose like an outlandish bracelet. Her method of gripping her gardener is this: he crooks his right arm, pointing his elbow toward her shoulder, and she shakily brings her left forearm up within his and bears down heavily on his wrist with her lumpish and freckled fingers. Her hold is like that of a vine to a wall; one good pull will destroy it, but otherwise it will survive all weathers. He feels her body jolt with every step, and every word twitches her head. Not that the effort of speaking is so great; it is the excitement of communication that seizes her, wrinkling the arch of her nose fiercely, making her lips snarl above her snaggle-teeth with a comic overexpressiveness that is self-conscious, like the funny faces made by a thirteen-year-old girl in constant confession of the fact that she is not beautiful. She sharply tips her head to look up at Harry, and in tiny brown sockets afflicted by creases like so many drawstrings, her crackled blue eyes bulge frantically with captive life as she speaks: "Oh, I *don't* like Mrs. R. S. Holford; she always looks so washed-out and flossy to me. Harry loved those salmon colors so; I'd say to him, 'If I want red, give me red; a fat red rose. And if I want white, give me white, a tall white lily; and don't bother me with all these in-betweens and would-be-pinks and almost-purples that don't know what their mind is. Rhody's a mealymouthed plant,' I'd say to Harry, 'she doesn't have a brain, so she gives you some of everything' just to tease him. But in truth I meant it." The thought seems to strike her. She stops dead on the path of grass and her eyes, the irises a kind of broken-glass white within rings of persisting blue, roll nervously, looking from one side of him to the other. "In truth I meant every word of it. I'm a farmer's daughter, Mr. Angstrom, and I would have rather seen this land gone under to alfalfa. I'd say to him, 'Why don't you plant buckwheat if you must fuss in the ground? Now there's a real crop. You raise the wheat, I'll bake the bread.' I would have, too. 'What do we want with all these corsages that after they've gone we have to look at their ugly leaves all the year round?' I'd say to him, 'What pretty girl are you growing these for?' He was younger than I, that's why I took advantage of my right to tease him. I won't say by how much. What are we standing here for? Old body like mine, stand still in one place you'll be rooted fast." She jabs the cane into the grass, his signal to extend his arm. They move on down the alley of bloom. "Never thought I'd outlive him. That was his weakness. Come in out of the garden he'd be forever sitting. A farmer's daughter never learns the meaning of sit."

Her unsteady touch on his wrist bobs like the swaying tops of the giant spruces. He associates these trees with forbidden estates; it gives him pleasure to be within their protection. "Ah. Now here is a *plant*." They stop at a corner and she lifts her dangling cane toward a small rhododendron clothed in pink of penetrating purity, a color through whose raw simplicity, as through stained glass, you seem to look into the ideal subsoil of reality. "Harry's Bianchi" Mrs. Smith says. "The only rhody except some of the whites, I forget their names, silly names anyway, that says what it means. It's the only true pink there is. When Harry first got it he set it among the other so-called pinks and it showed them up as just so muddy he tore them out and backed the Bianchi with crimsons. The crimsons are by, aren't they? Is today June?" Her wild eyes fix him crazily and her grip tightens.

"I don't know. I don't think so. Memorial Day's next Saturday."

"Oh, I remember so well the day we got that silly plant. Hot! We drove to New York City to take it off the boat and put it in the back seat of the Packard like a favorite aunt or some such thing. It came in a big blue wooden tub of earth. There was only one nursery in England that carried the stock and it cost two hundred dollars to ship. A man came down to the hold to water it every day. Hot, and all that vile traffic through Jersey City and Trenton and this scrawny bush sitting in its blue tub in the back seat like a prince of the realm! There weren't any of these turnpikes then so it was a good six-hour trip to New York. The middle of the Depression and it looked like everybody in the world owned an automobile. You came over the Delaware at Burlington. This was before the war. I don't suppose when I say 'the war' you know which one I mean. You probably think of that Korean thing as the war."

"No I think of the war as World War Two."

"So do I! So do I! Do you really remember it?"

"Sure. I mean I was pretty old. I flattened tin cans and bought War Stamps and we got awards at grade school."

"Our son was killed."

"Gee. I'm sorry."

"Oh he was old, he was old. He was almost forty. They made him an officer right off."

"Still—"

"I know. You think of only young men being killed."

"Yeah, you do."

"It was a good war. It wasn't like the first. It was ours to win, and we won it. All wars are hateful things but that one was satisfying to win." She gestures with her cane again at the pink plant. "The day we came over from the boat docks it of course wasn't in flower that late in the summer so it looked like just foolishness to me, to have it riding in the back seat like a"—she realizes she is repeating herself, falters, but goes on—"like a prince of the realm." In her almost transparent blue eyes there is pinned this little sharpness watching his face to see if he smiles at her addlement. Seeing nothing she snaps roughly, "It's the only one."

"The only Bianchi?"

"Yes! Right! There's not another in the United States. There's not another good pink from the Golden Gate to—wherever. The Brooklyn Bridge, I suppose they say. All the truly *good* pink in the nation is right here under our eyes. A florist from Lancaster took some cuttings but they died. Probably smothered them in lime. Stupid man. A Greek."

She claws at his arm and moves on more heavily and rapidly. The sun is high and she probably feels a need for the house. Bees swim in the foliage; hidden birds scold.

The tide of leaf has overtaken the tide of blossom, and a furtively bitter smell breaths from the fresh walls of green. Maples, birches, oaks, elms, and horse-chestnut trees compose a thin forest that runs, at a varying depth, along the far property-line. In the damp shaded fringe between the lawn and this copse, the rhododendrons are still putting forth, but the unsheltered clumps in the center of the lawn have already dropped petals, in oddly neat rows, along the edge of the grass paths. "I don't like it, I don't like it," Mrs. Smith says, hobbling with Rabbit down such a trench of overblown brilliance. "I appreciate the beauty but I'd rather see alfalfa. A woman—I don't know why it should vex me so—Horace used to encourage the neighbors to come in and see the place in blooming time, he was like a child in many ways. This woman, Mrs. Foster, from down the hill in a little orange shack with a metal cat climbing up the shutters, used to in*va*riably say, turn to me with lipstick halfway up to her nose and say"—she mimics a too-sweet voice with a spirited spite that shakes her frame——" 'My, Mrs. Smith, this must be what Heaven is like!' One year I said to her, I couldn't hold my tongue any longer, I said, 'Well if I'm driving six miles back and forth to St. John's Episcopal Church every Sunday just to get into another splash of rhodies, I might as well save the mileage because I don't want to *go*.' Now wasn't that a dreadful thing for an old sinner to say?"

"Oh, I don't know—"

"To this poor woman who was only trying to be civil? Hadn't a bean of a brain in her head, of course; painting her face like a young fool. She's passed on now, poor soul; Alma Foster passed on two or three winters back. Now she knows the truth and I don't."

"Well, maybe what looks like rhododendrons to her will look like alfalfa to you."

"*Heh!* Eh-HA! Exactly! Exactly! You know, Mr. Angstrom, it's *such* a pleasure—" She stops them in the walk and caresses his forearm awkwardly; in the sunshine the tiny tan landscape of her face tips up toward his, and in her gaze, beneath the fumbling girlish flirtatiousness and the watery wander, there glitters the edge of an old acuteness, so that Rabbit standing there easily feels a stab of the unkind force that drove Mr. Smith out to the brainless flowers. "You and I, we think alike. Don't we? Now *don't we?*"

"You have it pretty good, don't you?" Ruth asks him. They have gone on the afternoon of this Memorial Day to the public swimming pool in West Brewer. She was self-conscious about getting into a bathing suit but in fact she looks great, up to her thighs in turquoise water and soaked licks of red hair sneaking out of her bathing cap. She swims easily, her big legs kicking slowly and the water flowing in bubbling transparence over her shoulders and her clean arms lifting and her back and bottom shimmering black under the jiggled green. Sometimes, when she stops and floats a moment, putting her face down in the water in a motion that quickens his heart with its slight danger, her bottom of its own buoyance floats up and breaks the surface—nothing much, just a round black island glistening there, a clear image suddenly in the water wavering like a blooey television set, but the solid sight swells his heart with pride, makes him harden all over with a chill clench of ownership. His, she is his, he knows her as well as the water, like the water has been everywhere on her body. When she does the backstroke the water breaks and pours down her front into her breastcups, flooding her breasts with touch; the arch of her submerged body tightens, thrusting her breasts fitfully into air; she closes her eyes and moves blindly. Two skinny boys dabbling at the shallow end of the pool splash away from her headfirst approach. She brushes one with a backsweep of her arm, awakes, and squats smiling in the water; her arms wave bonelessly to keep her balance in the nervous tides of the crowded pool. The air sparkles with the scent of chlorine. He rejoices in how clean she feels: clean, clean. What is it? Nothing touching you that is not yourself. Her in water, him in grass and air. Her head, bobbing like a hollow ball, makes a face at him. Himself, he is not a water animal. Wet is cold to him. Having got wet, he prefers to sit on the tile edge dangling his feet and imagining that high-school girls behind him are admiring the muscle-play of his broad back. He revolves his shoulders thoughtfully and feels the blades stretch his skin in the sun. Ruth wades to the end, through water so shallow the checker pattern of the pool floor is refracted to its surface. She climbs the little ladder, shedding water in great grape-bunches. He scrambles back to their blanket and lies down so that when she comes over he can see her standing above him as big as the sky, the black hair high on the inside of her thighs pasted into swirls by the water.

She tears off her cap and shakes out her hair and bends over for the towel. Water on her back flows upwards down soft valleys of fat and drips over her shoulders. As he watches her rub her arms the smell of grass comes up through the blanket and shouts make the crystalline air vibrate. She lies down beside him and closes her eyes and submits to the sun. Her face, seen so close, is built of great flats of skin pressed clean of color by the sun, except for a burnish of yellow that adds to their size mineral weight, the weight of some pure ungrained stone carted straight from quarries to temples. Words come from this monumental Ruth in the same scale, as massive wheels rolling to the porches of his ears, as mute coins spinning in the light. "You have it pretty good."

"How so?"

"Oh"—her words seem slightly delayed in passage from her lips; he sees them move, and then hears—"look at all you've got. You've got Eccles to play golf with every week and to keep your wife from chasing you. You've got your flowers, and you've got Mrs. Smith in love with you. You've got me."

"You think she really is in love with me? Mrs. Smith."

"All I know is what I get from you. You say she is."

"No, I never actually said that. Did I?"

She doesn't bother to answer him out of her huge face, magnified by her drowsy contentment. Chalk highlights run along her tanned skin.

He repeats, "Did I?" and pinches her arm, hard. He hadn't meant to do it so hard; something angered him at the touch of her skin. Her sullenness.

"Ow. You son of a bitch."

Still she lies there, paying more attention to the sun than him. He gets up on an elbow and looks across her dead body to the lighter figures of two sixteen-year-olds standing sipping orange crush from cardboard cones. The one in a white strapless peeks up at him from her straw with a brown glance. Her skinny legs dark as a Negro's. Her hipbones making gaunt peaks on either side of her slanted flat belly.

"Oh, all the world loves you," Ruth says suddenly. "What I wonder is why?"

"I'm lovable," he says.

"I mean why the hell *you*. What's so special about *you*?"

"I'm a mystic," he says. "I give people faith." Eccles has

told him this. Once, with a laugh, probably meaning it sarcastically. You never knew what Eccles was really meaning; you had to take what you wanted. Rabbit took this to heart. He never would have thought of it himself. He doesn't think much about what he gives other people.

"You give *me* a pain," she says.

"Well I'll be damned." The injustice: after he was so proud of her in the pool, loved her so much.

"What in hell makes you think you don't have to pull your own weight?"

"What's your kick? I support you."

"The hell you do. I have a job." It's true. A little after he went to work for Mrs. Smith she got a job as a stenographer with an insurance company that has a branch in Brewer. He wanted her to; he was nervous about how she'd spend her afternoons with him away. She said she never enjoyed that business; he wasn't so sure. She wasn't exactly suffering when he met her.

"Quit it," he says. "I don't care. Sit around all day reading mysteries. I'll support ja."

"You'll support me. If you're so big, why don't you support your wife?"

"Why should I? Her father's rolling in it."

"You're so smug, is what gets me. Don't you ever think you're going to have to pay the price?" She looks at him now, squarely with eyes bloodshot from being in the water. She shades them with her hand. These aren't the eyes he met that night by the parking meters, flat pale disks like a doll might have. The blue of her irises has deepened inward and darkened with a richness that, singing the truth to his instincts, disturbs him.

These eyes sting her and she turns her head away to hide the tears, thinking. That's one of the signs, crying easily. God, at work she has to get up from the typewriter and rush into the john like she had the runs and sob, sob, sob. Standing there in a booth looking down at a toilet laughing at herself and sobbing till her chest hurts. And sleepy. God, after coming back from lunch it's all she can do to keep from stretching out in the aisle right there on the filthy floor between Lilly Orff and Rita Fiorvante where that old horse's neck Honig would have to step over her. And hungry. For lunch an ice-cream soda with the sandwich and then a doughnut with the coffee and still she has to buy a candy bar at the cash register. After she's been trying to slim down for him and *had* lost six pounds, at least one scale said. For him, that was what was rich, changing herself for him when he was worth nothing, less than nothing, he was a menace, for all his mildness. He had that mildness. The others didn't. The thing was, when they knew you were one, they didn't think you were human, and thought they were entitled. Which they were, but still, some of the things. It was like they hated women and used *her*. But now she forgives them because it all melts, the next day is the next day and you're still the same and there, and they're away. The older they were, the more like presidents they looked, the wiser they should have been, the worse they were. Then they wanted some business their wives wouldn't give, in from the back which she didn't mind it was like being a hundred miles away once you get adjusted, or with the mouth. That. What do they see in it? It can't be as deep, she doesn't know. After all it's no worse than them at your bees and why not be generous, the first time it was Harrison and she was drunk as a monkey anyway but when she woke up the next morning wondered what the taste in her mouth *was*. But that was just being a superstitious kid there isn't much taste to it a little like seawater, just harder work than they probably think, women are always working harder than they think. The thing was, they wanted to be admired there. They really did want that. They weren't that ugly but they thought they were. That was the thing that surprised her in high school how ashamed they were really, how grateful they were if you just touched them there and how quick word got around that you would. What did they think, they were monsters? If they'd just thought they might have known you were curious too, that you could like that strangeness there like they liked yours, no worse than women in their way, all red wrinkles, my God, what was it in the end? No mystery. That was the great thing she discovered, that it was no mystery, just a stuck-on-looking bit that made them king and if you went along with it could be good and anyway put you with them against those others, those little snips running around her at hockey in gym like a cow in that blue uniform like a baby suit she wouldn't wear it in the twelfth grade and took the demerits. God she hated some of those girls. But she got it back at night, taking that urgency they didn't know existed like a queen. Boy, there wasn't any fancy business then, you didn't even need to take off your clothes, just a little rubbing through the cloth, your mouths tasting of the onion on the hamburgers you'd just had at the diner and the car heater ticking as it cooled, through all the cloth, everything, off they'd go. They couldn't have felt much it must have been just the *idea* of you. All their ideas. Sometimes just French kissing not that she ever really got with that, sloppy tongues and nobody can breathe, but all of a sudden you knew from the way their lips went hard and opened and then eased shut and away that it was over. That there was no more push for you and you better back off if you wanted to keep your dress dry. That made you dirty. You, their stickum. They couldn't forgive her that. Her forgiving them. She didn't blame them though that was their mothers making them write her name on the lavatory walls. Allie told her about that, kindly. But she had some sweet things with Allie; once after school with the sun still up they drove along a country road and up an old lane and stopped in a leafy place where they could see Mt. Judge, the town against the mountain both, dim in the distance, and he put his head in her lap, her sweater rolled up and her bra undone, and it was like a baby gently, her bees (who called them her bees? not Allie) firmer and rounder then, more sensitive; his waiting wet mouth so happy and blind and the birds making their warm noises overhead in the sunshine. Allie blabbed. He had to blab. She forgave him but it made her wiser. She began the older ones; the mistake if there was one but why not? Why not? was the question and still held; wondering if there was a mistake makes her tired just thinking, lying there wet from swimming and seeing red through her eyelids, trying to move back through all that red wondering if she was wrong. She was wise. With them being young did for being pretty, and them being older it wasn't such a rush. Boy some bastards you think *never*, like their little contribution's the greatest thing the world's ever going to see if it ever gets here.

But *this* one. What a nut. He had though that mildness. At least he saw you as being there. Boy that first night when he said that so sort of proudly "Hey" she didn't mind so much going under in fact it felt like she should. She forgave them all then, his face all their faces gathered into a scared blur and it felt like she was falling under to something better than she was. But then after all it turns out he's not that different, hanging on you all depressed and lovey and then sick of you or less just bored really when it's done. It's getting quicker, and quicker, more like a habit, he really hurries now when senses or she tells him she's lost it. Then she can just lie there and in a way listen and it's soothing; but then she can't go to sleep afterward. Some nights he tries to bring her up but she's just so sleepy and so heavy down there it's nothing; sometimes she just wants to push him off and shake him and shout, I *can't,* you dope, don't you know you're a *father!* But no. She mustn't tell him. Saying a word would make it final; it's just been one period and the next is coming up in a day maybe she'll have it and then she won't have anything. As much of a mess as it is she doesn't know how happy that would make her really. At least this way she's doing something, sending those candy bars down. God she isn't even sure she doesn't want it because *he* wants it from the way he acts, with his damn no stripper just a nice clean piece. She isn't even sure she didn't just deliberately bring it on by falling asleep under his arm just to show the smug bastard. For the thing about him he didn't mind her getting up when he was asleep and crawling into the lousy bathroom just so long as he didn't have to watch anything or do anything. That was the thing about him, he just lived in his skin and didn't give a thought to the consequences of anything. Tell him about the candy bars and feeling sleepy he'll probably get scared and off he'll go, him and his good clean piece and his cute little God and his cute little minister playing golf every Tuesday. For the damnedest thing about that minister was that, before, Rabbit at least had the idea he was acting wrong but with him he's got the idea he's Jesus Christ out to save the world just by doing whatever comes into his head. I'd like to get hold of the bishop or whoever and tell him that minister of his is a menace. Filling poor Rabbit full of something nobody can get at and even now, filling her ear, his soft cocksure voice answers her question with an idle remote smugness that infuriates her so the tears *do* come.

"I'll tell you," he says. "When I ran from Janice I made an interesting discovery." The tears bubble over her lids and the awful taste of the pool-water is sealed into her mouth. "If you have the guts to be yourself," he says, "other people'll pay your price."

Making awkward calls is agony for Eccles; at least anticipation of them is. Usually, the dream is worse than the reality: so God has disposed the world. The actual presences of people are always bearable. Mrs. Springer is a plump, dark, small-boned woman with a gypsy look about her. Both the mother and the daughter have a sinister aura, but in the mother this ability to create uneasiness is a settled gift, thoroughly meshed into the strategies of middle-class life. With the daughter it is a floating thing, useless and as dangerous to herself as to others. Eccles is relieved that Janice is out of the house; he feels guiltiest in her presence. She and Mrs. Fosnacht have gone into Brewer to a matinee of *Some Like It Hot*. Their two sons are in the Springers' back yard. Mrs. Springer takes him through the house to the screened-in porch, where she can keep an eye on the children. Her house is expensively but confusedly furnished; each room seems to contain one more easy chair than necessary. To get from the front door to the back they take a crooked path in the packed rooms. She leads him slowly; both of her ankles are bound in elastic bandages. The pained littleness of her steps reinforces his illusion that her lower body is encased in a plaster cast. She gently lets herself sink onto the cushions of the porch glider and startles Eccles by kicking up her legs as with a squeak and sharp sway the glider takes her weight. The action seems to express childish pleasure; her bald pale calves stick out stiff and her saddle shoes are for a moment lifted from the floor. These shoes are cracked and rounded, as if they've been revolved in a damp tub for years. He sits down in a trickily hinged aluminum-and-plastic lawn chair. Through the porch screen at his side, he can see Nelson Angstrom and the slightly older Fosnacht boy play in the sun around a swing-slide-sandbox set.

"It's nice to see you," Mrs. Springer says. "It's been so long since you came last."

"Just three weeks, isn't it?" he says. The chair presses against his back and he hooks his heels around the pipe at the bottom to keep it from folding. "It's been a busy time, with the confirmation classes and the Youth Group deciding to have a softball team this year and a series of deaths in the parish." His previous contacts with this woman have not disposed him to be apologetic. Her having so large a home offends his sense of place; he would like her better if this were the porch of a shanty.

"Yes I wouldn't want your job for the world."

"I enjoy it most of the time."

"They say you do. They say you're becoming quite an expert golf player."

Oh dear. And he thought she was relaxing. He thought for the moment they were on the porch of a shabby peeling house and she was a long-suffering fat factory wife who had learned to take things as they came. That is what she looked like; that is easily what she might have been. Fred Springer when he married her was probably less likely-looking than Harry Angstrom when her daughter married him. He tries to imagine Harry four years ago, and gets an attractive picture: tall, fair, famous in his school days, clever enough—a son of the morning. His air of confidence must have especially appealed to Janice. David and Michal. Husbands are a woeful lottery. He scratches his forehead and says, "Playing golf with someone is a good way to get to know him. That's what I try to do, you understand—get to know people. I don't think you can lead someone to Christ unless you know him."

"Well now what do you know about my son-in-law that I don't?"

"That he's a good man, for one thing."

"Good for what?"

"Must you be good *for* something?" He tries to think. "Yes, I suppose you must."

"Nelson! Stop that this minute!" She turns rigid in the glider but does not rise to see what is making the boy cry. Eccles, sitting by the screen, can see. The Fosnacht boy stands by the swing, holding two red plastic trucks. Angstrom's son, some inches shorter, is batting with an open hand toward the bigger boy's chest, but does not quite dare to move forward a step and actually strike him. Young Fosnacht stands with the maddening invulnerability of the stupid, looking down at the flailing hand and contorted face of the smaller boy without even a smile of satisfaction, a true scientist, observing without passion the effect of his experiment. Mrs. Springer's voice leaps to a frantic hardness and cuts through the screen: "Did you hear me I said stop that bawling!"

Nelson's face turns up toward the porch and he tries to explain, "Pilly have—Pilly—" But just trying to describe the injustice gives it unbearable force, and as if struck from behind he totters forward and slaps the thief's chest and receives a mild shove that makes him sit on the ground. He rolls on his stomach and spins in the grass, revolved by his own incoherent kicking. Eccles' heart seems to twist with the child's body; he knows so well the propulsive power of a wrong, the way the mind batters against it and each futile blow sucks the air emptier until it seems the whole frame of blood and bone must burst in a universe that can be such a vacuum.

"The boy's taken his truck," he tells Mrs. Springer.

"Well let him get it himself," she says. "He must learn. I can't be getting up on these legs and running outside every minute; they've been at it like that all afternoon."

"Billy." The boy looks up in surprise toward Eccles' male voice. "Give it back." Billy considers this new evidence and hesitates indeterminately. *"Now,* please." Convinced, Billy walks over and pedantically drops the toy on his sobbing playmate's head.

The new pain starts fresh grief in Nelson's throat, but seeing the truck on the grass beside his face chokes him. It takes him a moment to realize that the cause of his anguish is removed and another moment to rein the emotion in his body. His great dry gasps as he rounds these corners seem to heave the sheet of trimmed grass and the sunshine itself. A wasp bumping persistently against the screen dips and the aluminum chair under Eccles threatens to buckle; as if the wide world participates in Nelson's readjustment.

"I don't know why the boy is such a sissy," Mrs. Springer says. "Or maybe I do."

Her sly adding this irks Eccles. "Why?"

The purple skin under her eyes lifts and the corners of her mouth pull down in an appraising scowl. "Well, he's like his dad: spoiled. He's been made too much of and thinks the world owes him what he wants."

"It was the other boy; Nelson only wanted what was his."

"Yes and I suppose you think with his dad it was all Janice's fault." She pronounces "Janice" with German juice, Channiss, making the girl seem thicker, darker, more precious and important than the tenuous, pathetic image in Eccles' mind. He wonders if she's not, after all, right: if he hasn't gone over to the other side.

"No I don't," he says. "I think his behavior has no justification. This isn't to say, though, that his behavior doesn't have reasons, reasons that in part your daughter could have controlled. With my Church, I believe that we are all responsible beings, responsible for ourselves and for each

much we try to do on the fringes, we're *outside*." In imitation of his father he has clasped his hands behind him and turned his back on his auditor; through the screen he watches the one other who, perhaps, is not outside, Nelson, lead the Fosnacht boy across the lawn in pursuit of a neighbor's dog. Nelson's laughter spills from his head as his clumsy tottering steps jar his body. The dog is old, reddish, small, and slow; the Fosnacht boy is puzzled yet pleased by his friend's cry of "Lion! Lion!" It interests Eccles to see that under conditions of peace Angstrom's boy leads the other. The green air seen through the muzzy screen seems to vibrate with Nelson's noise. Eccles feels the situation: this constant translucent outpour of selfish excitement must naturally now and then dam in the duller boy's narrower passages and produce a sullen backflow, a stubborn bullying act. He pities Nelson, who will be stranded in innocent surprise many times before he locates in himself the source of this strange reverse tide. It seems to Eccles that he himself was this way as a boy, always giving and giving and always being suddenly swamped. The old dog's tail wags as the boys approach. It stops wagging and droops in an uncertain wary arc when they surround it like hunters, crowing. Nelson reaches out and beats the dog's back with both hands. Eccles wants to shout; the dog might bite; he can't bear to watch.

"Yes but he drifts further *away*," Mrs. Springer is whining. "He's well off. He has no reason to come back if we don't give him one."

Eccles sits down in the aluminum chair again. "No. He'll come back for the same reason he left. He's fastidious. He has to loop the loop. The world he's in now, the world of this girl in Brewer, won't continue to satisfy his fantasies. Just in seeing him from week to week, I've noticed a change."

"Well not to hear Peggy Fosnacht tell it. She says *she* hears he's leading the life of Riley. I don't know how many women he has."

"Just one, I'm sure. The strange thing about Angstrom, he's by nature a domestic creature. *Oh dear.*"

There is a flurry in the remote group; the boys run one way and the dog the other. Young Fosnacht halts but Nelson keeps coming, his face stretched large by fright.

Mrs. Springer hears his sobbing and says angrily, "Did

they get Elsie to snap again? That dog must be sick in the head the way she keeps coming over here for more."

Eccles jumps up—his chair collapses behind him—and opens the screen door and runs down to meet Nelson in the sunshine. The boy shies from him. He grabs him. "Did the dog bite?"

The boy's sobbing is paralyzed by this new fright, the man in black grabbing him.

"Did Elsie bite you?"

The Fosnacht boy hangs back at a safe distance.

Nelson, unexpectedly solid and damp in Eccles' arms, releases great rippling gasps and begins to find his voice.

Eccles shakes him to choke this threat of wailing and, wild to make himself understood, with a quick lunge clicks his teeth at the child's cheek. "Like that? Did the dog do that?"

The boy's face goes rapt at the pantomime. "Like dis," he says, and his fine little lip lifts from his teeth and his nose wrinkles and he jerks his head an inch to one side.

"No bite?" Eccles insists, relaxing the grip of his arms.

The little lip lifts again with that miniature fierceness, as if this tells the whole delightful story. Eccles feels mocked by a petite facial alertness that recalls, in tilt and cast, Harry's. Sobbing sweeps over Nelson again and he breaks away and runs up the porch steps to his grandmother. Eccles stands up; in just that little time of squatting the sun has started sweat on his black back.

As he climbs the steps he is troubled by something pathetic, something penetratingly touching, in the memory of those tiny square teeth bared in that play snarl. The harmlessness yet the reality of the instinct. The kitten's instinct to kill the spool with its cotton paws.

He comes onto the porch to find the boy between his grandmother's legs, his face buried in her belly. In worming against her warmth he has pulled her dress up from her knees, and their exposed breadth and pallor, undesired, laid bare defenselessly, superimposed upon the tiny, gamely gritted teeth the boy exposed for him, this old whiteness strained through this fine mesh, make a milk that feels to Eccles like his own blood. Strong—as if pity is, as he has been taught, not a helpless outcry but a powerful tide that could purge the dust and rubble from every corner of the world—he steps forward and promises to the two bowed heads, "If he doesn't come back when she has the baby, then we'll get the law after him. There *are* laws, of course; quite a few."

"Elsie snaps," Mrs. Springer says, "because you and Billy tease her."

"Naughty Elsie," Nelson says.

"Naughty Nelson," Mrs. Springer corrects. She lifts her face to Eccles and continues in the same correcting voice, "Yes well she's a week due now and I don't see him running in."

His moment of fondness for her has passed; he leaves her on the porch. *Love never ends,* he tells himself, using the Revised Standard Version. The King James has it that it never fails. Mrs. Springer's voice carries after him into the house, "Now the next time I catch you teasing Elsie you're going to get a whipping from your grandmom."

"No, Mom-mom," the child begs coyly, fright gone.

Eccles thought he would find the kitchen and take a drink of water from the tap but the kitchen slips by him in the jumbled rooms. He makes a mouth that works up saliva and swallows it as he leaves the stucco house. He gets into his Buick and drives down Joseph Street and then a block along Jackson Road to the Angstroms' address.

Mrs. Angstrom has four-cornered nostrils. Lozenge-shape, they are set in a nose that is not so much large as extra-anatomical; the little pieces of muscle and cartilage and bone are individually emphatic and divide the skin into many facets in the sharp light. Their interview takes place in her kitchen amid several burning light bulbs. Burning in the middle of day; their home is the dark side of a two-family brick house. She came to the door wearing suds on her red forearms and returns with him to a sink full of bloated shirts and underwear. She plunges at these things vigorously while they talk. She is a vigorous woman. Mrs. Springer's fat, soft, aching excess, had puffed out from little bones, the bones once of a slip of a girl like Janice; Mrs. Angstrom's is packed on a great harsh frame. Harry's size must come from her side. Eccles is continually conscious of the long faucets, heraldic of cool water, shielded by her formidable body; but the opportunity never arises for a request so small.

"I don't know why you come to me," she says. "Harold's one and twenty. I have no control over him."

"He hasn't been to see you?"

"No sir." She displays her profile above her left shoulder.

"You've made him so ashamed I suppose he's embarrassed to."

"He *should* be ashamed, don't you think?"

"I wouldn't know why. I never wanted him to go with the girl in the first place. Just to look at her you know she's two-thirds crazy."

"Oh now, that's not true, is it?"

"Not true! Why the first thing that girl said to me was Why don't I get a washing machine? Comes into my kitchen, takes one look around, and starts telling me how to manage my life."

"Surely you don't think she meant anything?"

"No, she didn't mean anything. All she meant was, What was I doing living in such a run-down half-house when she came from a great big barn on Joseph Street with the kitchen full of gadgets, and Wasn't I lucky to be fobbing off my boy on such a well-equipped little trick? I never liked that girl's eyes. They never met your face full-on." She turns her face on Eccles and, warned, he returns her stare. Beneath her misted spectacles—an old-fashioned type, circles of steel-rimmed glass in which the bifocal crescents catch a pinker tint of light—her arrogantly tilted nose displays its meaty, intricate underside. Her broad mouth is stretched slightly by a vague expectation. Eccles realizes that this woman is a humorist. The difficulty with humorists is that they will mix what they believe with what they don't; whichever seems likelier to win an effect. The strange thing is how much he likes her, though in a way she is plunging at him as roughly as she plunges the dirty clothes. But that's it, it's the same to her. Unlike Mrs. Springer, she doesn't really see him at all. Her confrontation is with the whole world, and secure under the breadth of her satire, he can say what he pleases.

He bluntly defends Janice. "The girl is shy."

"Shy! She wasn't too shy to get herself pregnant so poor Hassy has to marry her when he could scarcely tuck his shirttail in."

"He was one and twenty, as you say."

"Yes, well, years. Some die young; some are born old."

Epigrams, everything. My, she is funny. Eccles laughs out loud. She doesn't acknowledge hearing him, and turns to her wash with furious seriousness. "About as shy as a snake," she says, "that girl. These little women are poison. Mincing around with their sneaky eyes getting everybody's sympathy. Well she doesn't get mine; let the men weep. To hear her father-in-law talk she's the worst martyr since Joan of Arc."

He laughs again; but isn't she? "Well uh, what does Mr. Angstrom think Harry should do?"

"Crawl back. What else? He will, too, poor boy. He's just like his father underneath. All soft heart. I suppose that's why men rule the world. They're all heart."

"That's an unusual view."

"Is it? It's what they keep telling you in church. Men are all heart and women are all body. I don't know who's supposed to have the brains. God, I suppose."

He smiles, wondering if the Lutheran church gives everyone such ideas. Luther himself was a little like this, perhaps—overstating half-truths in a kind of comic wrath. The whole black Protestant paradox-thumping maybe begins there. Deep fundamental hopelessness in such a mind. Hubris in shoving the particular aside. Maybe: he's forgotten much theology. It occurs to him that he should see Angstrom's pastor.

Mrs. Angstrom picks up a dropped thread. "Now my daughter Miriam is as old as the hills and always was; I've never worried about her. I remember, on Sundays long ago when we'd walk out by the quarry Harold was so afraid—he wasn't more than twelve then—he was so afraid she'd fall over the edge. I knew she wouldn't. You watch her. She won't marry out of pity like poor Hassy and then have all the world jump on him for trying to get out."

"I don't think the world *has* jumped on him. The girl's mother and I were just discussing that it seemed quite the contrary."

"Don't you think it. That girl gets no sympathy from me. She has everybody on her side from Eisenhower down. They'll talk him around. *You'll* talk him around. And there's another."

The front door has opened with a softness she alone hears. Her husband comes into the kitchen wearing a white shirt and a tie but with his fingernails ringed in black; he's a printer. He's as tall as his wife but seems shorter. His mouth works self-deprecatorily over badly fitted false teeth. His nose is Harry's, a neat smooth button. "How do you do, Father," he says; either he was raised as a Catholic or among Catholics.

"Mr. Angstrom, it's very nice to meet you." The man's

hand has tough ridges but a soft, dry palm. "We've been discussing your son."

"I feel terrible about that." Eccles believes him. Earl Angstrom has a gray, ragged look. This business has blighted him. He thins his lips over his slipping teeth like a man with stomach trouble biting back gas. He is being nibbled from within. Color has washed from his hair and eyes like cheap ink. A straight man, who has measured his life with the pica-stick and locked the forms tight, he has returned in the morning and found the type scrambled.

"He goes on and on about that girl as if she was the mother of Christ," Mrs. Angstrom says.

"That's not true," Angstrom says mildly, and sits down in his white shirt at the porcelain kitchen table. Four settings, year after year, have worn black blurs through the enamel. "I just don't see how Harry could make such a mess. As a boy he was always so trim. He wasn't like other boys, sloppy. He was a neat worker."

Wtih raw sudsy hands Mrs. Angstrom has set about heating coffee for her husband. This small act of service seems to bring her into harmony with him; they begin, in the sudden way of old couples apparently at odds, to speak as one. "It was the Army," she says. "When he came back from Texas he was a different boy."

"He didn't want to come into the shop," Angstrom says. "He didn't want to get dirty."

"Reverend Eccles, would you like some coffee?" Mrs. Angstrom asks.

At last, his chance. "No, thank you. What I would *love*, though, is a glass of water."

"Just water? With ice?"

"Any way. Any way would be lovely."

"Yes, Earl is right," she says. "People now say how lazy Hassy is, but he's not. He never was. When you'd be proud of his basketball in high school you know, people would say, 'Yes well but he's so tall, it's easy for him.' But they didn't know how he had worked at it. Out back every evening banging the ball way past dark; you wondered how he could see."

"From about twelve years old on," Angstrom says, "he was at that night and day. I put a pole up for him out back; the garage wasn't high enough."

"When he set his mind to something," Mrs. Angstrom says,

"there was no stopping him." She yanks powerfully at the lever of the ice-cube tray and with a brilliant multiple crunch that sends chips sparkling the cubes come loose. "He wanted to be best at that and I honestly believe he was."

"I know what you mean," Eccles says. "I play a little golf with him and already he's become better than I am."

She puts the cubes in a glass and holds the glass under a spigot and brings it to him. He tilts it at his lips and Earl Angstrom's palely vehement voice wavers through the liquid. "Then he comes back from the Army and all he cares about is chasing ass. He won't come work in the print shop because it'll get his fingernails dirty." Eccles lowers the glass and Angstrom says full in his face across the table, "He's become the worst kind of Brewer bum. If I could get my hands on him, Father, I'd try to thrash him if he killed me in the process." His ashen face bunches defiantly at the mouth; his colorless eyes swarm with glitter.

"Your language, Earl," his wife says, setting coffee in a flowered cup on the table between his hands.

He looks down into the steam and says, "Excuse me. When I think of what that boy's doing my stomach does somersaults."

Eccles lifts his glass and says "No" into it like a megaphone and then drinks until no more water can be sucked from under the ice cubes that bump under his nose. He wipes the moisture from his mouth and says, "There's a great deal of goodness in your son. When I'm with him—it's rather unfortunate, really—I feel so cheerful I quite forget what the point of my seeing him is." He laughs, first at Mr., and, failing here to rouse a smile, at Mrs.

"This golf you play," Angstrom says. "What is the point? Why don't the girl's parents get the police after him? In my opinion a good swift kick is what he needs."

Eccles glances toward Mrs. Angstrom and feels the arch of his eyebrows like drying paste on his forehead. He didn't expect, a minute ago, to be looking toward her as an ally and toward this worn-out good man as a rather vulgar and disappointing foe.

"Mrs. Springer wants to," he tells Angstrom. "The girl and her father want to wait."

"Don't talk nonsense, Earl," Mrs. Angstrom says. "What does old Springer want with his name in the papers? The way you talk you'd think poor Harry was your enemy."

"He is my enemy," Angstrom says. He touches the saucer from both sides with his stained fingertips. "That night I spent walking the streets looking for him he became my enemy. You can't talk. You didn't see the girl's face."

"What do I care about her face? You talk about tarts: they don't become ivory-white saints in my book just by having a marriage license. That girl wanted Harry and got him with the only trick she knew and now she's run out of tricks."

"Don't *talk* that way, Mary. It's just words with you. Suppose I had acted the way Harry has."

"Ah," she says, and turns, and Eccles flinches, seeing her face taut to release a special missile. "I didn't want *you;* you wanted *me*. Or wasn't it that way?"

"Yes of course it was that way," Angstrom mutters.

"Well then: there's no comparison."

Angstrom has hunched his shoulders over the coffee, drawn himself in very small; as if she has painted him into a tiny corner. "Oh Mary," he sighs, not daring move with words.

Eccles tries to defend him; he goes to the weaker side of a fight almost automatically. "I don't think you can say," he tells Mrs. Angstrom, "that Janice didn't imagine that her marriage was built on mutual attraction. If the girl was such a clever schemer she wouldn't have let Harry slip away so easily."

Mrs. Angstrom's interest in this discussion, now that she knows she pressed her husband too hard, has waned; she maintains a position—that Janice is in control—so obviously false that it amounts to a concession. "She hasn't let him slip away," she says. "She'll have him back, you watch."

Eccles turns to the man; if he will agree they will all three be united and he can leave. "Do you think too that Harry will come around?"

"No," Angstrom says, looking down, "never. He's too far gone. He'll just slide deeper and deeper now until we might as well forget him. If he was twenty, or twenty-two; but at his age . . . In the shop sometimes you see these young Brewer bums. They can't stick it. They're like cripples only they don't limp. Human garbage, they call them. And I sit there at the machine for two months wondering how the hell it could be my Harry, that used to hate a mess so much."

Eccles looks over at Harry's mother and is jarred to see her leaning against the sink with soaked cheeks gleaming under the glasses. He gets up in shock. Is she crying because she thinks her husband is speaking the truth, or because she thinks he is saying this just to hurt her, in revenge for making him admit that he had wanted her? "I hope you're wrong," Eccles says. "I must go now; I thank you both for discussing this with me. I realize it's painful."

Angstrom takes him back through the house and in the dark of the dining-room touches his arm. "He liked things just so," he says. "I never saw a boy like him. Any rumpus in the family he'd take hard out of all reason—when Mary and I, you know would have our fun." Eccles nods, but doubts that "fun" describes what he's seen.

In the living-room shadows a girl stands in a bare-armed summer dress. "Mim! Did you just get in?"

"Yeah."

"This is Father—I mean Reverend—"

"Eccles."

"Eccles, he came to talk about Harry. My daughter Miriam."

"Hello, Miriam. I've heard Harry speak very fondly of you."

"Hi."

With that word the big window behind her takes on the intimate glaze of the big window in a luncheonette. Flip greetings seem to trail behind her with wisps of cigarette smoke and drugstore perfume. Mrs. Angstrom's nose has delicacy on the girl's face, a sharpness Saracen or even more ancient, barbaric. Taken with the prominent nose her height at first glance seems her mother's, but when her father stands beside her, Eccles sees that it is his height; their bodies, the beautiful girl's and the weary man's, are the same. They have the same narrowness; a durable edge that, Eccles knows after seeing the wounds open under Mrs. Angstrom's spectacles, can cut. That narrowness, and a manageable vulgarity that offends him. They'll get through. They know what they're doing. It's a weakness of his, to prefer people who don't know what they're doing. The helpless: these, and the people on top, beyond help. The ones who maneuver more or less well in the middle seem to his feudal instincts to be thieving from both ends. When they bunch at the door, Angstrom puts his arm around his daughter's waist and Eccles thinks of Mrs. Angstrom silent in the kitchen with her wet cheeks and red arms.

It's just a flash; an impression. From the pavement turning to wave at the two of them in the doorway he is grateful for the fine picture they make and laughs at their incongruous symmetry, the earringed Arab boy with her innocent contempt for his Christian collar and the limp-faced old woman of a printer, paired in slenderness, interlocked.

He gets into the car thirsty and vexed. There was something pleasant said in the last half-hour but he can't remember what it was. He's scratched, hot, confused, and dry; he's spent an afternoon in a bramble patch. He's seen half a dozen people and a dog and nowhere did an opinion tally with his own, that Harry Angstrom was worth saving and could be saved. Instead down there between the brambles there seemed to be no Harry at all: nothing but stale air and last year's dead stalks. Mrs. Angstrom's ice water has left him thirstier than before; his palate seems coated with cobwebs. The day is declining through the white afternoon to the long blue spring evening. He drives past a corner where someone is practicing on a trumpet behind an open upstairs window. *Du du do do da da dee. Dee dee da da do do du.* Cars are whispering home from work. He drives across the town, tacking on the diagonal streets along a course parallel to the distant ridge of the mountain. Fritz Kruppenbach, Mt. Judge's Lutheran minister for twenty-seven years, lives in a high brick house not far from the cemetery. The motorcycle belonging to his college-age son is on its side in the driveway, partly dismantled. The sloping lawn, graded in fussy terraces, has the unnatural chartreuse evenness that comes with much fertilizing, much weed-killing, and much mowing. Mrs. Kruppenbach—will Lucy ever achieve that dimpled, obedient look?—comes to the door in a gray dress that makes no compromise with the season. Her gray hair girdles her head with braids of great compactness. When she lets all that hair down, she must be a witch. "He's mowing out back" she says.

"I'd like to talk to him for just a few minutes. It's a problem that involves our two congregations."

"Go up to his room, why do-an tcha? I'll fetch him."

The house—foyer, halls, staircase, even the minister's leathery den upstairs—is flooded with the smell of beef roasting. As if every day, when the house is cleaned, the odor is rubbed into the wood with a damp rag. Eccles sits by the window of Kruppenbach's den on an oak-backed choir pew left over from some renovation. Seated on the bench he feels an adolescent compulsion to pray but instead peers across the valley at the pale green fragments of the golf course where he would like to be, with Harry. He lied somewhat to Mrs. Angstrom. Harry does not play golf better than he. He seems to have trouble in making the club part of himself, to be tense with the fear that this stick of steel will betray him. Between Harry's alternately fine and terrible shots and his own consistent weakness there is a rough equality that makes each match unpredictable. Eccles has found other partners either better or worse than he; only Harry is both, and only Harry gives the game a desperate gaiety, as if they are together engaged in an impossible, startling, bottomless quest set by a benevolent but absurd lord, a quest whose humiliations sting them almost to tears but one that is renewed at each tee, in a fresh flood of green. And for Eccles there is an additional hope, a secret determination to trounce Harry. He feels that the thing that makes Harry unsteady, that makes him unable to repeat his beautiful effortless swing every time, is the thing at the root of all the problems that he has created; and that by beating him decisively he, Eccles, will get on top of this weakness, this flaw, and hence solve the problems. In the meantime there is the pleasure of hearing Harry now and then cry, "Yes, yes," or "That's the one!" Their rapport at moments attains for Eccles a pitch of pleasure, a harmless ecstasy, that makes the world with its endless circumstantiality seem remote and spherical and green.

The house shudders to the master's step. Of the ministers in the town, he likes Kruppenbach least. The man is rigid in his creed and a bully in manner. Eccles loves rectories; he grew up in one. But in this one he feels all the humorlessness, the pious oppression, that people falsely imagine. Yet Kruppenbach's son must not have found it so: witness the motorcycle.

The man comes up the stairs into his den, angry at being taken from his lawn-mowing. He wears old black pants and an undershirt soaked with sweat. His shoulders are coated with wiry gray wool and a wide tangled bush of black-speckled hair bubbles out of the U of the undershirt neck and froths across the wet red skin of his chest.

"Hello, Chack," he says at pulpit volume, with no intonation of greeting. His German accent makes his words seem stones, set angrily one on top of another. "What is it?"

Eccles doesn't dare "Fritz" with the older man, and instead laughs and exclaims, "Hello!"

Kruppenbach grimaces. He has a massive square head, crew-cut. He is a man of brick. As if he was born as a baby literally of clay and decades of exposure have baked him to the color and hardness of brick. He repeats, "What?"

"You have a family called Angstrom."

"Yes."

"The father's a printer."

"Yes."

"Their son, Harry, deserted his wife over two months ago; her people, the Springers, are in my church."

"Yes, well. The boy. The boy's a *Schussel*."

Eccles isn't certain what that means. He supposes that Kruppenbach doesn't sit down because he doesn't want to stain his furniture with his own sweat. His continuing to stand puts Eccles in a petitionary position, sitting on the bench like a choirboy. The odor of meat cooking grows more insistent as he explains what he thinks happened: how Harry has been in a sense spoiled by his athletic successes; how the wife, to be fair, had perhaps showed little imagination in their marriage; how he himself, as minister, had tried to keep the boy's conscience in touch with his wife without pressing him into a premature reunion—for the boy's problem wasn't so much a lack of feeling as an uncontrolled excess of it; how the four parents, for various reasons, were of little help; how he had witnessed, just minutes ago, a quarrel between the Angstroms that perhaps offered a clue as to why their son—

"Do you think," Kruppenbach interrupts; Jack hadn't expected him to be quiet this long—the man certainly was no listener; even in his undershirt he somehow wore vestments —"do you think this is your job, to meddle in these people's lives? I know what they teach you at seminary now: this psychology and that. But I don't agree with it. You think now your job is to be an unpaid doctor, to run around and plug up the holes and make everything smooth. I don't think that. I don't think that's your job."

"I only—"

"No now let me finish. I've been in Mt. Judge twenty-seven years and you've been here two. I've listened to your story but I wasn't listening to what it said about the people, I was listening to what it said about you. What I heard was this: the story of a minister of God selling his message for a few scraps of gossip and a few games of golf. What do you think now it looks like to God, one childish husband leaving one childish wife? Do you ever think any more what God sees? Or have you grown beyond that?"

"No, of course not. But it seems to me our role in a situation like this—"

"It seems to you our role is to be cops, cops without handcuffs, without guns, without anything but our human good nature. Isn't it right? Don't answer, just think if I'm not right. Well, I say that's a Devil's idea. I say, let the cops be cops and look after their laws that have nothing to do with us."

"I agree, up to a point—"

"There *is* no up to a point! There is no reason or measure in what we must do." His thick forefinger, woolly between the knuckles, has begun to tap emphasis on the back of a leather chair. "If Gott wants to end misery He'll declare the Kingdom now." Jack feels a blush begin to burn on his face. "How big do you think your little friends look among the billions that God sees? In Bombay now they die in the streets every minute. You say role. I say you don't know what your role is or you'd be home locked in prayer. *There* is your role: to make yourself an exemplar of faith. *There* is where comfort comes from: faith, not what little finagling a body can do here and there, stirring the bucket. In running back and forth you run from the duty given you by God, to make your faith powerful, so when the call comes you can go out and tell them, 'Yes, he is dead, but you will see him again in Heaven. Yes, you suffer, but you must *love* your pain, because it is *Christ's* pain.' When on Sunday morning then, when we go before their faces, we must walk up not worn out with misery but full of Christ, *hot*"—he clenches his hairy fists—"with Christ, on *fire: burn* them with the force of our belief. That is why they come; why else would they pay us? Anything else we can do or say anyone can do and say. They have doctors and lawyers for that. It's all in the Book—a thief with faith is worth all the Pharisees. Make no mistake. Now I'm serious. Make no mistake. There is nothing but Christ for us. All the rest, all this decency and busyness, is nothing. It is Devil's work."

"Fritz," Mrs. Kruppenbach's voice calls carefully up the stairs. "Supper."

The red man in his undershirt looks down at Eccles and asks, "Will you kneel a moment with me and pray for Christ to come into this room?"

"No. No. I won't. I'm too angry. It would be hypocritical."

The refusal, unthinkable from a layman, makes Kruppenbach, not softer, but stiller. "Hypocrisy," he says mildly. "You have no seriousness. Don't you believe in damnation? Didn't you know when you put that collar on, what you risked?" In the brick skin of his face his eyes seem small imperfections, pink and glazed with water as if smarting in intense heat.

He turns without waiting for Jack to answer and goes downstairs for supper. Jack descends behind him and continues out the door. His heart is beating like a frightened child's and his knees are weak with fury. He had come for an exchange of information and been flagellated with an insane spiel. Unctuous old thundering Hun had no conception of the ministry as a legacy of light and probably himself scrambled into it out of a butcher's shop. Jack realizes that these are spiteful and unworthy thoughts but he can't stop them. His depression is so deep that he tries to gouge it deeper by telling himself *He's right, he's right* and thus springing tears and purging himself, however absurdly, above the perfect green circle of the Buick steering wheel. But he can't cry; he's parched. His shame and failure hang downward in him heavy but fruitless.

Though he knows that Lucy wants him home—if dinner is not quite ready he will be in time to give the children their baths—he instead drives to the drugstore in the center of town. The poodle-cut girl behind the counter is in his Youth Group and two parishioners buying medicine or contraceptives or Kleenex hail him gaily. He feels at home in public places; he rests his wrists on the cold clean marble and orders a vanilla ice-cream soda with a scoop of maple-walnut ice cream, and drinks two Coca-Cola glasses full of delicious clear water before it comes.

Club Castanet was named during the war when the South American craze was on and occupies a triangular building where Warren Avenue crosses Running Horse Street at an acute angle. It's in the south side of Brewer, the Italian-Negro-Polish side, and Rabbit doesn't like it. With its glass-brick windows grinning back from the ridge of its face it looks like a fortress of death; the interior is furnished in the glossy low-lit style of an up-to-date funeral parlor, potted green plants here and there, music piping soothingly, and the same smell of strip rugs and fluorescent tubes and Venetian-blind slats and, the most inner secretive smell, of alcohol. We drink it and then we're embalmed in it. Ever since a man down from them on Jackson Road lost his job as an under-taker's assistant and became a bartender, Rabbit thinks of the two professions as related; men in both talk softly, look very clean, and are always seen standing up. He and Ruth sit at a booth near the front, where they get through the win-dow a faint fluctuation of red light as the neon castanet on the sign outside flickers back and forth between its two positions, that imitate clicking.

This pink tremor takes the weight off Ruth's face. She sits across from him. He tries to picture the kind of life she was leading; a creepy place like this probably seems as friendly to her as a locker room would to him. But just the thought of it that way makes him nervous; her sloppy life, like his having a family, is something he's tried to keep be-hind them. He was happy just hanging around her place at night, her reading mysteries and him running down to the delicatessen for ginger ale and some nights going to a movie but nothing like this. That first night he really used that Daiquiri but since then he didn't care if he ever had another and hoped she was the same way. For a while she was but lately something's been eating her; she's heavy in bed and once in a while looks at him as if he's some sort of pig. He doesn't know what he's doing different but knows that somehow the ease has gone out of it. So tonight her so-called friend Margaret calls up. It scares him out of his skin when the phone rings. He has the idea lately it's going to be the cops or his mother or somebody; he has the feeling of some-thing growing on the other side of the mountain. A couple times after he first moved in, the phone rang and it was some thick-voiced man saying "Ruth?" or just hanging up in sur-prise at Rabbit's voice answering. When they hung on, Ruth just said a lot of "No's" into the receiver and they never had any trouble luckily. She knew how to handle them and any-way there were only about five that ever called. Like the past was a vine hanging on by just these five shallow roots and it tore away easily, leaving her clean and blue and blank. But tonight it's Margaret out of this past and she wants them to come down to the Castanet and Ruth wants to and Rabbit goes along. Anything for a little change. He's bored.

He asks her, "What do you want?"

"A Daiquiri."

"You're sure? You're sure now it won't make you sick?" He's noticed that, that she seems a little sick sometimes, and won't eat, and sometimes eats the house down.

"No, I'm not sure but why the hell shouldn't I be sick?"

"Well I don't know why you shouldn't. Why shouldn't anybody?"

"Look let's not be a philosopher for once. Just get me the drink."

A colored girl in an orange uniform that he guesses from the frills is supposed to look South American comes and he tells her two Daiquiris. She flips shut her pad and walks off and he sees her back is open halfway down her spine. So a little bit of black bra shows. Compared with this her skin isn't black at all, just a nice thick soft color that brings a little honest life into here. Purple shadows swing on the flats of her back where the light hits. She has a pigeon-toed way of sauntering, swinging those orange frills. She doesn't care about him; he likes that, that she doesn't care. The thing about Ruth is lately she's been trying to make him feel guilty about something.

"Don't fall in," she tells him.

"I'm not doing anything."

"You're right you're not doing anything."

If this is a threat, he doesn't like threats.

Margaret comes and the guy with her, he isn't very happy to see, is Ronnie Harrison. Margaret says to him, "Hello, you. Are you still hanging on?"

"Hell," Harrison says, "it's the great Angstrom," as if he's trying to take Tothero's place in every way. "I've been hearing about you," he adds slimily.

"Hearing what?"

"Oh. The word."

Harrison was never one of Rabbit's favorites and has not improved. In the locker room he was always talking about making out and playing with himself under his little hairy pot of a belly and that pot has really grown. Harrison is fat. Fat and half bald. His kinky brass-colored hair has thinned and the skin of his scalp shows, depending on how he tilts his head. This pink showing through seems obscene to Rabbit, like the pink bald idea that is always showing through Harrison's talk. Still, he remembers one night when Harrison came back into the game after losing two teeth to somebody's elbow and tries to be glad to see him. There were just five of you out there at one time and the other four for that time were unique in the world.

But it seems long ago, and every second Harrison stands there smirking it seems longer. He is wearing a narrow-shouldered summer suit of some linen imitation and having this nifty self-satisfied cloth hanging beside his ear annoys Rabbit. He feels hemmed in. The problem is, who shall sit where? He and Ruth have gotten on opposite sides of the table, which was the mistake. Harrison decides, and ducks down to sit beside Ruth, with a little catch in the movement that betrays the old limp from his football injury. Rabbit becomes obsessed by Harrison's imperfections. He's ruined the effect of his Ivy League suit by wearing a black wool tie like a wop. When he opens his mouth the two false teeth don't quite match the others.

"Well, how's life treating the old Master?" he says. "The word is you got it made." His eyes make his meaning by flicking sideways to Ruth, who sits there like a lump, her hands folded around the Daiquiri. Her knuckles are red from washing dishes. When she lifts the glass to drink, her chin shows through distorted.

Margaret wriggles at Rabbit's side. She feels somehow like Janice: jumpy. Her presence in the left corner of his vision feels like a dark damp cloth approaching that side of his face.

"Where's Tothero?" he asks her.

"Totherwho?"

Ruth giggles, damn her. Harrison bends his head toward her, pink showing, and whispers a remark. Her lips tuck up in a smile; it's just like that night in the Chinese place, anything he says will please her, except that tonight he is Harrison and Rabbit sits across from them married to this girl he hates. He's sure what Harrison whispers is about him, "the old Master." From the second there were four of them it was clear he was going to be the goat. Like Tothero that night.

"You know damn well who," he tells Margaret. "Tothero."

"Our old coach, Harry!" Harrison cries, and reaches across the table to touch Rabbit's fingertips. "The man who made us immortal!"

Rabbit curls his fingers an inch beyond Harrison's reach and Harrison, with a satisfied smirk, draws back, pulling his palms along the slick-top table so they make a slippery screech of friction.

"Me, you mean," Rabbit says. "You were nothing."

"Nothing. That seems a little stern. That seems a little stern, Harry old bunny. Let's cast our minds back. When Tothero wanted a guy roughed up, who did he send in to do it? When he wanted a hot shot like you guarded nice and close, who was his boy?" He slaps his chest. "You were too much of a queen to dirty your hands. No, you never touched anybody, did you? You didn't play football either, and get your knee scrambled, either, did you? No sir, not Harry the bird; he was on wings. Feed him the ball and watch it go in."

"It went in, you noticed."

"Sometimes. Sometimes it did. Harry now don't wrinkle your nose. Don't think we all don't appreciate your ability." From the way he's using his hands, chopping and lifting with practiced understatement, getting a quiet symphony of sarcasm and patience and emphasis out of the play of his palms, Rabbit thinks he must do a lot of talking around a table. Yet there's a tremor; and in seeing that Harrison is afraid of him, Rabbit loses interest. The waitress comes—Harrison orders Bourbon-on-the-Rocks for himself and Margaret and another Daiquiri for Ruth—and Rabbit watches her back recede as if it is the one real thing in the world: the thick notched rope of her spine between two blue-brown pillows of muscle. He wants Ruth to see him looking.

Harrison is losing his salesman's composure. "Did I ever tell you what Tothero once said to me about you? Ace, are you listening?"

"What did Tothero say?" God this guy is a middle-aged bore.

"He said to me, 'This is in confidence, Ronnie, but I depend on you to spark the team. Harry is not a team player.' "

Rabbit looks down at Margaret and over at Ruth. "Now I'll

tell ya what really happened," he says to them. "Old Harrison here went in to Tothero and he said, 'Hey, I'm a real spark plug, ain't I coach? A real play-maker, huh? Not like that lousy showboat Angstrom, huh?' And Tothero was probably asleep and didn't answer, so Harrison goes through the rest of his life thinking, 'Gee, I'm a real hero. A real playmaker.' On a basketball team, you see, whenever you have a little runty clumsy guy that can't do anything he's called the play-maker. I don't know where he's supposed to be making all these plays. In his bedroom I guess." Ruth laughs; he's not sure he wanted her to.

"That's not true." Harrison's practiced palms flicker more hastily. "He volunteered it to me. Not that it was anything I didn't know; the whole school knew it."

Did it? Nobody ever told him.

Ruth says, "God, let's not talk *bas*ketball. Every time I go out with this bastard we talk nothing but."

He wonders, Did doubt show on his face, and she say that to reassure him? Does she in any part of her pity him?

Harrison perhaps thinks he's been uglier than befits his sales-conference suavity. He takes out a cigarette and a lizardskin Ronson.

Rabbit turns to Margaret—something in the way this arranges the nerves in his neck rings a bell, makes him think he turned to her exactly like this a million years ago—and says, "You never answered me."

"Nuts, I don't know where he is. I guess he went home. He was sick."

"Just sick, or—" Harrison's mouth does a funny thing, smiling and pursing both, as if he is introducing, with deference, this bit of Manhattan cleverness to his rural friends for the first time, and taps his head to make sure they will "get it"— "sick, sick, sick?"

"All ways," Margaret says. A serious shadow crosses her face that seems to remove her and Harry, who sees it, from the others, and takes them into that strange area of a million years ago from which they have wandered; a strange guilt pierces Harry at being here, instead of there, where he never was. Ruth and Harrison across from them, touched by staccato red light, seem specters glimpsed from the heart of damnation.

"Dear Ruth," Harrison says, "how have you been? I often worry about you."

"Don't worry about *me*," she says, yet seems pleased.

The Negress brings their drinks and Harrison sets his lizard-skin Ronson beside his glass, as if suggesting it's for sale. "Did you know," he asks Harry, with a sweet smile, as if he's chatting with a child, "that Ruth and I once went to Atlantic City together?"

"There was another couple," she tells Harry.

"A disgusting pair," Harrison says, "who preferred the shabby privacy of their own bungalow to the golden sunshine outdoors. The male of this twosome later confided to me, with ill-concealed pride, that he had enjoyed the orgasmatic climax eleven times in the all-too-short period of thirty-six hours."

Margaret laughs. "Honestly, Ronnie, to hear you talk sometimes you'd think you went to Harvard."

"Princeton," he corrects. "Princeton is the effect I want to give. Harvard is suspect around here."

Rabbit looks toward Ruth to see if she is still on his side. With dismay he sees that the second Daiquiri is on its way and the first has been delivered. She titters. "The awful thing about them," she says, "was that they did it in the car. Here was poor Ronnie, trying to drive through all this Sunday-night traffic, and I looked back at a stoplight and Betsy's dress was up around her neck."

"I didn't drive all the way," Harrison tells her. "Remember we *finally* got him to drive." His head tips toward her for confirmation and his pink scalp glints.

"Yeah." Ruth looks into her glass and titters again, maybe at the thought of Betsy naked.

Harrison watches narrowly the effect of this on Rabbit. "This guy," he says, in the pushy-quiet voice of offering a deal, "had an interesting theory. He thought"—Harrison's hands grip air—"that right at the crucial, how shall I say?—development, you should *slap* your partner, as hard as you can, right in the face. If you're in a position to. Otherwise slap what you can."

Rabbit blinks; he really doesn't know what to do about this awful guy. And just there, in the space of blinking, with the alcohol vaporizing under his ribs, he feels himself pass over. He laughs, really laughs. They can all go to Hell. "Well what did he think about biting?"

Harrison's I've-got-your-number-buddy grin grows fixed; his

reflexes aren't quick enough to take this sudden turn. "Biting? I don't know."

"Well he couldn't have given it much thought. A good big bloody bite: nothing better. Of course I can see how you're handicapped, with those two false teeth."

"Do you have false teeth, Ronnie?" Margaret cries. "How exciting! You've never told."

"Of course he does," Rabbbit tells her. "You didn't think those two piano keys were his, did you? They don't even come close to matching."

Harrison presses his lips together but he can't afford to give up that forced grin and it sharply strains his face. His talking is hampered too.

"Now there was this place we used to go to in Texas," Rabbit says, "where there was this girl whose backside had been bitten so often it looked like a piece of old cardboard. You know, after it's been out in the rain. It's all she did. She was a virgin otherwise." He looks around at his audience and Ruth shakes her head minutely, one brief shake, as if to say, "No, Rabbit," and it seems extremely sad, so sad a film of grit descends on his spirit and muffles him.

Harrison says, "It's like that story about this whore that had the biggest—ah—you don't want to hear it, do you?"

"Sure. Go ahead," Ruth says.

"Well, this guy, see, was making out and he loses his, ahem, device." Harrison's face bobbles in the unsteady light. His hands start explaining. Rabbit thinks the poor guy must have to make a pitch five times a day or so. He wonders what he sells; ideas, he guesses; nothing as tangible as the MagiPeel Peeler. ". . . up to his elbow, up to his shoulder, then he gets his whole head in, and his chest, and starts crawling along this tunnel . . ." Good old MagiPeel, Rabbit thinks, he can almost feel one in his hand. Its handle came in three colors, turquoise, scarlet, and gold. The funny thing about it, it really did what they said, really took the skin off turnips and stuff as neat and quick—". . . sees this *other* guy and says, 'Hey, have you seen . . .'" Ruth sits there resigned and with horror he believes it's all the same to her in her mind there's no difference between Harrison and him and for that matter *is* there a difference? The whole interior of the place muddles and runs together red like the inside of a stomach in which they're all being digested ". . . and the other guy says, 'Stripper, hell. I've been in here three weeks looking for my motorcycle!' "

Harrison, waiting to join the laughter, looks up in silence. He's failed to sell it. "That's too fantastic," Margaret says.

Rabbit's skin is clammy under his clothes; this makes the breeze from the door opening behind him chilling. Harrison says, "Hey, isn't that your sister?"

Ruth looks up from her drink. "Is it?" He makes no sign and she says, "They have the same horsy look."

One glance told Rabbit. Miriam and her escort luckily walk a little into the place, past their table, and wait there to see an empty booth. The place is shaped like a wedge and widens out from the entrance. The bar is in the center, and on either side there is an aisle of booths. The young couple heads for the opposite aisle. Mim wears bright white shoes with very high heels. The boy with her has woolly blond hair cut just long enough to comb, and a self-consciously brown face, a somehow *bought* tan. I went south this winter, it says.

"Is that your sister?" Margaret says. "She's attractive. You and her must take after different parents."

"How do *you* know her?" Rabbit asks Harrison.

"Oh—" His hand flicks diffidently, as if his fingertips slide across a streak of grease in the air. "You see her around."

Rabbit's instinct was to freeze at first but this suggestion of Harrison's that she's a tramp makes him get up and walk across the orange tile floor and around the bar.

"Mim."

"Well, *hi*."

"What are you doing here?"

She tells the boy with her, "This is my brother. He's back from the dead."

"Hi, big brother." Rabbit doesn't like the boy's saying this and he doesn't like the way the kid is sitting on the inside of the booth with Mim on the outside in the man's place. He doesn't like the whole feel of the thing, that Mim is showing him around. The kid is wearing a seersucker coat and a narrow tie and looks very innocent, in a smirched prep-school way. His lips are too thick. Mim doesn't give his name.

"Harry, Pop and Mom fight all the time about you."

"Well if they knew you were in a joint like this they'd have something else to talk about."

"It's not so bad, for this section of town."

"It stinks. Why don't you and Junior get out?"

"Say. Who's in charge here?" the kid asks, drawing his shoulders up and making his lips thicker.

Harry reaches over, hooks his finger around the kid's striped necktie, and snaps it up. It flies up and hits his thick mouth and makes his manicured face go slightly fuzzy. He starts to rise and Rabbit puts his hand on top of his tidy narrow head and pushes him down again and walks away, with the hardness of the kid's head still in his fingertips. At his back he hears the sweetest sound he's heard that night, his sister calling, "Harry."

His ears are so good he hears, as he rounds the bar, Junior explain to her, in a voice made husky with cowardice, "He's in love with you."

To his own table he says, "Come on, Ruth. Get on your motorcycle."

She protests, "I'm happy."

"Come on."

She moves to collect her things and Harrison, after looking around in doubt, gets out of the booth to let her up. He stands there beside Rabbit and Rabbit on an impulse puts his hand on Ronnie's unpadded pseudo-Princeton shoulder. In comparison with Mim's kid he likes him. "You're right, Ronnie," he tells him, "you were a real play-maker." It comes out nasty but he meant it well, for the sake of the old team.

Harrison, too slow to feel that he means it, knocks his hand away and says, "When are you gonna grow up?" It's telling that lousy story that has rattled him.

Outside on the summer-warm steps of the place Rabbit starts laughing. "Looking for my motorcycle," he says, and lets go, "Hwah hwah hyaaa," under the neon light.

Ruth is in no humor to see it. "Well you *are* a nut," she says.

It annoys him that she is too dumb to see that he is really furious. The way she shook her head "No" at him when he was gagging it up annoys him; his mind goes back over the minute again and again and every time snags on it. He is angry about so many things he doesn't know where to begin; the only thing clear is he's going to give her hell.

"So you and that bastard went to Atlantic City together."

"Why is he a bastard?"

"Oh. He's not and I am."

"I didn't say you were."

"You did too. Right back in there you did."

"It was just an expression. A *fond* expression, though I don't know why."

"You don't."

"No I don't. You see your sister come in with some boy friend and practically pee in your pants."

"Did you see the punk she was with?"

"What was the matter with him?" Ruth asks. "He looked all right."

"Just about everybody looks all right to you, don't they?"

"Well I don't see what you're doing going around like some almighty judge."

"Yes sir, just about anything with hair in its armpits looks all right to you."

They are walking up Warren Avenue. Their place is seven blocks away. People are sitting out on their steps in the warm night; their conversation is in this sense public and they fight to keep their voices low.

"Boy, if this is what seeing your sister does to you I'm glad we're not married."

"What brought that up?"

"What brought what up?"

"Marriage."

"You did, don't you remember, the first night, you kept talking about it, and kissed my ring finger."

"That was a nice night."

"All right then."

"All right then nothing." Rabbit feels he's been worked into a corner where he can't give her hell without giving her up entirely, without obliterating the sweet things. But she did that by taking him to that stinking place. "You've laid for Harrison, haven't you?"

"I guess. Sure."

"You guess. You don't know?"

"I said sure."

"And how many others?"

"I don't know."

"A hundred?"

"It's a pointless question."

"Why is it pointless?"

"It's like asking how many times you've been to the movies."

"They're about the same to you, is that it?"

"No they're not the same but I don't see what the count matters. You knew what I was."

"I'm not sure I did. You were a real hooer?"

"I took some money. I've told you. There were boy friends when I was working as a stenographer and they had friends and I lost my job because of the talk maybe I don't know and some older men got my number I guess through Margaret, I don't know. Look. It's by. If it's a question of being dirty or something a lot of married women have had to take it more often than I have."

"Did you pose for pictures?"

"You mean like for high-school kids? No."

"Did you blow guys?"

"Look, maybe we should say bye-bye." At the thought of that her chin softens and eyes burn and she hates him too much to think of sharing her secret with him. Her secret inside her seems to have no relation to him, this big body loping along with her under the street lamps, hungry as a ghost, wanting to hear the words to whip himself up. That was the thing about men, the importance they put on the mouth. Rabbit seems like another man to her, with this difference: in ignorance he has welded her to him and she can't let go.

With degrading gratitude she hears him say, "No I don't *want* to say bye-bye. I just want an answer to my question."

"The answer to your question is yes."

"Harrison?"

"Why does Harrison mean so much to you?"

"Because he stinks. And if Harrison is the same to you as me then I stink."

They are, for a moment, the same to her—in fact she would prefer Harrison, just for the change, just because he doesn't insist on being the greatest thing that ever was—but she lies. "You're not at all the same. You're not in the same league."

"Well I got a pretty funny feeling sitting across from you two in that restaurant. What all did you do with him?"

"Oh, I don't know, what *do* you do? You make love, you try to get close to somebody."

"Well, would you do everything to me that you did to him?"

This stuns her skin in a curious way, makes it contract so that her body feels squeezed and sickened inside it. "If you want me to." After being a wife her old skin feels tight.

His relief is boyish; his front teeth flash happily. "Just once," he promises, "honest. I'll never ask you again." He tries to put his arm around her but she pulls away. Her one hope is that they aren't talking about the same thing.

Up in the apartment he asks plaintively, "Are you going to?" She is struck by the helplessness in his posture; in the interior darkness, to which her eyes have not adjusted, he seems a suit of clothes hung from the broad white knob of his face.

She asks, "Are you sure we're talking about the same thing?"

"What do you think we're talking about?" He's too fastidious to mouth the words.

She says.

"Right," he says.

"In cold blood. You just want it."

"Uh-huh. Is it so awful for you?"

This glimmer of her gentle rabbit emboldens her. "May I ask what I've done?"

"I didn't like the way you acted tonight."

"How did I act?"

"Like what you were."

"I didn't mean to."

"Even so. I saw you that way tonight and I felt a wall between us and this is the one way through it."

"That's pretty cute. You just want it, really." She yearns to hit out at him, to tell him to go. But that time is past.

He repeats, "Is it so awful for you?"

"Well it is because you think it is."

"Maybe I don't."

"Look, I've loved you."

"Well I've loved *you*."

"And now?"

"I don't know. I want to still."

Now those damn tears again. She tries to hurry the words out before her voice crumbles. "That's good of you. That's heroic."

"Don't be smart. Listen. Tonight you turned against me. I need to see you on your knees."

"Well just that—"

"No. Not just that."

The two tall drinks have been a poor experiment; she wants to go to sleep and her tongue tastes sour. She feels in her stomach her need to keep him and wonders, Will this frighten him? Will this kill her in him?

"If I did it what would it prove?"

"It'd prove you're mine."

"Shall I take my clothes off?"

"Sure." He takes his off quickly and neatly and stands by the dull wall in his brilliant body. He leans awkwardly and brings one hand up and hangs it on his shoulder not knowing what to do with it. His whole shy pose has these wings of tension, like he's an angel waiting for a word. Sliding her last clothes off, her arms feel cold touching her sides. This last month she's felt cold all the time; her temperature being divided or something. In the growing light he shifts slightly. She closes her eyes and tells herself, They're not ugly. Not.

Mrs. Springer called the rectory a little after eight. Mrs. Eccles told her Jack had taken the young people's softball team to a game fifteen miles away and she didn't know when he'd be home. Mrs. Springer's panic carried over the wire and Lucy spent nearly two hours calling numbers in an attempt to reach him. It grew dark. She finally reached the minister of the church whose softball team they were playing and he told her the game had been over for an hour. The darkness thickened outside; the window whose sill held the phone became a waxy streaked mirror in which she could see herself, hair unpinning, slump back and forth between the address book and the phone. Joyce, hearing the constant ticking of the dial, came downstairs and leaned on her mother. Three times Lucy took her up to bed and twice the child came down again and leaned her damp weight against her mother's legs in frightened silence. The whole house, room beyond room surrounding with darkness the little island of light around the telephone, filled with menace and when, the third time, Joyce failed to come down from her bed, Lucy felt guilty and forsaken both, as if she had sold her only ally to the shadows. She dialed the number of every problem case in the parish she could think of, tried the vestrymen, the church secretary, the three co-chairmen of the fund-raising drive, and even the organist, a piano-teaching professional who lived in Brewer.

The hour-hand has moved past ten; it's getting embarrassing. It's sounding as if she's been deserted. And in fact it frightens her, that her husband seems to be nowhere in the world. She makes coffee and weeps weakly, in her own kitchen. How did she get into this? What drew her in? His gaiety, he was always so gay. To know him back in seminary you would never think he would take all this so seriously; he and his friends sitting in their drafty old rooms lined with handsome blue exegetical works made it all seem an elegant joke. She remembers playing with them in a softball game that was the Athanasians against the Arians. And now she never saw his gaiety, it was all spent on other people, on this grim gray intangible parish, her enemy. Oh, how she hates them, all those clinging quaint quavering widows and Christing young people; the one good thing if the Russians take over is they'll make religion go extinct. It should have gone extinct a hundred years ago. Maybe it shouldn't have, maybe our minds need it, but let somebody else carry it on. On Jack it was so dreary. Sometimes she feels sorry for him and abruptly, this is one of the times.

When he does come in, at quarter of eleven, it turns out he's been sitting in a drugstore gossiping with some of his teenagers; the idiotic kids tell him everything, all smoking like chimneys, so he comes home titillated silly with "how far" you can "go" on dates and still love Jesus.

Eccles sees at once she is furious. He had been having far too happy a time in the drugstore. He loves kids; their belief is so real to them and sits so light.

Lucy delivers her message as sufficient rebuke, but it fails as that; for, with hardly a backward glance at the horrid evening she has, implicitly, spent, he rushes to the phone.

He takes his wallet out and between his driver's license and his public-library card finds the telephone number he has been saving, the key that could be turned in the lock just once. He wonders, dialing it, if it will fit, if he was a fool to lean the entire weight of the case on the word of young Mrs. Fosnacht, with her mirroring, perhaps mocking sunglasses. The distant phone rings often, as if electricity, that amazingly trained mouse, has scurried through miles of wire only to gnaw at the end of its errand on an impenetrable plate of metal. He prays, but it is a bad prayer, a doubting prayer; he fails to superimpose God upon the complexities of electricity. He concedes them their inviolable laws. Hope has vanished, he is hanging on out of numbness, when the gnawing ringing stops, the metal is lifted, and openness, an impression of light and air, washes back through the wires to Eccles' ear.

"Hello." A man's voice, but not Harry's. It is heavier and more brutal than that of his friend.

"Is Harry Angstrom there?" Sunglasses mock his sunk heart; this is not the number.

"Who's this?"

"My name is Jack Eccles."

"Oh. Hi."

"Is that you, Harry? It didn't sound like you. Were you asleep?"

"In a way."

"Harry, your wife has started to have the baby. Her mother called here around eight and I just got in." Eccles closes his eyes; in the dark tipping silence he feels his ministry, sum and substance, being judged.

"Yeah," the other breathes in the far corner of the darkness. "I guess I ought to go to her."

"I wish you would."

"I guess I should. It's mine I mean too."

"Exactly. I'll meet you there. It's St. Joseph's in Brewer. You know where that is?"

"Yeah, sure. I can walk it in ten minutes."

"You want me to pick you up in the car?"

"No, I'll walk it."

"All right. If you prefer. Harry?"

"Huh?"

"I'm very proud of you."

"Yeah. O.K. I'll see you."

Eccles had reached for him, it felt like, out of the ground. Voice had sounded tinny. Ruth's bedroom is dim; the street lamp like a low moon burns shadows into the inner planes of the armchair, the burdened bed, the twisted sheet he tossed back finally when it seemed the phone would never stop. The bright rose window of the church opposite is still lit: purple red blue gold like the notes of different bells struck. His body, his whole frame of nerves and bone, tingles, as if with the shaking of small bells hung up and down his silver skin. He wonders if he had been asleep, and how long, ten minutes or five hours. He finds his underclothes and trousers draped on a chair and fumbles with them; not only his fingers but his vision itself trembles in the luminous gloom. His white shirt seems to crawl, like a cluster of glow-worms in grass. He hesitates a second before poking his fingers into the nest, that turns under his touch to safe cloth, dead. He carries it in his hand to the sullen laden bed.

"Hey. Baby."

The long lump under the covers doesn't answer. Just the top of Ruth's hair peeks up out of the pillow. He doesn't feel she is asleep.

"Hey. I got to go out."

No answer, no motion. If she wasn't asleep she heard everything he said on the phone, but what did he say? He remembers nothing except this sense of being reached. Ruth lies heavy and silent and her body hidden. The night is hot enough for just a sheet but she put a blanket on the bed saying she felt cold. It was just about the only thing she did say. He shouldn't have made her do it. He doesn't know why he did except it felt right at the time. He thought she might like it or at least like the humbling. If she didn't want to, if it made her sick, why didn't she say no like he halfhoped she would anyway? He kept touching her cheeks with his fingertips. He kept wanting to lift her up and hug her in simple thanks and say Enough you're mine again but somehow couldn't bring himself to have it stop and kept thinking the *next* moment, until it was too late, done. With it went instantly that strange floating feeling of high pride. Shame plunged in.

"My wife's having her baby. I got to go see her through it I guess. I'll be back in a couple of hours. I love you."

Still the body under the covers and the frizzy crescent of hair peeking over the top edge of the blanket don't move. He is so sure she is not asleep he thinks, *I've killed her.* It's ridiculous, such a thing wouldn't kill her, it has nothing to do with death; but the thought paralyzes him from going forward to touch her and make her listen.

"Ruth. I got to go this once, it's my baby she's having and she's such a mutt I don't think she can do it by herself. Our first one came awfully hard. It's the least I owe her."

Perhaps this wasn't the best way to say it but he's trying to explain and her stillness frightens him and is beginning to make him sore.

"Ruth. Hey. If you don't say anything I'm not coming back. Ruth."

She lies there like some dead animal or somebody after a car accident when they put a tarpaulin over. He feels if he went over and lifted her she would come to life but he doesn't like being manipulated and is angry. He puts on his shirt and doesn't bother with a coat and necktie but it seems to take forever putting on his socks; the soles of his feet are tacky.

When the door closes the taste of seawater in her mouth is swallowed by the thick grief that mounts in her throat so fully she has to sit up to breathe. Tears slide from her blind eyes and salt the corners of her mouth as the empty walls of the room become real and then dense. It's like when she was fourteen and the whole world trees sun and stars would have swung into place if she could lose twenty pounds just twenty pounds what difference would it make to God Who guided every flower in the fields into shape? Only now it's not that she's asking she knows now that's superstitious all she wants is what she had a minute ago *him* in the room him who when he was good could make her into a flower who could undress her of her flesh and turn her into sweet air Sweet Ruth he called her and if he had just said "sweet" talking to her she might have answered and he'd still be between these walls. No. She had known from the first night the wife would win they have the hooks and anyway she feels really lousy: a wave of wanting to throw up comes over her and washes away caring much about anything. She goes into the john and kneels on the tiles and watches the still oval of water in the toilet as if *it's* going to do something. She doesn't think after all she has it in her to throw up but stays there anyway because it pleases her, her bare arm resting on the icy porcelain lip, and grows used to the threat in her stomach, which doesn't dissolve, which stays with her, so in her faint state it comes to seem that this thing that's making her sick is some kind of friend.

He runs most of the way to the hospital. Up Summer one block, then down Youngquist, a street parallel to Weiser on the north, a street of brick tenements and leftover business places, shoe-repair nooks smelling secretively of leather, darkened candy stores, insurance agencies with photographs of tornado damage in the windows, real-estate offices lettered in gold, a bookshop. On an old-fashioned wooden bridge Youngquist Street crosses the railroad tracks, which slide between walls of blackened stone soft with soot like moss through the center of the city, threads of metal deep below in a darkness like a river, taking narrow sunset tints of pink from the neon lights of the dives along Railway Street. Music rises to him. The heavy boards of the old bridge, waxed black with locomotive smoke, rumble under his feet. Being a small-town boy, he always has a fear of being knifed in a city slum. He runs harder; the pavement widens, parking meters begin, and a new drive-in bank faces the antique Y.M.C.A. He cuts up the alley between the Y. and a limestone church whose leaded windows show the reverse sides of Biblical scenes to the street. He can't make out what the figures are doing. From a high window in the Y.M.C.A. fall the clicks of a billiard game; otherwise the building's broad side is lifeless. Through the glass side door he sees an old Negro sweeping up in green aquarium light. Now the pulpy seeds of some tree are under his feet. Its tropically narrow leaves are black spikes against the dark yellow sky. Imported from China or Brazil or somewhere because it can endure soot and fumes. The St. Joseph's parking lot is a striped asphalt square whose sides are lined with such city trees; and above their tops, in this hard open space, he sees the moon, and for a second stops and communes with its mournful face, stops stark on his small scrabbled shadow on the asphalt to look up toward the heavenly stone that mirrors with metallic brightness the stone that has risen inside his hot skin. *Make it be all right*, he prays to it, and goes in the rear entrance.

He walks down a linoleum hall perfumed with ether to the

front desk. "Angstrom," he tells the nun behind the type-writer. "I think my wife is here."

Her plump face is rimmed like a cupcake with scalloped linen. She surveys her cards and says "Yes" and smiles. Her little wire spectacles perch way out from her eyes on the pads of fat at the top of her cheeks. "You may wait over there." She points with a pink ball-point pen. Her other hand rests, beside the typewriter, on a string of black beads the size of the necklace of beads carved in Java he once got Janice for Christmas. He stands there staring, expecting to hear her say, *She's been here hours, where were you?* He can't believe she'll just accept him. As he stares, her nerve-less white hand, that has never seen the sun, slides the black necklace off the desktop into her lap.

Two other men are already established in the waiting end of the room. This is the front entrance hall; people drift in and out. Rabbit sits down on an imitation leather chair with chrome arms and gets the idea he's in a police court and these other two men are the cops who made the arrest. In his nervousness he plucks a magazine from the table. It's a Catholic magazine the size of *The Reader's Digest*. He tries to read a story about a lawyer in England who becomes so interested in how legally un*fair* it was for Henry VIII to confiscate the property of the monasteries that he becomes a Roman Catholic convert and eventually a monk. The two men whisper together; one maybe is the other's father. The younger one keeps kneading his hands together and nodding to what the older man whispers.

Eccles comes in, blinking and looking scrawny in his col-lar. He greets the sister behind the desk by name, Sister Bernard. Rabbit stands up on ankles of air and Eccles comes over with that familiar frown in his eyebrows made harsh by the hospital light. His forehead is etched in purple. He's had a haircut that day; as he turns his skull, the shaved planes above his ears shine like the blue throat feathers of a pigeon.

Rabbit asks, "Does she know I'm here?" He wouldn't have predicted that he would whisper too. He hates the panicked sound of his voice.

"I'll see that she's told if she's still conscious," Eccles says in a loud voice that makes the whispering men look up. He goes over to Sister Bernard. The nun seems happy to chat, and both laugh, Eccles in the startled guffaw Rabbit knows

well and Sister Bernard with a pure and girlish fat woman's
fluting that springs from her throat slightly retracted, curbed
by the frame of stiff frills around her face. When Eccles
moves away she lifts the phone by her skirted elbow.

Eccles comes back and looks him in the face, sighs, and
offers him a cigarette. The effect is somehow of a wafer of
repentance and Rabbit accepts. The first drag, after so many
clean months, unhinges his muscles and he has to sit down.
Eccles takes a hard chair nearby and makes no effort at conversation. Rabbit can't think of much to say to him off the
golf course and, shifting the smoking cigarette awkwardly to
his left hand, pulls another magazine off the table, making
sure it's unreligious, *The Saturday Evening Post*. It opens to
an article in which the author, who from the photograph
looks Italian, tells how he took his wife and four children
and mother-in-law on a three-week camping trip to the Ca-
nadian Rockies that only cost them $120 not counting the
initial investment of a Piper Cub. His mind can't keep with
the words but keeps skidding up and branching away and
flowering into little soft visions of Janice screaming, of the
baby's head blooming out of blood, of the wicked ridged blue
light Janice must be looking into if she's conscious, *if she's
conscious* Eccles said, of the surgeon's red rubber hands and
gauze face and Janice's babyish black nostrils widening to take
in the antiseptic smell he smells, the smell running everywhere along the whitewashed walls, of being washed, washed,
blood washed, retching washed until every surface smells like
the inside of a bucket but it will never come clean because
we will always fill it up again with our filth. A damp warm
cloth seems wrapped around his heart. He is certain that as
a consequence of his sin Janice or the baby will die. His
sin a conglomerate of flight, cruelty, obscenity, and conceit;
a black clot embodied in the entrails of the birth. Though
his bowels twist with the will to dismiss this clot, to retract,
to turn back and undo, he does not turn to the priest beside
him, but instead reads the same sentence about delicious
fried trout again and again.

On the extreme edge of his tree of fear Eccles perches,
black bird, flipping the pages of magazines and making
frowning faces to himself. He seems unreal to Rabbit, everything seems unreal that is outside of his sensations. His
palms tingle; a strange impression of pressure darts over
his body, seizing now his legs, now the base of his neck.

His armpits itch the way they used to when he was little and late for school, running up Jackson Road.

"Where's her parents?" he asks Eccles.

Eccles looks surprised. "I don't know. I'll ask the sister." He moves to get up.

"No no, sit still for Chrissake." Eccles' acting like he half-owns the place annoys him. Harry wants to be unnoticed; Eccles makes noise. He rattles the magazine so it sounds like he's tearing orange crates apart. And flips cigarettes around like a juggler.

A woman in white, not a man, comes into the waiting-room and asks Sister Bernard, "Did I leave a can of furniture polish in here? I can't find it anywhere. A green can, with one of those pushy things on top that makes it spritz."

"No, dear."

She looks for it and goes out and after a minute comes back and announces, "Well that's the mystery of the world."

To the distant music of pans, wagons, and doors, one day turns through midnight into another. Sister Bernard is relieved by another nun, a very old one, dressed in dark blue, signifying some mysterious inferiority of holiness. The two whispering men go to the desk, talk, and leave, their crisis unresolved. Eccles and he are left alone. Rabbit strains his ears to catch the cry of his child somewhere deep in the hushed hospital maze. Often he thinks he hears it; the scrape of a shoe, a dog in the street, a nurse giggling—any of these are enough to fool him. He does not expect the fruit of Janice's pain to make a very human noise. His idea grows, that it will be a monster, a monster of his making. The thrust whereby it was conceived becomes confused in his mind with the perverted entry a few hours ago he made into Ruth. Momentarily drained of lust, he stares at the remembered contortions to which it had driven him. His life seems a sequence of grotesque poses assumed to no purpose, a magic dance empty of belief. *There is no God; Janice can die*: the two thoughts come at once, in one slow wave. He feels underwater, caught in chains of transparent slime, ghosts of the urgent ejaculations he has spat into the mild bodies of women. His fingers on his knees pick at persistent threads.

Mary Ann. Tired and stiff and tough somehow after a game he would find her hanging on the front steps under the school motto and they would walk across mulching wet leaves through white November fog to his father's car and drive to get the heater warmed and park. Her body a branched tree of warm nests yet always this touch of timidity, as if she wasn't sure but he was much bigger, a winner. He came to her as a winner and that was the feeling he missed since. In the same way she was the best of them all because she was the one he brought most to, so tired. Some times the shouting glare of the gym would darken behind his sweat-burned eyes into a shadowed anticipation of the careful touchings that would come under the padded gray car roof and once there the bright triumph of the past game flashed across her quiet skin streaked with the shadows of rain on the windshield. So that the two kinds of triumph were united in his mind. She married when he was in the Army; a P.S. in a letter from his mother shoved him out from shore. That day he was launched.

But he feels joy now; cramped from sitting on the eroded chrome-armed chair sick with cigarettes he feels joy in re-membering his girl; the water of his heart has been poured into a thin vase of joy that Eccles' voice jars and breaks.

"Well I've read this article by Jackie Jensen all the way to the end and I don't know what he said," Eccles says.

"Huh?"

"This piece by Jackie Jensen on why he wants to quit baseball. As far as I can tell the problems of being a baseball player are the same as those of the ministry."

"Say, don't you want to go home? What time is it?"

"Around two. I'd like to stay, if I may."

"I won't run off if that's what you're afraid of."

Eccles laughs and keeps sitting there. Harry's first impres-sion of him had been tenacity and now all the intervening companionship has been erased and it's gone back to that.

Harry tells him, "When she had Nelson the poor kid was at it for twelve hours."

Eccles says, "The second child is usually easier," and looks at his watch. "It hasn't quite been six hours."

Events create events. Mrs. Springer passes through from the privileged room where she has been waiting and stiffly nods at Eccles; seeing Harry in the corner of her eye makes her stumble on her sore legs and tumbledown saddle shoes. Eccles gets up and goes with her through the door to the outside. After a while the two of them come back in along with Mr. Springer, who wears a tiny-knotted necktie and a spandy-fresh shirt. At two a.m. he looks like he just came from the tailor's. His little sandy mustache has been trimmed so often his upper lip has turned gray under it. He says, "Hello, Harry."

This acknowledgment from her husband, despite some talking-to they've probably had from Eccles, goads the old lady into turning on Harry and telling him, "If you're sitting there like a buzzard young man hoping she's going to die, you might as well go back to where you've been living because she's doing fine without you and has been all along."

The two men hustle her away while the old nun peers with a smile across her desk, deaf? Mrs. Springer's attack, though it ached to hurt him, is the first thing anybody has said to Harry since this began that seems to fit the enormity of the event going on somewhere behind the screen of hospital soap-smell. Until her words he felt alone on a dead planet encircling the great gaseous sun of Janice's labor; her cry, though a cry of hate, pierced his solitude. The dreadful thought of Janice's death: hearing it voiced aloud had halved its weight. The strange scent of death Janice breathed: Mrs. Springer also smelled it, and this sharing seems the most precious connection he has with anybody in the world.

Mr. Springer returns and passes through to the outside, bestowing upon his son-in-law a painfully complex smile, compounded of a wish to apologize for his wife (we're both men; I know), a wish to keep distant (nevertheless you've behaved unforgivably; don't touch me), and the car salesman's mechanical reflex of politeness. Harry thinks, *You crumb;* hurls the thought at the slammed door. *You slave.* Where is everybody going? Where are they coming from? Eccles comes back and feeds him another cigarette and goes away again. Smoking it makes the floor of his stomach tremble. His throat feels like it does when you wake up after sleeping all night with your mouth open. His own bad breath now and then brushes his nostrils. A doctor with a barrel chest and unimaginably soft small hands, held curled in front of the pouch of his smock, comes into the anteroom uncertainly. He asks Harry, "Mr. Angstrom?" This would be Dr. Crowe. Harry has never met him. Janice used to go off and visit him once a month, bringing home tales of how gentle he was, how delicate.

"Yes."

"Congratulations. You have a beautiful little daughter."

He offers his hand so hastily Harry has only time to half-rise, and so absorbs the news in a crouching position. The scrubbed pink of the doctor's face—his sterile mask is unknotted and hangs from one ear, exposing pallid beefy lips—becomes enmeshed in the process of trying to give shape and tint to the unexpected word "daughter."

"I do? It's O.K.?"

"Seven pounds ten ounces. Your wife was conscious throughout and held the baby for a minute after delivery."

"Really? She held it? Was it—did she have a hard time?"

"No-o. It was normal. In the beginning she seemed tense, but it was normal."

"That's wonderful. Thank you. Good grief, thank you."

Crowe stands there smiling uneasily. Coming up from the pit of creation, he stammers in the open air. Strange: here he has been for the last hours closer to Janice than Harry ever was, has been grubbing right in her roots, yet he has brought back no secret, no wisdom to confide; just a bland sterile blessing. Harry dreads that the doctor's eyes will release with thunder the horror they have seen; but Crowe's gaze contains no wrath. Not even a reprimand. He seems to see Harry as just another in the parade of more or less dutiful husbands whose brainlessly sown seed he spends his life trying to reap.

Harry asks, "Can I see her?"

"Who?"

Who? That "her" is a forked word now startles him. The world is thickening. "My my wife."

"Of course, surely." Crowe seems in his soft way puzzled that Harry asks for permission. He must know the facts, yet seems oblivious of the gap of guilt between Harry and humanity. "I thought you might mean the baby. I'd rather you waited until visiting hours tomorrow for that; there's not a nurse to show her right now. But your wife is conscious, as I say. We've given her some Equanil. That's just a tranquilizer. Meprobamate. Tell me"—he moves closer gently, pink skin and clean cloth—"is it all right if her mother sees her for a moment? She's been on our necks all night." He's asking *him*, him, the runner, the fornicator, the monster. He must be blind. Or maybe just being a father makes everyone forgive you.

"Sure. She can go in."

"Before or after you?"

Harry hesitates, and remembers the way Mrs. Springer came and visited him on his empty planet. "She can go in before."

"Thank you. Good. Then she can go home. We'll get her out in a minute. It'll be about ten minutes all told. Your wife is being prepared by the nurses."

"Swell." He sits down to show how docile he is and rises again. "Say, thanks by the way. Thank you very much. I don't see how you doctors do it."

Crowe shrugs. "She was a good girl."

"When we had the other kid I was scared silly. It took ages."

"Where did she have it?"

"At the other hospital. Homeopathic."

"Nn-*huh*." And the doctor, who had gone into the pit and brought back no thunder, emits a spark of spite at the thought of the rival hospital, and utters his grunt of disapproval with a sharp wag of his scrubbed head and, still wagging it, walks away.

Eccles comes into the room grinning like a schoolboy and Rabbit can't keep his attention on his silly face. He suggests thanksgiving and Rabbit bows his head blankly into his friend's silence. Each heartbeat seems to flatten against a wide white wall. When he looks up, objects seem infinitely solid and somehow tip, seem so full they are about to leap. His real happiness is a ladder from whose top rung he keeps trying to jump still higher, because he knows he should.

Crowe's phrase about nurses "preparing" Janice has a weird May Queen sound. When they lead him to her room he expects to find her with ribbons in her hair and paper flowers twined into the bedposts. But it's just old Janice, lying between two smooth sheets on a high metal bed. She turns her face and says, "Well look who it isn't."

"Hey," he says, and goes over to kiss her; he intends it so gently. Her mouth swims in the sweet stink of ether. To his surprise her arms come out from the sheets and she puts them around his head and presses his face down into her soft happy swimming mouth. "Hey take it easy," he says.

"I have no legs," she says, "it's the funniest feeling." Her hair is drawn against her skull in a sanitary knot and she has no makeup. Her small skull is dark against the pillow.

"No legs?" He looks down and there they are under the sheets, stretched out flat in a motionless V.

"They gave me a spinal or whatever at the end and I didn't feel anything. I was lying there hearing them say push and the next thing here's this teeny flubbly *baby* with this big moon face looking cross at me. I told Mother it looks like you and she didn't want to hear it."

"She gave me hell out there."

"I wish they hadn't let her in. I didn't want to see her. I wanted to see *you*."

"Did you, God. Why, baby? After I've been so crummy."

"No you haven't. They told me you were here and all the while I was thinking then it was your baby and it was like I was having *you*. I'm so full of ether it's just like I'm floating; without any legs. I could just talk and talk." She puts her hands on her stomach and closes her eyes and smiles. "I'm really quite drunk. See, I'm flat."

"Now you can wear your bathing suit," he says, smiling and entering the drift of her ether-talk, feeling himself as if he has no legs and is floating on his back on a great sea of cleanness light as a bubble amid the starched sheets and germless surfaces before dawn. Fear and regret are dissolved, and gratitude is blown so large it has no cutting edge. "The doctor said you were a good girl."

"Well isn't that silly; I wasn't. I was horrible. I cried and screamed and told him to keep his hands to himself. Though the thing I minded worst was when this horrible old nun shaved me with a dry razor."

"Poor Janice."

"No it was wonderful. I tried to count her toes but I was so dizzy I couldn't so I counted her eyes. Two. Did we want a girl? Say we did."

"I did." He discovers this is true, though the words discover the desire.

"Now I'll have somebody to side with me against you and Nelson."

"How is Nelson?"

"Oh. Every day, 'Daddy home day?' until I could belt him, the poor saint. Don't make me talk about it, it's too depressing."

"Oh, damn," he says, and his own tears, that it seemed didn't exist, sting the bridge of his nose. "I can't believe it was me. I don't know why I left."

"Vnnn." She sinks deeper into the pillow as a lush grin spreads her cheeks apart. "I had a little baby."

"It's terrific."

"You're lovely. You look so tall." She says this with her

eyes shut, and when she opens them, they brim with an inebriated idea; he has never seen them sparkle so. She whispers, "Harry. The girl in the other bed in here went home today so why don't you sneak around when you go and come in the window and we can lie awake all night and tell each other stories? Just like you've come back from the Army or somewhere. Did you make love to other women?"

"Hey I think you ought to go to sleep now."

"It's all right, now you'll make better love to me." She giggles and tries to move in the bed. "No I didn't mean that, you're a good lover you've given me a baby."

"It seems to me you're pretty sexy for somebody in your shape."

"That's how you feel," she says. "I'd invite you into bed with me but the bed's so narrow. Ooh."

"What?"

"I just got this terrible thirst for orangeade."

"Aren't you funny?"

"*You're* funny. Oh that baby looked so *cross*."

A nun fills the doorway with her wings. "Mr. Angstrom. Time."

"Come kiss," Janice says. She touches his face as he bends to inhale her ether again; her mouth is a warm cloud that suddenly splits and her teeth pinch her lower lip. "Don't leave," she says.

"Just for now. I'll be back tomorrow."

"Love you."

"Listen. I love *you*."

Waiting for him in the anteroom, Eccles asks, "How was she?"

"Terrific."

"Are you going to go back now, to uh, where you were?"

"No," Rabbit answers, horrified, "for Heaven's sake. I can't."

"Well, then, would you like to come home with me?"

"Look, you've done more than enough. I can go to my parents' place."

"It's late to get them up."

"No, really, I couldn't put you to the trouble." He has already made up his mind to accept. Every bone in his body feels soft.

"It's no trouble; I'm not asking you to live with us," Eccles says. The long night is baring his nerves. "We have *scads* of room."

"O.K. O.K. Good. Thanks."

They drive back to Mt. Judge along the familiar highway. At this hour it is empty even of trucks. Harry sits wordless staring through the windshield, rigid in body, rigid in spirit. The curving highway seems a wide straight road that has opened up in front of him. There is nothing he wants to do but go down it.

He is taken to a room that has tassels on the bedspread. He uses the bathroom stealthily and in underclothes curls up between the sheets, making the smallest possible volume of himself. Thus curled near one edge, he draws backward into sleep like a turtle drawing into his shell. Sleep this night is not a dark haunted domain the mind must consciously set itself to invade, but a cave inside himself, into which he shrinks while the claws of the bear rattle like rain outside.

Sunshine, the old clown, rims the room. Two pink chairs flank the gauze-filled window buttered with light that smears a writing desk furry with envelope-ends. Above it a picture of a lady in pink stepping toward you. A woman's voice is tapping the door. "Mr. Angstrom. Mr. Angstrom."

"Yeah. Hi," he calls, hoarse.

"It's twelve-twenty. Jack told me to tell you the visiting hours at the hospital are one to three." He recognizes Eccles' wife's crisp little curly tone, like she was adding, "And what the hell are you doing in my house anyway?"

"Yeah. O.K. I'll be right out." He puts on the cocoa-colored trousers he wore last night and, displeased by the sense of these things being dirty, he carries his shoes and socks and shirt into the bathroom with him, postponing putting them against his skin, giving them another minute to air. Still foggy despite splashing water all around, he carries them out of the bathroom and goes downstairs in his bare feet and a T shirt.

Eccles' little wife is in her big kitchen, wearing khaki shorts this time and sandals and painted toenails. "How did you sleep?" she asks from behind the refrigerator door.

"Like death. Not a dream or anything."

"It's the effect of a clear conscience," she says, and puts

a glass of orange juice on the table with a smart click. He imagines that seeing how he's dressed, with just the T shirt over his chest, makes her look away quickly.

"Hey don't go to any bother. I'll get something in Brewer."

"I won't give you eggs or anything. Do you like Cheerios?"

"Love 'em."

"All right."

The orange juice burns away some of the fuzz in his mouth. He watches the backs of her legs; the white tendons behind her knees jump as she assembles things at the counter. "How's Freud?" he asks her. He knows this could be bad, because if he brings back that afternoon he'll bring back how he nicked her fanny; but he has this ridiculous feeling with Mrs. Eccles, that he's in charge and can't make mistakes.

She turns with her tongue against her side teeth, making her mouth lopsided and thoughtful, and looks at him levelly. He smiles; her expression is that of a high-school tootsie who wants to seem to know more than she's telling. "He's the same. Do you want milk or cream on the Cheerios?"

"Milk. Cream is too sticky. Where is everybody?"

"Jack's at the church, probably playing ping-pong with one of his boys. Joyce and Bonnie are asleep, Heaven knows why. They kept wanting to look at the naughty man in the guest room all morning. It took real love to keep them out."

"Who told them I was a naughty man?"

"Jack did. He said to them at breakfast, 'I brought home a naughty man last night who's going to stop being naughty.' The children have names for all of Jack's problems—you're the Naughty Man, Mr. Carson, an alcoholic, is the Silly Man, Mrs. MacDaniel is the Woman Who Calls Up in the Night. Then there's the Droopsy Lady, Mr. Hearing-Aid, Mrs. Side-Door, and Happy Beans. Happy Beans is just about the least happy man you ever wanted to see, but once he brought the children some of those celluloid capsules with a weight in them, so they jiggle around. Ever since that he's Happy Beans."

Rabbit laughs, and Lucy, having delivered the Cheerios—too much milk; he is used to living with Ruth, who let him pour his own milk; he likes just enough to take away the dryness, so that the milk and cereal come out even—chats on gaily. "The worst thing that happened, in connection with some committee or other Jack was talking with one of the vestrymen over the phone and had the idea that it would buck this poor soul up to be given a church job so he said, 'Why not make Happy Beans the chairman of something or other?' Well, the man on the other end of the line said "Happy Who?" and Jack realized what he'd said but instead of just sluffing it off like anybody else would have, Jack tells the whole story about the children calling him Happy Beans and of course this stuffy old vestryman doesn't think it's at all funny. He was a friend, you see, of Happy Beans; they weren't exactly business associates but often had lunch together over in Brewer. That's the thing about Jack; he always tells people too much. Now this vestryman is probably telling everybody how the rector pokes fun of this poor miserable Happy Beans."

He laughs again. His coffee comes, in a thin shallow cup monogrammed in gold, and Lucy sits down opposite him at the table with a cup of her own. "He said I'm going to stop being naughty," Rabbit says.

"Yes. He's overjoyed. He went out of here virtually singing. It's the first constructive thing he thinks he's done since he came to Mt. Judge."

Rabbit yawns. "Well I don't know what he did."

"I don't either," she says, "but to hear him talk the whole thing was on his shoulders."

This suggestion that he's been managed rubs him the wrong way. He feels his smile creak. "Really? Did he talk about it?"

"Oh, all the time. He's very fond of you. I don't know why."

"I'm just lovable."

"That's what I keep hearing. You have poor old Mrs. Smith wrapped around your little finger. She thinks you're marvelous."

"And you don't see it?"

"Maybe I'm not old enough. Maybe if I were seventy-three." She lifts the cup to her face and tilts it and the freckles on her narrow white nose sharpen in proximity to the steaming brown coffee. She is a naughty girl. Yes, it's very clear, a naughty girl. She sets the cup down and looks at him with round green eyes, and the triangular white space between her eyebrows seems to look and mock too. "Well tell me. How does it feel? To be a new man. Jack's always hoping I'll reform and I want to know what to expect. Are you 'born anew'?"

"Oh, I feel about the same."

"You don't act the same."

He grunts "Well" and shifts in his chair. Why does he feel so awkward? She is trying to make him feel foolish and sissy, just because he's going to go back to his wife. It's quite true, he doesn't act the same; he doesn't feel the same with her, either; he's lost the nimbleness that led him so lightly into tapping her backside that day. He tells her, "Last night driving home I got this feeling of a straight road ahead of me; before that it was like I was in the bushes and it didn't matter which way I went."

Her small face above the coffee cup held in two hands like a soup bowl is perfectly tense with delight; he expects her to laugh and instead she smiles silently. He thinks, *She wants me.*

Then he thinks of Janice with her legs paralyzed talking about toes and love and orangeade and this perhaps seals shut something in his face, for Lucy Eccles turns her head impatiently and says, "Well you better get going down that nice straight road. It's twenty of one."

"How long does it take to walk to the bus stop?"

"Not long. I'd drive you to the hospital if it weren't for the children." She harks. "Speak of the devil: here comes one."

As he's pulling on his socks the older girl sneaks into the kitchen, dressed just in underpants.

"Joyce." Her mother halts halfway to the sink with the empty cups. "You get right back up to bed."

"Hello, Joyce," Rabbit says. "Did you come down to see the naughty man?"

Joyce stares and hugs the wall with her shoulder blades. Her long golden stomach protrudes thoughtfully.

"Joyce," Lucy says. "Didn't you hear me?"

"Why doesn't he have his shirt on?" the child asks distinctly.

"I don't know," her mother says. "I suppose he thinks he has a nice chest."

"I have a T shirt on," he protests. It's as if neither of them see it.

"Is that his boo-zim?" Joyce asks.

"No, darling: only ladies have bosoms. We've been through that."

"Hell, if it makes everybody nervous," Rabbit says, and puts on his shirt. It's rumpled and at the collar and cuffs gray; he puts it on clean to go to the Club Castanet. He has no coat, he left Ruth too hastily. "O. K.," he says, tucking in the tail. "Thank you very much."

"You're very welcome," Lucy says. "Be good now." The two girls walk with him down the hall. Lucy's white legs mix in pallor with the child's naked chest. Little Joyce keeps staring up at him. He wonders what she's puzzling about. Children and dogs smell things. He tries to calculate how much sarcasm was in that "Be good now" and what it meant, if anything. He wishes she could drive him; he wants, he really wants, to get into a car with her. Not so much to do anything as just feel how things set. His reluctance to leave pulls the air between them taut.

They stand at the door, he and Eccles' baby-skinned wife and under them Joyce's face looking up with her father's wide lips and arched eyebrows and under them all Lucy's painted toenails, tiny scarlet shells in a row on the carpet. He strums the air with a vague disclaimer and puts his hand on the hard doorknob. The thought that only ladies have bosoms haunts him foolishly. He looks up from the toenails to Joyce's watching face and from there to her mother's bosom, two pointed bumps under a buttoned blouse that shows through its airy summer weave and white shadow of the bra. When his eyes reach Lucy's an amazing thing enters the silence. The woman winks. Quick as light: maybe he imagined it. He turns the knob and retreats down the sunny walk with a murmur in his chest as if a string in there had snapped.

At the hospital they say Janice has the baby with her for a moment and would he please wait? He is sitting in the chair with chrome arms leafing through a *Woman's Day* backwards when a tall woman with beautiful gray hair and somehow silver, finely wrinkled skin comes in and looks so familiar he stares. She sees this and has to speak; he feels she would have preferred to ignore him. Who is she? Her familiarity has touched him across a great distance. She looks into his face reluctantly and tells him, "You're an old student of Marty's. I'm Harriet Tothero. We had you to dinner once, I can almost think of your name."

Yes, of course, but it wasn't from that dinner he remembers her, it was from noticing her on the streets. The students at Mt. Judge High knew, most of them, that Tothero played around, and his wife appeared to their innocent eyes wreathed in dark flame, a walking martyr, a breathing shadow of sin. It was less pity than morbid fascination that singled her out; Tothero was himself such a clown and windbag, such a speechifier, that the stain of his own actions slid from him, oil off a duck. It was the tall, silver, serious figure of his wife that accumulated the charge of his wrongdoing, and released it to their young minds with an electrical shock that snapped their eyes away from the sight of her, in fear as much as embarrassment. Harry stands up, surprised to feel that the world she walks in is his world now. "I'm Harry Angstrom," he says.

"Yes, that's your name. He was so proud of you. He often talked to me about you. Even recently."

Recently. What did he tell her? Does she know about him? Does she blame him? Her long schoolmarmish face, as always, keeps its secrets in. "I've heard that he was sick."

"Yes, he is, Harry. Quite sick. He's had two strokes, one since he came into the hospital."

"He's here?"

"Yes. Would you like to visit him? I know it would make him very happy. For just a moment. He's had very few visitors; I suppose that's the tragedy of teaching school. You remember so many and so few remember you."

"I'd like to see him, sure."

"Come with me, then." As they walk down the halls she says, "I'm afraid you'll find him much changed." He doesn't take this in fully; he is concentrating on her skin, trying to see if it *does* look like a lot of little lizard skins sewed together. Just her hands and neck show.

Tothero is in a room alone. White curtains seem to hang expectantly around his bed. Green plants on the windowsills dutifully exhale oxygen. Canted panes of glass lift the smells of summer into the room. Footsteps crunch on the gravel below.

"Dear, I've brought you someone. He was waiting outside in the most miraculous way."

"Hello, Mr. Tothero. My wife's had her baby." He speaks these words and goes toward the bed with blank momentum; the sight of the old man lying there shrunken, his tongue sliding in his lopsided mouth, has stunned him. Tothero's face, spotted with white stubble, is yellow in the pillows, and his thin wrists stick out from candy-striped pajama sleeves beside the shallow lump of his body. Rabbit offers his hand.

"He can't lift his arms, Harry," Mrs. Tothero says. "He is helpless. But talk to him. He can see and hear." Her sweet patient enunciation has a singing quality that is sinister, like a voice humming in empty rooms.

Since he has extended his hand, Harry presses it down on the back of one of Tothero's. For all its dryness, the hand, under a faint scratchy fleece, is warm, and to Harry's horror moves, revolves stubbornly, so the palm is presented upward to Harry's touch. Harry takes his fingers back and sinks into the bedside chair. His old coach's eyeballs shift with scattered quickness as he turns his head an inch toward the visitor. The flesh under them has been so scooped that they are weakly protrusive. *Talk,* he must talk. "It's a little girl. I want to thank you"—he speaks loudly—"for the help you gave in getting me and Janice back together again. You were very kind."

Tothero retracts his tongue and shifts his face to look at his wife. A muscle under his jaw jumps, his lips pucker, and his chin crinkles repeatedly, like a pulse, as he tries to say something. A few dragged vowels come out; Harry turns to see if Mrs. Tothero can decipher them, but to his surprise she is looking elsewhere. She is looking out the window, toward an empty green courtyard. Her face is like a photograph.

Is it that she doesn't care? If so, should he tell Tothero about Margaret? But there was nothing to say about Margaret that might make Tothero happy. "I'm straightened out now, Mr. Tothero, and I hope you're up and out of this bed soon."

Tothero's head turns back with an annoyed quickness, the mouth closed, the eyes in a half-squint, and for this moment he looks so coherent Harry thinks he will speak, that the pause is just his old disciplinarian's trick of holding silent until your attention is complete. But the pause stretches, inflates, as if, used for sixty years to space out words, it at last has taken on a cancerous life of its own and swallowed the words. Yet in the first moments of the silence a certain force flows forth, a human soul emits its invisible and scentless rays with urgency. Then the point in the eyes fades, the brown lids lift and expose pink jelly, the lips part, the tip of the tongue appears.

"I better go down and visit my wife," Harry shouts. "She just had the baby last night. It's a girl." He feels claustrophobic, as if he's inside Tothero's skull; when he stands up, he has the fear he will bump his head, though the white ceiling is yards away.

"Thank you very much, Harry. I know he's enjoyed seeing you," Mrs. Tothero says. Nevertheless from her tone he feels he's flunked a recitation. He walks down the hall springingly, dismissed. His health, his reformed life, make space, even the antiseptic space in the hospital corridors, delicious. Yet his visit with Janice is disappointing. Perhaps he is still choked by seeing poor Tothero stretched out as good as dead; perhaps out of ether Janice is choked by thinking of how he's treated her. She complains a lot about how much her stitches hurt, and when he tries to express his repentance again she seems to find it boring. The difficulty of pleasing someone begins to hem him in. She asks why he hasn't brought flowers. He had no time; he tells her how he spent the night and, sure enough, she asks him to describe Mrs. Eccles.

"About your height," he says. "Freckles."

"Her husband's been wonderful," she says. "He seems to love everybody."

"He's O.K.," Rabbit says. "He makes me nervous."

"Oh, everybody makes you nervous."

"No now that's not true. Marty Tothero never made me nervous. I just saw the poor old bastard, stretched out in a bed up the hall. He can't say a word or move his head more than an inch."

"He doesn't make you nervous but I do, is that right?"

"I didn't say that."

"Oh no. Ow. These damn stitches they feel like barbed wire. I just make you so nervous you desert me for two months. Over two months."

"Well Jesus Janice. All you did was watch television and

drink all the time. I mean I'm not saying I wasn't wrong, but it felt like I had to. You get the feeling you're in your coffin before they've taken your blood out. On that first night, when I got in the car in front of your parents' place, even then I might just as easy have gone down to get Nelson and driven it home. But when I let the brake out—" Her face goes into that bored look again. Her head switches from side to side, as if to keep flies from settling. He says, "Shit."

This gets her. She says, "I see your language hasn't been improved by living with that prostitute."

"She wasn't a prostitute, exactly. She just kind of slept around. I think there are a lot of girls like her around. I mean if you're going to call everybody who isn't married a prostitute—"

"Where are you going to stay now? Until I get out of the hospital."

"I thought Nelson and me would move into our apartment."

"I'm not sure you can. We didn't pay any rent on it for two months."

"Huh? You didn't?"

"Well my *good*ness, Harry. You expect a lot. You expect Daddy to keep paying rent? I didn't have any money."

"Well did the landlord call? What happened to our furniture? Did he put it out on the street?"

"I don't know."

"You don't *know*? Well what *do* you know? What have you been doing all this time? Sleeping?"

"I was carrying your baby."

"Well hell, I didn't know you had to keep your whole mind on *that* all the time. The trouble with you, kid, is you just don't give a damn. Really."

"Well listen to you."

He does listen to what he's been sounding like, remembers how he felt last night, and after a pause tries to begin all over again. "Hey," he says, "I love you."

"I love you," she says. "Do you have a quarter?"

"I guess. I'll look. What do you want it for?"

"If you put a quarter in that"—she points toward a small television set on a high stand, so patients can see it over the foot of their beds—"it'll play for an hour. There's a silly program on at two that Mother and I got to watching when I was home."

So for thirty minutes he sits by her bed watching some curly-haired M.C. tease a lot of elderly women from Akron, Ohio, and Oakland, California. The idea is all these women have tragedies they tell about and then get money according to how much applause there is, but by the time the M.C. gets done delivering commercials and kidding them about their grandchildren and their girlish hairdos there isn't much room for tragedy left. Rabbit keeps thinking that the M.C., who has that way of a Jew of pronouncing very distinctly, no matter how fast the words, is going to start plugging the MagiPeel Peeler but the product doesn't seem to have hit the big time yet. It's not too bad; a pair of peroxide twins with twitchy tails push the women around to various microphones and booths and applause areas. It even makes for a kind of peace; he and Janice hold hands. The bed is almost as high as his shoulders when he sits down, and he enjoys being in this strange relation to a woman. As if he's carrying her on his shoulder but without the weight. He cranks her bed up and pours her a drink of water and these small services suit some need he has. The program isn't over when some nurse comes and says, "Mr. Angstrom, if you want to see your baby the nurse is holding them to the window now."

He goes down the hall after her; her square hips swing under the starched white. From just the thickness of her neck he figures her for a good solid piece: haunchy. Big above the knee. He does like women big above the knee. Also he's worrying about what a woman from Springfield, Illinois, was going to say happened after her son's dreadful automobile accident, in which he lost an arm. So he's quite unprepared when the nurse in the baby room, where little bundles with heads like oranges lie in rows of supermarket baskets, some tilted, brings his girl to the viewing window, and it's like a damper being slid back in his chest. A sudden stiff draft freezes his breath. People are always saying how ugly new babies are, maybe this is the reason for the amazement. The baby is held by the nurse so her profile is sharp red against the buttoned white bosom of the uniform. The folds around the nostril, worked out on such a small scale, seem incredibly precise; the tiny stitchless seam of the closed eyelid runs diagonally a great length, as if the eye, when it is opened, will be huge and see everything and know everything. As if behind the bulge of membrane a quantity of the most precious and clear liquid in the world is held in suspense. In the suggestion of pressure behind the tranquil lid and in the tilt of the protruding upper lip he reads a delightful hint of disdain. She knows she's good. What he never expected, he can feel she's feminine, feels something both delicate and enduring in the arc of the long pink cranium, furred in bands with black licked swatches. Nelson's head had been full of lumps and frightening blue veins and bald except at the base of the neck. Rabbit looks down through the glass with a timidity in the very act of seeing, as if rough looking will smash the fine machinery of this beautiful life.

The smile of the nurse, foreshortened and flickering cutely between his eyes and the baby's nose, reassures him that he is the father. Her painted lips wrinkle a question through the glass, and he calls, "O. K., yeah," and gestures, throwing his hands, fingers splayed, to the height of his ears. "She's great," he adds, in a forced voice meant to carry through glass, but the nurse is already returning his daughter to her supermarket basket. Rabbit turns the wrong way, into the pink-lidded face of the father next in line, and laughs outright. He goes back to Janice with the wind swirling through him and fire the red of the baby's skin blazing. In the soap-scented hall he gets the idea: they should call the girl June. This is June, she was born in June. He's never known a June. It will please Janice because of the J. But Janice has been thinking about names too and wants to call her after her mother. Harry never thinks of Mrs. Springer as having a first name. It is Rebecca. His warm gust of pride in his child turns Janice soft in the bed, and he in turn is sweetened by her daughterly wish; it worries him at times that she does not seem to love her mother. They compromise: Rebecca June Angstrom.

The straight path is made smooth. Mr. Springer had been paying rent on the apartment all along, it turns out; he is a personal friend of the landlord and had arranged it without troubling his daughter. He always had a hunch Harry would come back but didn't want to advertise it in case he was wrong. Harry and Nelson move in and start housekeeping. Rabbit has a gift for housekeeping; the sensation of dust sucking into the vacuum cleaner, down the cloth hose, into a paper bag that when it is full of compact gray fluff will pop the cover of the Electrolux, like a gentleman tipping his hat, pleases him. He was not entirely miscast as a barker for the MagiPeel Peeler; he has an instinctive taste for the small appliances of civilization, the little grinders and slicers and holders. Perhaps the oldest child should always be a girl; Mim, coming after him to the Angstrom household, was never exposed direct to the bright heart of the kitchen, but was always in his shadow with the housework, and sullen about assuming her share, which eventually became the greater share, because he was, after all, a boy. He supposes it will be the same with Nelson and Rebecca.

Nelson is a help. Closer to three now than two, the child can carry out orders that do not take him out of the room, understands that his toys belong in the bushel basket, and feels the happiness in cleanness, order, and light. The June breeze sighs at the screens of the long-closed windows. The sun dots the mesh with hundreds of sparkling T's and L's. Beyond the windows Wilbur Street falls away. The flat tin-and-tar roofs of their neighbors, weathered into gentle corrugations, glitter with mysterious twists of rubble, candy-bar wrappers and a pool of glass flakes, litter that must have fallen from the clouds or been brought by birds to this street in the sky, planted with television aerials and hooded chimneys the size of fire hydrants. There are three of these roofs on the down side, tipped like terraces for drainage, three broad dirty steps leading to a brink below which the better homes begin, the stucco and brick forts, rugged with porches and dormer windows and lightning rods, guarded by conifers, protected by treaties with banks and firms of lawyers. It was strange that a row of tenements had been set above them; they had been tricked by growth. But in a town built against a mountain, height was too common to be precious; above them all there was the primitive ridge, the dark slum of forest, separated from the decent part of town by a band of unpaved lanes, derelict farmhouses, a cemetery, and a few raw young developments. Wilbur Street was paved for a block past Rabbit's door, and then became a street of mud and gravel between two short rows of ranch-houses of alternating color erected in 1953 on scraped red earth that even now gives scant support to the blades of grass that speckle it. The land grows steeper still, and the woods begin.

Straight out from the windows Rabbit can look in the opposite direction across the town into the wide farm valley, with its golf course. He thinks, *My valley, my home.* The blemished green-papered walls, the scatter-rugs whose corners keep turning under, the closet whose door bumps the television set, absent from his senses for months, have returned with unexpected force. Every corner locks against a remembered corner in his mind; every crevice, every irregularity in the paint clicks against a nick already in his brain. This adds another dimension of neatness to his housecleaning.

Under the sofa and chairs and behind doors and in the footspace under the kitchen cabinets he finds old fragments of toys that delight Nelson. The child has a perfect memory for his own possessions. "Mom-mom gay me dis." Holding up a plastic duck that had lost its wheels.

"She did?"

"Yop. Mom-mom did."

"Wasn't that nice of Mom-mom?"

"Yop."

"You know what?"

"What?"

"Mom-mom is Mommy's mommy!"

"Yop. Where Mommy?"

"At the hospital."

"At hop-pital? Come back Fi-day?"

"That's right. She'll come back Friday. Won't she be happy to see how clean we make everything?"

"Yop. Daddy at hop-pital?"

"No. Daddy wasn't at the hospital. Daddy was away."

"Daddy away"—the boy's eyes widen and his mouth drops open as he stares into the familiar concept of "away"; his voice deepens with the seriousness of it—"very, very *long.*" His arms go out to measure the length, so far his fingers bend backward. It is as long as he can measure.

"But Daddy's not away now, is he?"

"Nope."

He takes Nelson with him in the car the day he goes to tell Mrs. Smith he has to quit working in her garden. Old man Springer has offered him a job in one of his lots. The rhododendron trees by the crunching driveway look dusty and barren with a few brown corsages still pinned to their branches by fronds of light green new growth. Mrs. Smith herself comes to the door. "Yes, yes," she croons, her brown face beaming.

"Mrs. Smith, this is my son Nelson."

"Yes, yes, how do you do, Nelson? You have your father's head." She pats the small head with a hand withered like a tobacco leaf. "Now let me think. Where did I put that jar of old candy? He can eat candy, can't he?"

"I guess a little but don't go looking for it."

"I will too, if I want to. The trouble with you, young man, you never gave me credit for any competence whatsoever." She totters off, plucking with one hand at the front of her dress and poking the other into the air before her, as if she's brushing away cobwebs.

While she's out of the room he and Nelson stand looking at the high ceiling of this parlor, at the tall windows with mullions as thin as chalk-lines, through whose panes, some of which are tinted lavender, they can see the pines and cypresses that guard the far rim of the estate. Paintings hang on the shining walls. One shows, in dark colors, a woman wrapped in a whipping strip of silk apparently having an argument, from the way her arms are flailing, with a big swan that just stands there pushing. On another wall there is a portrait of a young woman in a black gown sitting in a padded chair impatiently. Her face, though squarish, is fine-looking, with a triangular forehead caused by her hairdo. Round white arms curve into her lap. Rabbit moves a few steps closer to get a less oblique view. She has that short puffy little upper lip that is so good in a girl. The way it lifts to let a dab of dark come between her lips. Lifted like the top petal of a blossom. There is this readiness about her all over. He feels that she's about to get out of the chair and step forward toward him with a frown on her triangular forehead. Mrs. Smith, returning with a crimson glass ball on a stem like a wineglass, sees where he's looking and says, "What I always minded was Why did he have to make me look so irritable? I didn't like him a whit and he knew it. A slick little Italian. Thought he knew about women. Here." She has crossed to Nelson with the candy glass. "You try one of these. They're old but good like a lot of old things in this world." She takes off the lid, a knobbed hemisphere of turquoise glass, and holds it waggling in her hand. Nelson looks over and Rabbit nods at him to go ahead and he chooses a piece wrapped in colored tinfoil.

"You won't like it," Rabbit tells him. "That's gonna have a cherry inside."

"Shoosh," Mrs. Smith says. "Let the boy have the one he wants." So the poor kid goes ahead and takes it, bewitched by the tinfoil.

"Mrs. Smith," Rabbit begins, "I don't know if Reverend Eccles has told you, but my situation has kind of changed and I have to take another job. I won't be able to help around here any more. I'm sorry."

"Yes, yes," she says, alertly watching Nelson fumble at the tinfoil.

"I've really enjoyed it," he goes on. "It was sort of like Heaven, like that woman said."

"Oh that foolish woman Alma Foster," Mrs. Smith says. "With her lipstick halfway up to her nose. I'll never forget her, the dear soul. Not a brain in her body. Here, child. Give it to Mrs. Smith." She sets the dish down on a round marble table holding only an oriental vase full of peonies and takes the piece of candy from Nelson and with a frantic needling motion of her fingers works the paper off. The kid stands there staring up with an open mouth; she thrusts her hand down jerkily and pops the ball of chocolate between his lips. With a crease of satisfaction in one cheek she turns, drops the tinfoil on the table, and says to Rabbit, "Well, Harry. At least we brought the rhodies in."

"That's right. We did."

"It pleased *my* Harry, I know, wherever he is."

Nelson bites through to the startling syrup of the cherry and his mouth curls open in dismay; a dribble of brown creeps out one corner and his eyes dart around the immaculate palace room. Rabbit cups a hand at his side and the kid comes over and silently spits the mess into it, bits of chocolate shell and stringy warm syrup and the broken cherry.

Mrs. Smith sees none of this. Her eyes with their transparent irises of crazed crystal burn into Harry's as she says, "It's been a religious duty to me, to keep Horace's garden up."

"I'm sure you can find somebody else. Vacation's started; it'd be a perfect job for some high-school kid."

"No," she says, "no. I won't think about it. I won't be here next year to see Harry's rhodies come in again. You kept me alive, Harry; it's the truth; you did. All winter I was fighting the grave and then in April I looked out the window and here was this tall young man burning my old stalks and I knew life hadn't left me. That's what you have, Harry: life. It's a strange gift and I don't know how we're supposed to use it but I know it's the only gift we get and it's a good one." Her crystal eyes have filmed with a liquid thicker than tears and she grabs his arms above his elbows with hard brown claws. "Fine strong young man," she murmurs, and her eyes come back into focus as she adds, "You have a proud son; take care."

She must mean he should be proud of his son and take care of him. He is moved by her embrace; he wants to respond and did moan "No" at her prediction of death. But his right hand is full of melting mashed candy, and he stands helpless and rigid hearing her quaver, "Good-by. I wish you well. I wish you well."

In the week that follows this blessing, he and Nelson are often happy. They go for walks around the town. One day they watch a softball game played on the high-school lot by men with dark creased faces like millworkers, dressed in gaudy felt-and-flannel uniforms, one team bearing the name of a fire hall in Brewer and the other the name of the Sunshine Athletic Association, the same uniforms, he guesses, that he saw hanging in the attic the time he slept in Tothero's bedroom. The number of spectators sitting on the dismantleable bleachers is no greater than the number of players. All around, behind the bleachers and the chickenwire-and-pipe backstop, kids in sneakers scuffle and run and argue. He and Nelson watch a few innings, while the sun lowers into the trees. It floods Rabbit with an ancient, papery warmth, the oblique sun on his cheeks, the sparse inattentive crowd, the snarled pepper chatter, the spurts of dust on the yellow infield, the girls in shorts strolling past with chocolate popsicles. Brown adolescent legs thick at the ankle and smooth at the thigh. They know so much, at least their skins do. Boys their age scrawny sticks in dungarees and Keds arguing frantically if Williams was washed up or not. Mantle 10,000 times better. Williams 10,000,000 times better. He and Nelson share an orange soda bought from a man in a Boosters' Club apron who has established a bin in the shade. The smoke of dry ice leaking from the ice-cream section, the *ffp* of the cap being pulled from the orange. The artificial sweetness fills his heart. Nelson spills on his chest trying to get it to his lips.

Another day they go to the playground. Nelson acts

frightened of the swings. Rabbit tells him to hold on and pushes very gently, from the front so the kid can see. Laughs, pleads, "Me out," begins to cry, "me out, me out, Da-dee." Dabbling in the sandbox gives Rabbit a small headache. Over at the pavilion the rubber thump of Roofball and the click of checkers call to his memory, and the forgotten smell of that narrow plastic ribbon you braid bracelets and whistle-chains out of and of glue and of the sweat on the handles on athletic equipment is blown down by a breeze laced with children's murmuring. He feels the truth: the thing that had left his life had left irrevocably; no search would recover it. No flight would reach it. It was here, beneath the town, in these smells and these voices, forever behind him. The best he can do is submit to the system and give Nelson the chance to pass, as he did, unthinkingly, through it. The fullness ends when we give Nature her ransom, when we make children for her. Then she is through with us, and we become, first inside, and then outside, junk. Flower stalks.

They visit Mom-mom Springer. The child is delighted; Nelson loves her, and this makes Rabbit like her. Though she tries to pick a fight with him he refuses to fight back, just admits everything; he was a crumb, a dope, he behaved terribly, he's lucky not to be in jail. Actually there's no real bite in her attack. Nelson is there for one thing, and for another she is relieved he has come back and is afraid of scaring him off. For a third, your wife's parents can't get at you the way your own can. They remain on the outside, no matter how hard they knock, and there's something relaxing and even comic about them. He and the old lady sit on the screened sunporch with iced tea; her bandaged legs are up on a stool and her little groans as she shifts her weight make him smile. It feels like he's visiting a silly girl friend. Nelson and Billy Fosnacht are inside the house playing quietly. They're too quiet. Mrs. Springer wants to see what's happening but doesn't want to move her legs; in her torment she starts to complain about what a crude child little Billy Fosnacht is, and from this shifts over to the kid's mother. Mrs. Springer doesn't like her, doesn't trust her around the corner; it isn't just the sunglasses, though she thinks that's a ridiculous affectation; it's the girl's whole creepy manner, the way she came cozying around to Janice just because it looked like juicy gossip. "Why, she came around here so much that I had more charge of Nelson than Janice did, with those two off to the movies every day like high-school girls that don't have the responsibility of being mothers." Now Rabbit knows from school that Peggy Fosnacht, then Peggy Gring, wears sunglasses because she is freakishly, humiliatingly walleyed. And Eccles has told him that her company was a great comfort to Janice during the trying period now past. But he does not make either of these objections; he listens contentedly, pleased to be united with Mrs. Springer, the two of them against the world. The cubes in the iced tea melt, making the beverage doubly bland; his mother-in-law's talk leaves his ears like the swirling mutter of a brook. Lulled, he lets his lids lower and a smile creeps into his face; he sleeps badly at nights, alone, and drowses now on the grassy breadth of day, idly blissful, snug on the right side at last.

It is quite different at his own parents' home. He and Nelson go there once. His mother is angry about something; her anger hits his nostrils as soon as he's in the door, like a lining of dust on everything. This house looks shabby and small after the Springers'. What ails her? He assumes she's always been on his side and tells her in a quick gust of confiding how terrific the Springers have been, how Mrs. Springer is really quite warmhearted and seems to have forgiven him everything, how Mr. Springer kept up the rent on their apartment and now has promised him a job selling cars in one of his lots. He owns four lots in Brewer and vicinity; Rabbit had no idea he was that much of an operator. He's really kind of a jerk but a successful jerk at least; at any rate he thinks he, Harry Angstrom, has gotten off pretty easily. His mother's hard arched nose and steamed spectacles glitter bitterly. Her disapproval nicks him whenever she turns from the sink. At first he thinks it's that he never got in touch with her but if that's so she should be getting less sore instead of more because he's in touch with her now. Then he thinks it's that she's disgusted he slept with Ruth, and committed adultery; she's getting religious as she gets older and probably thinks of him as around twelve years old anyway, but out of a clear sky she explodes that by asking abruptly, "And what's going to happen to this poor girl you lived with in Brewer?"

"Her? Oh, she can take care of herself. She didn't expect nothing." But he tastes his own saliva saying it. It makes his

life seem cramped, that Ruth can be mentioned out of his
mother's mouth.

Her mouth goes thin and she answers with a smug flirt
of her head, "I'm not saying anything, Harry. I'm not saying
one word."

But of course she is saying a great deal only he doesn't
know what it is. There's some kind of clue in the way she
treats Nelson. She as good as ignores him, doesn't offer him
toys or hug him, just says, "Hello, Nelson," with a little nod,
her glasses snapping into white circles. After Mrs. Springer's
warmth this coolness seems brutal. Nelson feels it and acts
hushed and frightened and leans against his father's legs.
Now Rabbit doesn't know what's eating his mother but she
certainly shouldn't take it out on a two-year-old kid. He
never heard of a grandmother acting this way. It's true, just
the poor kid's being there keeps them from having the kind
of conversation they used to have, where his mother tells
him something pretty funny that happened in the neighborhood and they go on to talk about him, the way he used to be
as a kid, how he dribbled the basketball all afternoon until
after dark and was always looking after Mim. Nelson's being
half Springer seems to kill all that. For the moment he stops
liking his mother; it takes insanity to snub a tiny kid that
just learned to talk. He wants to say to her, What is this
anyway? You act like I've gone over to the other side.
You're acting insane. Don't you know it's the right side
and why don't you praise me?

But he doesn't say this; he has a stubbornness to match
hers. He doesn't say much at all to her, after telling her what
good sports the Springers are doesn't go over. He just hangs
around, him and Nelson rolling a lemon back and forth in
the kitchen. Whenever the lemon wobbles over toward his
mother's feet he has to get it; Nelson won't. The silence makes
Rabbit blush, for himself or for her he doesn't know. When
his father comes home it isn't much better. The old man isn't
angry but he looks at Harry like there isn't anything there.
His weary hunch and filthy fingernails annoy his son; it's as
if he's willfully aging them all. Why doesn't he get false teeth
that fit? His mouth works like an old woman's. But one
thing at least, his father pays some attention to Nelson, who
hopefully rolls the lemon toward him. He rolls it back. "You
going to be a ballplayer like your Dad?"

"He can't, Earl," Mom interrupts, and Rabbit is happy to

hear her voice, thinks the ice has broken, until he hears what she says. "He has those little Springer hands." These words, spoken hard as steel, strike a flurry of sparks off Rabbit's heart.

"The hell he does," he says, and regrets it, being trapped. It shouldn't matter what size hands Nelson has. Now he discovers it does matter; he doesn't want the boy to have his mother's hands, and, if he does—and if Mom noticed it he probably does—he likes the kid a little less. He likes the kid a little less but he hates his mother for making him do it. It's as if she wants to pull down everything, even if it falls on her. And he admires this, her willingness to have him hate her, so long as he gets her message. But he rejects her message, he feels it probing at his heart and rejects it. He doesn't want to hear it. He doesn't want to hear her say another word. He just wants to get out with a little piece of his love of her left.

At the door he asks his father, "Where's Mim?"

"We don't see much of Mim any more," the old man says. His blurred eyes sink and he touches the pocket of his shirt, which holds two ballpoint pens and a little soiled packet of cards and papers. Just in these last few years his father has been making little bundles of things, cards and lists and receipts and tiny calendars that he wraps rubber bands around and tucks into different pockets with an elderly fussiness. Rabbit leaves his old home depressed, with a feeling of his heart having slumped off center.

The days go all right as long as Nelson is awake. But when the boy falls asleep, when his face sags asleep and his breath drags in and out of helpless lips that deposit spots of spit on the crib sheet and his hair fans in fine tufts and the perfect skin of his fat slack cheeks, drained of animation, lies sealed under a heavy flush, then a dead place opens in Harry, and he feels fear. The child's sleep is so heavy he fears it might break the membrane of life and fall through to oblivion. Sometimes he reaches into the crib and lifts the boy's body out, just to reassure himself with its warmth and the responsive fumbling protest of the tumbled limp limbs.

He rattles around in the apartment, turning on all the lights and television, drinking ginger ale and leafing through old *Life*'s, grabbing anything to stuff into the emptiness. Before going to bed himself he stands Nelson in front of the toilet, running the faucet and stroking the taut bare bottom

until wee-wee springs from the child's irritated sleep and
jerkily prinkles into the bowl. Then he wraps a diaper
around Nelson's middle and returns him to the crib and braces
himself to leap the deep gulf between here and the moment when in the furry slant of morning sun the boy will
appear, resurrected, in sopping diapers, beside the big bed,
patting his father's face experimentally. Sometimes he gets
into the bed, and then the clammy cold cloth shocking Rabbit's skin is like retouching a wet solid shore. The time in
between is of no use to Rabbit. But the urgency of his wish to
glide over it balks him. He lies in bed, diagonally, so his feet
do not hang over, and fights the tipping sensation inside
him. Like an unsteered boat, he keeps scraping against the
same rocks: his mother's ugly behavior, his father's gaze of
desertion, Ruth's silence the last time he saw her, his mother's oppressive not saying a word, what ails her? He rolls over
on his stomach and seems to look down into a bottomless sea,
down and down, to where crusty crags gesture amid blind
lead. Good old Ruth in the swimming pool. That poor jerk
Harrison sweating it out Ivy-League style the son of a bitch.
Margaret's weak little dirty hand flipping over into Tothero's
mouth and Tothero lying there with his tongue floating
around under twittering jellied eyes: No. He doesn't want to
think about that. He rolls over on his back in the hot dry bed
and the tipping sensation returns severely. Think of something pleasant. Basketball and cider at that little school down
at the end of the country Oriole High but it's too far back he
can't remember more than the cider and the way the crowd
sat up on the stage. Ruth at the swimming pool; the way she
lay in the water without weight, rounded by the water, slipping backwards through it, eyes shut and then out of the
water with the towel, him looking up her legs at the secret
hair and then her face lying beside him huge and yellow
and still: dead. No. He must blot Tothero and Ruth out of
his mind both remind him of death. They make on one side
the vacuum of death and on the other side the threat of Janice coming home grows: that's what makes him feel tipped,
lopsided. Though he's lying there alone he feels crowded, all
these people troubling about him not much their faces or
words as their mute dense presences, pushing in the dark
like crags under water and under everything like a faint high
hum Eccles' wife's wink. That wink. What was it? Just a little joke in the tangle at the door, the kid coming down in

her underpants and maybe she conscious of him looking at
her toenails, a little click of the eye saying On your way Good
luck or was it a chink of light in a dark hall saying come
in? Funny wise freckled piece he ought to have nailed her
that steady high hum bothering him ever since she wanted
him to really nail her the shadow of her bra tipped bumps,
in a room full of light slips down the shorts over the childish thighs fat butt two globes hanging of white in the light
Freud in the white-painted parlor hung with watercolors of
canals; come here you primitive father canals on the sofa
she sits spreads like two white gates parted—what a nice
chest you have and here and here and here. He rolls over
and the dry sheet is the touch of her anxious hands, himself tapering tall up from furred velvet, ridges through which
the thick vein strains, and he does what he must with a tight
knowing hand to stop the high hum and make himself slack
for sleep. A woman's sweet froth. Nails her. Passes through the
diamond standing on his head and comes out on the other
side wet. How silly. He feels sorry. Queer where the wet is,
nowhere near where you'd think, on the top sheet instead
of the bottom. He puts his cheek on a fresh patch of pillow.
He tips less, Lucy undone. Her white lines drift off like un-
raveled string. He must sleep; the thought of the far shore
approaching makes a stubborn lump in his glide. Think of
things pleasant. Out of all his remembered life the one place
that comes forward where he can stand without the ground
turning into faces he is treading on is that lot outside the
diner in West Virginia after he went in and had a cup of
coffee the night he drove down there. He remembers the
mountains around him like a ring of cutouts against the
moon-bleached blue of the night sky. He remembers the diner, with its golden windows like the windows of the trolley
cars that used to run from Mt. Judge into Brewer when he
was a kid, and the air, cold but soft with the beginnings of
spring. He hears the footsteps tapping behind him on the
asphalt, and sees the couple running toward their car, hands
linked. One of the red-haired girls that sat inside with her
hair hanging down like seaweed. And it seems right here
that he made the mistaken turning, that he should have
followed, and it seems to him in his disintegrating state that he
did follow, that he *is* following, like a musical note that all
the while it is being held seems to travel though it stays in
the same place. On this note he carries into sleep.

But awakes before dawn being tipped again, frightened on the empty bed, with the fear that Nelson has died. He tries to sneak back into the dream he was having but his nightmare fear dilates and he at last gets up and goes to hear the boy breathe and then urinates with slight pain and returns to a bed whose wrinkles the first stirrings of light are etching into black lines. On this net he lies down and steals the hour left before the boy comes to him, hungry and cold.

On Friday Janice comes home. For the first days the presence of the baby fills the apartment as a little casket of incense fills a chapel. Rebecca June lies in a bassinet of plaited rushes painted white and mounted on a trundle. When Rabbit goes over to look at her, to reassure himself that she is there, he sees her somehow dimly, as if the baby has not gathered to herself the force that makes a silhouette. Her averted cheek, drained of the bright red he glimpsed at the hospital, is mottled gray, yellow, and blue, marbled like the palms of his hands when he is queasy; when Janice suckles Rebecca, yellow spots well up on her breast as if in answer to the fainter shadows of this color in the baby's skin. The union of breast and baby's face makes a globular symmetry to which both he and Nelson want to attach themselves. When Rebecca nurses, Nelson becomes agitated, climbs against them, pokes his fingers into the seam between the baby's lips and his mother's udder and, scolded and pushed away, wanders around the bed intoning, a promise he has heard on television, "Mighty Mouse is on the way." Rabbit himself loves to lie beside them watching Janice manipulate her swollen breasts, the white skin shiny from fullness. She thrusts the thick nipples like a weapon into the blind blistered mouth, that opens and grips with birdy quickness. "Ow!" Janice winces, and then the glands within the baby's lips begin to bubble in tune with her milk-making glands; the symmetry is established; her face relaxes into a downward smile. She holds a diaper against the other breast, mopping the waste milk it exudes in sympathy. Those first days, full of rest and hospital health, she has more milk than the baby takes. Between feedings she leaks; the bodices of all her nighties bear two stiff stains. When he sees her naked, naked all but for the elastic belt that holds her Modess pad in place, her belly shaved and puffed and soft, his whole stomach stirs at the fierce sight of her breasts, braced high by the tension of their milk, jutting from her slim body like glossy green-veined fruit with coarse purple tips. Top-heavy, bandaged, Janice moves gingerly, as if she might spill, jarred. Though with the baby her breasts are used without shame, tools like her hands, before his eyes she is still shy, and quick to cover herself if he watches too openly. But he feels a difference between now and when they first loved, lying side by side on the borrowed bed, his eyes closed, together making the filmy sideways descent into one another. Now, she is intermittenly careless, walks out of the bathroom naked, lets her straps hang down while she burps the baby, seems to accept herself with casual gratitude as a machine, a white, pliant machine for loving, hatching, feeding. He, too, leaks, thick sweet love burdens his chest, and he wants her—just a touch, he knows she's a bleeding wound, but just a touch, just enough to get rid of his milk, give it to her. Though in her ether trance she spoke of making love, she turns away from him in bed, and sleeps with a heaviness that feels sullen. He is too grateful, too proud of her, to disobey. He in a way, this week, worships her.

Eccles comes calling and says he hopes to see them in church. Their debt to him is such that they agree it would be nice of them, at least one of them, to go. The one must be Harry. Janice can't; she has been, by this Sunday, out of the hospital nine days, and, with Harry off at his new job since Monday, is beginning to feel worn out, weak, and abused. Harry is happy to go to Eccles' church. Not merely out of affection for Eccles, though there's that; but because he considers himself happy, lucky, blessed, forgiven, and wants to give thanks. His feeling that there is an unseen world is instinctive, and more of his actions than anyone suspects constitute transactions with it. He dresses in his new gray suit and steps out at quarter of eleven into a broad blue Sunday morning a day before the summer solstice. He always envied those people parading into church across from Ruth's place and now he is one of them. Ahead of him is the first hour in over a week when he won't be with a Springer, either Janice at home or her father at work. The job at the lot is easy enough, if it isn't any work for you to lie. He feels exhausted by midafternoon. You see these clunkers come in with 80,000 miles on them and the pistons so loose the oil just pours through and they get a washing and the speedometer turned back and you hear yourself saying this represents a real bargain, owned by a man with two cars and not 30,000 miles of wear in it. He'll ask forgiveness.

He hates all the people on the street in dirty everyday clothes, advertising their belief that the world arches over a pit, that death is final, that the wandering thread of his feelings leads nowhere. Correspondingly he loves the ones dressed for church; the pressed business suits of portly men give substance and respectability to his furtive sensations of the invisible; the flowers in the hats of their wives seem to begin to make it visible; and their daughters are themselves whole flowers, their bodies each a single flower, petaled in gauze and frills, a bloom of faith, so that even the plainest, sandwiched between their parents with olive complexions and bony arms, walk in Rabbit's eyes glowing with beauty, the beauty of relief, he could kiss their feet in gratitude; they release him from fear. By the time he enters the church he is too elevated with happiness to ask forgiveness. As he kneels in the pew on a red stool that is padded but not enough to keep his weight from pinching his knees painfully, his head buzzes with joy, his blood leaps in his skull, and the few words he frames, "God," "Rebecca," "thank you," bob inconsecutively among senseless eddies of gladness. He is surrounded by people who know God; he has come into a field of flowers. When he sinks back into sitting position the head in front of him takes his eye. A woman in a wide straw hat. Smaller than average with narrow freckled shoulders, probably young, though women tend to look young from the back. The straw hat is so fresh, so pleasing. The way it broadcasts the gentlest tilt of her head, the way it turns the twist of blond hair at the nape of her neck into a kind of peeping secret he alone knows. She *is* young; her neck and shoulders are given a faint, shifting lambency by their coat of fine white hairs, invisible except where the grain lies with the light. He smiles, remembering Tothero talking about women being covered all over with hair. He wonders if Tothero is dead now and quickly prays not. He becomes impatient for the woman to turn so he can see her profile under the rim of the hat, a great woven sun-wheel, garnished with an arc of paper violets. She turns to look down at something beside her; his breath catches; the thinnest crescent of cheek gleams, and is eclipsed again. Something in a pink ribbon pops up beside her shoulder. He stares into the inquisitive, delighted face of little Joyce Eccles. His fingers fumble for the hymnal as the organ heaves into the service; it is Eccles' wife rising within reach of his arm.

Eccles comes down the aisle shuffling behind a flood of acolytes and choristers. Up behind the altar rail he looks absentminded and grouchy, remote and insubstantial and stiff, like a Japanese doll in his vestments. The affected voice, nasal-pious, in which he intones prayers affects Rabbit disagreeably; there is something disagreeable about the whole Episcopal service, with its strenuous ups and downs, its canned petitions, its cursory little chants. He has trouble with the kneeling pad; the small of his back aches; he hooks his elbows over the back of the pew in front of him to keep from falling backward. He misses the familiar Lutheran liturgy, scratched into his heart like a weathered inscription. In this service he blunders absurdly, balked by what seem willful dislocations of worship. He feels too much is made of collecting the money. He scarcely listens to the sermon at all.

It concerns the forty days in the Wilderness and Christ's conversation with the Devil. Does this story have any relevance to *us*, here, now? In the Twentieth Century, in the United States of America. Yes. There exists a sense in which *all* Christians must have conversations with the Devil, must learn his ways, must hear his voice. The tradition behind this legend is very ancient, was passed from mouth to mouth among the early Christians. Its larger significance, its greater meaning, Eccles takes to be this: suffering, deprivation, barrenness, hardship, lack are all an indispensable part of the education, the initiation, as it were, of any of those who would follow Jesus Christ. Eccles wrestles in the pulpit with the squeak in his voice. His eyebrows jiggle as if on fishhooks. It is an unpleasant and strained performance, contorted, somehow; he drives his car with an easier piety. In his robes he seems the sinister priest of a drab mystery. Harry has no taste for the dark, tangled, visceral aspect of Christianity, the *going through* quality of it, the passage *into* death and suffering that redeems and inverts these things, like an umbrella blowing inside out. He lacks the mindful will to walk the straight line of a paradox. His eyes turn toward the light however it glances into his retina.

Lucy Eccles' bright cheek ducks in and out of view under its shield of straw. The child, hidden—all but her ribbon—behind the back of the pew, whispers to her, presumably that he is behind them. Yet the woman never turns her head

directly to see. This needless snub excites him. The most he
gets is her profile; the soft tuck of doubleness in her chin
deepens as she frowns down at the child beside her. She
wears a dress whose narrow blue stripes meet at the seams
in numerous sharp V's. The smart fabric and cut of the cloth
on her shoulders clash with the church yet submit to it;
there is something sexed in her stillness in the church, in her
obedience to its manly, crusted, rigid procedure. He flatters
himself that her true attention radiates backwards at him.
Against the dour patchwork of subdued heads, stained glass,
yellowing memorial plaques on the wall, and laboriously
knobbed and beaded woodwork, her hair and skin and hat
glow singly, their differences in tint like the shades of brilliance within one flame.

So that when the sermon yields to a hymn, and her bright
nape bows to receive the benediction, and the nervous moment
of silence passes, and she stands and faces him, it is anti-
climactic to see her face, with its pointed collection of dots—
eyes and nostrils and freckles and the tight faint dimples that
bring a sarcastic tension to the corners of her mouth. That
she wears a facial expression at all shocks him slightly; the
luminous view he had enjoyed for an hour did not seem
capable of being so swiftly narrowed into one small person.

"Hey. Hi," he says.

"Hello," she says. "You're the last person I ever expected
to see here."

"Why?" He is pleased that she thinks of him as an ultimate.

"I don't know. You just don't seem the institutional type."

He watches her eyes for another wink. He has lost belief
in that first one, weeks ago. She returns his gaze until his
eyes drop. "Hello, Joyce," he says. "How are you?"

The little girl halts and hides behind her mother, who
continues to maneuver down the aisle, walking with small
smooth steps, brightly distributing smiles to the faces of the
sheep. He has to admire her social co-ordination.

At the door Eccles clasps Harry's hand with his broad
grip, a warm grip that tightens at the moment it should
loosen. "It's exhilarating to see you here," he says, hanging
on. Rabbit feels the whole line behind him bunch and push.

"Nice to be here," he says. "Very nice sermon."

Eccles, who has been peering at him with a feverish smile

and a blush that seems apologetic, laughs; the roof of his mouth glimmers a second and he lets go.

Harry hears him tell Lucy, "In about an hour."

"The roast's in now. Do you want it cold or overdone?"

"Overdone," he says. He solemnly takes Joyce's tiny hand and says, "How do you do, Mrs. Pettigrew? How splendid you look this morning!"

Startled, Rabbit turns and sees that the fat lady next in line is startled also. His wife is right, Eccles is indiscreet. Lucy, Joyce behind her, walks up beside him. Her straw hat comes up to his shoulder. "Do you have a car?"

"No. Do you?"

"No. Walk along with us."

"O.K." Her proposition is so bold there must be nothing in it; nevertheless the harpstring in his chest tuned to her starts trembling. Sunshine quivers through the trees; in the streets and along unshaded sections of the pavement it leans down with a broad dry weight. It has lost the grainy milkiness of morning sun. Mica fragments in the pavement glitter; the hoods and windows of hurrying cars smear the air with white reflections. She pulls off her hat and shakes her hair. The church crowd thins behind them. The waxy leaves, freshly thick, of the maples planted between the pavement and curb embower them rhythmically; in the broad gaps of sun her face, his shirt, feel white, white; the rush of motors, the squeak of a tricycle, the touch of a cup and saucer inside a house are sounds conveyed to him as if along a bright steel bar. As they walk along he trembles in light that seems her light.

"How are your wife and baby?" she asks.

"Fine. They're just fine."

"Good. Do you like your new job?"

"Not much."

"Oh. That's a bad sign, isn't it?"

"I don't know. I don't suppose you're supposed to like your job. If you did, then it wouldn't be a job."

"Jack likes his job."

"Then it's not a job."

"That's what he says. He says it's not a job, as I would treat it. But I'm sure you know his lines as well as I do."

He knows she's needling him, but he doesn't feel it, tingling all over anyway. "He and I in some ways I guess are alike," he says.

"I know. I know." Her odd quickness in saying this sets his heart ticking quicker. She adds, "But naturally it's the differences that I notice." Her voice curls dryly into the end of this sentence; her lower lip goes sideways.

What is this? He has a sensation of touching glass. He doesn't know if they are talking about nothing or making code for the deepest meanings. He doesn't know if she's a conscious or unconscious flirt. He always thinks when they meet again he will speak firmly, and tell her he loves her, or something as blunt, and lay the truth bare; but in her presence he is numb; his breath fogs the glass and he has trouble thinking of anything to say and what he does say is stupid. He knows only this: underneath everything, under their minds and their situations, he possesses, like an inherited lien on a distant piece of land, a dominance over her, and that in her grain, in the lie of her hair and nerves and fine veins, she is prepared for this dominance. But between that preparedness and him everything reasonable intervenes. He asks, "Like what?"

"Oh—like the fact that you're not afraid of women."

"Who is?"

"Jack."

"You think?"

"Of course. The old ones, and the teenagers, he's fine with; the ones who see him in his collar. But the others he's very leery of; he doesn't like them. He doesn't really think they even ought to come to church. They bring a smell of babies and bed into it. That's not just in Jack; that's in Christianity. It's really a very neurotic religion."

Somehow, when she fetches out her psychology, it seems so foolish to Harry his own feeling of foolishness leaves him. Stepping down off a high curb, he takes her arm. Mt. Judge, built on its hillside, is full of high curbs difficult for little women to negotiate gracefully. Her bare arm remains cool in his fingers.

"Don't tell that to the parishioners," he says.

"See? You sound just like Jack."

"Is that good or bad?" There. This seems to him to test her bluff. She must say either good or bad, and that will be the fork in the road.

But she says nothing. He feels the effort of self-control this takes; she is accustomed to making replies. They mount the opposite curb and he lets go of her arm awkwardly.

Though he is awkward, there is still this sense of being nestled against a receptive grain, of fitting.

"Mommy?" Joyce asks.

"What?"

"What's rottic?"

"Rottic. Oh. *Neu*rotic. It's when you're a little bit sick in the head."

"Like a cold in the head?"

"Well yes, in a way. It's about that serious. Don't worry about it, sweetie. It's something most everybody is. Except our friend Mr. Angstrom."

The little girl looks up at him across her mother's thighs with a spreading smile of self-conscious impudence. "He's naughty," she says.

"Not very," her mother says.

At the end of the rectory's brick walk a blue tricycle has been abandoned and Joyce runs ahead and mounts it and rides away in her aqua Sunday coat and pink hair ribbon, metal squeaking, spinning ventriloquistic threads of noise into the air. Together they watch the child a moment. Then Lucy asks, "Do you want to come in?" In waiting for his reply, she contemplates his shoulder; her white lids from his angle hide her eyes. Her lips are parted and her tongue, a movement in her jaw tells him, touches the roof of her mouth. In the noon sun her features show sharp and her lipstick looks cracked. He can see the inner lining of her lower lip wet against her teeth. A delayed gust of the sermon, its anguished exhortatory flavor, like a dusty breeze off the desert, sweeps through him, accompanied grotesquely by a vision of Janice's breasts, green-veined, tender. This wicked snip wants to pluck him from them.

"No thanks, really. I can't."

"Oh come on. You've been to church, have a reward. Have some coffee."

"No, look." His words come out soft but somehow big. "You're a doll, but I got this wife now." And his hands, rising from his sides in vague explanation, cause her to take a quick step backward.

"I beg your pardon."

He is conscious of nothing but the little speckled section of her green irises like torn tissue paper around her black pupildots; then he is watching her tight round butt jounce up the walk. "But thanks anyway," he calls in a hollowed, gutless voice. He dreads being hated. She slams the door behind her so hard the knocker clacks by itself on the empty porch.

He walks home blind to the sunlight. Was she mad because he had turned down a proposition, or because he had shown that he thought she had made one? Or was it a mixture of these opposites, that had somehow exposed her to herself? His mother, suddenly caught in some confusion of her own, would turn on the heat that way. In either case he smiles; he feels tall and elegant and potential striding along under the trees in his Sunday suit. Whether spurned or misunderstood, Eccles' wife has jazzed him, and he reaches his apartment clever and cold with lust.

His wish to make love to Janice is like a small angel to which all afternoon tiny lead weights are attached. The baby scrawks tirelessly. It lies in its crib all afternoon and makes an infuriating noise of strain, *hnnnnnah ah ah nnnnh*, a persistent feeble scratching at some interior door. What does it want? Why won't it sleep? He has come home from church carrying something precious for Janice and keeps being screened from giving it to her. The noise spreads fear through the apartment. It makes his stomach ache; when he picks up the baby to burp her he burps himself; the pressure in his stomach keeps breaking and reforming into a stretched bubble as the bubble in the baby doesn't break. The tiny soft marbled body, weightless as paper, goes stiff against his chest and then floppy, its hot head rolling as if it will unjoint from its neck. "Becky, Becky, Becky," he says, "go to sleep. Sleep, sleep, sleep."

The noise makes Nelson fretful and whiny. As if, being closest to the dark gate from which the baby has recently emerged, he is most sensitive to the threat the infant is trying to warn them of. Some shadow invisible to their better-formed senses seems to grab Rebecca as soon as she is left alone. Rabbit puts her down, tiptoes into the living-room; they hold their breath. Then, with a bitter scratch, the membrane of silence breaks, and the wobbly moan begins again, *Nnnh, A-nnnnnih!*

"Oh my God," Rabbit says. "Son of a bitch. Son of a bitch."

Around five in the afternoon, Janice begins to cry. Tears burble down her dark pinched face. "I'm dry," she says. "I'm dry. I just don't have anything to feed her." The baby has been at her breasts repeatedly.

"Forget it," he says. "She'll conk out. Have a drink. There's some old whisky in the kitchen."

"Say; what is this Have a drink routine of yours? I've been trying not to drink. I thought you didn't like me to drink. All afternoon you've been smoking one cigarette after another and saying, 'Have a drink. Have a drink.' "

"I thought it might loosen you up. You're tense as hell."

"I'm no tenser than you are. What's eating you? What's on your mind?"

"What's happened to your milk? Why can't you give the kid enough milk?"

"I've fed her three times in four hours. There's nothing there any more." In a plain, impoverished gesture, she presses her breasts through her dress.

"Well have a drink of something."

"Say what did they tell you at church? 'Go on home and get your wife soused'? You have a drink if that's on your mind."

"I don't need a drink."

"Well you need something. You're the one's upsetting Becky. She was fine all morning until you came home."

"Forget it. Just forget it. Just forget the whole stinking thing."

"Baby *cry!*"

Janice puts her arm around Nelson. "I know it honey. She's hot. She'll stop in a minute."

"Baby hot?"

They listen for a minute and it does not stop; the wild feeble warning, broken by tantalizing gaps of silence, goes on and on. Warned, but not knowing of what, they blunder about restlessly through the wreckage of the Sunday paper, inside the apartment, whose walls sweat like the walls of prison. Outside, the sky holds a wide queenly state, blue through the hours, and Rabbit is further panicked by the thought that on such a day his parents used to take them on long pleasant walks, that they are wasting a beautiful Sunday. But they can't get organized enough to get out. He and Nelson could go but Nelson's strange fright makes him reluctant to leave his mother, and Rabbit, hoping to possess her eventually, hovers near her like a miser near treasure. His lust glues them together.

She feels this and is oppressed by it. "Why don't you go out? You're making the baby nervous. You're making *me* nervous."

"Don't you want a drink?"

"No. *No.* I just wish you'd sit down or stop smoking or rock the baby or something. And stop touching me. It's too hot. I think I should be back at the hospital."

"Do you hurt? I mean down there."

"Well I wouldn't if the baby would stop. I've *fed* her three times. Now I must feed you supper. Ohh. Sundays make me sick. What did you *do* in church that makes you so busy?"

"I'm not busy. I'm trying to be helpful."

"I know. That's what's so unnatural. Your skin smells funny."

"How?"

"Oh I don't know. Stop bothering me."

"I love you."

"Stop it. You can't. I'm not lovable right now."

"You just lie down on the sofa and I'll make some soup."

"No no no. You give Nelson his bath. I'll try to nurse the baby again. Poor thing there's nothing there."

They eat supper late but in broad light; the day is one of the longest of the year. They sip soup by the flickering light of Rebecca's urgent cries; her fragile voice is a thin filament burning with erratic injections of power. But as, amid the stacked dishes on the sink, under the worn and humid furniture, and in the coffin-like hollow of the plaited crib, the shadows begin to strengthen, the grip of the one with which Becky has been struggling all afternoon relaxes, and suddenly she is quiet, leaving behind a solemn guilty peace. They had failed her. A foreigner speaking no English but pregnant with a great painful worry had been placed among them and they had failed her. At last, night itself had swept in and washed her away like a broken piece of rubbish.

"It couldn't have been colic, she's too young for colic," Janice says. "Maybe she was just hungry, maybe I'm out of milk."

"How could that be, you've been like footballs."

She looks at him squinting, sensing what's up. "Well don't think you're going to play." But he thinks he spies a smile there.

Nelson goes to bed as he does when he's sick, willingly,

whimpering. His sister was a drain on him today. Sunk in the pillow, Nelson's brown head looks demure and compact. As the child hungrily roots the bottle in his mouth, Rabbit hovers, seeking what you never find, the expression with which to communicate, to transfer, those fleeting burdens, ominous and affectionate, that are placed upon us and as quickly lifted, like the touch of a brush. Obscure repentance clouds his mouth, a repentance out of time and action, a mourning simply that he exists in a world where the brown heads of little boys sink gratefully into narrow beds sucking bottles of rubber and glass. He cups his hand over the bulge of Nelson's forehead. The boy drowsily tries to brush it off, waggles his head with irritation, and Harry takes it away and goes into the other room.

He persuades Janice to have a drink. He makes it—he doesn't know much about alcoholic things—of half whisky and half water. She says it tastes hateful. But after a while consumes it.

In bed he imagines that he can feel its difference in her flesh. There is that feeling of her body coming into his hand, of fitting his palm, that makes a welcome texture. All under her nightie up to the pit of her throat her body is still for him. They lie sideways, facing each other. He rubs her back, first lightly, then toughly, pushing her chest against his, and gathers such a feel of strength from her pliancy that he gets up on an elbow to be above her. He kisses her dark hard face scented with alcohol. She does not turn her head, but he reads no rejection in this small refusal of motion, that lets him peck away awkwardly at a profile. He stifles his tide of resentment, reschooling himself in her slowness. Proud of his patience, he resumes rubbing her back. Her skin keeps its secret, as does her tongue; is she feeling it? She is mysterious against him, a sullen weight whose chemistry is impervious to ideas, impregnable to their penetration. Is he kindling the spark? His wrist aches. He dares undo the two buttons of her nightie front and lifts the leaf of cloth so a long arc is exposed in the rich gloom of the bed, and her warm breast flattens against the bare skin of his chest. She submits to this maneuver and he is filled with the joyful thought that he has brought her to this fullness. He is a good lover. He relaxes into the warmth of the bed and pulls the bow on his pajama waist. She has been shaved and scratches; he settles lower, on the cotton patch. This unnaturalness, this reminder of her wound makes his confidence delicate, so he is totally destroyed when her voice—her thin, rasping, dumb-girl's voice —says by his ear, "Harry. Don't you know I want to go to sleep?"

"Well why didn't you tell me before?"

"I didn't know. I didn't know."

"Didn't know what?"

"I didn't know what you were doing. I thought you were just being nice."

"So this isn't nice."

"Well, it's not nice when I can't *do* anything."

"You can do *some*thing."

"No I can't. Even if I wasn't all tired and confused from Rebecca's crying all day I can't. Not for six weeks. You know that."

"Yeah, I know, but I thought—" He's terribly embarrassed.

"What did you think?"

"I thought you might love me anyway."

After a pause she says, "I *do* love you."

"Just a touch, Jan. Just let me touch you."

"Can't you go to sleep?"

"No I can't. I can't. I love you too much. Just hold still."

It would have been easy a minute ago to get it over with but all this talk has taken the fine point off. It's a bad contact and her stubborn limpness makes it worse; she's killing it by making him feel sorry for her and ashamed and foolish. The whole sweet thing is just sweat and work and his ridiculous inability to finish it against the dead hot wall of her belly. She pushes him back. "You're just using me," she says. "It feels horrible."

"Please, baby. I'm almost there."

"It feels so cheap."

Her daring to say this infuriates him; he realizes she hasn't had it for three months and in all that time has gotten an unreal idea of what love is. She exaggerates its importance, has imagined it into something rare and precious she's entitled to half of when all he wants is to get rid of it so he can move on, on into sleep, down the straight path, for her sake. It's for her sake.

"Roll over," he says.

"I love you," she says with relief, misunderstanding, thinking he's dismissing her. She touches his face in farewell and turns her back.

He scruches down and fits himself between her buttocks, cool. It's beginning to work, steady, warm, when she twists her head and says over her shoulder, "Is this a trick your whore taught you?"

He thumps her shoulder with his fist and gets out of bed and his pajama bottoms fall down. The night breeze filters in through the window screen. She turns on her back into the center of the bed and explains out of her dark face, "I'm not your whore, Harry."

"Damn it," he says, "that was the first thing I've asked from you since you came home."

"You've been wonderful," she says.

"Thanks."

"Where are you going?"

He is putting on his clothes. "I'm going out. I've been cooped up in this damn hole all day."

"You went out this morning."

He finds his suntans and puts them on. She asks, "Why can't you try to imagine how I *feel*? I've just had a baby."

"I can. I can but I don't want to, it's not the thing, the thing is how *I* feel. And I feel like getting out."

"Don't. Harry. Don't."

"You can just lie there with your precious ass. Kiss it for me."

"Oh for God's sake," she cries, and flounces under the covers, and smashes her face down into her pillow.

Even this late he might have stayed if she hadn't accepted defeat by doing this. His need to love her is by, so there's no reason to go. He's stopped loving her at last so he might as well lie down beside her and go to sleep. But she asks for it, lying there in a muddle sobbing, and outside, down in the town, a motor guns and he thinks of the air and the trees and streets stretching bare under the streetlamps and goes out the door.

The strange thing is she falls asleep soon after he goes; she's been used to sleeping alone lately and it's a physical relief not having him in bed kicking his hot legs and twisting the sheets into ropes. That business of his with her bottom

made her stitches ache and she sinks down over the small
pain all feathers. Around four in the morning Becky cries
her awake and she gets up; her nightie taps her body lightly.
Her skin feels unnaturally sensitive as she walks about. She
changes the baby and lies down on the bed to nurse her. As
Becky takes the milk it's as if she's sucking a hollow place
into her mother's body; Harry hasn't come back. By this time
if he just went out to cool off he would be back.

The baby keeps slipping off the nipple because she can't
keep her mind on her; a taste like dry toast keeps touching
her lips; she keeps listening for Harry's key to scratch at the
door.

Mother's neighbors will laugh their heads off if she loses
him again, she doesn't know why she should think of Mother's neighbors except that all the time she was home Mother
kept reminding her of how they sneered and there was always that with Mother the feeling she was dull and plain
and a disappointment, and she thought when she got a husband it would be all over, all that. She would be a woman
with a house on her own. And she thought when she gave
this baby her name it would settle her mother but instead
it brings her mother against her breast with her blind mouth
poor thing and she feels she's lying on top of a pillar where
everyone in the town can see she is alone. She feels cold.
The baby won't stay on the nipple nothing will hold to her.

She gets up and walks around the room with the baby on
her shoulder patting to get the air up and the baby poor thing
so floppy and limp keeps sliding and trying to dig its little
boneless legs into her to hold tight and the nightie blown by
the breeze keeps touching her calves the backs of her legs
her ass as he called it. Makes you feel filthy they don't even
have decent names for parts of you.

If there would be a scratch at the lock and he would come
in the door he could do whatever he wanted with her have
any part of her if he wanted what did she care that was
marriage. But when he tried tonight it just seemed so unfair,
she still aching and him sleeping with that prostitute all those
weeks and him just saying Roll over in that impatient voice
like it was just something he wanted to have done with and
who was she not to let him after she had let him run off
what right had she to any pride? Any self-respect. That was
just why she had to have some because he didn't think she
dared have any after she let him run off that was the funny

thing it was his bad deed yet she was supposed not to have any pride afterwards to just be a pot for his dirt. When he did that to her back it was so practiced and reminded her of all those weeks he was off doing what he pleased and she was just helpless Mother and Peggy feeling sorry for her and everybody else laughing she couldn't bear it.

And then his going off to church and coming back full of juice. What right did he have to go to church? What did he and God talk about behind the backs of all these women exchanging winks that was the thing she minded if they'd just think about love when they make it instead of thinking about whatever they do think about think about whatever they're going to do whenever they've got rid of this little hot clot that's bothering them. You can feel in their fingers if they're thinking about you and tonight Harry was at first and that's why she let him go on it was like lying there in an envelope of yourself his hands going around you but then he began to be rough and it made her mad to feel him thinking about himself what a good job he was doing sucking her along and not at all any more about how she felt exhausted and aching, poking his thing at her belly like some elbow. It was so *rude*.

Just plain rude. Here he called her dumb when he was too dumb to have any idea of how she felt any idea of how his going off had changed her and how he must nurse her back not just wade in through her skin without having any idea of what was there. That was what made her panicky ever since she was little this thing of nobody knowing how you felt and whether nobody could know or nobody cared she had no idea. She didn't like her skin, never had it was too dark made her look like an Italian even if she never did get pimples like some of the others girls and then in those days both working at Kroll's she on the salted nuts when Harry would lie down beside her on Mary Hannacher's bed the silver wallpaper he liked so much and close his eyes it seemed to melt her skin and she thought it was all over she was with somebody. But then they were married (she felt awful about being pregnant before but Harry had been talking about marriage for a year and anyway laughed when she told him and said Great she was terribly frightened and he said Great and lifted her put his arms around under her bottom and lifted her like you would a child he could be so wonderful when you didn't expect it in a way it seemed important that you didn't expect it there was so much nice in him she couldn't explain to anybody she had been so frightened about being pregnant and he made her be proud) they were married and she was still little clumsy dark-complected Janice Springer and her husband was a conceited lunk who wasn't good for anything in the world Daddy said and the feeling of being alone would melt a little with a drink. It wasn't so much that it dissolved the lump as made the edges nice and rainbowy.

She's been walking around patting the baby until her wrists and ankles hurt and poor tiny Rebecca is asleep with her legs around the breast that still has its milk in it. She wonders if she should try to make her take some and thinks no if she can sleep let her sleep. She lifts the poor tiny thing weighing nothing off the sweaty place on her shoulder and lays her down in the cool shadows of the crib. Already the night is dimming, dawn comes early to the town facing east on its mountainside. Janice lies down on the bed but the sense of light growing beside her on the white sheets keeps her awake. Pleasantly awake at first; the coming of morning is so clean and makes her feel like she did through the second month Harry was hiding. Mother's great Japanese cherry tree blooming below her window and the grass coming up and the ground smelling wet and ashy and warm. She had thought things out and was resigned to her marriage being finished. She would have her baby and get a divorce and never get married again. She would be like a kind of nun she had just seen that beautiful picture with Audrey Hepburn. And if he came back it would be equally simple: she would forgive him everything and stop her drinking which annoyed him so though she didn't see why and they would be very nice and simple and clean together because he would have gotten everything out of his system and love her so because she had forgiven him and she would know now how to be a good wife. She had gone to church every week and talked with Peggy and prayed and had come to understand that marriage wasn't a refuge it was a sharing and she and Harry would start to share everything. And then, it was a miracle, these last two weeks had been that way.

And then Harry had suddenly put his whore's filthiness into it and asked her to love it and the unfairness makes her cry aloud softly, as if startled by something in the empty bed with her.

The last hours are like some narrow turn in a pipe that she can't force her thought through. Again and again she comes up to the sound of him saying "Roll over" and can't squeeze through it, can't not feel panicked and choked. She gets out of bed and wanders around with her one tight breast the nipple stinging and goes into the kitchen in her bare feet and sniffs the empty glass Harry made her drink whisky out of. The smell is dark and raw and soft and deep, and she thinks maybe a sip will cure her insomnia. Make her sleep until the scratch at the door awakens her and she sees his big white body ramble in sheepishly and she can say Come to bed, Harry it's all right, do me, I want to share it, I really want it, really.

She puts just an inch of whisky in, and not much water because it would take too long to drink, and no ice cubes because the noise of the tray might wake up the children. She takes this dose to the window and stands looking down past the three tar roofs at the sleeping town. Already a few kitchen and bedroom lights show pale here and there. A car, its headlights dull disks that do not throw beams into the thinning darkness, eases down Wilbur toward the center of town. The highway, half-hidden by the silhouettes of houses, like a river between banks of trees, this early swishes with traffic. She feels the workday approaching like an army of light, feels the dark ridged houses beneath her as potentially stirring, waking, opening like castles to send forth their men, and regrets that her own husband is unable to settle into the nationwide rhythm of which one more beat is about to sound. Why him? What was so precious about him? Anger at Harry begins to bloom, and to stifle it she drains the glass and turns in the dawn; everything in the apartment is a shade of brown. She feels lopsided; the pressure in the unused breast pulls her.

She goes into the kitchen and makes another drink, stronger than the first, thinking that after all it's about time she had a little fun. She hadn't had a moment to herself since she came back from the hospital. The thought of fun makes her movements quick and airy; she fairly runs in her bare feet across the gritty carpet back to the window, as if to a show arranged just for her. Mounted in her white gown above everything she can see, she touches her fingers to her tight breast so that the milk starts to leak, stains the white cloth with slow warmth.

The wetness slides down her front and turns cold in the air by the window. Her varicose veins ache from standing. She goes and sits in the moldy brown armchair and is sickened by just the angle at which the mottled wall meets the pasty ceiling. The angle tips her, muddles up and down. The pattern on the wallpaper swarms; the flowers are brown spots that swim in the murk and chase each other and merge hungrily. It's hateful. She turns her face away and studies the calm green globe of the dead television set. The front of her nightie is drying; the crusty stiffness scratches her. Baby book said keep nipples clean, soap gently: germs enter scratches. She sets the drink on the round chair arm and stands up and pulls her nightgown over her head and sits down again. It gives her nakedness a mossy hug. She puts the bunched nightgown in her lap on top of her Modess pad and belt and pulls the footstool over cleverly with her toes and rests her ankles on it and admires her legs. She always thought she had good legs. Straight small nice even thighs. She does have good legs. Their tapering wavering silhouettes are white against the deep shadow of the rug. The dim light erases the blue veins left from carrying Becky. She wonders if her legs are going to go as bad as Mother's. She tries to imagine the ankles as thick as the knees and they do seem to swell. She reaches down to reassure herself by feeling the ankles' hard narrow bones and her shoulder knocks the whisky glass off the chair arm. She jumps up, startled to feel the air embrace her bare skin, cool space sweep around her wobbly, knobbed body. She giggles. If Harry could see her now. Luckily there wasn't much in the glass. She tries to walk boldly into the kitchen with no clothes on like a whore but the sense of somebody watching her, which began when she stood at the window and made her milk flow, is too strong; she ducks into the bedroom and wraps the blue bathrobe around her and then mixes the drink. There is still a third of the bottle left. Tiredness makes the rims of her lids dry but she has no desire to go back to bed. She has a horror of it because Harry should be there. This absence is a hole that widens and she pours a little whisky into it but it's not enough and when she goes to the window for the third time it is now light enough to see how drab everything is. Someone has smashed a bottle on one of the tar roofs. The gutters of Wilbur Street are full of mud that washes down from the new development. While she looks the streetlights, great pale strings of them, go off in patches. She pictures the man at the power plant pulling the switches, little and gray and hunchbacked and very sleepy. She goes to the television set and the band of light that suddenly flares in the green rectangle sparks joy in her breast but it's still too early, the light is just a speckling senseless brightness and the sound is nothing but static. As she sits there watching the blank radiance a feeling of some other person standing behind her makes her snap her head around several times. She is very quick about it but there is always a space she can't see which the other person could dodge into if he's there. It's the television has called him into the room but when she turns off the set she starts to cry immediately. She sits there with her face in her hands, her tears crawling out between her fingers and her sobs shaking through the apartment. She doesn't stifle them because she wants to wake somebody; she is sick of being alone. In the bleaching light the walls and furniture are clear and regain their colors and the merging brown spots have gone into herself.

She goes and looks at the baby, the poor thing lying there snuffling the crib sheet, its little hands twitching up by its ears, and reaches down and strokes its hot membranous head and lifts it out its legs all wet and takes it to nurse in the armchair that looks toward the window. The sky beyond is a pale smooth blue that looks painted on the panes. There is nothing to see but sky from this chair, they might be a hundred miles up, in the basket of a great balloon. A door on the other side of the partition slams and her heart leaps but then of course it's just another tenant maybe grumpy Mr. Cappello going off to work, the stairs rumbling reluctantly. This wakes Nelson and for a time her hands are full. In making breakfast for them she breaks an orange-juice glass, it just drifts away from her thumb into the brittle sink. When she bends over Nelson to serve him his Rice Krispies he looks up at her and wrinkles his nose; he smells sadness and its familiar odor makes him timid with her. "Daddy go away?" He's such a good boy saying this to make it easy on her, all she has to do is answer "Yes."

"No," she says. "Daddy went out to work early this morning before you got up. He'll be home for supper like he always is."

The child frowns at her and then parrots with sharp hope, "Like always is?"

Worry has stretched his head high, so his neck seems a stem too thin to support the ball of his skull with its broad whorl of pillow-mussed hair. "Daddy will be home," she repeats. Having taken on herself the burden of lying, she needs a little more whisky for support. There is a murk inside her which she must tint a bright color or collapse. She takes the dishes out to the kitchen but they slide so in her hands she doesn't try to wash them. She thinks she must change out of her bathrobe into a dress but in taking the steps into the bedroom forgets her purpose and begins making the bed. But something whose presence she feels on the wrinkled bed frightens her so that she draws back and goes into the other room to be with the children. It's as if in telling them Harry would be back as normal she's put a ghost in the apartment. But the other person does not feel like Harry, it feels like a burglar, a teasing burglar dancing from room to room ahead of her.

When she picks up the baby again she feels its wet legs and thinks of changing it but cleverly realizes she is drunk and might stab it with the pins. She is very proud of thinking this through and tells herself to stay away from the bottle so she can change the baby in an hour. She puts good Becky in her crib and, wonderfully, doesn't hear her cry once. She and Nelson sit and watch the tail end of Dave Garroway and then a program about Elizabeth and her husband entertaining a friend of his who is always going away on camping trips being a bachelor and turns out to be a better cook than Elizabeth. For some reason watching this makes her so nervous that just out of television-watching habit she goes to the kitchen and makes herself a little drink, mostly ice cubes, just to keep sealed shut the great hole that is threatening to pull open inside of her again. She takes just a sip and it's like a swallow of blue light that makes everything clear. She must just arch over this one little gap and at the end of the day after work Harry will be back and no one will ever know, no one will laugh at Mother. She feels like a rainbow arching protectively over Harry, who seems infinitely small under her, like some children's toy. She thinks how good it would be to play with Nelson;

it is bad for him to watch television all morning. She turns it off and finds his coloring book and crayons and they sit on the rug and color opposite pages.

Janice repeatedly hugs him and talks to make him laugh and is very happy doing the actual coloring. In high school, art was the one subject she wasn't afraid of and she always got a B. She smiles in the delight of coloring her page, a barnyard, so well, of feeling the little rods of color in her fingers make such neat parallel strokes and her sons's small body intent and hard beside hers. Her bathrobe fans out on the floor around her and her body seems beautiful and broad. She moves to get her shadow off the page and sees that she has colored one chicken partly green and not stayed within the lines at all well and her page is ugly; she starts to cry; it is so un*fair,* as if someone standing behind her without understanding a thing has told her her coloring is ugly. Nelson looks up and his quick face slides wide and he cries, "Don't! Don't, Mommy!" She prepares to have him pitch forward into her lap but instead he jumps up and runs with a lopsided almost crippled set of steps into the bedroom and falls on the floor kicking.

She pushes herself up from the floor with a calm smile and goes into the kitchen, where she thinks she left her drink. The important thing is to complete the arch to the end of the day, to be a protection for Harry, and it's silly not to have the one more sip that will make her long enough. She comes out of the kitchen and tells Nelson, "Mommy's stopped crying, sweet. It was a joke. Mommy's not crying. Mommy's very happy. She loves you very much." His rubbed stained face watches her. Like a stab from behind the phone rings. Still carrying that calmness she answers it. "Hello?"

"Darling? It's Daddy."

"Oh, Daddy!" Joy just streams through her lips.

He pauses. "Baby, is Harry sick? It's after eleven and he hasn't shown up at the lot yet."

"No, he's fine. We're all fine."

There is another pause. Her love for her father flows toward him through the silent wire. She wishes the conversation would go on forever. He asks, "Well, where is he? Is he there? Let me speak to him, Janice."

"Daddy, he's not here. He went out early this morning."

"Where did he go? He's not at the lot." She's heard him say the word "lot" a million times it seems; he says it like no other man; it's dense and rich from his lips, as if all the world is concentrated in it. All the good things of her growing up, her clothes, her toys, their house, came from the "lot."

She is inspired; car-sale talk is one thing she knows. "He went out early, Daddy, to show a station wagon to a prospect who had to go to work or something. Wait. Let me think. He said the man had to go to Allentown early this morning. He had to go to Allentown and Hary had to show him a station wagon. Everything's all right, Daddy. Harry loves his job."

The third pause is the longest. "Darling. Are you sure he's not there?"

"Daddy, aren't you funny? He's not here. See?" As if it has eyes she thrusts the receiver into the air of the empty room. It's meant as a daughter's impudent joke but unexpectedly just holding her arm out makes her feel sick. When she brings the receiver back to her ear he is saying in a remote ticky voice, "darling. All right. Don't worry about anything. Are the children there with you?"

Feeling dizzy, she hangs up. This is a mistake, but she thinks on the whole she's been clever enough. She thinks she deserves a drink. The brown liquid spills down over the smoking ice cubes and doesn't stop when she tells it to; she snaps the bottle angrily and blot-shaped drops topple into the sink. She goes into the bathroom with the glass and comes out with her hands empty and a taste of toothpaste in her mouth. She remembers looking into the mirror and patting her hair and from that she went to brushing her teeth. With Harry's toothbrush.

She discovers herself making lunch, like looking down into a food advertisement in a magazine, bacon strips sizzling in a pan at the end of a huge blue arm. She sees the BB's of fat flying in the air like the pretty spatter of a fountain in a park and wonders at how quick their arcs are. They prick her hand on the handle and she turns the purple gas down. She pours a glass of milk for Nelson and pulls some leaves off of a head of lettuce and sets them on a yellow plastic plate and eats a handful herself. She thinks she won't set a place for herself and then thinks she will because maybe this trembling in her stomach is hunger and gets another plate and stands there holding it with two hands in front of her chest wondering why Daddy was so sure Harry was here. There *is* another person in the apartment she knows but it's not Harry and the person has no business here anyway and she determines to ignore him and continues setting lunch with a slight stiffness operating in her body. She holds on to everything until it is well on the table.

Nelson says the bacon is greasy and asks again if Daddy go away and his complaining about the bacon that she was so clever and brave to make at all annoys her so that after his twentieth refusal to eat even a bit of lettuce she reaches over and slaps his rude face. The stupid child can't even cry he just sits there and stares and sucks in his breath again and again and finally does burst forth. But luckily she is equal to the situation, very calm, she sees the unreason of his whole attempt and refuses to be bullied. With the smoothness of a single great wave she makes his bottle, takes him by the hand, oversees his urinating, and settles him in bed. Still shaking with the aftermath of sobs, he roots the bottle in his mouth and she is certain from the glaze on his watchful eyes that he is locked into the channel to sleep. She stands by the bed, surprised by her stern strength.

The telephone rings again, angrier than the first time, and as she runs to it, running because she does not want Nelson disturbed, she feels her strength ebb and a brown staleness washes up the back of her throat. "Hello."

"Janice." Her mother's voice, even and harsh. "I just got back from shopping in Brewer and your father's been trying to reach me all morning. He thinks Harry's gone again. Is he?"

Janice closes her eyes and says, "He went to Allentown."

"What would he do there?"

"He's going to sell a car."

"Don't be silly. Janice. Are you all right?"

"What do you mean?"

"Have you been drinking?"

"Drinking what?"

"Now don't worry, I'm coming right over."

"Mother, don't. Everything is fine. I just put Nelson into his nap."

"I'll have a bite to eat out of the icebox and come right over. You lie down."

"Mother, *please* don't come over."

"Janice, now don't talk back. When did he go?"

"Stay away, Mother. He'll be back tonight." She listens and adds, "And stop crying."

Her mother says, "Yes you say stop when you keep bringing us all into disgrace. The first time I thought it was all his fault but I'm not so sure any more. Do you hear? I'm not so sure."

Hearing this speech has made the sliding sickness in her so steep she wonders if she can keep her grip on the phone. "Don't come over, Mother," she begs. "Please."

"I'll have a bite of lunch and be over in twenty minutes. You go to bed."

Janice replaces the receiver and looks around her with horror. The apartment is horrible. Coloring books on the floor, glasses, the bed unmade, dirty dishes everywhere. She runs to where she and Nelson crayoned, and tests bending over. She drops to her knees, and the baby begins to cry. Panicked with the double idea of not disturbing Nelson and of concealing Harry's absence, she runs to the crib and nightmarishly finds it smeared with orange mess. "Damn you, damn you," she moans to Rebecca, and lifts the little filthy thing out and wonders where to carry her. She takes her to the armchair and biting her lips unpins the diaper. "You little pig," she murmurs, feeling that the sound of her voice is holding off the other person who is gathering in the room. She takes the soaked daubed diaper to the bathroom and drops it in the toilet and dropping to her knees fumbles the bathtub plug into its hole. She pulls on both faucets as wide as they will go, knowing from experiment that both opened wide make the right tepid mixture. The water bangs out of the faucet like a fist. She notices the glass of watery whiskey she left on the top of the toilet and takes a long stale swallow and then puzzles how to get it off her hands. All the while Rebecca screams. As if she has mind enough to know she's filthy. Janice takes the glass with her and spills it on the rug with her knee while she strips the baby of its nightie and sweater. She carries the sopping clothes to the television set and puts them on top while she drops to her knees and tries to stuff the crayons back into their box. Her head aches with all this jarring up and down. She takes the crayons to the kitchen table and dumps the uneaten bacon and lettuce into the paper bag under the sink but the mouth of the bag leans partly closed and the lettuce falls behind into the darkness in back of the can and she crouches down with her head pounding to try to see it or get it with her fingers and is unable. Her knees sting from so much kneeling. She gives up and to her surprise sits flatly on a kitchen chair and looks at the gaudy soft noses of the crayons poking out of the Crayola box. Hide the whisky. Her body doesn't move for a second but when it does she sees her hands with the little lines of dirt on her fingernails put the whisky bottle into a lower cabinet with some old shirts of Harry's she was saving for rags he would never wear a mended shirt not that she was any good at mending them. She shuts the door, it bangs but doesn't catch, and on the edge of linoleum beside the sink the cork cap of the whisky bottle stares at her like a little top hat. She puts it in the garbage bag. Now the kitchen is clean enough. In the living-room Rebecca is lying naked in the fuzzy armchair with her belly puffing out sideways to yell and her lumpy curved legs clenched and red. Janice's other baby was a boy and it still seems unnatural to her, between the girl's legs, those two little buns of fat instead of a boy's triple business (when the doctor had Nelson circumcised Harry hadn't wanted him to he hadn't been and thought it was unnatural she had laughed at him he was so mad). The baby's face goes red with each squall and Janice closes her eyes and thinks how really horrible it is of Mother to come and ruin her day just to make sure she's lost Harry again. She can't wait a minute to find out and this awful baby can't wait a minute and there are the clothes on top of the television set. She takes them into the bathroom and drops them into the toilet on top of the diaper and turns off the faucets. The wavery gray line of the water is almost up to the lip of the tub. On the skin quick wrinkles wander and under it a deep mass waits colorless. She wishes she could have the bath. Brimful of composure she returns to the living-room. She tips too much trying to dig the tiny rubbery thing out of the chair so drops to her knees and scoops Rebecca into her arms and carries her into the bathroom held sideways against her breasts. She is proud to be carrying this to completion; the baby will be clean. She drops gently to her knees by the big calm tub and does not expect her sleeves to be soaked. The water wraps around her forearms like two large hands; under her amazed eyes the pink baby sinks down like a gray stone.

With a sob of protest she grapples for the child but the water pushes up at her hands, her bathrobe tends to float, and the slippery thing squirms in the sudden opacity. She has a hold, feels a heartbeat on her thumb, and then loses it, and the skin of the water leaps with pale refracted oblongs that she can't seize the solid of; it is only a moment, but a moment dragged out in a thicker time. Then she has Becky squeezed in her hands and it is all right.

She lifts the living thing into air and hugs it against her sopping chest. Water pours off them onto the bathroom tiles. The little weightless body flops against her neck and a quick look of relief at the baby's face gives a fantastic clotted impression. A contorted memory of how they give artificial respiration pumps Janice's cold wet arms in frantic rhythmic hugs; under her clenched lids great scarlet prayers arise, wordless, monotonous, and she seems to be clasping the knees of a vast third person whose name, Father, Father, beats against her head like physical blows. Though her wild heart bathes the universe in red, no spark kindles in the space between her arms; for all of her pouring prayers she doesn't feel the faintest tremor of an answer in the darkness against her. Her sense of the third person with them widens enormously, and she knows, knows, while knocks sound at the door, that the worst thing that has ever happened to any woman in the world has happened to her.

JACK comes back from the telephone a shocking color.

"Janice Angstrom has accidentally drowned their baby."

"How *could* she?"

"I don't know. I'm afraid she was drunk. She's unconscious now."

"Where was *he?*"

"Nobody knows. I'm supposed to find him. That was Mrs. Springer."

He sits down in the great walnut-armed chair that had been his father's and Lucy realizes with resentment that her husband is middle-aged. His hair is thinning, his skin is dry, he looks exhausted. She cries, "Why must you spend your life chasing after that worthless heel?"

"He's not worthless. I love him."

"You love him. That's sickening. Oh I think that's sickening, Jack. Why don't you try loving me, or your children?"

"I do."

"You *don't,* Jack. Let's face it, you don't. You couldn't bear to love anybody who might return it. You're afraid of that, aren't you? Aren't you afraid?"

They had been drinking tea in the library when the phone rang and he picks his empty cup off the floor between his feet and looks into the center. "Don't be fancy, Lucy," he says. "I feel too sick."

"You feel sick, yes, and I feel sick. I've felt sick ever since you got involved with that animal. He's not even in your church."

"Any Christian is in my church."

"Christian! If he's a Christian thank God I'm not one. Christian. Kills his baby and that's what you call him."

"He didn't kill the baby. He wasn't there, it was an accident."

"Well he as good as did. Runs off and sends his idiot wife on a bender. You never should have brought them back together. The girl had adjusted and something like this never would have happened."

Eccles blinks; shock has put a great analytic distance between him and things. He's rather impressed by the way she has reconstructed what must have happened. He wonders a little why her speech is so vengeful. "Heel" was a strange word for her to have used. "So you're saying I really killed the baby," he says.

"Of course not. I didn't mean to say that at all."

"No. I think you're probably right," he says, and lifts himself out of the chair. He goes into the hall to the telephone and again draws out of his wallet the number written in pencil below the faint name, Ruth Leonard. The number worked once but this time the mouse of electricity gnaws at the remote membrance of metal in vain. He lets it ring twelve times, hangs up, dials the number again, and hangs up after seven rings. When he returns to the study Lucy is ready for him.

"Jack, I'm sorry. I didn't mean to suggest you were responsible at all. Of course you're not. Don't be silly."

"It's all right, Lucy. The truth shouldn't be able to hurt us." These words are a shadow of his idea that if Faith is true, then nothing that is true is in conflict with Faith.

"Oh mercy, the martyr. Well I can see it's an idea you have that it's your fault and nothing I can say will change your mind. I'll save my breath."

He keeps silent to help her save her breath but after a moment she asks in a softer voice, "Jack?"

"What?"

"Why *were* you so anxious to get them back together?"

He picks the slice of lemon up from the saucer of his teacup and tries to squint through it into the room. "Marriage is a sacrament," he says.

He half-expects her to laugh but instead she asks earnestly, "Even a bad marriage?"

"Yes."

"But that's ridiculous. That's not common sense."

"I don't believe in common sense," he says. "If it'll make you happy, I don't believe in anything."

"That doesn't make me happy," she says. "You're being psychopathic. But I'm sorry this has happened." She takes away their cups and swishes into the kitchen and leaves him alone. Afternoon shadows gather like cobwebs on the walls of books, most of them belonging not to him but to his predecessor in the rectory, the noble and much admired Dr. Langhorne. He sits waiting numbly but not too long. The phone rings. He hurries to answer it before Lucy can; through the window above the sill where the phone rests he can see his neighbor unpinning her wash from the line.

"Hello?"

"Hey, Jack? This is Harry Angstrom. I hope I'm not interrupting anything."

"No, you're not."

"You don't have any old ladies sitting around sewing or anything, do you?"

"No."

"Why, I've been trying to call my apartment and nobody answers and I'm kind of nervous about it. I didn't spend last night there and I'm getting sort of a prickly feeling. I want to go home but I want to know if Janice has done anything like call the cops or anything. Do you know?"

"Harry, where are you?"

"Oh, at some drugstore in Brewer."

The neighbor has bundled the last sheet into her arms and Jack's sight leans on the bare white line. One of the uses society seems to have for him is to break tragic news and the cave of his mouth goes dry as he braces for the familiar duty. *No man, having put his hand to the plough ...* He keeps his eyes wide open so he will not seem too close to the presence by his ear. "I guess to save time I'd better tell you over the phone," he begins. "Harry. A terrible thing has happened to us."

When you twist a rope and keep twisting, it begins to lose its straight shape and suddenly a kink, a loop leaps up in it. Harry has such a hard loop in himself after he hears Eccles out. He doesn't know what he says to Eccles; all he is conscious of is the stacks of merchandise in jangling packages he can see through the windows of the phone-booth door. On the drugstore wall there is a banner bearing in red the one word PARADICHLOROBENZENE. All the while he is trying to understand Eccles he is rereading this word, trying to see where it breaks, wondering if it can be pronounced. Right when he finally understands, right at the pit of his life, a fat woman comes up to the counter and pays for two boxes of Kleenex. He steps into the sunshine outside the drugstore swallowing, to keep the loop from rising in his body and choking him. It's a hot day, the first of summer; the heat comes up off the glittering pavement into the faces of pedestrians, strikes them sideways off the store windows and hot stone façades. In the white light faces wear the American expression, eyes squinting and mouths sagging open in a scowl, that makes them look as if they are about to say something menacing and cruel. In the street under glaring hardtops drivers bake in stalled traffic. Above, milk hangs in a sky that seems too exhausted to clear. Harry waits at a corner with some red sweating shoppers for a Mt. Judge bus, number 16A; when it hisses to a stop it is already packed. He hangs from a steel bar in the rear, fighting to keep from doubling up with the kink inside. Curved posters advertise filtered cigarettes and sun-tan lotion and an international charity.

He had ridden one of these buses last night into Brewer and gone to Ruth's apartment but there was no light on and nobody answered his ring, though there was a dim light behind the frosted glass lettered F. X. Pelligrini. He sat around on the steps, looking down at the delicatessen until the lights went out and then looking at the bright church window. When the lights went out behind that he felt cramped and hopeless and thought of going home. He wandered up to Weiser Street and looked down at all the lights and the great sunflower and couldn't see a bus and kept walking, over to the south side, and became afraid of getting knifed and robbed and went into a low-looking hotel and bought a room. He didn't sleep very well with a neon tube with a taped connection buzzing outside and some woman laughing and woke up early enough to go back to Mt. Judge and get a suit and go to work but something held him back. Something held him back all day. He tries to think of what it was because whatever it was murdered his daughter. Wanting to see Ruth again was some of it but it was clear after he went around to her address in the morning that she wasn't there probably off to Atlantic City with some madman and still he wandered around Brewer, going in and out of department stores with music piping from the walls and eating a hot dog at the five and ten and hesitating outside a movie house but not going in and keeping an eye out for Ruth. He kept expecting to see her shoulders that he kissed jostle out of a crowd and the ginger hair he used to beg to unpin shining on the other side of a rack of birthday cards. But it was a city of over a hundred thousand and the odds were totally against him and anyway there was tons of time he could find her another day. No, what kept him in the city despite the increasing twisting inside that told him something was wrong back home, what kept him walking through the cold air breathed from the doors of movie houses and up and down between counters of perfumed lingerie thinking of all the delicate ass these veils would flavor the little tits to be tucked into these cups and jewelry and salted nuts poor old Jan and up into the park along paths he walked once with Ruth to watch from under a horse-chestnut tree five mangy kids play cat with a tennis ball and a broomstick and then finally back down Weiser to the drugstore he called from, what kept him walking was the idea that somewhere he'd find an opening. For what made him mad at Janice wasn't so much that she was in the right for once and he was wrong and stupid but the closed feeling of it, the feeling of being closed in. He had gone to church and brought back this little flame and had nowhere to put it on the dark damp walls of the apartment, so it had flickered and gone out. And the feeling that he wouldn't always be able to produce this flame. What held him back all day was the feeling that somewhere there was something better for him than listening to babies cry and cheating people in used-car lots and it's this feeling he tries to kill, right there on the bus, he grips the chrome bar and leans far over two women with white pleated blouses and laps of packages and closes his eyes and tries to kill it. The kink in his stomach starts to take the form of nausea and he clings to the icy bar bitterly as the bus swings around the mountain. He gets off, in a sweat, blocks too soon. Here in Mt. Judge the shadows have begun to grow deep, the sun baking Brewer rides the crest of the mountain, and his sweat congeals, shortening his breath. He runs to keep his body occupied, to joggle his mind blank. Past a dry-cleaning plant with a little pipe hissing steam at the side. Through the oil and rubber smells riding above the asphalt pond around the red pumps of an Esso station. Past the Mt. Judge town-hall lawn and the World War II honor roll with the name plaques crumbled and blistered behind glass.

When he gets to the Springers' house Mrs. comes to the door and shuts it in his face. But he knows from the olive Buick parked outside that Eccles is in there and in a little while Jack comes to the door and lets him in. He says softly in the dim hall, "Your wife has been given a sedative and is asleep."

"The baby . . ."

"The undertaker has her."

Rabbit wants to cry out, it seems indecent, for the undertaker to be taking such a tiny body, that they ought to bury it in its own simplicity, like the body of a bird, in a small hole dug in the grass. But he nods. He feels he will never resist anything again.

Eccles goes upstairs and Harry sits in a chair and watches the light from the window play across an iron table of ferns and African violets and cacti. Where it hits the leaves they are bright yellow-green; the leaves in shadow in front of them look like black-green holes cut in this golden color. Somebody comes down the stairs with an erratic step. He doesn't turn his head to see who it is; he doesn't want to risk looking anybody in the face. A furry touch on his forearm and he meets Nelson's eyes. The child's face is stretched shiny with curiosity. "Mommy sleep," he says in a deep voice imitating the tragedy-struck voices he has been hearing.

Rabbit pulls him up into his lap. He's heavier and longer than he used to be. His body acts as a covering; he pulls the boy's head down against his neck. Nelson asks, "Baby sick?"

"Baby sick."

"Big, big water in tub," Nelson says, and struggles to sit up so he can explain with his arms, which go wide. "Many, many water," he says. He must have seen it. He wants to get off his father's lap but Harry holds him fast with a kind of terror; the house is thick with a grief that seems to threaten the boy. Also the boy's body wriggles with an energy that threatens the grief, might tip it and bring the whole house crashing down on them. It is himself he is protecting by imprisoning the child.

Eccles comes downstairs and stands there studying them. "Why don't you take him outside?" he asks. "He's had a nightmare of a day."

They all three go outdoors. Eccles takes Harry's hand in a long quiet grip and says, "Stay here. You're needed, even if they don't tell you." After Eccles pulls away in his Buick, he and Nelson sit in the grass by the driveway and throw bits of gravel down toward the pavement. The boy laughs and talks in excitement but out here the sound is not so loud. Harry feels thinly protected by the fact that this is what Eccles told him to do. Men are walking home from work along the pavement; Nelson nearly gets one with a pebble. They change their target to a green lawn-seeder leaning against the wall of the garage. Harry hits it four times running. Though the air is still light the sunshine has shrunk to a few scraps in the tops of trees. The grass is growing damp and he wonders if he should sneak Nelson in the door and go.

Mr. Springer comes to the door and calls, "Harry." They go over. "Becky's made a few sandwiches in place of supper," he says. "You and the boy come in." They go into the kitchen and Nelson eats. Harry refuses everything except a glass of water. Mrs. Springer is not in the kitchen and Harry is grateful. Her hate of him lingers in the room like a smell. "Harry," Mr. Springer says, and stands up, patting his mustache with two fingers, like he's about to make a financial concession, "Reverend Eccles and Becky and I have had a talk. I won't say I don't blame you because of course I do. But you're not the only one to blame. Her mother and I somehow never made her feel secure, never perhaps you might say made her welcome, I don't know"—his little pink crafty eyes are not crafty now, blurred and chafed—"we tried, I'd like to think. At any rate"—this comes out harsh and crackly; he pauses to regain quietness in his voice—"life must go on. Am I making any sense to you?"

"Yes sir."

"Life must go on. We must go ahead now with what we

have left. Though Becky's too upset to see you now, she
agrees. We had a talk and agree that it's the only way.
I mean, what I meant to say, I can see you're puzzled, is that
we consider you in our family, Harry, despite"—he lifts an
arm vaguely toward the stairs—"this." His arm slumps back
and he adds the word "accident."

Harry shields his eyes with his hand. They feel hot and
vulnerable to light. "Thank you," he says, and almost moans
in his gratitude to this man, whom he has always despised, for
making a speech so generous. He tried to frame, in accord-
ance with an etiquette that continues to operate in the thick
of grief as if underwater, a counter-speech. "I promise I'll
keep my end of the bargain," he brings out, and stops, sti-
fled by the abject sound of his voice. What made him say
bargain?

"I know you will," Springer says. "Reverend Eccles assures us you will."

"Dessert," Nelson says distinctly.

"Nelly, why don't you take a cooky to bed?" Springer
speaks with a familiar jollity that, though strained, reminds
Rabbit that the kid lived here for months. "Isn't it your bed-
time? Shall Mom-mom take you up?"

"Daddy," Nelson says, and slides off his chair and comes
to his father.

Both men are embarrassed. "O.K.," Rabbit says. "You
show me your room."

Springer gets two Oreo cookies out of the pantry and
unexpectedly Nelson runs forward to hug him. He stoops to
accept the hug and his withered dandy's face goes blank
against the boy's cheek; his unfocused eyes stare at Rabbit's shoes, and big black square cuff links, thinly rimmed
and initialed S in gold, creep out of his coat sleeves as his
arms tighten the hug.

As Nelson leads his father to the stairs they pass the room
where Mrs. Springer is sitting. Rabbit has a glimpse of a
puffed face slippery with tears and averts his eyes. He whispers to Nelson to go in and kiss her good-night. When the boy
returns to him they go upstairs and down a smooth corridor
papered with a design of old-style cars into a little room
whose white curtains are tinted green by a tree outside. On
either side of the window symmetrical pictures, one of kit-
tens and one of puppies, are hung. He wonders if this was
the room where Janice was little. It has a musty innocence,

and a suspense, as if it stood empty for years. An old teddy-bear, the fur worn down to cloth and one eye void, sits in a broken child's rocker. Had it been Janice's? Who pulled the eye out? Nelson becomes queerly passive in this room. Harry undresses the sleepy body, brown all but the narrow bottom, puts it into pajamas and into bed and arranges the covers over it. He tells him, "You're a good boy."

"Yop."

"I'm going to go now. Don't be scared."

"Daddy go way?"

"So you can sleep. I'll be back."

"O.K. Good."

"Good."

"Daddy?"

"What?"

"Is baby Becky dead?"

"Yes."

"Was she frightened?"

"Oh no. No. She wasn't frightened."

"Is she happy?"

"Yeah, she's very happy now."

"Good."

"Don't you worry about it."

"O.K."

"You snuggle up."

"Yop."

"Think about throwing stones."

"When I grow up, I'll throw them very *far*."

"That's right. You can throw them pretty far now."

"I know it."

"O.K. Go to sleep."

Downstairs he asks Springer, who is washing dishes in the kitchen, "You don't want me to stay here tonight, do you?"

"Not tonight, Harry. I'm sorry. I think it would be better not tonight."

"O.K., sure. I'll go back to the apartment. Shall I come over in the morning?"

"Yes, please. We'll give you breakfast."

"No, I don't want any. I mean, to see Janice when she wakes up."

"Yes of course."

"You think she'll sleep the night through."

"I think so."

"Uh—I'm sorry I wasn't at the lot today."

"Oh, that's nothing. That's negligible."

"You don't want me to work tomorrow, do you?"

"Of course not."

"I still have the job, don't I?"

"Of course." His talk is gingerly; his eyes fidget; he feels his wife is listening.

"You're being awfully good to me."

Springer doesn't answer; Harry goes out through the sunporch, so he won't have to glimpse Mrs. Springer's face again, and around the house and walks home in the soupy, tinkling dark. He lets himself into the apartment with his key and turns on all the lights as rapidly as he can. He goes into the bathroom and the water is still in the tub. Some of it has seeped away so the top of the water is an inch below a faint gray line on the porcelain but the tub is still more than half full. A heavy, calm volume, odorless, tasteless, colorless, the water shocks him like the presence of a silent person in the bathroom. Stillness makes a dead skin on its unstirred surface. There's even a kind of dust on it. He rolls back his sleeve and reaches down and pulls the plug; the water swings and the drain gasps. He watches the line of water slide slowly and evenly down the wall of the tub, and then with a crazed vortical cry the last of it is sucked down. He thinks how easy it was, yet in all His strength God did nothing. Just that little rubber stopper to lift.

In bed he discovers that his legs ache from all the walking he did in Brewer today. His shins feel splintered; no matter how he twists, the pain, after a moment of relief gained by the movement, sneaks back. He tries praying to relax him but it doesn't do it. There's no connection. He opens his eyes to look at the ceiling and the darkness is mottled with an unsteady network of veins like the net of yellow and blue that mottled the skin of his baby. He remembers seeing her neat red profile through the window at the hospital and a great draft of horror sweeps through him, brings him struggling out of bed to turn on the lights. The electric glare seems thin. His groin aches to weep. He is afraid to stick even his hand into the bathroom; he fears if he turns on the light he will see a tiny wrinkled blue corpse lying face up on the floor of the drained tub. Fear presses on his kidneys and he is at last forced to dare; the dark bottom of the tub leaps up blank and white.

He expects never to go to sleep and, awaking with the slant of sunshine and the noise of doors slamming downstairs, feels his body has betrayed his soul. He dresses in haste, more panicked now than at any time yesterday. The event is realer. Invisible cushions press against his throat and slow his legs and arms; the kink in his chest has grown thick and crusty. *Forgive me, forgive me,* he keeps saying silently to no one.

He goes over to the Springers' and the tone of the house has changed; he feels everything has been rearranged slightly to make a space into which he can fit by making himself small. Mrs. Springer serves him orange juice and coffee and even speaks, cautiously.

"Do you want cream?"

"No. No. I'll drink it black."

"We have cream if you want it."

"No, really. It's fine."

Janice is awake. He goes upstairs and lies down on the bed beside her; she clings to him and sobs into the cup between his neck and jaw and the sheet. Her face has been shrunk; her body seems small as a child's, and hot and hard. She tells him, "I can't stand to look at anyone except you. I can't bear to look at the others."

"It wasn't your fault," he tells her. "It was mine."

They cling together in a common darkness; he feels the walls between them dissolve in a flood of black; but the heavy knot of apprehension remains in his chest, his own.

He stays in the house all that day. Visitors come, and tiptoe about. Their manner suggests that Janice upstairs is very sick. They sit, these women, over coffee in the kitchen with Mrs. Springer, whose petite rounded voice, oddly girlish divorced from the sight of her body, sighs on and on in indistinct syllables, like the mourning chant of an ancient tribe. Peggy Fosnacht comes, her sunglasses off, her wall eyes wild, wide to the world, and goes upstairs. Her son Billy plays with Nelson, and no one moves to halt their squeals of anger and pain in the back yard, which, neglected, in time die, and revive, after a pause, in the form of laughter. Even Harry has a visitor. The doorbell rings and Mrs. Springer goes and comes into the dim room where Harry is sitting looking at magazines and says, in a surprised and injured voice, "A man for you."

She leaves the doorway and he gets up and walks a

few steps forward to greet the man coming into the room,
Tothero, leaning on a cane his face half paralyzed; but
talking, walking, alive. "Hi! Gee, how are you?"

"Harry." With the hand that is not on the cane he grips
Harry's arm. He brings a long look to bear on Harry's face;
his mouth is tweaked downward on one side, the skin over
his eye on this side is dragged down diagonally so it nearly
curtains the glitter, and it may be the bad light but this
whole side looks the color of stone. The gouging grip of his
fingers trembles.

"Let's sit down," Rabbit says, and helps him into an easy
chair. Tothero knocks off a doily in arranging his arms. Rabbit brings over a straight chair and sits close so he won't have
to raise his voice. "Should you be running around?" he asks
when Tothero says nothing.

"My wife brought me. In the car. Outside, Harry. We
heard your terrible news. Didn't I warn you?" Already his
eyes are bulging with water.

"When?"

"When?" The stricken side of his face is turned away,
perhaps consciously, into shadow, so his smile seems wholly
alive, wise, and sure. "That fight night. I said go back. I
begged you."

"I guess you did. I've forgotten."

"No you haven't. No you haven't, Harry." His breath
chuffs on the "Ha" of "Harry." "Let me tell you something.
Will you listen?"

"Sure."

"Right and wrong," he says, and stops; his big head shifts,
and the stiff downward lines of his mouth and bad eye
show. "Right and wrong aren't dropped from the sky. We. We
make them. Against misery. Invariably, Harry, invariably"—
his pride at negotiating the long word shows, simple as a
boy's—"misery follows their disobedience. Not our own, often
at first not our own. Now you've had an example of that in
your own life." Rabbit wonders when the tear-trails appeared
on Tothero's cheeks; there they are. "Do you believe me?"

"Sure. Sure. Look, I know this has been my fault. I've
felt like a, like an insect ever since the thing happened."

Tothero's tranquil smile deepens; a faint rasping purr comes
out of his face. "I warned you," he says, his diction quicken-
ing, "I warned you, Harry, but youth is deaf. Youth is careless."

Harry blurts, "But what can I do?"

Tothero doesn't seem to hear. "Don't you remember? My begging you to go back?"

"I don't know, I guess so."

"Good. Ah. You're still a fine man, Harry. You have a healthy body. When I'm dead and gone, remember how your old coach told you to avoid suffering. Remember." The last word is intoned coyly, with a little wag of the head; on the thrust of this incongruous vivacity he rises from his chair, and prevents himself from pitching forward by quick use of his cane. Harry jumps up in alarm, and the two of them stand for the moment very close. The old man's big head breathes a distressing scent, not so much medicine as a sweet vegetable staleness. "You young people," he says with a rising intonation, a schoolteacher's tone, scolding yet sly, even encouraging, "tend to forget. Don't you? Now don't you?"

He wants this admission mysteriously much. "Sure," Rabbit says, praying he'll go.

Harry helps him to his car, a '57 blue-and-cream Dodge waiting in front of the orange fire hydrant. Mrs. Tothero offers, rather coolly, her regrets at the death of his infant daughter. She looks harried and noble. Gray hair straggles down across her finely wrinkled silver temple. She wants to get away from him, away with her prize. Beside her on the front seat Tothero looks like a smirking gnome, brainlessly stroking the curve of his cane. Rabbit returns to the house feeling depressed and dirtied by the visit. Tothero's revelation chilled him. He wants to believe in the sky as the source of all things.

Eccles comes in the late afternoon, to complete the arrangements for the funeral: it will be held tomorrow afternoon, Wednesday. As he leaves Rabbit catches his attention and they talk in the front hall a moment. "What do you think?" Rabbit asks.

"About what?"

"What shall I do?"

Eccles glances up nervously. He is very tired; Harry has never seen him look so tired. His face has that pale babyish look of someone who has not slept enough. "Do what you are doing," he says. "Be a good husband. A good father. Love what you have left."

"And that's enough?"

"You mean to earn forgiveness? I'm sure it is, carried out through a lifetime."

"I mean"—he's never before felt *pleading* with Eccles—"remember that thing we used to talk about? The thing behind everything."

"Harry, you know I don't think that thing exists in the way you think it does."

"O.K." He realizes that Eccles wants to get away too, that the sight of himself is painful, disgusting.

Eccles must see that he senses this, for he abruptly summons up mercy and makes an attempt. "Harry, it's not for me to forgive you. You've done nothing to me *to* forgive. I'm equal with you in guilt. We must work for forgiveness; we must *earn* the right to see that thing behind everything. Harry, I *know* that people are brought to Christ. I've seen it with my eyes and tasted it with my mouth. And I do think this. I think marriage is a sacrament, and that this tragedy, terrible as it is, has at last united you and Janice in a sacred way."

Through the next hours Rabbit clings to this belief, though it seems to bear no relation to the colors and sounds of the big sorrowing house, the dabs and arcs of late sunshine in the little jungle of plants on the glass table, or the almost wordless supper he and Janice share in her bedroom.

He spends that night in the Springers' house, sleeping with Janice. Her sleep is so solid. A thin snore out of her black mouth sharpens the moonlight and keeps him awake. He gets up on an elbow and studies her face; it is frightening in the moonlight, small and smeared by patches of dark cut it seems in a soft substance that lacks the edges of a human presence. He resents her sleep. When, in sunlight, he feels her weight stir and slide off the bed, he turns his face deeper into the pillow, retracts his head half under the covers, and goes back to sleep stubbornly. Sleep is a safe cave. Today is the last day of his abnormal life, today is the funeral; tomorrow he is scheduled to go back to work.

He has a vivid dream. He is alone on a large sporting field, or vacant lot, littered with small pebbles. In the sky two perfect disks, identical in size but the one a dense white and the other slightly transparent, move toward each other slowly; the pale one is directly above the dense one. At the moment they touch he feels frightened and a voice like over a loudspeaker at a track meet announces, "The cowslip swallows up the elder." The downward gliding of the top one continues steadily until the other, though the stronger, is totally eclipsed, and just one circle is before his eyes, pale and pure. He understands: "the cowslip" is the moon, and "the elder" the sun, and that what he had witnessed is the explanation of death: lovely life eclipsed by lovely death. With great excitement he realizes he must go forth from this field and found a new religion. There is a feeling of the disks, and the echo of the voice, bending over him importunately, and he opens his eyes. Janice stands by the bed in a brown skirt and a pink sleeveless blouse. There is a drab thickness of fat under her chin he has never noticed before. He is surprised to be on his back; he almost always sleeps on his stomach. He realizes it was a dream, that he has nothing to tell the world, and the knot regathers in his chest. In getting out of bed he kisses the back of her hand, which is hanging by her side helpless and raw.

She makes him breakfast, the cereal drowned in milk, the coffee scalded in her style. With Nelson they walk over to the apartment to get clothes for the funeral. Rabbit resents her being able to walk; resents her not dying of remorse and shame. What kind of grief is it that permits them to walk? The sense of their thick bodies just going on, wrapping their hearts in numbness and small needs, angers him. They walk with their child through streets they walked as children. The gutter along Potter Avenue where the slime-rimmed ice-plant water used to run is dry. The houses, many of them no longer lived in by the people whose faces he all knew, are like the houses in a town you see from the train, their brick faces blank in posing the riddle, Why does anyone live here? Why was he set down here, why is this town, a dull suburb of a third-rate city, for him the center and index of a universe that contains immense prairies, mountains, deserts, forests, coastlines, cities, seas? This childish mystery—the mystery of "any place," prelude to the ultimate, "Why am I me?"—starts panic in his heart. Coldness spreads through his body and he feels detached, as if at last he is, what he's always dreaded, walking on air. The details of the street—the ragged margin where the pavement and grass struggle, the tarry scarred trunks of the telephone poles—no longer speak to him in a child's intimate, excited voice. He is no one; it is as if he stepped outside of his body and brain a moment to watch the engine run and stepped into nothingness, for this "he" had been merely a refraction, a vibration within the engine, and now can't get back in. He feels he is behind the windows of the houses they walk by, watching this three-cornered family walk along solidly with no sign that their universe has convulsed other than the woman's quiet tears. Janice's tears have come as gently as dew comes; the sight of the morning-fresh streets seems to have sprung them.

When they get inside the apartment she gives a sharp sigh and collapses against him. Perhaps she didn't expect the place to be full of sunshine; buttresses of dust drifting in milky light slant from the middle of the floor to the tops of the windows and touch everything with innocence and newness and hopefulness. The door to his closet is near the entry door so they needn't go very deep into the apartment at first. He opens the closet door as far as he can without bumping the television set and reaches far in and unzips a plastic zippered storage bag and takes out his blue suit, a winter suit made of wool, but the only dark one he owns. Nelson ranges through the apartment, going wee-wee in the bathroom, finding an old rubber panda in his bedroom that he wants to take along. His exploring drains enough of the menace from the rooms for them to go into their bedroom, where Janice's clothes hang. On the way she indicates a chair. "Here I sat," she says, "yesterday morning, watching the sun come up." Her voice is lifeless; he doesn't know what she wants him to say and says nothing. He is holding his breath.

In the bedroom there is a pretty moment. She takes off her skirt and blouse to try on an old black suit she has, and as she moves about in her slip, barefoot on the carpet, she reminds him of the girl he knew, with her narrow ankles and wrists and small shy head. The black suit, bought when she was in high school, doesn't fit; her stomach is still too big from having the baby. And maybe her mother's plumpness is beginning. Standing there trying to get the waist of the suit skirt to link at her side, the tops of her breasts pushing above her bra as she bends into the effort, the space between them dimpling into a dark crease, she does have a plumpness, a sweet plumpness that pleases him. He thinks *Mine, my woman,* but then she straightens up and her smeared frantic face blots out his pride of possession. She becomes a liability that painfully weights the heaviness already below his chest. This is the wild woman he must steer with care down a lifelong path, away from yesterday. "It won't *do* it!" she screams, and jerks her legs out of the skirt and flings it, great twirling bat, across the room.

"You have nothing else?"

"What am I going to *do?*"

"Come on. Let's get out of here and go back to your place. This place is making you nervous."

"But we're going to have to *live* here!"

"Yeah, but not today. Come on."

"We *can't* live here," she says.

"I know we can't."

"But where *can* we live?"

"We'll figure it out. Come on."

She stumbles into her skirt and puts her blouse over her arms and turns away from him meekly and asks, "Button my back."

Buttoning the pink cloth down her quiet spine somehow makes him cry; the hotness in his eyes works up to a sting and he sees the little babyish buttons through a cluster of disks of watery light like petals of apple blossoms. Water hesitates on his lids and then runs down his cheeks; the wetness is delicious. He wishes he could cry for hours, for just this tiny spill relieves him. But a man's tears are rare and his stop before they are out of the apartment. As he closes the door he feels he has already spent his whole dry life opening and closing this door.

Nelson takes the rubber panda along and every time he makes it squeak it makes Rabbit's stomach ache. The town now is bleached by a sun nearing the height of noon.

Mrs. Springer, when Janice tells what happened, bustles around and finds an old black dress of hers that, with skillful pinning and a little sewing, she thinks will do. She and Janice go upstairs and after half an hour Janice comes down wrapped in black. "Harry. Does it look all right?"

"What in hell do you think this is going to be? A fashion show?" The idea that she can wear her mother's clothes infuriates him. He adds regretfully, "You look fine," but the damage is done. Janice is wounded and collapses upstairs and Mrs. Springer revokes the small measure of tolerance she had extended to him. The house again fills with the unspoken thought that he is the murderer. He accepts the thought gratefully; it's true, he is, he is, and hate suits him better than forgiveness. Immersed in hate he doesn't have to do anything; he can be paralyzed, and the rigidity of hatred makes a kind of shelter for him.

He reads Nelson a Little Golden Book about a little choo-choo who was afraid of tunnels but finally became courageous. Mrs. Springer comes in and bites off the word "Lunch." Harry says he doesn't want any but, taking courage from the storybook, goes into the kitchen to supervise and guard Nelson. Mrs. Springer manages to keep her back to him all the time. When Nelson is finished with his soup and raw carrots and Lebanon balony sandwich Harry takes him upstairs and settles him in bed and then resumes sitting in the living-room chair. Janice has fallen asleep and the sound of Mrs. Springer's sewing machine spins out into the birdsong and murmur of the early afternoon. Mr. Springer comes home, comes in and says, "I've been down at Town Hall, Harry. They're satisfied. Accidental. Al Horst's the coroner; he guarantees there won't be a manslaughter charge. He's been talking to just about everybody. He wants to talk to you sometime. Unofficially."

"O. K." It disgusts him to feel the net of law slither from him. He wants jail: to be locked in place. Springer trots upstairs. Footfalls pad above. Fancy dishes in the glass-fronted cupboard behind Harry vibrate.

He wonders if the pain in his stomach comes from eating so little in the last two days and goes out to the kitchen and eats two crackers. He can feel each bite hit a scraped floor inside. The pain increases. The bright porcelain fixtures, the steel doors, all seem charged with a negative magnetism that pushes against him and makes him extremely thin. He goes into the shadowy living-room and at the front window watches two teen-age girls in snug shorts shuffle by on the sunny sidewalk. Their bodies are already there but their faces are still this side of being good. Funny about girls about fourteen, their faces have this kind of eager bunchy business. Too much candy, sours their skin. The girls' long legs and slow, developed motions seem distasteful and unreal. He himself, watching them behind the window, seems a smudge on the glass. He wonders why the universe doesn't just erase a thing so dirty and small. He looks at his hands and they seem fantastically ugly.

He goes upstairs and with intense care washes his hands and face and neck. He doesn't dare use one of their fancy towels. Coming out with wet hands he meets Springer in the muted hallway and says, "I don't have a clean shirt." Springer says "Wait" and brings him a shirt and black cuff links. Harry dresses in the room where Nelson sleeps. Sunlight under the drawn shades; the boy's heavy breath. It takes less time to dress than he hoped it would. The wool suit is uncomfortably hot, but something stubborn in him refuses to take off the coat. He sits, immaculately dressed, the shirt too tight, in the living-room looking at the tropical plants on the glass table, moving his head so that now this leaf eclipses that, now that this, and wondering if he is going to throw up. His insides are a clenched mass of dread, a tough bubble that can't be pricked.

Of the things he dreads, he is most conscious of seeing his parents. He hasn't had the courage to call them or see them since the thing happened; Mrs. Springer called Mom Monday night and asked her to the funeral. The silence from his home since then has frightened him. It's one thing to get hell from other people and another from your own parents. Ever since he came back from the Army Pop had been nibbling at a grudge because he wouldn't go to work in the shop and in a way had nibbled himself right into nothing in Harry's heart. All the mildness and kindness the old man had ever shown him had faded into nothing. But his mother was something else; she was still alive, and was still attached to the cord of his life. If she comes in and gives him hell he thinks he'll die rather than take it. And of course what else is there to give him? Whatever Mrs. Springer says he can slip away from because in the end she has to stick with him and anyway he feels somehow she wants to like him but with his mother there's no question of liking him they're not even in a way separate people he began in her stomach and if she gave him life she can take it away and if he feels that withdrawal it will be the grave itself. Of all the people in the world he wants to see her least. He wishes she'd die.

At last they're ready, Mr. Springer in a spiffy dark gray drip-and-dry and Nelson in a sissy suit with straps and Mrs. in a black felt hat with a veil and a stem of purple

berries and Janice all pinned and hemmed in but still looking broad and sooty in her mother's fat dress. She doesn't
wear a hat. The undertaker's black Cadillac comes and
takes them to the funeral parlor. It was once a house but
now is carpeted the way no house ever was, pale green
carpets that deaden your steps like an inch of dust on the
floor. Little silver tubes on the wall shield a yellowish light
and the colors everywhere, on all the walls and curtains
you can see, are colors no one would live with, salmon and
aqua and the violet that kills germs on toilet seats. They
come up a flagstone walk in the sunshine past frothy green
bushes into this, and wait in a little pink sideroom. Harry
can see into the main room; on a few rows of auditorium
chairs about six people sit, five of them women. The only
one he knows is Peggy Gring. Her little boy wriggling beside her makes seven. It was meant to be at first nobody
but the families, but the Springers then asked a few close
friends. His parents are not here. Somewhere someone's
boneless hands trail up and down the keys of an electric
organ. The unnatural coloring of the interior comes to a
head in the hothouse flowers arranged around a little white
coffin. The coffin, with handles of painted gold, rests on a
platform covered with a deep purple curtain; he thinks the
curtain might draw apart and reveal, like a magician's trick,
the living baby underneath. Janice looks in and yields a
startled whimper and an undertaker's man, blond and young
with an unnaturally red face, conjures a bottle of spirits of
ammonia out of his side pocket. Her mother holds it under
her nose and she suppresses a face of disgust; her eyebrows
stretch up, showing the bumps her eyeballs make under the
thin membrane. Harry takes her arm and turns her so
she can't see into the next room.

The side-room has a window through which they can look
at the street, where children and cars are running. "Hope
the minister hasn't forgotten," the young red-faced man says,
and to his own embarrassment chuckles. He can't help being
at his ease here.

"Does that happen often?" Mr. Springer asks. He is standing behind his wife, and his face tips forward with curiosity,
a birdy black gash below his pale mustache. Mrs. Springer
has sat down on a chair is pressing her palms against her
face through the veil. The purple berries tremble in their
stem of wire.

"About twice a year," is the answer.

A familiar old Plymouth slows against the curb outside and Rabbit's mother gets out and looks up and down the sidewalk angrily. His heart leaps and trips his tongue: "Here come my parents." As if giving a warning. And they do all come to attention, as if to withstand an attack. Mrs. Springer gets up and Harry places himself between her and Janice. Standing in formation with the Springers like this, he can at least show his mother that he's reformed, that he's accepted and been accepted. The undertaker's man goes out to bring them in; Harry can see them standing on the bright sidewalk, arguing which door to go into; Mim a little to one side. Dressed in a quiet suit and with no make-up, she reminds him of the little sister he once had. The sight of his parents makes him wonder why he was afraid of them.

His mother comes through the door first; her eyes sweep the line of them and she steps toward him with reaching curved arms. "Hassy, what have they done to you?" She asks this out loud and wraps him in a hug as if she would carry him back to the sky from which they have fallen.

This quick it opens, and seals shut again. In a boyish reflex of embarrassment he pushes her away and stands to his full height. As if unaware of what she has said, his mother turns and embraces Janice. He is relieved to see her act courteously, normally. Pop, murmuring, shakes Springer's hand. Mim comes and touches Harry on the shoulder and then squats and whispers to Nelson, these two the youngest. All under him Harry feels these humans knit together. His wife and mother cling together. His mother began the embrace automatically but has breathed a great life of grief into it. Her face creases in pain; Janice, rumpled and smothered, yet responds; her weak black arms try to encircle the great frame yearning against her. Mrs. Angstrom yields up two words to her. The others are puzzled; only Harry from his tall cool height sees. His mother had been propelled by the instinct that makes us embrace those we wound, and then she had felt this girl in her arms as a member with her of an ancient abused slave race, and then she had realized that, having restored her son to herself, she too must be deserted.

He had felt in himself these stages of grief unfold in her as her arms tightened. Now she releases Janice, and speaks, sadly and properly, to the Springers. They have let her first outcry pass as madness, they of course have done nothing to Harry, what has been done he has done to them. His liberation is unseen by them. They become remote beside him. The words his mother spoke to Janice, "My daughter," recede. Mim rises from squatting; his father takes Nelson into his arms. Their motions softly jostle him.

And meanwhile his heart completes its turn and turns again, a wider turn in a thinning medium to which the outer world bears a decreasing relevance.

Eccles comes, panting from some drugstore or tormented home, and the seven of them file with Nelson into the room of flowers and take their seats on the front row. Black Eccles reads before the white casket. It annoys Rabbit that Eccles should stand between him and his daughter. It occurs to him, with a strange deep soft probe of guilt, what no one has mentioned, the child was never baptized. "I am the resurrection and the life, saith the Lord: he that believeth in me, though he were dead, yet shall he live: and whosoever liveth and believeth in me, shall never die."

The angular words walk in Harry's head like clumsy blackbirds; he feels their possibility. Eccles doesn't; his face is humorless and taut. His voice is false. All these people are false: except his dead daughter, the white box with gold trim.

"He shall feed his flock like a shepherd: he shall gather the lambs with his arms, and carry them in his bosom."

Shepherd, lamb, arms: Harry's eyes fill with tears. It is as if at first the tears are everywhere about him, a sea, and that at last the saltwater gets into his eyes. His daughter is dead; June gone from him; his heart swims in grief, that had skimmed over it before, dives deeper and deeper into the limitless volume of loss. Never hear her cry again, never see her marbled skin again, never balance her faint weight in his arms again and watch for the blue knives of her eyes to widen at his words. Never, the word never stops, there is never a gap in its thickness.

They go to the cemetery. He and his father and Janice's father and the undertaker's man carry the white box to the hearse. There is weight to it but the weight is all wood. The cemetery is beautiful at four o'clock. Its nurtured green nap slopes down somewhat parallel to the rays of the sun. Tombstones cast long slate shadows. Up a crunching blue gravel lane moves the careful procession; their destination a meek green canopy smelling of earth and ferns. Beyond them at a distance a crescent sweep of black woods; the cemetery is high on the hill, between the town and the forest. Below their feet chimneys smoke. Harry can see across the valley but from here it looks different, more blue. A man on a power lawnmower rides between the worn teeth of tombstones far off. Swallows in a wide ball dip and toss themselves above a stone cottage, a crypt. The white coffin is artfully rolled on casters from the hearse's deep body onto crimson straps that hold it above the small nearly square-mouthed but deep-dug grave. The small creaks and breaths of effort scratch on a pane of silence. Silence. A cough. The flowers have followed them; here they are under the tent. Behind Harry's feet a neat mound of dirt topped with squares of sod waits to be replaced and meanwhile breathes a deep word of earth. The undertaking men look pleased, fold their pink hands in front of their flies. Silence.

"The Lord is my shepherd; therefore can I lack nothing."

Eccles' voice made fragile by the outdoors; the distant buzz of the power mower halts respectfully. Rabbit's chest vibrates with excitement and strength; he is sure his girl has ascended to Heaven. This feeling fills Eccles' recited words like a living body a skin. "O God, whose most dear Son did take little children into his arms and bless them; Give us Grace, we beseech thee, to entrust the soul of this child to thy neverfailing care and love, and bring us all to the heavenly kingdom; through the same thy Son, Jesus Christ, our Lord. Amen."

"Amen," Mrs. Springer whispers.

Yes. That is how it is. He feels them all, the heads as still around him as tombstones, he feels them all one, all one with the grass, with the hothouse flowers, all, the undertaker's men, the unseen caretaker who has halted his mower, all gathered into one here to give his unbaptized baby force to leap to Heaven.

An electric switch is turned, the straps begin to lower the casket into the grave and stop. Eccles makes a cross of sand on the lid; stray grains roll one by one down the curved lid into the hole. A pink hand throws crumpled petals. "Deal graciously, we pray thee, with all those who mourn, that, casting every care on thee..." The straps

whine again. Janice at his side staggers. He holds her arm
and even through the cloth it feels hot. A small breath of
wind makes the canopy fill and flap like a sail. The smell of
flowers rises toward them. ". . . and the Holy Ghost, bless
you and keep you, now and for evermore. Amen."

Eccles closes his book. Harry's father and Janice's, standing
side by side, look up and blink. The undertaker's men begin
to be busy with their equipment, retrieving the straps from
the hole. Mourners move into the sunshine. "Casting every
care on thee." He has done that; he feels full of strength.
The sky greets him. It is as if he has been crawling in a
cave and now at last beyond the dark recession of crowding rocks he has seen a patch of light; he turns, and Janice's
face, dumb with grief, blocks the light. "Don't look at *me*,"
he says. "I didn't kill her."

This comes out of his mouth clearly, in tune with the
simplicity he feels now in everything. Heads talking softly
snap around at a voice so sudden and cruel.

They misunderstand. He just wants this straight. He explains to the heads, "You all keep acting as if *I* did it. I
wasn't anywhere near. *She's* the one." He turns to her, and
in her face, slack as if slapped, sees that she too is a victim,
that everyone is; the baby is gone, is all he's saying, he had
a baby and his wife drowned it. "Hey it's O.K.," he tells her.
"You didn't mean to." He tries to take her hand but she
snatches it back like from a trap and looks toward her
parents, who step toward her.

His face burns; forgiveness had been big in his heart and
now it's hate. He hates her dumb face. She doesn't *see*. She
had a chance to join him in truth, just the simplest factual
truth, and turned away in horror. He sees that among the
heads even his own mother's is horrified, blank with shock,
a wall against him; she asks him what have they done to
him and then she does it too. A suffocating sense of injustice
blinds him. He turns and runs.

Uphill with broad strength. He dodges among gravestones
exultantly. Dandelions grow bright as butter among the
graves. Behind him his name is called in Eccles' voice:
"Harry! Harry!" He feels Eccles chasing him but does not
turn to look. He cuts diagonally through the stones across
the grass toward the woods. The distance to the dark crescent of trees is greater than it seemed from beside the
grave. The romping of his body turns heavy; the slope of

land grows steeper. Yet there is a softness in the burial ground that sustains his flight, a gentle settled bumpiness that buoys him up with its reminiscence of the dodging spurting runs down a crowded court. He arrives between the arms of the woods and aims for the center of the crescent. Once inside, he is less sheltered than he expected; turning, he can see through the leaves back down the graveyard to where, beside the small green tent, the human beings he has left cluster. Eccles is halfway between them and him. His black chest heaves. His wide-set eyes concentrate into the woods. The others, thick stalks in dark clothes, jiggle: maneuvering, planning, testing each other's strengths, holding each other up. Their pale faces flash mute signals toward the woods and turn away, in disgust or despair, and then flash again full in the declining sun, fascinated. Only Eccles' gaze is steady. He may be gathering energy to renew the chase.

Rabbit crouches and runs raggedly. His hands and face are scratched from plowing through the bushes and saplings that rim the woods. Deeper inside there is more space. The pine trees smother all other growth. Their brown needles muffle the rough earth with a slippery blanket; sunshine falls in narrow slots on this dead floor. It is dim but hot in here, like an attic; the unseen afternoon sun bakes the dark shingles of green above his head. Dead lower branches thrust at the level of his eyes. His hands and face feel hot where they were scratched. He turns to see if he has left the people behind. No one is following. Far off, through a tiny patch at the end of the aisle of pines he is in, a green glows which is perhaps the green of the cemetery; but it seems as far off as the patches of sky he can glimpse above the treetops. In turning he loses some sense of direction. But the tree-trunks are at first in neat rows that carry him along between them, and he walks always against the slope of the land. If he walks far enough uphill he will in time reach the scenic drive that runs along the ridge. Only by going downhill can he be returned to the others.

The trees cease to march in rows and grow together more thickly. These are older trees. The darkness under them is denser and the ground is steeper. Rocks jut up through the blanket of needles, scabby with lichen; collapsed trunks hold intricate claws across his path. At places where a hole has been opened up in the roof of evergreen, berrying bushes and yellow grass grow in a hasty sweet-smelling tumble. These patches, some of them broad enough to catch a bit of sun slanting down the mountainside, make the surrounding darkness darker, and in pausing in them he becomes conscious, by its cessation, of a whisper that fills the brown tunnels all around him. Midges circle thickly in the sunshine above these holes. The surrounding trees are too tall for him to see any sign, even a remote cleared landscape, of civilization. Islanded in light he becomes frightened. He is conspicuous; the bears and nameless menaces that whisper through the forest can see him clearly. Rather than hang vulnerable in these wells of visibility he rushes toward the menaces across the rocks and rotting trunks and slithering needles. Insects follow him out of the sun; his sweat is a strong perfume. His chest binds and his shins hurt from jarring uphill into pits and flat rocks that the needles conceal. He takes off his coat and carries it in a twisted bundle. He struggles against his impulse to keep turning his head, to see what is behind him; there is never anything, just the hushed, deathly life of the woods, but his fear fills the winding space between the tree-trunks with agile threats, that just dodge out of the corner of his eye each time he whips his head around. He must hold his head rigid. He's terrorizing himself. As a kid he often went up through the woods. But maybe as a kid he walked under a magic protection that has now been lifted; he can't believe the woods were this dark then. They too have grown. Such an unnatural darkness, clogged with spider-fine twigs that finger his face incessantly, a darkness in defiance of the broad daylight whose sky leaps in jagged patches from treetop to treetop above him like a blue monkey.

The small of his back aches from crouching. He begins to doubt his method. As a kid he never entered from the cemetery. Perhaps walking against the steepest slope is stupid, carrying him along below the ridge of the mountain when a few yards to his left the road is running. He bears to his left, trying to keep himself in a straight path; the whisper of woods seems to swell louder and his heart lifts with hope: he was right, he is near a road. He hurries on, scrambling ruthlessly, expecting the road to appear with every step, its white posts and speeding metal to gleam. The slope of the ground dies unnoticed under his feet. He stops, stunned, on the edge of a precipitate hollow whose near bank is strewn with the hairy bodies of dead trees locked against trunks that have managed to cling erect to the steep soil and that cast into the hollow a shadow as deep as the last stage of twilight. Something rectangular troubles this gloom; it dawns on him that on the floor of the hollow lie the cellarhole and the crumbled sandstone walls of a forgotten house. To his shrill annoyance at having lost his way and headed himself downhill again is added a clangorous horror, as if this ruined evidence of a human intrusion into a world of blind life tolls bells that ring to the edges of the universe. The thought that this place was once self-conscious, that its land was tramped and cleared and known, blackens the air with ghosts that climb the ferny bank toward him like children clambering up from a grave. Perhaps there were children, fat girls in calico fetching water from a nearby spring, taming the trees, scarring them with marks of play, growing old on boards stretched above the cellarhole, dying with a last look out the window at the bank where Harry stands. He feels more conspicuous and vulnerable than in the little clearings of sunshine: he obscurely feels lit by a great spark, the spark whereby the blind tumble of matter recognized itself, a spark struck in the collision of two opposed realms, an encounter a terrible God willed. His stomach slides; his ears seem suddenly open to the sound of a voice. He scrambles back uphill, thrashing noisily in the deepening darkness to drown out the voice that wants to cry out to him from a source that flits from tree to tree in the shadows. He runs always against the rise of land, chasing it in treacherous light, the steep solid land like some fleeing, twisting thing.

The light widens enough for him to spy off to his right a nest of old tin cans and bottles sunken into the needles and then he strikes the road. He jacks his long legs over the guard fence and straightens up. Gold spots are switching on and off in the corners of his eyes. The asphalt scrapes under his shoes and he seems entered, with the wonderful resonant hollowness of exhaustion, on a new life. Cold air strokes his shoulder blades; somewhere in there he split old man Springer's shirt right down the back. He has come out of the woods about a half-mile below the Pinnacle Hotel. As he swings along, jauntily hanging his blue coat over his shoulder on the hook of one finger, Janice and Eccles and his mother and his sins seem a thousand miles behind. He decides to call Eccles, like you'd send somebody a postcard. Eccles had liked him and put a lot of trust in him and deserves at least a phone call. Rabbit rehearses what he'll say. "It's O.K.," he'll tell him, "I'm on the way. I mean, I think there are several ways; don't worry. Thanks for everything." What he wants to get across is that Eccles shouldn't be discouraged.

On the top of the mountain it is still broad day. Up in the sea of sky a lake of fragmented mackerel clouds drifts in one piece like a school of fish. There are only a couple cars parked around the hotel, jalopies, '52 Pontiacs and '51 Mercs like Springer Motors sells to these blotchy kids that come in with a stripper in their wallets and a hundred dollars in the bank. Inside the cafeteria a few of them are playing a pinball machine called BOUNCING BETSY. They look at him with their long hair and make wise faces and one of them even calls, "Did she rip your shirt?" But, it's strange, they don't really know anything about him except he looks mussed. You do things and do things and nobody really knows. The clock says twenty of six. He goes to the pay phone on the butterscotch wall and looks up Eccles' number in the book. His wife answers dryly, "Hello?" Rabbit shuts his eyes and her freckles dance in the red of his lids.

"Hi. Could I speak to Reverend Eccles please?"

"Who is this?" Her voice has gotten up on a hard little high horse; she knows who. He smiles and pictures her solid sweet butt, that he tapped.

"Hey, this is Harry Angstrom. Is Jack there?"

The receiver at the other end of the line is replaced; that bitch. Just because I wouldn't go into her frigging house with her. Poor Eccles probably sitting there his heart bleeding to hear the word from me and she going back and telling him wrong number, that poor bastard being married to that bitch. He hangs up himself, hears the dime rattle down, and feels simplified by this failure. He goes out across the parking lot.

He seems to leave behind him in the cafeteria all the poison she must be dripping into the poor tired guy's ears. He imagines her telling Eccles about how he slapped her fanny and thinks he hears Eccles laughing and himself smiles. He'll remember Eccles as laughing; there was that in him that held you off, that you couldn't reach, the nasal business, but through the laughter you could get to him. Sort of sneaking in behind him, past the depressing damp gripping clinging front. What made it depressing was that he wasn't sure, but couldn't tell you, and worried his eyebrows instead, and spoke every word in a different voice. All in all, a relief to be loose from him. Soggy.

From the edge of the parking lot, Brewer is spread out like a carpet, its flowerpot red going dusty. Some lights are already turned on. The great neon sunflower at the center of the city looks small as a daisy. Now the low clouds are pink but up above, high in the dome, tails of cirrus still hang pale and pure. As he starts down the steps he wonders, Would she have? Lucy.

He goes down the mountainside on the flight of log stairs and through the part where some people are still playing tennis and down Weiser Street, putting his coat back on, and up Summer. His heart is murmuring in suspense but it is in the center of his chest. That lopsided kink about Becky is gone, he has put her in Heaven, he felt her go. If Janice had felt it he maybe might have stayed. The outer door is open and an old lady in a Polish sort of kerchief is coming mumbling out of F. X. Pelligrini's door. He rings Ruth's bell.

The buzzer answers and he quickly snaps open the inner door and starts up the steps. Ruth comes to the banister and looks down and says, "Go away."

"Huh? How'd you know it was me?"

"Go back to your wife."

"I can't. I just left her."

She laughs; he has climbed to the step next to the top one, and their faces are on a level. "You're always leaving her," she says.

"No, this time it's different. It's really bad."

"You're bad all around. You're bad with me, too."

"Why?" He has come up the last step and stands there a yard away from her, excited and helpless. He thought when he saw her, instinct would tell him what to do but in a way it's all new, though it's only been a few weeks. She is changed, graver in her motions and thicker in the waist. The blue of her eyes is darker.

She looks at him with a contempt that is totally new. *"Why?"* she repeats in an incredulous hard voice.

"Let me guess," he says. "You're pregnant."

Surprise softens the hardness a moment.

"That's great," he says, and takes advantage of her softness to push her ahead of him into the room. Her arms and sweater give like little cushions when he pushes. "Great," he repeats, closing the door. He tries to embrace her and she fights him successfully and backs away behind a chair. She had meant that fight; his neck is scraped.

"Go away," she says. "Go *away*."

"Don't you need me?"

"Need you," she cries, and he squints in pain at the straining note of hysteria; he feels she has imagined this encounter so ofter she is determined to say everything, which will be too much. He sits down in an easy chair. His legs ache. She says, "I needed you that night you walked out. Remember how much I needed you? Remember what you made me do?"

"She was in the hospital," he says. "I had to go."

"God, you're cute. God, you're so holy. You had to go. You had to stay, too, didn't you? You know, I was stupid enough to think you'd at least call."

"I wanted to but I was trying to start clean. I didn't know you were pregnant."

"You didn't, why not? Anybody else would have. I was sick enough."

"When, with me?"

"God, yes. Why don't you look outside your own pretty skin once in a while?"

"Well why didn't you tell me?"

"Why should I? What would that have done? You're no help. You're nothing. You know why I didn't? You'll laugh, but I didn't because I thought you'd leave me if you knew. You wouldn't ever let me do anything to prevent it but I figured once it happened you'd leave me. You left me anyway so there you are. Why don't you get out? Please get out. I begged you to get out the first time. The damn first time I begged you. Why are you *here?*"

"I want to be here. It's right. Look. I'm happy you're pregnant."

"It's too late to be happy."

"Why? Why is it too late?" He's frightened, remembering how she wasn't here when he came before. She's here now, she had been away then. Women went away to have it done, he knew.

"How can you sit there?" she asks him. "I can't understand it, how you can sit there; you just killed your baby and there you sit."

"Who told you that?"

"Your ministerial friend. Your fellow saint. He called about a half-hour ago."

"God. He's still trying."

"I said you weren't here. I said you'd never be here."

"I didn't kill the poor kid. Janice did. I got mad at her one night and came looking for you and she got drunk and drowned the poor kid in the bathtub. Don't make me talk about it. Where *were* you, anyway?"

She looks at him with dull wonder and says softly, "Boy, you really have the touch of death, don't you?"

"Hey; have you done something?"

"Hold still. Just sit there. I see you very clear all of a sudden. You're Mr. Death himself. You're not just nothing, you're worse than nothing. You're not a rat, you don't stink, you're not enough to stink."

"Look, I didn't do anything. I was coming to see you when it happened."

"No, you don't do anything. You just wander around with the kiss of death. Get out. Honest to God, Rabbit, just looking at you makes me sick." Her sincerity in saying this leaves her kind of limp, and she grips the top slat of a straight chair bearing a Pennsylvania Dutch design stenciled in faded flowers.

He, who always took pride in dressing neatly, who had always been led to think he was all right to look at, blushes to feel this sincerity. The sensation he had counted on, of being by nature her master, of getting on top of her, hasn't come. He looks at his fingernails, with their big cuticle moons. His hands and legs are suffused with a paralyzing sense of reality; his child is really dead, his day is really done, this woman is really sickened by him. Realizing this much makes him anxious to have all of it, to be pressed tight against the wall. He asks her flat, "Did you get an abortion?"

She smirks and says hoarsely, "What do *you* think?"

He closes his eyes and while the gritty grained fur of the chair arms rushes up against his fingertips prays, *God, dear God, no, not another, you have one, let this one go.* A dirty knife turns in his intricate inner darkness. When he opens his eyes he sees, from the tentative hovering way she is standing there, trying to bring off a hard swagger in her stance, that she means to torment him. His voice goes sharp with hope: "Have you?"

A crumbling film comes over her face. "No," she says, "*no*. I should but I keep not doing it. I don't want to do it."

Up he gets and his arms go around her, without squeezing, like a magic ring, and though she stiffens at his touch and twists her head sideways on her muscled white throat, he has regained that feeling, of being on top. "Oh," he says, "good. That's so good."

"It was too ugly," she says. "Margaret had it all rigged up but I kept—thinking about—"

"Yes," he says, "Yes. You're so good. I'm so glad," and tries to nuzzle the side of her face. His nose touches wet. "You have it," he coaxes. "Have it." She is still a moment, staring at her thoughts, and then jerks out of his arms and says, "Don't touch me!" Her face flares; her body is bent forward like a threatened animal's. As if his touch *is* death.

"I love you," he says.

"That means nothing from you. Have it, have it, you say: how? Will you marry me?"

"I'd love to."

"You'd love to, you'd love to do anything. What about your wife? What about the boy you already have?"

"I don't know."

"Will you divorce her? No. You love being married to her too. You love being married to everybody. Why can't you make up your mind what you want to *do*?"

"Can't I? I don't know."

"How would you support me? How many wives can you support? Your jobs are a joke. You aren't worth hiring. Maybe once you could play basketball but you can't do *any*thing now. What the hell do you think the world is?"

"Please have the baby," he says. "You got to have it."

"Why? Why do you *care*?"

"I don't know. I don't know any of these answers. All I know is what feels right. You feel right to me. Sometimes Janice used to. Sometimes nothing does."

"Who cares? That's the thing. Who cares *what* you feel?"

"I don't know," he says again.

She groans—from her face he feared she would spit—and turns and looks at the wall that is all in bumps from being painted over peeling previous coats so often.

He says, "I'm hungry. Why don't I go out to the delicatessen and get us something. Then we can think."

She turns, steadier. "I've *been* thinking," she says. "You

know where I was when you came here the other day? I
was with my parents. You know I have parents. They're pretty poor parents but that's what they are. They live in West
Brewer. They know. I mean they know some things. They
know I'm pregnant. Pregnant's a nice word, it happens to
everybody, you don't have to think too much what you must
do to get that way. Now I'd like to marry you. I would. I
mean whatever I said but if we're married it'll be all right.
Now you work it out. You divorce that wife you feel so sorry
for about once a month, you divorce her or forget me. If
you can't work it out, I'm dead to you; I'm dead to you
and this baby of yours is dead too. Now; get out if you want
to." Saying all this unsteadies her and makes her cry, but she
pretends she's not. The sides of her nose shine but she
doesn't touch them.

He has nervously felt her watching him for some sign of
resolution inspired by this speech. In fact he has hardly listened; it is too complicated and, compared to the vision of a
sandwich, unreal. He stands up, he hopes with soldierly effect,
and says, "That's fair. I'll work it out. What do you want at
the store?" A sandwich and a glass of milk, and then un-
dressing her, getting her out of that hot cotton dress harried
into wrinkles and seeing that thickened waist calm in its pale
cool skin. He loves women when they're first pregnant; they
look so gentle. If he can just once more bury himself in her
he knows he'll come up with his nerves all combed.

"I don't want anything," she says.

"Oh you got to eat," he says.

"I've eaten," she says.

He tries to go kiss her but she says "No" and does not
look inviting, fat and flushed and her many-colored hair
straggled and damp.

"I'll be right back," he says.

As he goes down the stairs worries come as quick as the
sound of his footsteps. Janice, money, Eccles' phone call, the
look on his mother's face all clatter together in sharp dark
waves; guilt and responsibility slide together like two sub-
stantial shadows inside his chest. The mere engineering of
it—the conversations, the phone calls, the lawyers, the finan-
ces—seems to complicate, physically, in front of his mouth, so
he is conscious of the effort of breathing, and every action,
just reaching for the doorknob, feels like a precarious exten-
sion of a long mechanical sequence insecurely linked to his

heart. The doorknob's solidity answers his touch, and turns nicely.

Outside in the air his fears condense. Globes of ether, pure nervousness, slide down his legs. The sense of outside space scoops at his chest. Standing on the step he tries to sort his worries, tries to analyze the machinery behind him in the house, put his finger on what makes it so loud. Two thoughts comfort him, let a little light through the dense pack of impossible alternatives. Ruth has parents, and she will let his baby live: two thoughts that are perhaps the same thought, the vertical order of parenthood, a kind of thin tube upright in time in which our solitude is somewhat diluted. Ruth and Janice both have parents: with this thought he dissolves both of them. Nelson remains: here is a hardness he must carry with him. On this small fulcrum he tries to balance the rest, weighing opposites against each other: Janice and Ruth, Eccles and his mother, the right way and the good way, the way to the delicatessen—gaudy with stacked fruit lit by a naked bulb—and the other way, down Summer Street to where the city ends. He tries to picture how it will end, with an empty baseball field, a dark factory, and then over a brook into a dirt road, he doesn't know. He pictures a huge vacant field of cinders and his heart goes hollow.

Afraid, really afraid, he remembers what once consoled him by seeming to make a hole where he looked through into underlying brightness, and lifts his eyes to the church window. It is, because of church poverty or the late summer nights or just carelessness, unlit, a dark circle in a stone façade.

There is light, though, in the streetlights; muffled by trees their mingling cones retreat to the unseen end of Summer Street. Nearby, to his left, directly under one, the rough asphalt looks like dimpled snow. He decides to walk around the block, to clear his head and pick his path. Funny, how what makes you move is so simple and the field you must move in is so crowded. Goodness lies inside, there is nothing outside, those things he was trying to balance have no weight. He feels his inside as very real suddenly, a pure blank space in the middle of a dense net. I don't know, he kept telling Ruth; he doesn't know, what to do, where to go, what will happen, the thought that he doesn't know seems to make him infinitely small and impossible to capture. Its smallness fills him like a vastness. It's like when they heard you were great and put two men on you and no matter which way you turned you bumped into one of them and the only thing to do was pass. So you passed and the ball belonged to the others and your hands were empty and the men on you looked foolish because in effect there was nobody there.

Rabbit comes to the curb but instead of going to his right and around the block he steps down, with as big a feeling as if this little side-street is a wide river, and crosses. He wants to travel to the next patch of snow. Although this block of brick three-stories is just like the one he left, something in it makes him happy; the steps and window sills seem to twitch and shift in the corner of his eye, alive. This illusion trips him. His hands lift of their own and he feels the wind on his ears even before, his heels hitting heavily on the pavement at first but with an effortless gathering out of a kind of sweet panic growing lighter and quicker and quieter, he runs. Ah: runs. Runs.

ABOUT THE AUTHOR

John Updike was born in 1932, in Shillington, Pennsylvania. He graduated *summa cum laude* from Harvard in 1954, and spent a year in England on the Knox Fellowship, at the Ruskin School of Drawing and Fine Art in Oxford. From 1955 to 1957 he was a member of the staff of *The New Yorker*, to which he has contributed short stories, essays, and poems. His novel *The Centaur* received the National Book Award for Fiction in 1964; in the same year Updike was elected to the National Institute of Arts and Letters and travelled to the Soviet Union. He presently lives in Ipswich, Massachusetts, with his wife and four children. His most recent novel is *Couples*.